The Winter Runaway

Katie Flynn is the pen name of the much-loved writer Judy Turner, who published over ninety novels in her lifetime. Judy's unique stories were inspired by hearing family recollections of life in Liverpool during the early twentieth century, and her books went on to sell more than eight million copies. Judy passed away in January 2019, aged 82.

The legacy of Katie Flynn lives on through her daughter, Holly Flynn, who continues to write under the Katie Flynn name. Holly worked as an assistant to her mother for many years and together they co-authored a number of Katie Flynn novels.

Holly lives in the north east of Wales with her husband Simon and their two children. When she's not writing she enjoys walking her dog Tara in the surrounding countryside, and cooking forbidden foods such as pies, cakes and puddings! She looks forward to sharing many more Katie Flynn stories, which she and her mother devised together, with readers in the years to come.

Keep up to date with all her latest news on Facebook: Katie Flynn Author

Also available by Katie Flynn

A Liverpool Lass
The Girl from Penny Lane
Liverpool Taffy
The Mersey Girls
Strawberry Fields
Rainbow's End
Rose of Tralee
No Silver Spoon
Polly's Angel
The Girl from Seaforth Sands
The Liverpool Rose
Poor Little Rich Girl
The Bad Penny
Down Daisy Street
A Kiss and a Promise
Two Penn'orth of Sky
A Long and Lonely Road
The Cuckoo Child
Darkest Before Dawn
Orphans of the Storm
Little Girl Lost
Beyond the Blue Hills
Forgotten Dreams
Sunshine and Shadows
Such Sweet Sorrow
A Mother's Hope
In Time for Christmas

Heading Home
A Mistletoe Kiss
The Lost Days of Summer
Christmas Wishes
The Runaway
A Sixpenny Christmas
The Forget-Me-Not Summer
A Christmas to Remember
Time to Say Goodbye
A Family Christmas
A Summer Promise
When Christmas Bells Ring
An Orphan's Christmas
A Christmas Candle
Christmas at Tuppenny Corner
A Mother's Love
A Christmas Gift
Liverpool Daughter
Under the Mistletoe
Over the Rainbow
The Rose Queen
The Winter Rose
A Rose and a Promise
White Christmas
Winter's Orphan
A Mother's Secret

Available by Katie Flynn writing as Judith Saxton

You Are My Sunshine
First Love, Last Love
Someone Special
Still Waters
A Family Affair
Jenny Alone
Chasing Rainbows
All My Fortunes

Sophie
We'll Meet Again
Harbour Hill
The Arcade
The Pride
The Glory
The Splendour
Full Circle

Katie Flynn

The Winter Runaway

PENGUIN BOOKS

PENGUIN BOOKS

UK | USA | Canada | Ireland | Australia
India | New Zealand | South Africa

Penguin Books is part of the Penguin Random House group of companies
whose addresses can be found at global.penguinrandomhouse.com

First published by Century in 2024
Published in Penguin Books 2024
001

Typeset in 11.18/14.2pt Palatino LT Pro by JOUVE(UK), Milton Keynes

Printed and bound in Great Britain by Clays Ltd, Elcograf S.p.A.

The authorised representative in the EEA is Penguin Random House Ireland,
Morrison Chambers, 32 Nassau Street, Dublin D02 YH68

A CIP catalogue record for this book is available from the British Library

ISBN: 978–1–80494–247–5

www.greenpenguin.co.uk

MIX
Paper | Supporting
responsible forestry
FSC
www.fsc.org   FSC® C018179

Penguin Random House is committed to a
sustainable future for our business, our readers
and our planet. This book is made from Forest
Stewardship Council® certified paper.

The Winter Runaway

Prologue

13TH MARCH 1941

Tammy Blackwell watched in a trance-like state as her father's blood dripped from the flat iron in her hand to the parlour floor.

'Tammy?'

She blinked as her mother's frightened voice penetrated the air. Slowly turning her attention away from the flat iron, Tammy watched her father's lifeless hands slip from around her mother's throat as she desperately tried to push herself out from underneath his body.

'Tammy!' Grace cried out again, more urgently this time, her voice thick with tears.

Snapping out of her trance, Tammy hastened to her mother's aid and between the two of them they managed to roll her father onto his back, allowing Grace enough room to wriggle free. Tammy swallowed as she looked from the flat iron, now on the floor, to the bloodied gash on her father's temple.

'It was an accident,' she said, her voice barely above a whisper. 'He wouldn't let go of you . . .'

Grace wiped her tears with the backs of her hands as she stared at her husband. 'Is he . . . ?' She paused, unable to say the word. She glanced meaningfully at her daughter.

Tammy's lower lip trembled as she gingerly placed two fingers across the underneath of his wrist; failing to find a pulse, she tentatively made her way up his body until she was close enough to hear him breathe. She turned round, her frightened eyes looking to her mother. 'They'll hang me . . .'

The words appeared to sharpen Grace's focus, and she picked up the iron as she got to her feet. Taking great strides into the kitchen, she grabbed a tea towel and wrapped it around the iron as she walked back through to Tammy. 'We need to go.'

'We cannae just leave him here . . .' Tammy protested.

'Oh aye? And what do you suggest we do?' said Grace, who was busy unclipping her suitcase.

'I don't know, but somebody's bound to find him sooner or later, and when they do . . .'

'We'll be long gone,' said Grace. Hastily hiding the iron amongst her belongings, she added, 'With no weapon to be found, they'll assume he's fallen over after havin' too much to drink.'

Tammy stared at the earthen floor and its distinct lack of sharp edges. 'They're not that stupid.'

Clicking her suitcase closed, Grace motioned to Tammy. 'Help me get him into the kitchen.' Tammy did as her mother asked and together they dragged him through by his ankles. Positioning him by the stove, Grace looked to her daughter. 'It'll be hard for

2

them to prove otherwise when the iron's at the bottom of the Clyde.' She grabbed a half-empty bottle of beer from the table and put it down next to the body. 'It'll help if they think he's been drinkin'.'

'If that's the case then why run at all?'

Grace stared at her daughter aghast. 'Because we're women and they'd rather take the side of a corpse than us! Men always stick together, don't you ever forget that, and I will *not* see you hang for savin' my life, because there's not a doubt in my mind that I'd be dead if you hadn't stepped in when you did.'

Tammy practically jumped out of her skin as something thumped the floor of the room above their heads. 'The neighbours!' she gasped. With her hand half-covering her mouth, she spoke thickly through her fingers. 'Do you think they heard owt?'

'They'd have to be deaf not to have, which is why we must make haste,' said Grace, who was taking care that the door wouldn't creak as she cracked it open the merest of slits and peered through to the street outside. Holding her breath, she waited for the ARP warden to walk on by before turning back to Tammy. 'If we hurry we can be gone before he reaches the far end.'

Tammy picked up her suitcase and looked back to the body of her father for one last time. 'He wasn't meant to be here . . .'

Grace cast her daughter a rueful glance. 'But he was, and we'll have to live with the consequences of that for the rest of our lives.' Stepping out of the door, she indicated for Tammy to follow and they hurried into the night.

Chapter One

THREE MONTHS EARLIER
Tammy wrapped her shawl tighter around her shoulders as she hurried to meet her childhood sweetheart, Rory, who was waiting for her on the corner of the street.

Grinning as she came into view, he greeted her with a quick peck on the lips before putting his arm around her and pulling her close. 'You managed to get away all right then?'

'Once he'd drunk himself to sleep,' said Tammy, her teeth chattering from the cold. In the resigned tones of someone who'd trodden this particular path too many times previously, she continued, 'but not before he'd given Mammy a damned good hidin'.'

Rory faltered mid-step before ploughing on. 'For cryin' out loud! What was it over this time?'

'The usual; he reckoned he hadn't enough money to go down the pub because Mammy had been frivolous with the housekeepin'.' She thinned her lips. 'All she'd done was buy—' she'd stopped herself from saying 'sanitary ware' in the nick of time. Her

5

cheeks colouring, she changed her words to '. . . the sort of products that most women need throughout the year.'

Rory pulled a downward grimace. 'What the heck does he expect her to do? Or does it not matter as long as he has a skinful?'

'How did you guess?' she said, in heavy satirical tones.

'Call it a hunch,' said Rory with equal sarcasm. Feeling Tammy shiver beneath his arm, he took his jacket off and placed it around her shoulders.

'Don't be daft, you'll freeze to death,' Tammy objected as she tried to duck out from underneath the heavy donkey jacket.

'Don't you worry about me, I've plenty of woollies to keep me warm,' said Rory, his breath clouding as it penetrated the cold night air. He ensured she was sufficiently wrapped in the jacket before pressing on. 'I don't know why the two of you don't just up and leave him, I really don't. It's not as if you'd be any worse off money wise, or at least I don't reckon so.'

'How could we be no worse off when we've not got two pennies to rub together?' cried Tammy. 'He knows we'd be lost without his money, which is precisely why he doesn't allow either of us to work, and even if he did, it's not just the money that stops us from runnin' away.' She continued darkly. 'He's made it quite plain that Mammy's as good as dead if she even thinks of leavin', and as he knows, I won't go anywhere without her. Neither of us are goin' anywhere.'

Rory wrinkled his brow. 'I know what he can be

like, we all do, but do you really think he'd commit murder when he knows the noose would be waitin' for him?'

Seeing fresh flakes of snow begin to fall, Tammy dug her hands deeper into her skirt pockets. 'There's only one way to find out if he'd stay true to his word, and neither of us are prepared to take the risk!'

'There has to be some way of gettin' you away from him without there bein' any repercussions. Perhaps one of your neighbours could do summat to help?'

She shook her head firmly. 'No! I'm not askin' anyone for their help, because if he found out what they'd done for us, he'd take his temper out on them.' She sighed. 'It might have been different if Mammy had grown up around these parts, but as it is, she has no real friends to speak of, despite having lived here the best part of twenty years!'

'Your poor mammy. I bet she wishes she'd stayed in Wales.'

'That's what I said, but she insists she wouldn't have it any other way because if she hadn't met my father, I wouldn't be here.'

'Fair point.' He squeezed her hand in the crook of his elbow. 'But even though I echo her words, havin' you came at one heck of a price.'

'Tell me about it,' agreed Tammy, adding, 'I don't understand why he cannae see Mammy for the wonderful woman she is. Most men would love to have someone as loyal and smart as her on their arm, but Dad acts like she's some sort of dreadful burden that he's being forced to bear.'

'She's too good for him,' concluded Rory. 'And what's more, he knows it.'

'Then why not treat her like the queen that she is, instead of actin' like she's the dirt from beneath his shoes?'

'Because he's worried that she might realise the truth and leave him for someone who's worthy of her attention,' said Rory plainly.

'But Mammy would never do that, not if he treated her right,' insisted Tammy.

'I know, but it doesn't take away from the fact that he cannae be someone he isn't,' said Rory. 'Dennis was born to be a docker; always duckin' and divin' from one scam to the next, because that's who he is, and he doesn't respect himself let alone anyone else.'

'So, he'll never change no matter what we say or do?'

'Alas no, because he hasn't got it in him to be any different. If she wants out of the marriage there's only two ways that I can see, and that's either death or divorce.'

Tammy rolled her eyes. 'As he'll never agree to a divorce that only leaves one option and I swear he's got the luck of the devil when it comes to dodgin' the bullet.'

Rory eyed her curiously. 'What makes you say that?'

'He nearly kicked the bucket a good few years back when he was helpin' to guide a load down onto the dockside; his supervisor yelled at him to get into the office and Dad was halfway there when the rope snapped and the load came crashin' down right where he'd been standin'.'

Rory blew his cheeks out. 'That was a lucky escape!'

'It's not the only one. There was another time when part of the cargo he was helping to unload fell into the sea, taking him with it. He cannae swim a stroke and no one saw him fall, so by rights he should've drowned.'

'How come he didn't?'

'Luckily for him, the cargo happened to be lifebuoys.'

'Blimey! I see what you mean by his havin' the luck of the devil.'

'He'll outlive the lot of us,' agreed Tammy. She jerked her head towards the wall of the greyhound track as she hitched up her skirts. 'C'mon, let's take a gander.'

Knitting his fingers into the form of a stirrup, Rory helped Tammy over the wall before jumping over to join her.

'I used to hate the track because it was one of Dad's favourite hang-outs, until they barred him,' said Tammy conversationally.

Rory wiped the snow from one of the benches before sitting down. 'Serves him right for throwin' a hissy fit when his dog come in last.' He tapped his hands on his knees, indicating that Tammy should sit on his lap. 'Warmer than the bench,' he said with a broadening smile.

Doing as he suggested, she leaned her head into the crook of his neck as he placed his arm around her shoulders. 'At least he cannae blow his money down here any more . . .' She felt Rory's arm stiffen as the words left her lips, and sensing that all was not as it seemed she looked up at the underside of his chin. 'Rory . . . ?'

'Sorry, Tammy, but he gets the lads down the docks to place bets for him,' said Rory wretchedly. 'He's not asked me to do it, but only because he knows I'd tell him to sling his hook.'

'Don't worry. It's hardly your fault he cannae keep his money in his pocket.' A vision of her father and Rory working down the same dock formed in her mind. 'Do you see much of him in work?'

'Not if I can help it,' he said vehemently, 'although I dare say the feelin's pretty mutual.'

'He'd go berserk if he knew I was here with you now,' said Tammy with some satisfaction, 'but thanks to the booze he'll never know, cos he won't come to till the mornin'.'

'Does he get in that sort of state every night?'

'Without fail,' Tammy confirmed.

'Well, if he's like that every night, then why on earth don't you and your mammy leg it once he's out for the count? Eight hours should see you at least halfway across the country, and there's no way he'd be able to find you with that kind of head start!'

'Because we've not got the money for the fare, never mind the rest of it,' said Tammy simply.

'You could come to mine while you look for jobs to save up . . .' Rory began, but Tammy was quick to point out the flaw in his plan.

'Yours is the first place he'd go, because he knows that you're the only one who'd take us in.'

'There is that,' said Rory reluctantly, 'but even so, he cannae expect you to stay at home for ever. He must realise that you'll get married and move out at some point in your life.'

Her eyebrows shot towards her hairline. 'And leave Mammy on her own with him? I should cocoa!'

He leaned to one side so that he could see her better. 'You cannae seriously suggest that you're goin' to live at home for the rest of your life? Even if you tried, how much longer do you think the three of you can live together before one of you ends up six feet under?'

'I don't see that we have another choice,' said Tammy, 'unless he gets called up; but that'll never happen with him workin' down the docks.'

'There has to be some way of gettin' you away from him,' said Rory softly as she leaned back into the warmth of his chest.

But Tammy had grown weary of discussing her father. 'I know you're only tryin' to help, Rory, but it's bad enough we have to live with him, without talkin' about him too. Can't we talk about somethin' else? We have so little time together it seems a shame to waste it on him.'

Rory lifted her chin with the crook of his finger and kissed her tenderly, breaking off momentarily to whisper, 'Of course we can.' But he couldn't tear his thoughts away from freeing his belle. *I'm goin' to get Tammy and her mother away from her father, no matter what it takes!* he thought as he cuddled her close. *Cos I'm not goin' to let that man stand in the way of me and my girl.*

* * *

11

CHRISTMAS EVE 1940

Grace gazed at the falling snow as it slowly covered the icy pavement. Speaking to Tammy over her shoulder, she continued to keep a keen eye out for her husband. 'Perhaps it would be better for you to go to bed before he comes home. I cannae see him bein' in a good mood, especially if he goes a cropper on the ice like he did last year.'

'Serve him right if he does,' said Tammy waspishly. 'Not that he'll see it that way.'

'No. He'll blame one of us – more than likely me – before turnin' on the other, which is why I suggest you get yourself out of harm's way.'

'Why should I hide when I've done nothin' wrong?' said Tammy sullenly. 'For cryin' out loud, Mammy, most families are thrilled at the thought of spendin' Christmas together, but not us. I'd rather be anywhere other than here with him, and how miserable is that?'

'I know,' said Grace softly, 'but even dockers get Christmas Day off.'

'And he'll spend the whole day drinkin' himself into a stupor, while we do everythin' we can to keep out of his way, makin' sure we don't do anythin' to annoy him – such as breathe,' Tammy finished sarcastically.

Her face reflecting the guilt of having chosen such a rotten man to be the father of her child, Grace changed the subject to a more favourable topic. 'What time are you meetin' Rory?'

'Ten o'clock at the track, cos Dad should be out cold by then.'

Grace was in the middle of agreeing with her daughter when Dennis arrived home. Banging his fists against the door, he shouted for them to unlock it and let him in. Rolling her eyes, Tammy shouted back at him. 'It's not locked. You're turnin' the handle the wrong way – again!'

Seemingly unconvinced by Tammy's advice Dennis kicked the door repeatedly, causing the frame to splinter. Huffing that it had been locked all along, he staggered inside, only to be met by the door, which collided with his head after rebounding off the wall. Roaring his displeasure, Dennis held his head in his hands as he gave the door a backward kick.

Tammy glanced at her mother. 'And you wanted me to go to bed and leave you here with him? No chance!'

Grace grimaced briefly before hurrying through to the kitchen, speaking to her husband over her shoulder as she went. 'Sit yourself at the table, and I'll fetch your supper.' She took a bowl from one of the crates where they kept their kitchenware, and began to fill it with the hot stew which was simmering gently on the stove. 'It's still pipin' hot, so mind you take care,' she warned as she placed the bowl down in front of him.

'It'll still taste like shite, but I dare say it cannae be any worse hot than it is cold,' growled Dennis as he waited for his wife to bring a spoon from the crate that housed the cutlery.

As she handed it to him, she remembered the day she'd spent several hours cleaning the stew off the ceiling after Dennis had claimed it was too cold. 'Either way, I kept it on a low flame until you came home, so mind you don't burn yourself.'

Ignoring his wife's words, Dennis began gulping down his supper and was several mouthfuls in before the heat of the food overrode the numbing effect of the alcohol. Clutching at his throat, he bellowed incoherently while throwing the spoon with pinpoint accuracy at his wife, closely followed by the bowl and its steaming contents.

Holding her stew-sodden blouse away from her skin, Grace hurried back into the kitchen, only to be sent sprawling to the floor when Dennis knocked her out of his way as he followed her to fetch a bottle of beer. Breaking the top off, he didn't stop drinking until he had finished every last drop. Then, throwing the empty bottle into the sink, he stared at her accusingly as she scrambled to her feet. 'You done that on purpose!' he snarled.

Aghast that he could say such a thing when she'd done her best to warn him, she started to pick the bits of stew from her hair and clothes. 'I did say . . .' she began, but Dennis wasn't in the mood for explanations. He struck her hard across the cheek, and tutted his contempt as she fell heavily once more.

Diving defensively in front of her mother, Tammy held up a warning hand while fixing her father with a look of pure hatred. 'Don't!' was all she managed to say before being cut off by Grace who had scrambled to her feet.

'Go to your room, Tammy,' said Grace, her tone leaden, 'and don't come out until I tell you to.'

14

Tammy stared at her mother in disbelief. 'But Mammy . . .'

Once again, Grace interrupted her daughter. 'I said go to your room, now do as you're told!' she snapped, before adding in kinder, quieter tones, 'Please, Tammy, just do as I ask.' Rather than risk making matters worse, Tammy reluctantly slunk into her room and closed the door behind her.

Listening to her mother apologising profusely to her father, Tammy winced as she heard several loud thuds. Her fingers were clasped around the doorknob and her knuckles whitened as she restrained herself from rushing to her mother's aid. *The last time you tried to help her you ended up makin' things worse*, Tammy reminded herself, *which is why she wanted you out of the way this time*. Tears surging down her cheeks, she pricked her ears as she tried to make out what was happening on the other side of the door, but it seemed like an eternity before she heard the sound of her father's heavy footsteps as he stumbled his way to bed. Crossing her fingers, she sagged with relief as her mother gently called for her to come out.

'It's not as bad as it looks,' murmured Grace, as Tammy's gaze settled on the eye which was already ballooning beneath the deepening bruise; she then saw the blood which was oozing from the cut on her mother's lower lip. Her voice quavered as she tried to stop the tears.

'We cannae go on like this, Mammy. Rory's right: we've got to do somethin'.'

Grace nodded in an absentminded fashion, as she always did when her daughter made such a statement. 'Your father's gone to bed, so you needn't worry about him doin' anythin' else this evenin'.' She cupped Tammy's cheek in the palm of her hand and gazed lovingly at her. 'You said you were meetin' Rory at ten o'clock. If you hurry, you can still make it.'

'I don't want to leave you on your own, not after what *he* did,' Tammy protested, but Grace was adamant.

'And I don't want to see you stuck under the same roof with him when you could be out havin' yourself some fun.' She took her daughter in a warm embrace, and continued in reassuring tones, 'He's my problem not yours, and just knowin' that you're safe with Rory will make me happy.' She leaned back and caught Tammy's gaze. 'Please, if just for me?'

Tammy, who would do anything to make her mother happy, agreed a tad reluctantly before kissing her on the cheek, noting that Grace winced with pain as she did so. 'I'll go, but I shan't be long.'

'You take as long as you need,' said Grace, as she helped Tammy on with her thickest shawl and scarf. 'He'll not wake up before late tomorrow mornin'.'

It didn't take Tammy long to reach the dog track where Rory was waiting for her, and seeing her tear-stained cheeks he tutted his disgust as he came to greet her. 'He cannae leave either of you alone, even on Christmas Eve! What was it over this time?'

Tammy told him everything that had transpired,

finishing with, 'You should see Mammy's eye; it was nigh on swollen shut by the time I left. What makes it worse is that she won't raise a finger to stop him for fear he'll turn on me, and he knows it. Bearing that in mind, I honestly believe it's only a matter of time before he goes too far.'

'I agree,' said Rory stoutly, as he helped her over the wall, 'which is why I've been makin' a few enquiries.'

'Such as?' asked Tammy, nervously adding, as he landed softly beside her, 'You haven't told anyone about him, have you? He'll lose the plot completely if he thinks I've been tellin' tales, and it's Mammy he'll take it out on.'

'I don't need to tell people, Tammy, because they already know,' said Rory gently. 'The walls in that tenement block are as thin as paper.'

Tammy grimaced because she knew that Rory was right. 'That's why Edie's always bangin' on the floor, tellin' us to keep the noise down.' Her cheeks bloomed with embarrassment. 'What must they think?'

'Who cares what they think!' snapped Rory. 'It's you and your mam I'm worried about, which is why I've been doin' some diggin', and I think I've found a solution that might just work.'

'Oh?'

'Fake identities,' said Rory proudly. Seeing the look of doubt shrouding Tammy's face, he quickly pressed on. 'I know that you're worried your father will come after you if you leave him, but he won't be able to find you if you're livin' under new names.'

'That's all well and good, but we couldn't possibly afford to pay for summat like that!' said Tammy. 'I should imagine it costs an arm and a leg!'

Cheered by the thought that Tammy hadn't dismissed the idea out of hand, Rory was quick to press on. 'It's not cheap, but I could always loan you the money and you can pay me back when you start earnin'.'

'We couldn't ask you to do that,' protested Tammy somewhat hesitantly.

'You're not,' said Rory. 'I'm insistin'.'

Sitting down on one of the benches, she eyed him doubtfully through lowered lashes. 'You make it sound simple, but do you really think it's that easy?'

He smiled encouragingly as he joined her on the bench. 'I've already got the ball rollin'. There's a feller by the name of Sid who does this sort of thing for a livin' – under the counter, of course – and he reckons he can get you everythin' you need to start a new life within the next month or so. He'd do it sooner, but what with the war and all he's got a bit of a wait on stock.'

Tammy felt her heart rise in her chest. 'You're actually serious about this, aren't you?'

His eyes sparkled as he gazed down at her. 'Very much so. You know I'd do anythin' to get you out of there.'

'I'll have to run it by Mammy first, but . . .'

Rory crowed with anticipatory delight. 'Is that a yes?'

'As far as I'm concerned it is, but I'll have to speak to Mammy before I can commit to anythin'.'

He planted his lips a little clumsily against hers, before leaning back. 'This is the best Christmas present I could wish for! Talkin' of which, are we still on for tomorrow?'

Heartened by the thought of their freedom, Tammy spoke excitedly. 'Too right we are! If Mammy gives us the go-ahead I want to get the ball rollin' asap.'

'Fantastic! I'll wait for you on the corner of your street. Have you any idea what time you might be free?'

'Aye. Dad will be off to the pub as soon as they're open, and I'll just make sure he's out of sight before comin' to meet you.'

'Sounds good to me.' He frowned as she stood up. 'You don't have to go yet, surely?'

Her eyes glittered in the moonlight as she looked down at him. 'I want to tell Mammy what we've discussed. She deserves some good news after tonight.'

'I couldn't agree more,' said Rory. He helped her back over the wall before arriving lightly by her side. 'Any thoughts on what name you'll choose?'

She clasped his hand in hers. 'When I was born Mammy wanted to call me Tamsin, but Dad insisted on Tamara.'

He coddled her hand in his. 'So, I'm guessin' you want to be called Tamsin?'

'I do indeed, and I'd like my surname to be Lloyd, cos that was my great-grandmother's maiden name.'

'Smart thinkin'. You'll be changin' your name enough so that Dennis cannae find you, while still keeping ties to your heritage. I take it your father doesn't know your great-grandmother's maiden name?'

'He won't have the foggiest. He's never shown an interest in Mammy's side of the family, which is why I'm goin' to suggest that she does the same.'

'I wish I could be a fly on the wall when he realises that you've escaped and there's nothin' he can do about it!'

She hugged his arm as fresh snow began to fall. 'Personally speakin', I'm glad I won't be there!' She gazed up at him thoughtfully. 'What'll you do when we leave?'

He looked at her in surprise. 'I'm goin' with you!'

She stared at him in astonishment. 'But what about your job?'

He held her close as they continued to walk. 'I'm a crane driver, Tammy, which means I can get work just about anywhere.'

Tammy smiled blissfully. 'Once we're free of him, the world's our oyster!'

'Any ideas on where you'd like to go?'

'Not really. I suppose Mammy might want to go back to her home town – Llangollen – but seein' as that's where they met, I dare say it will be his first port of call after yours, cos he's bound to come lookin' for us.'

He squeezed her hand in his. 'I suppose it doesn't matter where you go, as long as it's far away from him.'

'I cannae imagine what it'll be like to wake up of a mornin' and not have to worry about whether he's in a bad mood, cos that's what I've done my whole life.'

'Your only worry will be the war, and that's how it should be.'

Talking nineteen to the dozen, they seemed to reach

the corner of her street in no time, and Rory took her in his arms. 'I cannae wait to hear what your mammy has to say,' he said, and he looked around to make sure they couldn't be seen before leaning in for a kiss.

Hearing the sound of approaching footsteps, Tammy hastily broke from their embrace. Keeping her head lowered, she smiled shyly at him. 'See you tomorrow, and keep your fingers crossed that she agrees.'

Rory watched as Tammy hurried down the street and entered the tenement building where she lived before turning on his heel and heading back to his own home. *I'll ask Sid to make their papers his top priority*, he thought as his feet crumped through the thick snow, *cos the sooner I get Tammy and her mammy away from that man, the better!*

Tammy carefully opened the door to their flat and tiptoed inside. Hoping that her mother would still be up, she was pleased to see Grace sitting beside the fire, a compress held to her blackened eye.

'Hello, luv. I didn't expect to see you back so soon.'

Tammy knelt down in front of her, so that she could talk without fear of waking her father. 'Rory's had the best idea . . .' She went on to tell her mother all about Rory's plan to obtain false identities for them, while Grace listened in silence. Only when Tammy had finished did she voice her opinion.

'It's very kind of Rory to offer to pay for everythin', but I'm afraid I cannae accept his offer,' she said. 'I won't be beholden to anyone – not even Rory.'

'But why on earth not?' cried Tammy, before hastily

lowering her voice. 'It's not as if we wouldn't pay him back!'

'The main reason for me stayin' with your father is because I can't afford to leave him.' Guessing that Tammy had opened her mouth to say that Rory was nothing like her father, Grace held up her hands to stop her while she continued. 'I know Rory wouldn't hold the debt over our heads, but once bitten twice shy, and I have to draw a line somewhere.'

Tammy stared at her mother in disbelief. 'So we have to stay here with *him* because of your pride?'

Grace clicked her tongue irritably. 'Pride has nothin' to do with it. And who said we had to stay here?'

'But you said—' Tammy began, before being cut off by her mother.

'I said I wouldn't be beholden to anyone, and I won't, but that doesn't mean to say I intend to stay here for the rest of my life.' Grace smiled wistfully. 'It won't half feel good to get rid of the name Blackwell!'

Flooded with relief to hear that her mother wasn't condemning them to a life with Dennis, Tammy clapped her hands together excitedly, but quietly so as not to wake him. 'I cannae wait to tell Rory of your decision.'

Grace tucked a lock of her daughter's hair back behind her ear. 'I'd do anythin' to keep you safe, but I cannae do that if I'm not around.'

Tammy glanced at her parents' bedroom door. 'You think he's goin' to go too far one of these days, don't you?'

Grace hesitated. 'I can tell by the glint in his eye that he'd like to do a lot more than he does, and I don't think it would take much for him to lose control. And if the worst came to the worst, there's only one other person besides me he could vent his anger on.'

'Me.'

'Exactly! Now, with that in mind, we need to find out how much these documents will cost.'

A thought occurred to Tammy which she immediately voiced to Grace. 'You say you won't be beholden to anyone, but how on earth do you plan on gettin' the money when you don't earn any?'

Grace raised a single eyebrow. 'I've been thinkin' about leavin' your father for the longest time, which is why I've been sneakin' money from the housekeepin'.'

Tammy's jaw dropped. 'So it wasn't him imaginin' things, then?'

Grace chuckled softly. 'Not always. I don't take much, just a few pence here, a farthin' there, but it soon adds up.'

'Do you think you might have enough to pay Sid outright?'

Grace pulled a doubtful face. 'I wouldn't have thought so, but it's a good start.'

Finding that they might be closer to leaving than she had previously imagined focused Tammy's thoughts somewhat. 'We need to plan everythin' right down to the last detail – such as where we'll live – so that we can be ready to leave at a moment's notice,' she said. 'I think we should rule Llangollen out, as that would be the first place Dad would look, do you agree?'

Grace was nodding thoughtfully. 'No doubt about it.'

Tammy was about to ask her mother where they

might go when a sudden thought caused her to hesitate. Eyeing her mother curiously, she asked: 'Was it horrible, livin' in Llangollen?'

'What on earth makes you think that?'

'Because I cannae think of another reason for you wantin' to move so far away from your home – especially with someone like Dad.'

'Llangollen is beautiful, but remote. Before I met your father I'd never even heard of Clydebank, so when he told me he lived in a city I imagined it would be like Chester, or Liverpool. Even though I knew it was a long way from home, I never realised how far until I came here for the first time.'

'I know you met Dad while he was down on his holidays, but you've never really elaborated on your time together before you got married. How well did you know each other before tyin' the knot?'

Grace shrugged. 'We didn't. What with him livin' so far away, we only had a short time together before he had to go back to Clydebank. We continued a long-distance relationship – letters and the occasional telephone call – for a few months after he left, but no more than that.'

'Didn't your mammy and daddy disapprove of you marryin' a man you hardly knew?'

'It wasn't long after the great war, and what with money bein' short an' all, my mam and dad were strugglin' to keep a roof over our heads. If anythin', they encouraged me to accept his proposal, sayin' that it was a good opportunity and that I'd be mad to turn him down.'

'And what about when Dad revealed his true colours, what did they say then?'

'That no marriage was perfect, and I should try harder to please him,' said Grace matter-of-factly.

Tammy gaped at her mother. 'How could anyone say that to their own daughter?'

'It was a different time,' said Grace kindly. 'Believe it or not, things were a lot harder then than they are now.'

'Talk about out of the fryin' pan into the fire,' said Tammy, somewhat stiffly. 'I don't care how hard things were, they shouldn't have turned their backs on you like that.'

'Well, it's all water under the bridge now,' said Grace, and in an effort to change the subject she added, 'What time are you meetin' Rory tomorrow?'

'When the pubs open, which brings me to another matter. I'm goin' to nip into the Red Lion on my way, to see if they've got any cleanin' jobs. What with that and the money you've saved, it shouldn't take us long to pay for the necessaries.'

The smiled vanished from Grace's lips. 'And what if your daddy were to find out?'

'Which is why I chose the Red Lion, cos I know he won't go in there.'

'Only because he's barred for not payin' his tab! But that wouldn't stop one of his drinking buddies from seein' you and tellin' him.'

'Rory and I have already discussed that, and he reckons the pubs only want cleaners before they open for business,' said Tammy eagerly.

'I know, but' – Grace rubbed her hands over her

face – 'could you not try somewhere a little further afield, just for good measure?'

'If it makes you happy, then of course I will.'

'Good girl.' She hesitated, a line creasing her brow. 'I know we'll have new papers an' all, but we cannae just magically appear in another city without someone askin' where we've sprung from. What are we meant to say when they do?'

'Rory and I spoke about that too; we'll tell them our house got bombed,' said Tammy. 'That should be enough to satisfy anyone.'

A tear trickled from Grace's unblackened eye. 'We're really goin' to do this, aren't we?'

'You bet your life we are!'

When Tammy awoke on Christmas morning, it took her a moment or two to remember what day it was. Her mind instantly filled with dread until she recalled her meeting with Rory the previous day and the plans for their escape, and then the frown dissipated and a slow smile etched her cheeks as she revelled in the knowledge that this would be the last Christmas she'd be waking up under her father's roof. *I may not know where I'll be this time next year*, she thought, *but I do know one thing: I won't be anywhere near my dad!* She glanced through the thick ice that lined the inside of her bedroom window to the snow-covered pavement. It was too early for her father to have left for the pub, but she was too excited at the thought of telling Rory the good news to stay in bed, so she stood up from her mattress and padded over to the ewer, which had small wisps of steam emanating from the top. *Mammy must've been in while I was asleep*, she thought as she dunked her flannel into the deliciously warm water. *I bet she was just as excited as me when she woke up this morning*. With the room being as cold on the inside as it was on the out, she had what her mother described as a cat's lick and a promise of a wash before hastily patting herself dry. *I'll wait for Dad to leave before goin' through*, she thought as she pulled a second woolly over her head. *That way I don't have to wish him a merry Christmas when I don't mean it*. She glanced around the room, which was furnished with an old mattress, and a large crate on top of which sat the ewer. Her clothes – most of which she was wearing – were kept in a small pile next to the crate. Her father had sold on the wardrobe that used to hold them; Tammy presumed for beer money. *It wasn't even his to sell, same as the bed*, she thought bitterly. *Goodness only knows what he'll tell the landlord should he ever discover that Dad's sold most of the furniture that came with the flat. Not that that's anythin' for me or Mammy to worry about, not any more*. She tried to envisage what sort of place the three of them would rent when they left Clydebank. *Wherever we end up, I'm goin' to do my best to make sure it's not somewhere like this*, she thought as she cast her eyes around the bare, damp-riddled walls, *and we shall have proper furniture, not crates and mattresses*. Her thoughts were interrupted by the slamming of the front door. Only one person left the house in that manner, but it was better to be safe than sorry, so she cracked open the bedroom door and peered through the gap.

27

Having come to tell her daughter that the coast was clear, Grace smiled as she locked eyes with Tammy. 'Merry Christmas, luv. Your dad's just left, although I expect you already know that.'

Tammy followed her mother back through to the kitchen. 'He's out early. The pubs don't open for another hour yet.'

'He's gone down Stinky Harris's to watch a bare-knuckle boxin' match with Shrimpy and a few of the others.'

'Watch? More like bet on it,' said Tammy, 'not that I'm bothered if it means he's out of our hair earlier than expected.'

'Amen to that!' agreed Grace, who was busy putting the top crate on the floor so that she could fetch something from the one beneath. Handing Tammy a brown paper bag, she added, 'It's not much, but I hope you like it.'

Taking the beautifully knitted shawl out of the bag, Grace beamed at her mother. 'It's gorgeous, Mammy, and just what I wanted. Would I be right in guessing that you made it?'

Grace wriggled her fingers. 'I did indeed. I used old jumpers and scarves for the wool – not that your father would believe me, of course, which is why I hid it from him.'

'Father?' protested Tammy. 'What kind of father would begrudge their daughter a Christmas present – especially one that didn't cost him anythin'?'

'One who puts booze above everythin' else,' said Grace tartly.

Tammy admired the multicoloured shawl as she wrapped it around her shoulders. 'Thank goodness I have you.' Examining the neat stitches, she glanced up at her mother. 'Wherever did you find the time?'

Grace gestured to a candle which sat next to the housekeeping jar on top of the mantel. 'When everyone was in bed.'

Tammy felt her cheeks warm. 'I wish I had summat to give you.'

Grace's eyes rounded in astonishment. 'You're gettin' me away from *him*. Quite frankly I couldn't think of a better present than that!'

'Not me; Rory,' corrected Tammy. 'We wouldn't be goin' anywhere if it wasn't for him.'

'But only because of you. He's doin' all of this for you.'

'I know he is, and I'd be lost without him,' Tammy admitted.

'I reckon the feelin's mutual,' said Grace, 'because he wouldn't be goin' to such great lengths otherwise.'

Tammy snuggled her cheek against the soft wool. 'Can I wear my new shawl to go and meet him?'

'Of course you can,' said Grace, 'but let's get some breakfast down you before you head off.'

Having to account for every penny, Grace rarely bought fresh food, instead opting for items that were well past their best. Cutting the last of the stale bread into slices, she carefully picked off the spots of mould before pushing it onto a toasting fork and handing it to Tammy, who held it to the fire. 'When we get a place of our own, we'll only ever have fresh bread,' Tammy said as she turned the fork, 'and alcohol won't be allowed past the threshold.'

'Sounds like heaven,' said Grace, who'd got some Marmite for Tammy to spread on her toast once it was ready.

After they had eaten their meagre breakfast, Tammy helped her mother to prepare the Scotch broth which they would have for their dinner. Popping the last chunks of potato into the pan, she glanced at the clock. 'It's time I was off.'

Rory was delighted to hear that Grace had given the go-ahead. 'I knew she'd say yes,' he said as he lifted Tammy from the floor in a celebratory embrace. 'This is goin' to be the start of a whole new life for all of us!'

'My only worry is that someone will realise that the documents are fakes,' said Tammy.

'You needn't worry about that with Sid makin' them,' Rory assured her. 'He's the best there is, which is why he charges more than the others.'

'That reminds me. Mammy's managed to save a few bob over the years, and she's insistin' that we pay Sid outright, so I'm hopin' my cleanin' jobs will pick up the shortfall.'

Rory placed his arm around her shoulders, pulling her close. 'Sid won't accept the job unless he's had the money upfront, so it makes more sense for me to pay him now and you and your mammy to pay me back as and when you can.'

'Thanks, Rory. It's probably best that we keep that between you and me for now, though, since with any luck I'll be able to pay you back before the papers come through.'

'Did your mam have any ideas on where she'd like to go?'

'Not as yet, but maybe plannin' everythin' down to the last detail isn't the best idea,' said Tammy thoughtfully.

'Why not? Surely the more you plan the easier it'll be?'

Tammy disagreed. 'If we just hop aboard the first train out of town, and keep doin' that at every station, it should be impossible for him to hunt us down, don't you think? After all, if we don't know where we're goin' to end up then neither will he.'

Rory held up his fingers, which were crossed. 'We can only try, although why he can't just leave the two of you be is beyond me,' he said sullenly as they walked towards the outdoor market. 'The way he batters your mammy about, you'd think he'd be grateful to see the back of her.'

'If it was him leavin' us, there wouldn't be a problem,' said Tammy. 'But he won't like the thought of us leavin' him, not one bit!'

'That's typical of men like him,' said Rory. 'He couldn't give a fig about people knowin' he knocks seven bells out of your mammy, but them knowin' that your mammy walked out on him would be more than he could bear!'

'Because if we leave him, they'd know that he was the one at fault,' said Tammy.

'They already know who's to blame,' said Rory, 'even if your father doesn't.'

They spent the next hour wandering the empty streets, fantasising about their future, but at last Tammy turned ruefully to Rory. 'I'd best be off. I hate the idea of leavin' Mammy on her own on Christmas Day.'

'I wish you could both come and live with me until your papers come through,' said Rory. Cupping her chin in his hand, he gently brushed his lips over hers before kissing her with tenderness.

Fervently wishing the same, Tammy felt herself melt into the kiss until the sound of approaching footsteps caused her to hastily break away for fear it might be her father or someone he knew.

Ducking her face from view, she tucked her hand into Rory's. 'I really should make a move.'

Rory sighed his disappointment. 'Come on, I'll walk you to the corner of your street.'

Tammy listened to the crump of their boots as they walked through the thick snow. 'It's so beautiful, don't you think?' she said, indicating the wintery scene with her free hand.

'It makes everythin' look crisp and clean,' agreed Rory. 'Even the docks look pretty under a blanket of snow.'

At the street corner, Tammy jerked her head in the direction of Jellicoe House. 'This time next year, eh?'

'Aye, and I cannae wait.'

Standing on tiptoe, Tammy went to kiss him on the cheek, but he quickly turned his head so that their mouths met. Gasping out loud, she wagged a reproving finger. 'You're takin' your life in your hands kissin' me this close to home.'

'Worth the risk though,' said Rory. Holding her hands in his, he went on, 'I cannae wait till we're far from here.'

'Me neither. No more gossips to worry about, or wonderin' whether me dad's goin' to turn up at any moment.'

'It cannae come soon enough!' said Rory.

She glanced up at him hopefully. 'Shall I see you tomorrow?'

'You will indeed, I'll meet you after work in the usual place.'

She bade him goodbye and hurried home before anyone could see them. Cautiously entering the parlour, she looked at her mother, who confirmed with a thumbs up that her father hadn't returned early.

'How did it go with Rory?'

Tammy told her mother everything except for the bit about Rory paying Sid up front.

Grace smiled approvingly. 'All we can do now is sit tight and make sure we do as little as possible to provoke his temper.'

'And how are we meant to do that, when we don't know what we do wrong in the first place?' said Tammy, annoyed by her mother's implication.

'I know, and of course you're right, but you know what I mean.'

'As far as he's concerned everythin' we do is wrong.' Tammy fell into silent thought. 'If Rory's right, we could be out of here by March.'

'Either way, this is our last Christmas without a tree or decorations, or spoiled by the fear of what will happen cos he's had one too many,' said Grace.

'Life will certainly be a lot sweeter without him, and once we settle somewhere new we can find proper jobs,' said Tammy, brightening as an idea struck her. 'We could even start up our own business.' She pushed her hands into the air before pulling them slowly apart, as if she were unfurling a large banner. 'Lloyd's Looms.'

Grace chuckled at her daughter's ambition. 'I'm not sure that we could afford to have our own loom.'

'Maybe not at first, but I don't see that there's anythin' to stop us once we get some money behind us,' said Tammy optimistically. 'Things are changin'; this isn't a man's world, not any more.'

Grace raised a cynical eyebrow. 'Whatever makes you think that?'

'The WAAF, the ATS, and the Wrens,' said Tammy. 'The men need us to win this war, and we must make sure that they never forget that we played our part, cos from where I'm standin' we're on an equal footin'.'

Grace's brow rose swiftly. 'We'll never have equal rights while men roam the planet.'

'Why ever not? We deserve recognition.'

Grace laughed without mirth. 'We might get a pat on the head, but don't hold your breath for anythin' more than that!'

'It's wrong!' said Tammy. 'And they're as bad as Hitler if they think all women are worthless.'

Grace shrugged. 'I'm not sure I'd go that far, but in a way you're right, because they do think we're below them, always have, always will – apart from men like Rory, of course, but they're few and far between.'

'Then it's up to us women to make them see differently,' said Tammy stoutly.

Grace smiled. 'Good job I raised a warrior, because you've one heck of a battle on your hands!'

Chapter Two

13TH MARCH 1941, 13:00 HRS

A lot had happened since Tammy had given Rory the go-ahead regarding the fake documents, and even though Rory had asked Sid to see if he could put the Blackwells at the top of his list they'd still had to wait a couple of months before the documents were ready. Now, Tammy's stomach was turning cartwheels as she stood waiting for Rory to arrive. When she saw him approaching in the distance, she trotted stealthily towards him. 'Where've you been?' she hissed. 'I've been imaginin' all sorts!'

He peered at his wristwatch. 'How long have you been waitin'?'

She grimaced apologetically. 'About twenty minutes. I know I'm early, but I couldn't sit in the house any longer; I've been like a cat on a hot tin roof all day.' She glanced at the envelope in his hands. 'Is that them?'

Nodding, Rory handed it over.

Peeking inside, she felt her heart quicken as her eyes fell on the name Tamsin Lloyd. She tucked the envelope into her skirt pocket and glanced at Rory. 'Oh my God, this is really happenin', isn't it?' she said, her voice full of trepidation.

Rory smiled. 'Have you got everythin' ready to go?'

'Aye, we packed everythin' – not that there's an awful lot to pack – as soon as he left the house this mornin'. We're just waitin' on you.' She eyed him pleadingly. 'Everythin' has gone so smoothly, is there no chance that we could go now, instead of havin' to wait? Only I'm scared summat will go wrong at the last minute if we hang on too long.'

'I wish we could, but the van I'm borrowin' won't be free until later on today.'

'Fair enough. I know we can't get the train from Clydebank in case one of Dad's cronies sees us, but . . .' She hesitated. 'What have you told them exactly, the people whose van you're borrowin'?'

'I've told them I'm takin' a pal to Glasgow and don't expect to be back till late,' Rory explained. 'I've arranged to drop the van off at his house, so I won't have to go back to the docks, or anywhere near your old house; as soon as I've done that I'll be hot on your tail!'

'You make it sound so easy.'

'It's only as difficult as you make it.' He arched an eyebrow. 'Talkin' of which, let's run through the plan once more. Where are we meetin'?'

'You're goin' to be parked down the side of Scott Street, ready to leave at eight o'clock,' said Tammy without hesitation.

'Spot on! Now, is there anythin' I can get you before we set off?'

She glanced up at him anxiously. 'A new heart would be good, because mine's hammerin' like it's goin' to burst.'

He gave her a sympathetic smile. 'Don't worry, it's not for too much longer. You'll be able to relax a bit more once you're free of Clydebank.'

'I wish it was time already,' said Tammy, wringing her hands nervously.

'How's your mammy copin'?'

'Better than me. She's still actin' as though it's a normal day,' said Tammy incredulously.

'Perfect! The best way to pull the wool over someone's eyes is to act normally. I bet he didn't suspect a thing when he left for work this mornin'?'

'Not an inklin'.' She patted the pocket which contained the envelope. 'Speakin' of Mammy, I'd best get back because she'll worry if I'm away for too long, plus I know she's eager to take a good look at the documents for herself.'

'Fair enough.' He smiled. 'The next time I see you, it'll all be over, or as near as damn it.'

She placed a hand to her tummy before clapping it to her forehead. 'Honest to goodness, I'd forget my own head if it weren't screwed on!' Delving into her other pocket she pulled out a similar envelope to the one he'd handed her, and passed it over.

He frowned at the envelope. 'What's in there?'

She beamed proudly. 'The money we owe you for the documents, right down to the last farthing.'

'That's very good of you, but there was no need to

rush. You could easily have given it to me when we meet later on.'

'That's what I told Mammy, but she was insistent that you should have it before we left, in case you needed it for summat.'

Tucking the envelope into his top pocket, he glanced at his wristwatch. 'I'd best get back to work before someone misses me.'

She was about to turn away when something made her hesitate. 'I love you, Rory. You do know that, don't you?'

He grinned. 'Course I do! Just like you know that I love you. What made you ask?'

'I dunno. I just wanted you to know, that's all.'

He chuckled softly. 'I think the pressure's gettin' to you; hardly surprisin' given the circumstances, I suppose. Now get you gone, and stop stallin'. We'll be together soon enough!'

She smiled fleetingly before turning on her heel and heading back to the house. Once inside she handed the envelope full of documents to her mother, who immediately compared them with the originals.

'Apart from the names, they're identical!' she breathed, with astonished approval.

'What shall we do with our old ones?'

'We cannae leave them here for him to find, because if we do he'll know we're usin' new identities, and I'd prefer to send him off on a wild goose chase than have him make enquiries with his ne'er-do-well pals, so we must take them with us and destroy them once we're

39

settled,' said Grace as she tucked both her old and her new documents into her handbag.

Tammy also compared her fake documents to the real ones, with equal admiration for Sid's work. 'Dad'll not suspect for a moment that we've changed our names, so he'll never find us cos he'll be lookin' for a couple of Blackwells.' She tucked her old identification papers into her pocket and put the fake ones into her purse, which she then tucked into her handbag. 'I don't want to get them mixed up,' she told her mother by way of explanation.

'Good thinking,' said Grace, who followed her daughter's example. With nothing left to do save sit and wait, she cast her eye around the parlour. 'I know I've asked you a hundred times already, but are you sure you've got everythin'?'

Tammy indicated the bag which was in the hall ready to go. 'Everythin' I own is in that suitcase.'

Grace drummed her fingers against her folded arms. 'We've a long wait until eight o'clock.'

'I know, and I did ask Rory if we could meet any sooner, but he said he cannae pick the van up until later on today, so we're goin' to have to be patient.' She patted her mother reassuringly on the shoulder. 'It's probably better this way, cos at least it'll be dark when we leave. The last thing we want is for someone to see us headin' off in his mate's van, cos you know what it's like around here for gossip – if Dad found out whose van it was, it wouldn't take him long to work out who we were with, plus he'd be there to ambush Rory when he drops the van back off.'

Grace sighed impatiently. 'I know. It's only that I'm just itchin' to be off.'

The hours passed slowly as the two women sat in the parlour watching the minutes tick by on the only clock they had. With just ten minutes to go before it struck five, Grace got to her feet for what felt like the hundredth time. 'Waitin' has to be the hardest part. I wish there was summat for me to do, cos I think I'm goin' to go doolally if I sit here much longer!'

'I still say we should take the housekeepin',' said Tammy, who had been eyeing the pot which stood on the mantel. 'It's not as if he'll spend it on anythin' other than beer.'

Grace shook her head fervently. 'If we take that, he'll be crowin' it from the rooftops, tellin' them all how we were nowt but a couple of thieves who left him high and dry, and I won't have them think badly of us when he's the one who's in the wrong!'

'I don't care what they think, and neither should you!' said Tammy stoutly. 'And besides, I reckon we've earned that money after havin' to put up with him for all these years.'

But Grace was adamant. 'He's already goin' to be gunnin' for us; we don't need to make matters worse by givin' him more ammunition, and that's precisely what we'll be doin' if we steal what he sees as bein' rightfully his.' She cast a wary eye in the direction of the front door. 'I'm goin' to wait in the hallway. I know we've only got a few hours left, but I've a sense that summat's goin' to go horribly wrong. You might say I can feel it in my bones.'

Tammy appeared nonplussed by her mother's words as she followed her through to the hall. 'It's because you cannae believe your luck,' she told Grace. 'I've been feelin' the same way all day, but as you say, there's only a few hours left to wait, and you know as well as I do that Dad'll be straight down the pub as soon as he finishes work. So stop your frettin', cos nothin' can go wrong, not this late in the day.'

* * *

13TH MARCH, 16:50 HRS

Dennis's anger was all-consuming as he left the docks for the final time. Furious that he had been sacked without any physical proof that he'd actually stolen the money, there was only one destination on his mind and that was the pub. Turning his collar up against the rain which was lashing down, he rued the moment he'd seen the other man drop his wallet.

I wish I'd left it where it was, Dennis told himself as he made his way to the pub where he intended to drown his sorrows, *and let's face it, if I hadn't picked it up some-one else would, and they'd have done the same as me!*

In his mind's eye he replayed the moment he'd stooped to pick the wallet up without breaking his stride before heading behind a stack of crates, where he'd swiftly pocketed the contents and discarded the wallet before emerging on the other side. Confident that nobody had seen him, he'd continued about his work until being called into the office where his supervisor – an older man by the name of Callaghan – had told him to turn his pockets out. Dennis had done so with-out hesitation, believing that nobody could prove the money wasn't his, but as it turned out, one of the crane drivers had witnessed the whole thing.

'You cannae prove that money's not mine!' cried Dennis as they informed him of his fate.

'Not only were you seen, but the man who lost his wallet told us how much he had in it, and it just so hap-pens to be the exact same amount you've just turfed out of your pockets.' His supervisor pointed towards the door. 'We've got you bang to rights this time, Dennis. If you don't want to find yourself up in court, I suggest you leave without a fuss.'

Dennis had wanted to argue a case for 'finders keep-ers', but he could tell by the look on his supervisor's face that it would be futile to even attempt to fight his corner. So embroiled was he in his thoughts that he made it halfway to the pub before he realised he hadn't been paid and therefore had no beer money. Cursing beneath his breath, he turned on his heel and headed for home. With it not yet being five of the clock he knew that Grace would want to know why he was home earl-ier than usual, and he was not in the mood to answer her questions. *If she so much as opens her mouth, I'll bleedin' well shut it for her, cos I ain't havin' her judge me as well as them lot down the docks*, he thought bitterly, *although I dare say she'll find out in the fullness of time, either from the dockers or that bleedin' Rory*. He faltered mid-step. Rory was a crane driver – was he the one who'd reported Dennis for stealing the wallet? He clenched his jaw as flecks of spittle formed in the corners of his mouth. Of course Rory had been the one who'd reported him, and had he had the presence of mind at the time, he'd have put two and two together. Being caught on the hop had left him in a state of disarray. He struck a stone with the toe of his boot, causing it to ricochet off a passing bus. *If I'd realised it was Rory who'd reported me, I could've claimed that he'd made the whole thing up to get me back for not allowin' him to see Tammy. I reckon they'd believe me too, cos they all know me and him have got beef* . . . He paused in his thoughts. Bearing in mind that they knew about Rory and Dennis being at loggerheads, why hadn't it occurred to any of them to question Rory's accusation? *Because they wanted an excuse to get rid of me, that's why*, Dennis told himself; *they even said they'd got me bang to rights 'this time'.* He dug his hands deep into his pockets as his anger grew. If Grace were to so much as mention his being home early he would tell her why, and he'd make sure that Tammy knew who was to blame for his sacking. *See how she feels about her precious Rory when she learns that he's the reason for us not havin' money to put food in our bellies or keep a roof over our heads.* Dennis fumed as he strode in the direction of his home. *That'll show her that he's a no-good*— His thoughts were interrupted by a female voice.

'You're home early.'

Dennis swung round to see who'd spoken and grunted his displeasure as his eyes fell on Stella Warbeck, a neighbour who liked to nose into other people's affairs.

'Piss off, and mind your own business.'

Stella bristled. 'That's the last time *I* make an observation!'

He cast her a long cynical look which ran from the rollers partly hidden beneath her headscarf to the worn toes of her boots. Looking back up, his eyes narrowed as they met hers. 'I very much doubt that.'

Hefting her bosom with her folded arms, she walked off stiff-backed, muttering reprovingly to herself.

Feeling somewhat pleased that he had managed to upset his neighbour, he approached the door to his house and pushed it open, only to find himself staring at his wife and daughter standing in the hallway, with their suitcases close by.

* * *

13TH MARCH, 17:00 HRS

Back at the docks, Rory joined the other workers who were having a brew. Conscious of the need to steer clear of Dennis, he had no knowledge of what had transpired just a short while earlier until he heard his colleagues discussing the man's dismissal.

'Did you see the look on Dennis's face when they told him to sling his hook?' said one of the men as he passed Rory a mug of tea. 'I thought he was goin' to swing for old Callaghan.'

Rory spoke in even tones, the mug of tea poised before his lips. 'Are you talkin' about Dennis Blackwell?'

The man nodded. 'He got caught thievin' some feller's wallet.'

'No surprises there,' muttered another of the workers.

45

Rory lowered his mug as he stared at the man who was telling the story. 'Where is he now?'

'Down the pub.'

'Are you sure?'

'Positive. Greg Robins seen him headin' to the Alexander. Why, what's it to you?'

Breathing a sigh of relief, Rory shrugged the question off. 'Just wondered. You know what Dennis is like for takin' his wrath out on the nearest person.'

'And with you bein' a crane driver, you worried he might think it was you what grassed him up?' said the man. 'I s'pose that stands to reason. Should he start, you'll just have to tell him he's got it wrong.'

Rory sank into deep thought. If Dennis had gone down the pub it would be a long time before he went back home, so he needn't worry about him thwarting their plans of escape. *Of all the days to get caught, though*, Rory thought now. *It's a good job we're leavin', cos I should imagine he's intendin' to take his anger out on Grace and Tammy as soon as he gets back from the pub.*

* * *

13TH MARCH, 17:10 HRS

Dennis had realised their intention as soon as he'd laid eyes on the suitcases. Slamming the door hard behind him, he pointed an accusing finger at his wife as he strode down the hall, Tammy and Grace retreating before him into the parlour.

'You, sneaky, connivin', selfish bitch!' roared Dennis, looming over his wife as she backed herself against a wall. 'After everythin' I've done for you, and you think you can just walk away?'

'All you've done for me?' cried Grace in disbelief. 'What've you done for me other than beat me black and blue?'

'No more than you deserve,' snarled Dennis. 'Not many men would put up with your selfish ways.'

She gaped at him. '*Me* selfish? I spend my whole day bendin' over backwards in a bid to make you happy, but nothin's ever good enough for you, is it, Dennis?'

'Scaldin' me with your disgusting cooking! Is that what you call bendin' over backwards to make me happy? Not to mention how you fritter away the money that I've worked my fingers to the bone for!'

'How can I fritter your money away when you barely give me enough to pay the bills in the first place?'

Their upstairs neighbour, Edie Brodie, banged the floor with her broom while shouting at them to 'Shut the hell up!' Shaking his fist at the ceiling, Dennis bellowed, 'Shurrup yourself!' before turning his attention back to his wife. 'It's my money, and I can do what I damned well please with it.'

'In which case you'll be better off without us,' said Grace plainly.

Not used to retaliative replies from Grace, Dennis found his temper growing hotter by the second. 'If you think you're goin' to just walk out of here then you've another thing comin'!'

'I don't *think* anythin',' said Grace defiantly. 'We're leavin' and there isn't a darned thing you can do to stop us.'

His eyes bulging, Dennis gripped his wife by the throat and pushed her up against the wall, leaving her feet dangling above the floor. Talking in tones of pure loathing, he stared at her with a hatred that burned. 'Can't I now? Well that's where you're wrong! I say who stays and who goes around here and the only way you're leavin' is in a wooden box.'

Seeing her mother struggling to breathe, Tammy begged her father to let go, but Dennis tightened his grip even further, cutting off Grace's airway. Fearing that he was about to do the unthinkable, Tammy grabbed his wrist and tried frantically to yank his hand from her mother's throat, but no matter how hard she tried she couldn't get him to let go. With tears coursing down her cheeks she continued to plead with her father to release his grip, but it seemed he was hell bent on committing murder, and she could only watch in horror as Grace's eyes rolled back in her head. Desperate to stop him before it was too late, she grabbed the nearest thing to hand and swung it at him, but he leaned towards her at the last second and the iron connected with the side of his head instead of his arm as she had intended.

* * *

13TH MARCH, 19:15 HRS
Rory glanced at his wristwatch before he picked up the last of the pallets to be loaded onto the ship. He'd never known the time to drag as much as it had today, and he'd be glad when his shift was over. Listening to

the men talk of Dennis's wrongdoings had unnerved him, and even though he knew that the man was drinking his sorrows away down the Alexander he couldn't shake the uneasy sense that all was not well. *You're being paranoid because you know how much is at stake*, he told himself. *Even if you'd turned up earlier than planned, you'd still have had to wait for the van to be available.* He put his thoughts to one side as he jerked his head in acknowledgement of the men who'd given him the thumbs up after securing the pallet to the crane's hook. Only once the shipment was on deck and the hook freed from the cargo did he turn his thoughts back to Dennis. *You've waited a long time for this day to come, and you cannae believe it's finally here, which is why you're determined Dennis is goin' to throw a spanner in the works, but you're worryin' needlessly. Dennis has more reason than ever to get bladdered and he won't be back from the pub until they chuck him out, by which time we'll be long gone!*

It was only after they turned the corner that Tammy realised her mother was running in the opposite direction from Scott Street. She called in vain for her to come back, but Grace wasn't stopping for anything or anyone until they were far away from the scene of the crime.

'We're goin' the wrong way!' panted Tammy as she eventually caught up. 'Rory's meetin' us on Scott Street.'

Glancing fearfully around her, Grace hastily hushed Tammy into silence. 'For cryin' out loud, Tammy, keep your voice down! And as for Rory, we cannae possibly meet up with him, not now.'

Tammy stared at her open-mouthed. 'Why on earth not? We need to get away from here as fast as we can!'

Grace pointed a trembling finger back in the direction of their home while hissing in a frantic whisper, 'Because your father's lyin' dead on the floor and it was you what killed him, that's why!'

'It was an accident!' cried Tammy, her voice shaking with suppressed emotion. 'Rory will understand!'

'I never thought for a moment that he wouldn't, and it's not him I'm worried about.' Grace endeavoured to steady her nerves. 'What do you think the polis would think if they found us with Rory?'

Tammy knew full well what her mother was getting at. 'We'll tell them he had nothin' to do with it. They cannae prove otherwise.'

'My darlin' child, they'll arrest him for aidin' and abettin' a couple of murderers. As far as they're concerned he'd be as guilty as us, and it's not fair for us to put him in that position. You know it isn't.'

Tears cascaded down Tammy's cheeks. 'But neither is it fair for us to leave without tellin' him what's gone on. We owe him that much at least.'

'Only you know as well as I do that Rory would insist on comin' with us.'

Since Rory had already told her the same thing, Tammy couldn't argue. 'Well, if he does, and we do get collared, then I'll tell them that I forced him to come.'

Grace eyed her daughter sternly. 'What would you prefer? To never see him again or for him to join you at the gallows? Because three people are a lot easier to find than two, and unlike you and me Rory hasn't got false papers.'

Tammy hung her head in her hands before looking back up at her mother. 'And what about you? If they see Rory as an accomplice, then why wouldn't they see you the same way?'

Grace swallowed the lump in her throat which was prohibiting the words she dreaded to speak. 'If anyone's goin' to take the blame for this then it's me, *not* you!' She held up a hand to quell Tammy's protests. 'But I'd prefer it if they got neither of us, which is why I think we should split up.'

Shaking her head frantically, Tammy grabbed her mother's hands. 'No! I am not leavin' you. We're in this together, come what may.'

Grace's eyes shone with unshed tears. 'My darlin' child, you must realise that two people are easier to find than one, which is why we have to go our separate ways if we've any hope of gettin' out of this unscathed.'

Tammy felt the blow of her mother's words as though she had delivered them physically. 'But we've already got new identities, and if we're careful—'

'As soon as they find Dennis's body they'll put a call out to arrest a mother and daughter matching our descriptions. They'll know we'll be usin' public transport to get as far away from Scotland as we can so don't kid yourself that you'll be scot free just because you're not in Clydebank any more. This is murder, Tammy; the call will be nationwide.'

Tammy nodded miserably. She knew her mother was

talking sense, even if it was a bitter pill to swallow. 'This was meant to be the start of a new life, but we're in a worse position than we were before . . . thanks to me.'

Unable to bear the pain in her daughter's face, Grace took Tammy in a tight embrace. 'It's nothin' of the sort. The only one to blame is your dad.'

'If we go our separate ways we'll never see each other again,' Tammy mumbled as the tears continued to form.

'It's only until the heat's off,' Grace assured her softly.

Tammy sniffed. 'And when will that be?'

Grace spoke slowly and deliberately. 'Give it till Christmas. If we haven't been collared by then, we should be all right to meet up, even if it's just for a few hours or so.'

'But how will I know where to find you?'

Grace fished a handkerchief out of her pocket and handed it to Tammy. 'D'you remember that photo-graph I had of the Liver Building in Liverpool?'

Tammy pictured the photograph of an elderly man standing on the steps to a building which had a large statue of a bird perched on top of the clock tower. 'Where my great-grandaddy used to work?'

'That's the one! How about we meet there at twelve noon on Christmas Eve?'

Tammy stared at her mother. 'That's nine months away! What am I supposed to do in the meantime?'

'Get as far away from here as you can.'

'What about you?' said Tammy, her voice cracking with emotion.

'I'll do the same.' Grace paused momentarily before

continuing. 'And I think we should start right away. I'll get on the first bus goin' out of town, and you can board the first train.'

Tammy rummaged in her pocket before handing her mother some coins, and Grace stared at her accusingly.

'Where did you get these from?'

'It's the housekeepin',' said Tammy, quickly adding, 'I know you said not to take it, but that was before Dad came home; things are different now.'

'I suppose if you put it that way . . .' Grace was beginning, when something caught her attention. She stared fixedly at a point behind her daughter as she tried to pick out the shadow which had moved within the darkness.

Tammy looked over her shoulder, following her mother's gaze. 'What is it?'

Grace waved a dismissive hand towards some flattened cardboard boxes. 'I thought I saw the boxes move, but it's probably my guilty conscience playin' tricks on me.'

Tammy peered into the darkness. She'd often seen tramps using cardboard boxes as blankets. If there was someone underneath, then . . . Her thoughts were interrupted as her mother cupped her cheek in the palm of her hand.

'If there were any other way . . .'

Tammy gulped the words which came out in a rush. 'I wish this wasn't happenin'.'

Taking her daughter in a tight embrace, Grace whispered: 'Me too, but we'll be back together one day, just you wait and see.' She fussed over the shawl she had given Tammy as a Christmas gift, making sure it was wrapped tightly around her daughter's shoulders. 'Take care of yourself, Tammy, and don't ever forget: I will always love you.'

Feeling her mother's arms slip from around her shoulders, Tammy murmured, 'I love you too,' before turning on her heel and hurrying away.

Blissfully unaware of these events, it was with a spring in his step that Rory left work to begin his new life with Tammy and her mother. As he said goodbye to his co-workers, some of whom he'd worked with since leaving school at the age of fourteen, he'd felt a sense of sorrow that he wasn't able to be completely honest with them, but had simply said it was time to move on. *I reckon most of them would cheer from the rooftops if they knew what I had planned, because they've all got beef with Dennis for one reason or another*, he thought as he hurried back to his room to pick up his belongings, which he had packed the night before. *I'd love to see the look on Dennis's face when he realises they've left him. I know Tammy thinks he'll be eager to track them down, but I'm not so certain; the way he treats them he might actually be happy that they've gone!* He dug his key out of his pocket and entered the room, gathered his bag and jacket, and did one final check before locking the door and heading off. He'd tell his landlord that he didn't intend to live there any more when he returned the borrowed van. *Dennis will already know they've gone by that time, so there'll be no need to skulk in the shadows, and I won't be bothered if someone does tell him that I've gone, because at least he'll know they're not on their own, which might make him less likely to come looking.*

He rounded the corner and smiled as he saw the small van parked up ahead. *This is it!* he thought as he jogged towards the van. *Twenty minutes from now we'll be on the road.*

Chapter Three

Having waited what felt like an eternity for a train to arrive, above all else Tammy was extremely glad to get out of the freezing cold and into a warm carriage when she snuck aboard the first one to leave the station. With no idea where it was headed, she gazed blindly out of the carriage window as the train made its way through the dark, bleak countryside. *Poor Rory will be worried sick, and I cannae do anythin' to let him know that I'm all right*, she thought as the wheels of the train clacked along the rails. *I wish he were here to give me one of his bear hugs, because they never fail to make me feel better, but I guess I'll never feel his arms around me again.* Tears trickled down her cheeks as she pictured him telling her that he'd take care of everything and she was not to worry, while enveloping her in his arms just as he always had. *If he'd been with me, I just know he'd have found a way for the three of us to stay together.* She turned her thoughts to what her mother had said about how the police would put a call out nationwide for two women fitting their descriptions on the run for murder. *I might be out of Clydebank, but I'm still not out of the woods,* thought Tammy, ashen-faced with terror that the police might come down the train at any moment and arrest her either for the murder of her father or for not having purchased a ticket. She had chosen to sit in the only empty carriage and had been on her own until a girl of around her own age had entered and taken the seat opposite. Briefly glancing at the newcomer, Tammy had taken in the large headscarf which hid her hair and ears and the woolly scarf which was wound around her neck, leaving just her eyes and nose on view. Keen not to give her an excuse to strike up a conversation, she had quickly averted her gaze from the other girl, but when gentle sobs reached her ears she found she couldn't possibly keep ignoring her.

Dipping her head to try to catch her eye, Tammy spoke in gentle tones. 'Hello? Is everythin' all right?' She knew it was a stupid question, but thought it was a good way to break the ice without appearing too intrusive.

Hastily drying her eyes on the cuffs of her coat, the girl spoke thickly through her scarf. 'I'll be fine. It's just that it's my first time away from home.'

'Mine too,' said Tammy who, having not spoken to anyone since leaving her mother, found the thought of taking on someone else's worries more appealing than addressing her own and so went on, 'Are you goin' anywhere nice?'

The girl hesitantly pulled the scarf down, revealing plump rosy lips. 'I hope so. I'm off to join the services. You?'

Tammy swallowed. She hadn't expected to have a

question thrown back at her, and this one had really caught her on the hop. Unable to think of a suitable lie, she said the first words that came into her head. 'Wherever the wind takes me.' She hoped that this made her sound interesting rather than evasive, and was pleased to see the other girl's lips twitch into a soft smile.

'That sounds more excitin' than the services.' She lowered her gaze to examine her fingernails before looking back up. 'I chose this carriage because I thought you looked how I felt – if that isn't too rude to admit.'

Tammy stared at her. 'How d'you mean?'

The other girl shrugged. 'That you look like you've got the weight of the world on your shoulders.'

Tammy was somewhat surprised by how intuitive the stranger was, given that she herself had purposely kept her gaze averted. Thinking it better to stick with half-truths, she looked pointedly at the night sky. 'We're livin' in dangerous times, and tonight's moon is perfect for the Luftwaffe.'

The girl followed her gaze. 'Is that why you keep lookin' out of the window?'

Pleased that her fib had provided the perfect excuse for having ignored her fellow passenger, Tammy spoke over her shoulder as she turned her attention back to the dark landscape. 'They say that forewarned is as good as forearmed, although I'm not sure what good I could do apart from raise the alarm.'

The girl leaned forward, her hand outstretched. 'I'm Georgina Anderson, but you can call me Gina.'

Tammy had taken Gina's hand in hers when she spied several police officers on the platform of the station they were pulling in to. Her cheeks paling, she murmured 'Bloody hell' beneath her breath as two of the officers boarded the train.

Gina, who had also been watching the officers, fixed Tammy with a look of grave concern. 'No wonder you look like you're carrying the weight of the world! I knew summat was up. Are you on the run from the polis?'

Momentarily stunned, but with Gina her only possible ally, Tammy decided to continue skimming the surface of the truth. 'Kind of. I've run away from home.'

Gina held a hand to her mouth. 'Oh my good God!' She glanced nervously to the reflections of the corridor windows to see if she could spy the policemen, but they were nowhere to be seen. 'D'you think they're after you?'

Tammy felt the colour drain from her cheeks. Half-truths were all well and good but it was only natural that Gina would want to know more, and unless Tammy wanted to alienate her new friend she would have to give her some kind of explanation. 'That depends.'

'On what?'

It was now or never as far as Tammy was concerned, so she stuck with the first story that sprang to mind. 'On whether my stepmother has realised I'm missin' yet. Usually she locks me in the cellar when she goes out but her daughters were making such a fuss this afternoon that she forgot, so I made good my escape while I could.'

'How awful! Why on earth does she lock you in the cellar?'

Thankful that Gina hadn't spotted the similarity between her story and that of Cinderella, Tammy pulled her collar up in a bid to hide her face from the policemen should they come their way. 'She hates me, because I remind her of my mammy, and while I dare say she'll be glad to find me gone she knows it would look bad if she didn't report me missin', so she's bound to tell the polis, if only to cover her back.'

Still keeping a close eye out for the policemen, who had yet to pass them by, Gina said, 'Didn't your dad do anythin' to help?'

'Too busy gettin' legless,' said Tammy.

Gina came to sit down next to Tammy. 'No wonder you're on the run with parents like that! If the polis ask, we're cousins, and you're comin' with me to sign up.'

Relieved that Gina was going along with the plan, yet disappointed that she'd had to lie to a possible ally, Tammy was halfway through thanking her for her help when something occurred to her. 'You say you're off to sign up for the services, but couldn't you have signed up in Clydebank?'

Gina hesitated slightly before replying. 'I could have,' she said slowly, 'but I wanted to show my parents that I can make my own way in the world.'

Tammy gave her a puzzled look. 'But surely you could have done that in Clydebank?'

Gina appeared to have an epiphany. 'My father's an admiral in the Navy and me mammy's in the Wrens, so they're both keen for me to follow in their footsteps, but I want to join the ATS, so rather than argue the toss I thought it easier if I just left without telling them.'

'Oh.' Tammy was still not quite sure why Gina felt she had to go to a different city to sign on, but she supposed that if it was important to Gina, then who was she to argue? 'I guess tradition can mean a lot to some folk,' she ventured, 'but it's your life not theirs.'

Gina appeared relieved that Tammy had seen things from her perspective. 'Exactly!' She glanced out of the window. 'I wonder how long it will take us to reach Kilmarnock?'

Tammy looked at her in surprise. 'Kilmarnock? Is that where this train's headed?'

Gina gaped at her. 'I know you said you were going wherever the wind took you, but I kind of assumed you at least knew what train you were on!'

'Not the foggiest,' admitted Tammy. 'I just jumped aboard the first one to pull up and hoped no one saw me.'

Gina's chin dropped even further. 'You haven't got a ticket?'

Tammy grimaced. Up until now Gina had been on her side, but would she feel the same way knowing that Tammy was a stowaway? 'I know it's wrong, but I don't have a lot of money, and what little I do have I need to keep for emergencies.'

Thinking that Tammy's sheltered life had left her somewhat naïve, Gina decided to fill her in on what was necessary in order to get by in today's world. 'If you've been locked away for goodness knows how long you're probably not aware of this, but it's impossible to do anything without some form of identification these days. You even need a card to buy groceries!'

Tammy patted her handbag. 'I've got everythin' I need to start anew.'

Gina appeared perplexed. 'I hope you don't mind my sayin', but you're awfully well organised for someone who escaped from a cellar.'

Stunned by her own stupidity, Tammy could've kicked herself for opening her mouth without thinking first, but it was too late to go back now; she would have to muddle her way through and hope for the best. 'I saw her hidin' my documents before she locked me in the cellar, and as for the money . . .' Here Tammy fell quiet while she tried to think of a plausible explanation, but luckily for her Gina had already found one.

'I wouldn't normally condone stealin', but your circumstances are exceptional to say the least, and I'm sure you wouldn't dream of doin' summat like that otherwise.'

Tammy felt her tummy plummet. Gina was lovely and she hated lying to her, but what choice did she have? She was so deep in thought she hadn't even realised the policemen had passed by their carriage until Gina brought it to her attention.

'Looks like they must be after someone else, because they barely gave either of us a second glance,' she said, indicating the officers, who were nearly lost from view. As she spoke, she opened her satchel and pulled out four rounds of shop-bought cheese and onion sandwiches, two of which she held out to Tammy. 'I bet you're starvin'. I know I am.' She glanced down at her ample waistline. 'Although I dare say it won't harm me to lose a pound or two before I sign up.'

Tammy was surprised to find that she was in fact hungry, despite everything she'd been through. 'Only if you're sure?'

Having already taken a large bite out of her own sandwich Gina spoke thickly, covering her mouth with her fingers. 'Positive! Besides, I bet it's been a long time since you've had any decent tucker.'

They both looked out of the window while they ate their sandwiches, despite the fact that there was nothing to see. Only when they had finished did Gina finally speak. 'Just a thought, but with you havin' nowhere to run to, and me off to join the services, why don't you come with me?'

Tammy stared at her. 'To join up, you mean?'

'Unless you've a better idea?'

Tammy blinked. If she were to join the services, she'd be dressed in the same uniform as countless others, which would make her a lot harder to find should the police come looking. Not only that, but she'd have a place to lay her head, food in her belly, and a wage to boot. In short, it seemed the answer to all her problems, and there was only one thing holding her back – something which she now addressed. 'But I thought you wanted to do this on your own?'

'Not on my own per se,' said Gina, 'just without my parents' input. So, what do you say?'

Tammy didn't need to think twice. 'I'm in.'

Gina gave a small crow of delight. 'Perfect! I cannae wait till we sign on the dotted line!'

'What did your parents say when you told them you were leavin' town in order to join the service of your choice?'

'They don't know,' replied Gina matter-of-factly.

Tammy stared at her. 'Won't they worry?'

Gina's cheeks were beginning to bloom. 'Do you mind if we talk about summat else?'

Tammy apologised hastily. 'Sorry. I didn't mean to pry.'

Gina gave her a reassuring smile before turning her gaze to the window and resting her forehead against the glass. 'Don't worry about it.'

Tammy stared thoughtfully at the other girl. When Gina had announced her father to be an important figure in the Navy, and her mother a servicewoman too, Tammy had automatically assumed them to be kind, loving, maybe a tad overbearing – the sort of people who would bend over backwards for their daughter – but the way Gina had reacted to Tammy's innocent question made her think again. *She must have been concerned they'd react badly for her not to tell them where she was going, which just goes to show that all that glitters is not gold*, she mused as she watched the different shadows flicker past the window, and even though she found it hard to believe that *anybody*'s father could be as bad as her own, she realised Gina must have chosen to keep her decision secret for a reason. She then turned her thoughts to her own life and the image she had portrayed to Gina versus the reality of her situation. Her eyelids fluttered as she recalled how she'd made her mother – or rather her stepmother – out to be a wicked woman. True, she had subconsciously been describing the family from *Cinderella*, but it was still upsetting for Tammy to realise she had portrayed her mother in a very bad light. Her jaw tightened as a vision of her father lying on the floor, a pool of blood seeping from his temple, flashed before her eyes. Her stomach dropped. How could everything have gone so wrong so quickly? She'd never raised a hand to anyone in her life, yet within a split second she'd murdered her own flesh and blood, albeit by accident. *Everything had been going so smoothly*, Tammy thought now. *One minute we were all set to start a new life, the next we're running for our lives with no idea where we're running to.* She wondered whether her mother had managed to flee the city unseen. *If I've got away without bein' caught then I'm sure she will have too, because she's a far wiser head on her shoulders than I have. I hope she manages to find a pal as good as Gina to help her out – I'd hate for her to be doin' this on her own.* An image of Rory sitting by himself in the car entered her head. *He won't have a clue as to why we didn't go to meet him, or not until they find Dad, that is. She sighed inwardly. I dare say he'll guess exactly why we left when they do, but it'll still be a bitter pill for him to swallow, knowin' we chose to leave without him.*

'Have you ever had a boyfriend?'

Tammy blinked. She knew that Gina couldn't possibly have read her mind and that her sudden question had fallen in line with her own thoughts by pure coincidence, but even so it did seem rather intuitive, as though some unknown force was orchestrating their conversation. Reluctant to deny Rory's existence, but keen to protect him, Tammy hoped that Gina was unable to see her fingers as she crossed them. 'Never. You?'

Gina glanced pointedly at her own ample figure. 'I'm not exactly fighting them off with sticks.'

Tammy tutted beneath her breath. 'Any man who only wants a woman for the way she looks is not the sort of man she needs.'

Gina wrinkled one side of her face. 'That's all well and good, but I'm nearly twenty and I'm worried the well's going to run dry before I get a sip of water, if you catch my drift?'

'All good things come to those who wait,' said Tammy. 'The right one will come along eventually, just you wait and see.'

'I hope so.' Gina glanced wistfully out of the carriage window. 'Maybe we'll meet our Mr Rights in the services.'

A pang of guilt flushed through Tammy as an image of Rory rose before her eyes. She'd already met Mr Right, not that she could tell that to Gina, of course.

'What's wrong with the stars?'

Snapping back into the present, Tammy followed her gaze. 'What do you mean, what's wrong with the stars?' Even as the words left her lips, she swallowed. She could see exactly what Gina meant. They kept disappearing from view, as though something was passing in front of them.

Gina turned wide, frightened eyes to Tammy. 'Please

tell me they're ours, because there must be hundreds if not thousands of them.'

Tammy returned Gina's gaze. 'If they are then they're flyin' in the wrong direction,' adding in the privacy of her own mind, *I hope to God Mammy's on her way out of Clydebank, and that Rory's found somewhere safe to shelter.*

Chapter Four

13TH MARCH, 21:00 HRS

Rory woke with a start as the air raid siren split the night air. Glancing at his wristwatch as he sat up behind the wheel of the car, he frowned at the dial, which read nine o'clock. Tammy and her mother should've been with him an hour ago! Cursing himself for having fallen asleep, he peered into the darkness and saw an air raid warden frantically beckoning to him. He was reluctant to leave the car, but the sound of a second siren persuaded him to do as the warden asked.

'What on earth are you playin' at?' the man yelled as Rory hurried towards him. 'Takin' a bleedin' nap when all hell's breakin' loose! Get down the shelter with everyone else.'

Rory glanced over to the tenement building where Tammy lived. 'Shouldn't we make sure everyone's got out first?'

The warden shook his head. 'Not everyone can sleep through an air raid,' he said pointedly. 'I was only checkin' to make sure nobody's left a light on. Now you come along with me.'

Rory hesitated. Should he go and check that the Blackwells weren't inside the building, or should he do the sensible thing and follow the warden? The distant sight of the night sky lighting up as the bombs thudded onto the ground below brought him to a hasty conclusion, and he jogged to catch up with the ARP officer. Whatever had happened to prevent them from meeting him as planned, he had no doubt that it wouldn't keep them from getting to one of the shelters. *Dennis might be a lot of things*, Rory thought now, *but he's not totally stupid, especially when it comes to looking out for himself. I dare say he's already got himself tucked safely down the pub cellar. No, wherever they are, it'll be somewhere safe, and there'll be plenty of time to find them after the air raid.*

Grace glanced nervously out of the back window of the bus as it wound its way round the sharp bends. Crossing her fingers as tightly as she could, she closed her eyes and prayed for Tammy and Rory to be out of harm's way, and so didn't see the clippie, who had just taken the last passenger's fare, tottering her way down the aisle of the bus until she half-tripped, half-fell into the only vacant seat.

Apologising for having practically sat on Grace, the woman jerked her head in the direction of the driver. 'I know it's dark out, but Dougal knows these roads like the back of his hand.'

Grace heard someone near the front of the bus blaspheme as he pointed to the cloud of Luftwaffe bombers which darkened the night sky as they headed towards the city. Following his line of sight, Grace heard several passengers offer up prayers to keep them safe, while others wept softly. A heavily pregnant woman laid a protective hand over her stomach, and said, 'Thank God we got out when we did.'

'I've never seen so many,' said Grace hollowly as her eyes followed the planes. 'I dread to think what will be left of Glasgow by the time they're through.'

'I hope someone warned the folk back home that this ain't no normal raid,' said the pregnant woman.

'They'll have got word from down south, don't you worry,' the clippie assured her. Hearing the revs of the engine quieten, she called out to those around her. 'Dougal's goin' to park under a disused railway bridge. We've done it on many an occasion, and it's never been struck yet.'

As several of the passengers protested at the idea of a railway bridge when they knew that the Luftwaffe targeted transport links in particular, a man two seats up from Grace voiced his own thoughts on the matter. 'They probably know there's no point in bombin' an old railway track when there's better targets to be had.'

'They'll be headin' for the docks,' agreed Grace, adding quietly, 'and the railway station.'

The driver pulled the bus to a halt under the bridge and turned the engine off. Taking a cigarette from his tobacco tin, he lit it before addressing the passengers. 'We're safe as we can be; all we can do now is wait.'

Having already had to wait a good couple of hours for a bus to arrive, Grace could only hope that Tammy hadn't encountered the same problem when it came to catching a train. *I don't care where she is as long as she's nowhere near Glasgow*, she thought now. An image of Rory crept into her mind, causing a shiver to run down her spine. She had no idea what he'd have chosen to do once he realised they weren't coming, but she hoped for his sake that wherever he was, he was far away from the docks.

As soon as he ducked through the curtained doorway Rory scoured the sea of heads for a sign of Tammy and her mother, but wherever they were it wasn't in this particular shelter. As the dull thud of the bombs grew ever nearer, he heard the whispered prayers of those around him call for either the heavens to show some mercy or better still the Luftwaffe to turn back. With nothing to do but sit and wait, he turned his mind back to what could have prevented the women from meeting him. The man who'd told him that Dennis had gone to the Alexander had seemed certain that he was correct, but what if Dennis had had a change of heart and instead had gone home for some reason? Knowing Tammy the way he did, Rory had no doubt that in that case she and Grace would carry on as normal and wait for him to go to the pub as usual before they hurried to meet himself. Tammy would know that Rory would guess something of the sort had happened, so she'd be confident that he'd stay put until she and Grace turned up. *I'll go back to the van as soon as the all-clear sounds, and wait for them to join me*, Rory told himself now, before the devil's advocate plagued his thoughts once more. What if they failed to turn up at all, what would he do then? A newer, darker question entered his mind. What if Dennis had discovered their plan to leave? But he quickly dismissed the thought. *They were paranoid that summat was goin' to go wrong at the last minute, so I bet they'd already thought of what they'd say and do if Dennis were to come home unexpectedly.* He continued to try to assure himself that all would be well, but he could not prevent the idle chatter of those around him from leaking into his consciousness.

'Them bloody neighbours of mine were at it again this afternoon. You should've heard him, Stella. Callin' her all sorts, he was!' huffed an elderly lady in disgusted tones.

'Not unusual in that household,' remarked Stella in a disinterested fashion.

'It was this time,' said the older woman with some satisfaction. 'She actually told him a few home truths!'

Stella raised an approving brow. 'And about time too! You should've 'eard the way he spoke to me when all I'd done was make an innocent observation.'

Rory glanced at the two women. Neither of them had mentioned their neighbours by name, but he had an uneasy feeling that they were talking about the Blackwells.

'He's got no respect!' sniffed the older woman. 'I've complained to the council more times than I care to count, but do they do anythin' about it? Do they 'eck as like!'

Stella gave a derisive snort before voicing her thoughts as far as the council were concerned. 'That lot are always the same, Edie; it's out of sight, out of mind with them. They couldn't give a monkey's what's goin' on as long as it's not happenin' on their doorstep.'

Rory leaned forward. 'Sorry to interrupt, but do you mind if I ask who you're talkin' about?'

The older woman eyed him suspiciously. 'Why, what's it to you?'

Realising that he'd put the woman on her guard, he thought quickly. 'I'm sorry to say they sound very much like my neighbours,' he told her, 'so much so I was wonderin' if they might be related somehow.'

'I doubt it. She's not from round here, and he's got no kith or kin to speak of,' remarked the older woman, before hastily adding, 'Not that I'm one to gossip, mind you . . .'

Stella gave Edie a friendly nudge. 'I don't think this nice young man would accuse you of gossipin', Edie; besides which, how can it be described as gossip when they were shoutin' their business for all to hear!'

Rory held his hands up in a placating fashion. 'I assure you, that was never my intention.'

Edie settled her gaze on Rory. 'It's not like it's a secret anyway, cos everyone knows what the Blackwells are like—' She stopped speaking abruptly as Rory jumped to his feet. 'You didn't hear it from me!' she cried after him as he strode towards the top of the shelter.

Hearing the commotion, the ARP warden stuck his arm across the doorway, blocking Rory's path. 'Whoa there, pal. Where do you think you're goin'? You cannae leave here till they sound the all-clear.'

'Bugger that!' snapped Rory, trying to push past the older man. 'I'm not goin' to sit around here when my Tammy and her mam are in danger.'

'As will you be, if you venture out there!' barked the warden, then continuing in kinder tones, 'Besides, they're probably down one of the other shelters—'

Rory spoke impatiently, cutting the warden short. 'I'm not talking about the Luftwaffe, I'm talkin' about the feller they live with.' He indicated the two women, who did their best to hide their faces from the warden. 'I've just been talkin' to those two . . .'

The warden tutted irritably. 'If you think I'm goin' to let you run out there cos you've been listenin' to the likes of Edie and Stella, then you've another thing coming!' He raised his voice so that the women could hear him. 'The pair of you should know better than to go spreadin' rumours, especially when there's more than likely no truth to them.'

Edie jutted her jaw in a defensive manner. 'There is too!' she snapped. 'Everyone knows what the Black-wells are like – especially *him*!'

Stella's eyes rounded as she tugged at Edie's sleeve. 'That's as may be, but I doubt Dennis will be too happy if he hears you've been shoutin' your mouth off to all and sundry.'

The warden held Rory by the shoulder. 'You're right, Edie, everyone does know what they're like, but that's still no excuse for you to be spreadin' the type of gossip that sends a young feller off on a suicide mission, cos that's what it'll be if he steps foot outside of here.' He gave Rory a sympathetic grimace. 'Don't pay any

attention to them, son; the Blackwells are always fallin'
out. You mark my words, this will be the same as every
other argument they've had over the years.'

But Rory wasn't so sure. If Dennis had come home to
find the women on their way out, his threats might
have become a reality. He very much wanted to say as
much to the warden, but if he was wrong and Dennis
didn't know of their plans, then Rory's own words
might well put them in danger.

The warden pointed to the bench he was sitting on,
cutting across Rory's thoughts. 'Sit here with me . . .'
He looked at Rory expectantly.

'Rory,' said Rory.

The warden nodded before continuing. 'Save you
listenin' to the likes of them two.'

Edie snorted her contempt, but said nothing.

Reluctantly, Rory did as the warden asked. He would
just have to hope for the raid to come to a swift end so
that he could get to the Blackwells' house and rescue
Tammy and Grace from Dennis. *There's bound to be loads
of people knockin' about after the raid*, Rory thought. *I shall
march up to Dennis's front door and tell him that I'm there
for Tammy and Grace and I don't intend to leave without
them.* He nodded to himself. Dennis wouldn't try anything stupid with so many witnesses to hand.

As Tammy had told Rory, Dennis Blackwell was like a
cat with nine lives when it came to cheating death.
Feeling the floor vibrate beneath him as heavy thuds
sounded in the distance, Dennis stared bleary-eyed
into the darkness. He tried calling out to Grace and

Tammy, but the small clouds of dust which rose from the earthen floor caught in his throat, causing his words to come out in the form of a cough. Realising that he was on his own, he attempted to get up, but the moment he lifted his head a sharp jab of pain seared straight through his temple. Raising a hand to the offending area, he swiftly withdrew his fingers when they touched a mess of congealed blood. Flummoxed as to how he'd got into such a state, he tried to recall what had happened before he came to, but try as he might nothing sprang to mind. *I bet that useless lump of a wife of mine knows*, he thought bitterly. *I bet she's keepin' her fingers crossed that I die, the ungrateful bitch.* At the last thought he experienced a sense of déjà vu, as if those words in particular held an important link to his current situation, and a vision of his wife and daughter on the point of running away rushed into his mind's eye. Anger searing through him, he could almost feel Grace's throat between his hands, while Tammy had cried out for him to stop. But what next? A line creased his brow as he tried to remember, but everything after that was a blank. *Not that it takes a genius to work out what happened next*, Dennis thought bitterly. *They obviously whacked me over the head and left me for dead!*

His thoughts were interrupted as the floor beneath him shook violently, and that's when the awful truth of his current situation hit him. Clydebank was being bombed, and if he didn't get out he might well be buried alive. *I'd bet a pound to a penny that they heard the sirens and thought they'd leave the Luftwaffe to finish me off,* he thought as he attempted to get to his feet. *I've clothed them, fed them, put up with all their whining and complaining, and for what? To be left to die like a rat, that's what.*

Using all his might, he pushed himself up onto his hands and knees. *Well, they ain't goin' to get away with it. As soon as I'm out of here I'll tell the polis what they've done and make sure they hang for it!* As he attempted to stand, his fingertips touched what felt like a glass bottle, and his nostrils flared as the scent of alcohol wafted towards him. Taking care not to spill a drop, he held the bottle to his lips and took a deep swig before glugging down the rest and getting to his feet.

Throwing the empty bottle to one side, he heard it smash as it hit something. He couldn't see what, and it occurred to him that he'd need some form of light if he were to get out safely. Patting his pockets, he withdrew a box of matches and struck one into life. He cupped his hand around the flame and looked about for one of the oil lamps, which he eventually spied in the middle of the kitchen table. Taking care to keep the match alight, he held his breath as he touched the flame to the wick and lit it. Then, waving the match out, he held the lamp aloft and took a good look around him.

It was then that he noticed the empty housekeeping jar sitting on one of the crates. Angry that he had been robbed whilst left to die, he kicked the crate from under the pot before marching to the front door and throwing it wide open, only to be blinded by the intensity of the white phosphorous flames from the incendiary bombs which were burning ferociously outside. He put the lamp down and shielded his eyes as best he could before hurrying out of the house and down the road. Even though he'd been the one who'd been left for dead, there was no doubt in his mind that his wife and daughter would find a way to twist things round to make him out to be the villain. With bombs continuing to rain down around him, he was determined to get as far away from the docks as possible. *As soon as they sound the all-clear*, he thought, *I'll be straight down the polis station to let them know they've two murderers on the loose.*

Hearing the rumours that were rife among the other passengers who'd entered their compartment at the last station, Tammy could do nothing but pray that her mother too had made it safely out of the city.

'How lucky are we to have got on this train,' remarked Gina as she looked out of the window.

'Very,' Tammy agreed, adding in what she hoped sounded like a casual afterthought, 'What will happen to those on the buses, do you think?'

'Depends on where they're headed,' said Gina. 'If they were already out of town – same as us – then they'll have found somewhere safe to park and wait, but if they're still in town the passengers'll head for the shelters along with everyone else.'

Tammy concurred, but it was good to hear that Gina thought the same. She gazed at the white inferno which could still be clearly seen, even though it was many miles away. Her thoughts turned to her neighbours in Clydebank. *I hope to God none of them think to call round and check we've gone down the shelter.* An image of the

ARP warden entering their kitchen made her shudder. *If anyone finds me dad dead on the floor, they'll soon realise that me and Mammy have scarpered, and it won't take the polis long to realise who's to blame.* Her thoughts turned to Rory. Would he still have been waiting for them in the car? She banished the idea without hesitation. Rory wasn't stupid, and she had no doubt that he would have gone to the nearest shelter, hoping to find her and her mother. Her stomach dropped as she imagined again someone telling Rory of her father's death. *He'll know that we had summat to do with it*, thought Tammy, *but what he won't know is why we left without telling him what happened.* Her eyelids fluttered as she envisaged him sitting alone in the car, wondering why they'd run off without so much as a goodbye. She wished that she could get word to him somehow, but to do so would put Rory at risk as well as herself. *Rory's not daft. If they find Dad's body he'll know why we left without sayin' good-bye*, she assured herself. *I just hope that he can find it in his heart to forgive me!*

Many hours had passed before the siren sounded the all-clear, and Rory made sure that he was one of the first to leave the shelter when it did. Heading straight for Jellicoe House, his heart sank as he saw the tenement reduced to a mass of rubble, fires blazing out of every gap. There was no doubt in his mind as to what must have become of his belle if she had remained in the building. Clasping his cap in his hands and looking around him wildly, he began to shout for Tammy and Grace.

'They're probably in one of the shelters round the back,' said the warden, who had followed him from the shelter. 'If I go and check, you can put word out that they might be missing while keepin' an eye out for them here.'

'Thanks . . . er?'

'Archie,' said the warden as he hurried away. 'Don't worry – I'm sure we'll find them soon enough.'

Rory continued to call out the women's names between waylaying passers-by to ask whether they'd seen either of them, and with every shake of the head he began to grow more frantic. Hoping that Archie would reappear with good news, he was disheartened to see the man walking towards him with his hands held up in a placating fashion. 'No one's seen hide nor hair of them, but you mustn't give up hope. For all we know they might've been in town when the sirens sounded.'

Tears glazing his eyes, Rory shook his head. Fighting to keep his emotions in check, he spoke in hoarse, hollow tones. 'You know how you found me waitin' in the car?' Archie nodded. 'I was helpin' them to leave Tammy's dad.' He went on to tell the warden about the planned escape, and finished, 'I don't care what you think of me, cos I know I was doin' the right thing, and tonight just proves it.'

The warden stared at him wide-eyed. 'Why on earth didn't you mention any of this before? If I'd thought for one minute that he might've been holdin' them against their will . . .'

Rory rubbed his hands over his face. 'Because I

could've been wrong, and if I'd mentioned it in front of Edie and Stella the whole of Clydebank would have known before we heard the all-clear!'

Archie grimaced. 'I grant you it doesn't look good, but we don't know anythin' for certain, not yet. Why don't we go and get a cup of tea and see whether anyone has any news of them? You never know your luck, and I still find it hard to believe that Dennis would be stupid enough to stay inside durin' an air raid, no matter what the circumstances.'

A single tear tracked its way through the grime which lined Rory's face. 'I don't want tea; I just want someone to tell me that this has been a horrible mix-up and that they're safe and well somewhere.'

'As do we all,' said Archie, 'which is why I suggest we go and get a cup of tea, cos the women in the WVS van get to hear all the gossip.' He looked up as a grave-faced warden approached them and nodded his head at Archie before addressing Rory.

'Are you the feller what's lookin' for the Blackwells?'

Rory swallowed. 'Have you found them?'

'I'm afraid not, but I've spoken to a lot of the neighbours and nobody recalls seein' them after the siren sounded. However, a few of them have said they heard a lot of screamin' and shoutin' some hours before the alarm.'

Rory clasped his head in his hands. 'Tammy said summat was goin' to go wrong. Why didn't I listen to her?'

'We still don't know—' Archie began, but Rory cut across him.

'Dennis got the sack for nickin' some feller's wallet earlier today. They told me he'd gone to the pub to drown his sorrows, but he obviously decided to call home first. I know for a fact that they were packed and ready to leave well before five o'clock, so he must've figured out what was goin' on, and . . .' He stopped speaking.

Archie blinked. 'You really think he's that stupid?'

'I don't think stupidity comes into it,' said Rory. 'This is down to pride, and yes, I think he'd sooner risk the Luftwaffe than watch his wife and daughter walk away.'

Unnoticed by Rory, Edie had been lurking nearby and eavesdropping on the entire conversation. 'So we were right!' she said aloud.

Archie jumped, and held up a hand to stop her from saying anything further. 'Not now, Edie. And before you go spreadin' gossip, we don't know anythin' for certain as yet.'

'You should've let him go and look for them,' said Edie, jerking her head towards Rory, 'I *told* you . . .'

But Archie had had enough. 'And what if I had, what then? He'd be in there with them . . .'

'So, you *do* think they're in there!' said Edie triumphantly.

The warden turned his eyes to the heavens before fixing her with a wooden stare. 'Go away, Edie. You're just makin' matters worse!'

Edie arched an eyebrow. 'Truth hurts, don't it?'

'She's right though,' said Rory softly as they watched Edie walk away, her nose turned up. 'I should've come here as soon as the sirens sounded. Had I done that things might be different.'

Archie's jaw flinched. 'If anyone's to blame it's Dennis bleedin' Blackwell, cos even if we're barkin' up the wrong tree – and by God I hope we are – he should've reported back to let us know that they're safe, to save us searchin' for their—' He had been about to say 'bodies', but had stopped himself in the nick of time.

Rory stared blindly at the rubble. 'Tammy always said he'd go too far one of these days.'

'You cannae give up hope, son. We've still to search the buildin'.'

But Rory had made up his mind. 'I'm not hangin' around to see them carry out my Tammy's body. I don't think I could bear it.'

'That's right – you get off home for a bit,' said Archie. 'If you give me your address I can let you know if there's any news.'

'You don't understand. When I say I'm not hangin' around, I mean I'm off to join the services. I might not be able to make Dennis pay for what he did to Tammy, but I can sure as hell make Hitler wish he'd never heard of Clydebank!'

Chapter Five

Keen to get as far away from the bombings as possible, Tammy and Gina had finally decided to make for Carlisle, which they hoped wouldn't attract the attention of the Luftwaffe.

Tammy nudged Gina awake as the train pulled into the station. 'This is our stop.'

Clutching her satchel close to her chest, Gina stared around her, bleary-eyed. 'Are we in Carlisle?'

'We most certainly are.'

Gina yawned behind the back of her hand. 'Thank goodness for that! I've had enough of racin' round tryin' to find the right train, scared that we'd get on the wrong one by mistake.' Stifling another yawn, she stared accusingly at Tammy. 'How come you're so bright-eyed and bushy-tailed?'

In truth, Tammy had been too scared to fall asleep for fear she would relive the moment she killed her father. That, and the thought of leaving Rory in the thick of it while she and her mother had fled to safety – or at least she hoped to goodness her mother had also made it out of the city in one piece – had meant she'd passed a restless night, but as she could hardly explain that to Gina she said instead: 'Excited to begin my new life?'

Gina got to her feet. 'I bet you'll not feel like that when they sound reveille for the first time.'

'Reveille? What's that?'

Gina led the way out of the carriage and onto the platform, still chatting away in a sleepy fashion. 'It's the bugle they play to get you up each morning. A bit like an alarm clock, only louder.'

'I see. So a bit like the piper who plays beneath the King's window every mornin'?' Tammy supposed.

'Kind of, only I don't think the piper gives the King a heart attack like what reveille does.' Gina stopped to look around her. 'Where do you suppose the recruiting office is?'

'Probably in a public place, such as a school or the town hall,' said Tammy, who was looking for some-one to ask. Her eyes settled on a railway guard standing on the platform. 'I bet he knows. Let's see.' Striding towards the man with Gina in her wake, she coughed to gain his attention before asking him where they should go.

He smiled approvingly. 'Joinin' up, are you, and very admirable too!' He gave them directions to the city hall, before asking why they'd come all this way when their accents were clearly Glaswegian.

Tammy looked to Gina, hoping that she could pro-vide an answer that wouldn't raise more questions, and Gina pulled a shocked face. 'Didn't you hear about the air raid?'

The man nodded gravely. 'It's all over the news. Was it as bad as they say?'

'Worse,' confirmed Gina, while casting an eye around her. 'You've obviously not seen much action here, thank goodness.'

He gave her a grim smile. 'We've been lucky so far; I just hope our luck holds out.'

The girls were about to walk away when another question raised itself. 'Is there a hotel close to the hall? Only we're goin' to need somewhere to stay while we wait for our papers to arrive.'

'The Crown and Mitre, on Castle Street,' he replied promptly. 'It's pretty grand, but it's the closest hotel to City Hall. If you'd prefer somewhere a bit cheaper . . .'

'That will do just fine, thank you,' said Gina. Tucking her arm through Tammy's, she bade the guard good-bye even as Tammy spluttered an objection.

'Hold on a mo. I cannae afford to splash out on a posh hotel . . .'

Gina waved a nonchalant hand. 'Not to worry. I'll cover the cost.'

Tammy stopped in her tracks, bringing Gina to a halt. 'I cannae ask you to do that. It's all right; I'll find somewhere that's cheaper close by.'

'First off, you didn't ask, I offered, and secondly you'll be doin' me a favour by keepin' me company while we wait for our papers to come through.'

'If you're sure,' said Tammy somewhat dubiously, 'but perhaps we should see how much it costs to stay there for a night first?'

'Don't worry about it. I've got it covered.'

Feeling that it would be rude to insist she pay her own way, when Gina had made it clear she was happy to foot the bill, Tammy changed the subject. 'So, what should we do first?' she said. 'City Hall or the hotel?'

'City Hall,' said Gina immediately. 'I'd rather get that part over and done with, and there's no point in forkin' out for a hotel if the services refuse to take us on.'

'Why might they do that?' mused Tammy. 'I thought they were desperate for volunteers.'

'They might want us to sign up in a different town or summat,' Gina supposed, 'and even though I'm sure everythin' will be fine, it's better to play it safe than sorry.'

'Fair point; City Hall it is,' said Tammy, adding as they crossed the busy road, 'I wonder how long it will take for our papers to come through.'

'I've heard some say at least a fortnight; others just over a week,' said Gina in a carefree manner.

'A fortnight? We cannae possibly stay in a hotel for a fortnight!' Tammy cried. 'You do realise that hotels don't come cheap?'

'Of course I do, but trust me when I say that money's no object.' She pointed to a magnificent building as they turned a corner. 'That looks like the place!'

They made their way into the building, and headed straight for a friendly-looking woman with gold-rimmed spectacles.

'May I help you?' she smiled.

'I hope so. We're here to sign up for the ATS,' said Gina, who was looking around her.

The woman gave them a look of approval before leaning forward in her seat and using her pencil to point down a long corridor. 'Down the hall, third door on the right.'

Thanking the woman for her assistance the girls followed her directions. 'Third on the right,' said Tammy, as she opened the door.

'Flippin' 'eck,' breathed Gina as her eyes fell on a queue which wound round the room. 'It's a good job we came here first.'

Tammy, who still couldn't get over Gina's generosity, harked back to their previous conversation. 'They're not goin' to get through this lot in a hurry. I reckon it'll be at least two weeks before they get the paperwork done and dusted. I know you said you could afford a hotel, but are you sure we wouldn't be better off rentin' a room somewhere?'

Gina rolled her eyes. 'For the last time, money's no object, so please stop worryin'!'

'But—'

'But me no buts!' said Gina. 'I'm payin' and that's an end to it.'

Resigned to the fact that her new friend was going to have the last say, Tammy caved in. 'Well, thank you. I really appreciate it.'

Gina pointed to another desk which had opened up across the way. 'Let's get over there before they all do!' Towing Tammy in her wake, she joined the new, far shorter queue, and it wasn't long before she was handing over her papers and going through the necessary details with the corporal on duty.

Up until now, Tammy had forgotten that she had been travelling under a false identity, having been more concerned with what had happened prior to her leaving Clydebank, but knowing that she was about to hand Sid's papers over to authority she felt beads of sweat begin to prick her forehead as she imagined the soldier yelling for the police to come and arrest her.

'Tammy?'

She jumped as Gina's voice cut across her thoughts. Realising that the corporal was waiting for her to hand over her identification, Tammy did just that, and watched with trepidation as he flicked through the documents while taking notes. Her heart in her mouth, she felt as though time itself had stood still as he gazed at her papers before handing them back and smiling up at her. 'I take it you're in Carlisle for the same reason as your pal?'

'I am,' said Tammy, so quietly she thought it a miracle he heard her.

'And are you stayin' at the same hotel?'

Stunned that she wasn't being carted off to the local nick, it took Tammy a second or two to reply, 'Aye.'

He raised his brow. 'Very nice. Your papers should arrive within the next couple of weeks.' He looked to the girl in line behind Tammy. 'Next.'

As they left the hall, Tammy noticed that Gina kept flicking her sidelong glances, although she said nothing. Worried that Gina had picked up on something the soldier hadn't, she broke the silence. 'Why d'you keep lookin' at me like that?'

'Because back there in the hall just now you looked

like a deer caught in the headlights. Surely you didn't think your stepmother had reported you to the army for runnin' away?'

Tammy, who had been expecting Gina to say something about her papers, frowned. 'Sorry?'

'I only ask because you looked like you was sweatin' cobs when he was goin' through your details.'

Remembering the story she had told Gina, Tammy shook her head. 'I guess I'm a little nervous about what's to come.'

'You've gone from excited to nervous in less than an hour, although I suppose that's only natural, cos in truth I'm nervous too, but at least we're doin' this together.' She pointed to the building ahead of them. 'The guard was right when he said it was close by.'

Tammy's cheeks bloomed as she took in the sheer size of the impressive-looking hotel. 'I know you said not to give it a second thought, but it looks frightfully expensive.'

'It's just as well I'm payin' then, isn't it?'

Rather than get into another difficult conversation about money, Tammy kept quiet, but that didn't stop her from wondering how Gina could possibly afford to pay for the two of them to stay in such a swanky-looking place. *It's not as if her parents gave her enough money to cover hotels and the like, because they didn't know she was leaving Clydebank in the first place*, thought Tammy, and it was then that the penny dropped. *No wonder she said that there could be an exception to the rules when it came to stealin'*, she realised. *Cos she's done it herself!*

Feeling more uncomfortable than ever at the thought of spending someone else's stolen money, Tammy reluctantly followed Gina to the reception desk. *If I say anythin' to her she'll only deny it, and what then? I've got no evidence to prove otherwise, on top of which I'll have alienated my only ally.* She rolled her eyes as she remembered the corporal asking if she was staying at the same hotel as her friend. *I'm goin' to have to put it out of my mind, because I cannae see as I've any other choice, and even if she did steal the money, who am I to judge after what I did? In the grand scheme of things, I'm guilty of far worse than she is!*

The sharp-faced woman who sat behind the desk rose as they walked towards her. 'May I help you?'

'We'd like a twin room for . . .' Gina paused while she looked to Tammy, '. . . a week, to start?'

Tammy nodded.

The woman looked from Gina to Tammy and back again before eyeing them both from head to toe in a slow, speculative manner. 'That'll be eight shillings and sixpence daily.' She glanced down at their meagre belongings in a pointed fashion before adding, 'That includes breakfast as well as hot and cold facilities.' She glanced towards the main door. 'There's a b&b—'

'If we'd wanted to stay in a b&b we'd have gone to one,' said Gina, standing to one side as she rummaged through her holdall. Stepping forward, she placed enough money for a week's stay onto the counter. 'I think you'll find that's right.'

The receptionist counted out the money in a some-what reluctant fashion before turning the guest book to face them. 'If you can sign here, I'll give you your room key. You're on the second floor.'

Gina looked to Tammy. 'Would you mind doin' the honours? Only I'm gaggin' for the lavvy.'

Tammy signed the book while the receptionist took their key from a row of hooks behind her. 'You're from Glasgow, am I right?'

'You are.'

'I didn't realise Glaswegian children were so wealthy,' said the woman, looking down the length of her nose at Tammy as Gina hurried towards the ladies'.

'That's the privilege of bein' the daughter of an admiral,' said Tammy, who didn't care for the woman's tone of voice.

The woman looked at Tammy in a disbelieving manner. 'Really? You do surprise me. I thought she sounded like someone from the tenements, a bit like yourself.'

Tammy was about to tell the receptionist that she should mind her own business and stop being so judgemental when she realised the woman had a point. Gina didn't talk like someone who'd had a posh upbringing, certainly not how you'd expect an admiral's daughter to speak, but there was no way she was going to agree with the snooty receptionist. 'If you think her money isn't good enough, we can easily take it elsewhere, but not until I've spoken with the manager.'

The woman's face immediately dropped. 'I didn't mean to offend—'

'Really? I'd hate to see what you're like when you do.'

The woman had opened her mouth to apologise further when Gina exited the powder room. 'Ready?'

Tammy cast the receptionist a scathing look, her eyebrows raised questioningly.

The woman swallowed. 'Just call down if you need anything.'

Snatching the key from the desk, Tammy jerked her head in the direction of the grand staircase. 'C'mon.'

As she led the way up the stairs, Tammy couldn't help but cast her mind back over Gina's behaviour. *I did think that she'd stolen the money from her parents, but now I'm findin' it hard to believe that she comes from a well-to-do background, because she definitely doesn't act like she does. But if that's the case, then where did the money come from?* Her eyes flicked to the satchel which, she now realised, Gina never let out of her sight, something that gave Tammy even more cause to pause. *Just how much money is there in that bag?* she thought now. *She certainly keeps it on her wherever she goes – includin' the lavvy – so I'm guessin' it must be a fair amount, and while I don't blame her for not wantin' to leave it with a relative stranger, I cannae help but think there's more to this than meets the eye.*

On that thought, she opened the door to their room and stepped inside. One glance was enough to let her know that it was nothing like Jellicoe House. The wallpaper was free from mould, and the beds . . . she walked over to the one nearest the window and sat down. 'It's as soft as a feather!' she told Gina, who had followed her into the room and immediately pushed her satchel under the other bed.

'Better than sleepin' in the cellar, eh?' said Gina, wandering over to the window.

'Just a bit,' said Tammy, as she unpacked the few

clothes she had into the top drawer of the dresser. She glanced at Gina's satchel, a corner of which was just visible beneath the bed. 'Aren't you goin' to unpack?'

'I didn't pack much in the way of clothes,' said Gina, 'so it hardly seems worthwhile puttin' them away.'

Disappointed that she wouldn't have a chance to take a sneaky glance inside the bag, Tammy joined Gina at the window. 'As you're payin' for the hotel, how about I take us out for a bite to eat?'

Gina wrinkled her nose. 'Would it be all right if we ate in the hotel? Only I'm still shattered from the journey.' Seeing the worried look on Tammy's face, she quickly added, 'Don't worry, it'll be my treat.'

'Like everythin' else,' objected Tammy. 'I know I haven't got the same kind of money as you, but I'd like to pay what I can. How about I buy us summat from a bakery?'

Gina gave her a reassuring smile. 'That would be lovely! But would you mind if I stay here? Only I'd like to get my head down for half an hour.'

Tammy swung her handbag over her shoulder. 'Not a problem. I shan't be long.'

Leaving Gina to have a sleep, Tammy glanced briefly at the receptionist as she passed by the desk. *The stupid woman was questioning Gina's background, but she should've been questioning mine*, she thought as she scanned the street for a bakery, *which just goes to show you cannae judge a book by its cover!* Spotting a baker's further down on the opposite side of the road, she set off at a brisk pace. She might be far away from Clydebank, but her heart still jumped whenever she saw a man in uniform. *And here I am joinin' the services*, she thought. *I'll be a nervous wreck by the time I've finished my initial training.* She was about to open the door to the shop when someone in a police uniform walked out. He dipped his head in greeting and said 'Good morning' as he held the door open for her to pass through.

Tammy swallowed as she replied: 'Good mornin'.' Her heart hammering in her chest, she waited for him to ask her whether everything was all right, because she was sure that she must look as guilty as she felt. But he simply continued on his way. Relieved that the encounter had come to nought, she had ordered a couple of pasties when a newspaper which sat on the counter caught her eye. As she looked round to see if it belonged to anyone, the server spoke from behind the counter.

'Jerry – the policeman what just left – left it here for others to read; feel free,' she said, indicating the newspaper with a jerk of her head.

Tammy picked up the paper and held her breath as she looked at the front page. Relieved yet surprised that the headline didn't read *Mother And Daughter Wanted For Murder In Clydebank*, she quickly flicked through the rest of the paper, but found nothing other than news of the war and advertisements in the pages. The woman placed the bagged pasties on the counter and Tammy handed her the money for them before heading back to the hotel. *They can't have found him yet*, she thought as she passed the reception desk, *but they will. It's just a matter of time.*

Entering their hotel room, she expected to find Gina

asleep; instead she was just in time to see her pushing her satchel back beneath her bed, leading Tammy to believe that she'd been checking over the contents.

'I know you like cheese, so I got us a cheese and onion pasty each,' she said, handing one to Gina and sinking her teeth into the other while trying not to look at the satchel, which was still just visible.

Using her feet to push the satchel fully out of sight, Gina finished her first bite before saying: 'It tastes heavenly.'

Her uneventful encounter with the policeman had left Tammy feeling far more confident as she jerked her head in the direction of the street. 'What would you like to do this evenin'? I thought it might be nice to go for a wander round the city, maybe take in a film – my treat, of course.'

'I'd rather stay in, if you don't mind.'

Disappointed that Gina didn't want to go exploring, Tammy finished her mouthful before replying. 'Not at all. We've plenty of time to have a look around.'

Gina held up a couple of bottles, which Tammy assumed must have been in her satchel. 'I don't suppose you'd have a go at dyein' my hair?'

Tammy's eyes grew wide. 'I don't think that's a good idea. I wouldn't have a clue where to start. Surely you'd be better off goin' to a hairdresser?'

'I'd rather you did it,' said Gina. She held out the bottle of what turned out to be peroxide mixed with ammonia, along with a pair of scissors. 'I thought you could give me a quick trim while you were about it.'

Tammy was flabbergasted that Gina would even

suggest that a non-professional like Tammy cut her hair. She was about to say as much when she thought of something else. 'You obviously bought this stuff before we met. What were you plannin' on doin'? Havin' a go yourself?'

'In short, yes. I've always wanted to be a blonde.'

Tammy cast a doubtful eye over Gina's beautiful dark locks. 'I don't think it's a good idea.'

Shrugging, Gina got up from her bed. 'Not to worry, I'm sure I'll manage.'

Rather than see Gina struggle on her own, Tammy got up reluctantly. 'I cannae promise you'll come out lookin' like Mae West, but I'll certainly do my best!'

It was several hours before Tammy declared she had done all she could. Admiring her new chin-length hairstyle in the mirror, Gina smiled. 'I think you've done a grand job,' she said, but Tammy was less convinced.

'I think a proper hairdresser would've made you more blonde than yellow.' She cast a worried eye over her attempt. 'Are you *sure* it's the colour you wanted?'

'As good as,' said Gina. 'How do I look?'

Tammy tried to answer in a positive manner. 'Nothin' like you did twenty-four hours ago!'

Gina's smile grew broader. 'Perfect! Goodbye borin' brunette, hello bubbly blonde.'

When they went to bed later that night, Tammy mulled over what had been the worst twenty-four hours of her life so far. She'd started off with a spring in her step, looking forward to her new life, only to have everything go wrong; in one fell swoop she'd lost both her mother and Rory and was currently on the run for murder. She thought she'd struck lucky when she met Gina, but it seemed as though Gina, too, was hiding something, because there was no way she had bought the dye and scissors simply because she wanted to be a blonde – or at least not in Tammy's opinion.

She's not tellin' the whole truth when it comes to her parents, but there again neither am I, she thought as she snuggled down between the sheets. Lying in the darkness she thought about the newspaper she'd glanced at while waiting for her pasties, and wondered what Gina would think if she were to read the headlines that Tammy had been expecting. *She'd probably think that the mother and daughter were terrible people*, she thought as she glanced across at her new friend, nestled cosily in the other bed. *But what would she think if she knew that I was the daughter? She'd probably still think that I was a cold-blooded murderer, because I'm not choked with grief, but that's because she didn't know my dad. If she did, then she'd know I only had two options: let him strangle Mammy or do what I did; quite frankly, he left me with no choice. I hate him for the way he treated me and Mammy, and I hate him even more for forcing me into a situation as dire as this.* Her eyes began to brim with tears as she lay gazing at the ceiling. Why had he chosen to get married and have a child when he clearly didn't want either? Tammy knew that she herself would never agree to marry someone unless it was for love, and her father clearly didn't love her mother. She turned her thoughts to Rory, and how much she wished she could explain everything to him, and suddenly she wondered whether Rory would come looking for her and what she would do if he did. *I'd tell him to run in the opposite direction*, she thought ruefully, *because Mammy's right: Rory would be charged with being an accomplice even though he's innocent.* The tears began to fall. *No matter which way you look at it, I've made a real hash of this, and Rory and Mammy are better off without me. One stupid mistake*, she thought bitterly, *and I've lost everyone I ever loved.*

Dennis held a hand to his head in an attempt to ease the throbbing pain which was emanating from his temple. *What the hell did they hit me with?* he wondered as he stumbled along the pavement. *It must've been summat solid whatever it was, cos it hurts like buggery.* Feeling fresh blood ooze down the side of his face, he decided it would be best for him to head to the hospital to see if he needed stitches. *As soon as I get out I'll go to the nick and report the two of them for attempted murder. If they ask what happened to cause the attack, I'll say they beat me with a poker for losin' me job, but legged it when I said I was goin' to report them, and that I fully intended on comin' straight to the polis station, but had to go to the hospital first to get stitched up. There's not a soul alive who wouldn't believe that story.*

Half an hour later, he staggered through the hospital doors, one hand clutched to his head, the other to his back. Howling in exaggerated pain, he called out for a doctor to come and tend to him.

Rushing to his aid, a nurse did her best to support him as he half-collapsed into her arms. 'I swear I didn't mean to lose my job,' he whimpered, 'but they wouldn't listen.'

Startled that his visible wound apparently wasn't caused by the air raid, the nurse stared at him wide-eyed. 'Who wouldn't listen?'

'Me wife and daughter,' wailed Dennis as he turned to face her. 'They beat me with the poker, but I managed to get out before they done me in.'

Smelling the alcohol which wafted off his breath, the nurse wrinkled her brow. 'Pardon me for askin', but have you been drinking?'

'What's that got to do with the price of fish?' snapped Dennis, his features turning sharp.

'We need to know before we can treat you,' said the nurse, who was taken aback by the speed with which he'd responded, in comparison to the way he'd acted when first coming through the doors of the hospital.

'Oh. Well, yes, I had some, but only for medicinal purposes. The pain in my head is terrible.'

She peered at the injury. 'You're lucky to be alive. If they'd struck you an inch or so higher it would be a very different story.' Leading him through to one of the cubicles, she instructed him to take a seat while she fetched something to clean the wound. When she returned she was with a doctor, who introduced himself while the nurse began to swab the gash.

'Nurse Mackay has told me what happened. Do you know where your wife and daughter are now?'

'They legged it when I threatened to report them to the polis.'

Nurse Mackay paused in her cleaning of the wound.

'I thought you said that you were the one who got away from them?'

Dennis glared at the nurse. 'In case you hadn't noticed I've got a ruddy great big hole in the side of my skull, so it's hardly surprisin' if I get a bit mixed up, is it?'

The nurse said nothing but continued to bathe the gash until it was free of blood. Leaning forward, the doctor examined the injury as Dennis whimpered, 'Is it broke, doc?'

Taking a needle and thread from the nurse, the doctor set about stitching the wound. 'It's impossible to tell without an X-ray, but I don't think so, no. Are you sure it was a poker they hit you with? Only it looks like you were struck with something sharp-edged.'

'I had my arms up tryin' to protect meself,' lied Dennis, 'but I'm pretty sure one of them would have had the poker, cos that's what they usually use.'

The nurse switched her attention from the doctor's stitching to Dennis. 'This has happened before?'

'Not as bad,' said Dennis, delighted that they were swallowing his story, 'but yes.'

'What did the polis say when you reported them last?' enquired the doctor, as he cut the thread.

'I've not reported them in the past,' said Dennis shortly. He was beginning to get annoyed at the sudden need for questions.

'So why report them now, when you've never bothered before?' asked the nurse, starting to bandage his head.

Dennis's jaw flinched. 'Because they nigh on bleedin' murdered me this time,' he growled. 'They're bleedin' lucky I decided to report them to the polis rather than take matters into my own hands, cos if I had—' He stopped himself in the nick of time.

Aware that the man he was treating had turned from victim to would-be assailant, the doctor asked for his address.

'What do you want to know that for?' Dennis snarled, all thoughts of playing the victim now gone.

'Because the polis will want to have a word with your wife and daughter, to get their side of the story,' said the doctor calmly.

Dennis stood up. 'Don't you worry, I'll be tellin' the polis everything.' Keen to get away before the doctor could ask more questions, he left the hospital at a brisk pace, just as the all-clear sounded. *Trust that bleedin' nurse to stick her nose in; typical woman*, he thought as he made his way to the police station. *I'll have to watch what I say to the polis, cos they're bound to ask more questions than they did at the hospital.*

When he arrived, he was surprised to find the police station practically deserted. 'Where the hell is everybody?' he asked the constable who was manning the desk.

'Off fighting fires,' said the constable, as he looked at Dennis's bandaged head. 'What happened to you?' He took a sip of his tea while waiting for Dennis's response.

'I'm glad you asked, Reg,' said Dennis. Puffing out his chest he continued importantly, 'I want to make a statement regardin' my attempted murder.'

Reg – who'd had various encounters with Dennis for being drunk and disorderly – choked on his tea. When it came to getting into fights, Dennis was always whining that he was the victim, even though they knew for a fact that he was the instigator more often than not, but attempted murder was a new high even for him. 'I've got to man the desk, and as there's no one else here to take your statement you'll have to come back later.'

The wind taken out of his sails, Dennis banged his fist on the desk. 'Did you not hear what I just said?'

'Aye. Did you not hear what *I* said?' Reg sighed impatiently. 'Go home, Dennis, and don't come back until you're sober.'

Dennis continued to thump his fist onto the desk. 'I demand to speak to your superior.'

Reg refrained from rolling his eyes. 'In which case you'll definitely have to come back later. As I said, I'm the only one here!'

'Oh, I will, and when I do, I'm gonna make sure you get the sack for allowin' two attempted murderers to flee the city! See how you like that!'

Reg watched as Dennis left the station. He'd lost count of the times he'd been called out by various landlords because Dennis had started a fight within their pub. *If somebody has tried to do him in – and it wouldn't surprise me if they had, given his track record – then he probably did summat to deserve their wrath in the first place*, Reg thought now. *Ten to one he owes money to the wrong person and they've given him a good hidin' to show him they're serious about bein' repaid. After all, it's not exactly the first time Dennis has failed to pay his debts.* The fact that Dennis had reeked of ale when he walked in had only validated such thoughts. Content that he had solved the supposed murder attempt, Reg turned his attention back to his doodling.

With the police uninterested in helping him bring his wife and daughter to justice, Dennis headed straight for Jellicoe House in the hope that he would find one of his drinking buddies who might lend him a bob or two. He was stunned by the sight which met his eyes. *I'd have been dead for sure if I hadn't got out when I did*, he told himself as he surveyed the broken rubble before him, *and those bitches would've got away with murder*.

He turned as a familiar voice called his name behind him.

'Bleedin' hell, Den, I thought you was dead,' said Shrimpy, one of Dennis's drinking pals. 'I reckon we all did.'

'I would've been had I not come to,' said Dennis, pointing to his bandaged head. 'That bitch of a wife of mine tried to do me in. I don't suppose you've seen her, have you?'

Shrimpy shook his head. 'Sorry, pal.'

'Her and Tammy run off after hittin' me over the head.' He gave his friend a calculating look. 'They'll have gone to her parents in Llangollen, but I haven't any money to chase after them. I don't suppose . . . ?'

Shrimpy rubbed his chin thoughtfully. He knew Dennis of old, and was aware that the likelihood of ever getting his money back was little to none, but Dennis had saved his skin once or twice when it came to fights down the pub, so . . . He dug his hand into his pocket. 'I ain't got much, but you've done me a few favours in the past.' He handed Dennis some coins.

Dennis clapped him on the shoulder. 'Thanks, pal. I owe you one.'

Shrimpy waved a dismissive hand. 'Don't worry about it. You've always had my back, so it's about time I returned the favour, and quite frankly I hate to see injustice go unpunished. Those bitches deserve whatever it is you've got planned for them.'

'They'll rue the day they decided to leave me for dead,' said Dennis. 'Thanks for this, Shrimpy.' With that, Dennis set off for the train station, where he sneaked aboard the first train to head off on what would undoubtedly prove to be a long and arduous journey to Wales.

The first few days in the hotel, Tammy had woken in a cold sweat, her heart hammering in her chest as she tried to get the image of her father out of her mind. Add to that the constant pictures of Rory looking sad and alone as he tried to work out just what had happened, coupled with the fear of her mother's ending up in a worse place than she'd been in before leaving Clydebank, and it was a wonder Tammy got any sleep at all. She'd been fearful that Gina would question why she woke up in such a state, but luckily Gina was a heavy sleeper, and with Tammy being the first to wake she was always washed and dressed before Gina opened her eyes.

Ten days after they'd signed up for the services,

Tammy went down to reception as usual to check for any mail while Gina slumbered on.

'One for you and one for your friend,' said the receptionist, and Tammy gave a squeak of excitement.

'It's our papers,' she informed the woman. 'Looks like we might be checkin' out soon!'

Taking the stairs two at a time, she rushed into their room to find Gina awake. 'This is it!' she squealed, handing Gina her letter. 'Good luck.'

Opening her envelope slightly ahead of Tammy, Gina was the first to speak. 'Where's Dalkeith?'

Tammy looked up from her own instructions. 'I've no idea, but I'm goin' there too!'

Gina beamed as she held the papers to her chest. 'I reckon that corporal made sure we were sent to the same camp because he could see we were friends.'

'Whatever the reason I think we've been jolly lucky,' said Tammy, 'cos they could've stationed us at opposite ends of the country. Talkin' of which, we'd better find out where this New Battle Abbey Training Camp is, because accordin' to this we've got to be there in three days' time!'

'What should we do to celebrate?'

'How about I go down the bakery and buy us a penny bun each and two of them cheese and onion pasties for our lunch?'

'Perfect!'

Having long given up any notion of asking Gina whether she wanted to join her or not, Tammy set off alone. Since arriving at the hotel her new friend hadn't stepped foot outside, saying that she was tired, or didn't feel well; there was always an excuse. Not that Tammy minded, but she failed to see why Gina was worried about her parents carting her back to Clydebank when she'd already signed on the dotted line. She'd even brought it up in conversation once.

'It's too late for them to do anythin' about it now,' she had assured her friend. 'I'm sure your parents would know that.'

'Dad would pull some strings, I know he would,' Gina had insisted. 'It'll be different once I'm based somewhere, but until that day comes I'm not takin' any chances.' Rather than argue, Tammy had gone along with things, even though she felt that Gina would be better telling her parents the truth.

Now, as she entered the bakery, she greeted the friendly owner, who raised a brow. 'Two cheese and onion pasties, am I right?'

Tammy smiled. 'Aye, and we'd like two penny buns to celebrate, as well.'

'Does that mean you've got your posting?'

Tammy nodded. 'Somewhere called Dalkeith. Have you heard of it?'

'That's where my hubby come from,' said the woman. 'It's not far from Edinburgh.'

'Oh,' said Tammy, disappointed they weren't going somewhere a lot further away from Glasgow.

'You'll not be there long, I shouldn't wonder,' the baker continued as she bagged their food.

'I was hopin' to be stationed somewhere further south,' admitted Tammy, 'see a bit more of England.'

'I've no doubt you will given the fullness of time, cos

that's where most of the action is.' She took the money from Tammy and placed it in the till. 'When are you off?'

'We've got to be there in three days' time,' said Tammy, 'so I should imagine we'll be leavin' tomorrow or the next day.'

'I'm sure I'll see you again before you go, but if not, good luck.'

Tammy thanked the woman before heading back to the hotel. When she entered their room, she was surprised to find that Gina was missing. Supposing that her friend must have stepped out to use the facilities, Tammy put the paper bags containing their food on the dresser and sat down to take her shoes off. It was then that she noticed the satchel beneath the bed. She sat bolt upright. Gina never went anywhere without it; she even took it to the bathroom. Wondering what could have caused her to leave it behind this time, Tammy's eyes flicked towards the door. If she wanted to see the contents she'd have to act quickly. Hating herself for what she was about to do, she leaned down and pulled the bag out from under the bed. Resting on her haunches, she pulled it open and peered inside.

Almost immediately, she wished she hadn't, because among a whole heap of money was something that gave Tammy cause for grave concern. Leaning forward, she picked it up, and nearly jumped out of her skin as the door was flung open.

Standing in the doorway, her eyes round like saucers, Gina stared at the blood-stained knife in Tammy's hand.

Chapter Six

Her face draining of colour, Gina didn't take her eyes off Tammy's as she hastily closed the door behind her. Leaning back against it, small beads of sweat pricking her brow, she said, 'I know what this must look like, but I promise you, none of that stuff is mine.'

Tammy put the knife back in the satchel and placed the bag on Gina's bed. The sheer look of anguish on Gina's face was enough to persuade her to give her friend the benefit of the doubt – provided she could supply a reasonable explanation.

'Then whose is it?'

Gina swiftly stowed the bag beneath the bed. 'I'd rather not say.'

Tammy stared at her. 'I know I haven't known you for very long, but your actions don't match those of a thief. That being said, if you didn't steal the money, then where did it come from? I doubt your father keeps bags of cash stashed about the house.'

Gina blew out a staggered breath. 'I don't even know who my father is – or my mother, come to that.'

Stunned by the sudden revelation, Tammy saw that

Gina's eyes were welling with tears. Whether it was the weight of her own guilt, or whether there truly was something about Gina that made Tammy want to believe her, she couldn't be sure, but she knew one thing: she had to give Gina the best possible chance to explain herself before making a judgement.

'I don't know what's happened here, Gina, but I do know there isn't a bad bone in your body. I don't know how you came into possession of that money – or the knife for that matter – but I know it wasn't dishonestly. I really want to help you, because it's clear to me that somethin' must've gone dreadfully wrong for you to end up with the contents of that satchel, but you're goin' to have to be honest with me if we've any hope of sortin' this out.'

'Please don't be kind to me, because I don't deserve it,' wailed Gina, tears flooding her eyes. 'I've put you in a terrible situation, and I shouldn't have.'

Tammy stared at her open-mouthed while pointing beneath the bed. 'Whose is the money in that bag, Gina?'

Tears streaming down her face, Gina managed to compose herself enough to say, 'It belongs to the Billy Boys – or at least that's who I think they were.'

Tammy backed away from the bed as though the satchel contained a bomb. '*The* Billy Boys?' she said, her tone heavy with uncomprehending disbelief. 'How the hell did you end up with their money?'

Burying her face in her hands, Gina spoke thickly through her fingers. 'Through one stupid mistake.'

Even though she was still unnerved to think that a

notorious criminal gang might be after Gina, Tammy was nothing if not a good friend. Sitting down next to Gina, she placed an arm around her shoulders. 'I think it best if you start from the beginnin'. Don't worry about me – I've got bigger things than the Billy Boys to worry about.' As she spoke, she pulled a handkerchief from her skirt pocket and handed it to Gina, who dried her eyes.

'It's all because of that stupid Woolton pie,' she sniffed, before blowing her nose noisily.

'What on earth has Woolton pie got to do with the Billy Boys?'

Gina spoke slowly, fiddling with the hem of her skirt. 'I made a Woolton pie with a bit of left-over liver I had.' She grimaced. 'I hate wastin' food, especially with rationin' and all, so I put the liver in despite thinkin' it had probably seen better days.' She held a hand to her stomach. 'I ate the pie over the course of a few days, and everythin' was fine until the last day. I'd popped home for my lunch, and even though I thought it tasted a bit funny I figured I'd been fine for the rest of it so I ate it anyway. Long story short, I was on my way back to work when my guts started rumblin' somethin' awful, so I ducked into this café.' She pulled a face. 'I'd been in once before, so I knew the lavvy was out back; I also knew that the owner was a stickler for not allowin' anyone to use the conveniences if they didn't spend money in the caff. I had no intention of gettin' anythin' to eat, not with my guts bein' in the state they were, so I figured I'd leave my satchel on the table nearest the lavvy, so that I could pretend I had every intention of

orderin' summat should I get caught on my way out.'
She pulled a disgruntled face. 'Without goin' into too
much detail, I was in there for quite some time; I did
worry that some of the other customers would want to
use the facilities, but luckily for me none of them did.
When I'd finished my business I pulled the chain, but
it wouldn't flush.' She rolled her eyes. 'I tried and tried,
but no joy. I was too embarrassed to walk out, so I
thought I'd wait until the café was empty then scarper
before anyone saw me.' She began to twist the hem of
her skirt around her finger in an agitated fashion.
'That's when I heard the gun go off. I nearly jumped
out of my skin, and I'm sure I screamed, but if I did no
one seemed to have heard.'

Tammy interrupted. 'How did you know it was a
gun?'

'I didn't, at first. I thought someone must've dropped
summat really heavy, so I stayed in the lavvy waitin' for
the coast to clear. It seemed like an age before I heard the
bell go above the shop doorway. I hung on for a couple
more minutes to make sure the place was empty before
venturing out.' The tears returned as Gina relived the
moment. 'I was so busy keepin' an eye out for the owner
I didn't look where I was goin', and that's when I fell
over the body.' Her bottom lip quivered as she continued, 'It was the café owner, and he had a bullet hole
in his chest. *That's* when I knew it was a gun.'

Tammy cupped her hand over her mouth. 'Someone
murdered him!' she hissed through her fingers.

Gina nodded. 'There was no way I was hangin'
around, so I grabbed the satchel and left.'

Thinking that Gina was making assumptions, Tammy interrupted again. 'Hang on a mo. How do you know it was the Billy Boys if you never saw them?'

'Because I cannoned into one of them as I legged it from the caff. He tried to grab hold of me but there was no way I was stoppin', not after what had just happened.' Seeing the confusion on Tammy's face, she elaborated further. 'I knew who he was because I'd seen his photograph in one of the papers, askin' folk to contact the police if they'd seen him.'

'Why on earth was he on his way back to the scene of the crime, *especially* knowin' he was already wanted?' Tammy asked incredulously.

Gina pulled the satchel from under the bed and placed it on her knee. 'He must've realised he'd taken the wrong bag long before I did. I only discovered the mix-up when I was on my way to the police station. The satchels weren't identical, but they were very alike, only his was heavier, somethin' I hadn't noticed until then.' She looked to the heavens. 'Well, I panicked, and instead of carrying on to the police I ran for the station and got on the first train I saw. And thank God I did, because I'd be a dead woman for sure otherwise.'

'So only one of them saw you,' said Tammy. 'But they cannae know who you are.'

'Only they do. You see, I had a copy of *Pride and Prejudice* in my satchel, and I'd written my name and address on the inside cover so that . . .'

'. . . If you ever lost it the finder would know who to return it to,' said Tammy, adding sympathetically, 'Oh, Gina.'

'Precisely. Not only do they know what I look – looked – like, but they also know my name and address. That's when I knew I had to leave. I bought the hair dye and scissors from a chemist, and the sarnies from a bakery on the way to the station.'

Tammy frowned. 'But you obviously have your papers, because you showed them to the corporal . . .'

'I took my handbag with me to the lavvy, because I know the sort of people who frequent the café,' said Gina. 'They'd swipe my papers toot-sweet, but they're hardly the kind to read *Pride and Prejudice*!' She shot Tammy a questioning glance. 'So now you know the truth warts and all, but what about you? You mentioned summat about your havin' bigger things than the Billy Boys to worry about – what did you mean by that?'

Tammy felt her cheeks redden. She had wanted Gina to feel better about her own situation, and the words had escaped her lips without thinking. When she remained silent, Gina pressed on incredulously. 'You cannae possibly think your stepmother's worse than the Billy Boys.'

Tammy knew she couldn't continue to lie to Gina after the girl had been so honest with her. Taking a deep breath, she hoped she was placing her trust in the right person. 'I haven't got a stepmother,' she said quietly.

The faintest of smiles twitched the corners of Gina's mouth. 'Blimey, we're as bad as each other when it comes to tellin' the truth!'

Tammy told Gina everything, from the beatings her father had dished out to her mother to the moment she stepped aboard the train. When she had finished she waited a few seconds for Gina to respond before saying, 'I swear to God I didn't mean to hurt him; I just wanted him to let Mammy go.'

Her head lowered, Gina appeared to be deep in thought before eventually locking eyes with Tammy's. 'I believe you, and not because you believed me, but because your story has a ring of truth to it, unlike the Cinderella yarn you spun me on the train when we first met.'

Tammy's lips parted. 'You knew I was lyin'?'

Gina nodded. 'I figured it was none of my business; besides, I was hardly one to judge!'

Tammy sagged with relief. 'I cannae tell you how good it is to be able to talk about what happened. I barely had more than a few minutes with Mammy before we had to go our separate ways. This past week or so has been a nightmare. I twitch every time I hear someone shout because I'm worried the polis have caught up with me.'

'If the polis do come knockin' I'll corroborate your story,' said Gina firmly, 'cos I know what it's like to live in fear when you've done nothin' wrong.'

'And I'll do the same for you,' said Tammy fervently, adding, 'It's a shame we cannae change your name the way I did mine.'

'Only it's not the police who are after me,' said Gina, 'and I doubt the Billy Boys will be able to find me once

I'm in the services, especially with my new do.' She pointed to her hair. 'The way I see it, as long as I don't return to Clydebank I should be fine.'

Tammy glanced at the satchel. 'I'm guessin' you've been generous with the money because you want to get rid of it, but there's still loads left. What are you goin' to do with the rest?'

'I cannae hand it in to the polis, cos they'll want to know where I got it and we all know what the Billy Boys do to people who grass. You're right in sayin' that I've been tryin' to get rid of it by payin' for everythin', but there's still too much left for us to spend, no matter how hard we try.'

'So, what *will* you do with it?'

'I haven't the foggiest.'

'I suppose you could give it away?' suggested Tammy, before almost immediately reneguing her suggestion. 'Scrap that. They'd want to know where it came from.'

'I could always hide it somewhere where nobody would ever find it.'

'But where?'

'God knows, but the thought of leavin' the hotel with it is givin' me the jitters,' Gina confessed.

'Me too, but what choice do we have?' Tammy was gazing at the floor as she spoke, and an idea occurred to her. 'What if we hid it under one of the floorboards in this room?'

Gina looked doubtful. 'What if someone finds it? It wouldn't take them long to put two and two together.'

But Tammy was already pulling one of the beds to

the side. 'If we hide it under one of the floorboards beneath the bed, nobody will ever know it's there.'

Gina pulled the rug back and together they began checking the floorboards.

'This one's loose,' said Tammy, 'but not enough to come up without a bit of help . . .' She took the large knife from Gina's satchel and dug the tip of the blade between two of the boards.

'Careful it doesn't slip,' warned Gina.

'I'm more worried about breakin' the blade,' said Tammy as she continued to prise the floorboard away from its neighbours. 'Got it!' she said as the board came free. 'Pass me the bag.'

Gina did as she was instructed, but Tammy held a few bob back for expenses.

'We'll need to get you a new satchel to put your things in,' said Tammy as she carefully placed the bag between the joists.

'What things? I literally have nothing else with me.'

Tammy slotted the floorboard back into place. 'Which is why we need to go and buy you a change of clothes.' She hesitated. 'How on earth you've been managing with only the one pair of knickers is beyond me!'

Gina grimaced. 'You get to be pretty ingenious when you're on the run.' She held up a finger. 'I've been usin' this as a toothbrush, and I've been washin' my smalls while you're asleep.'

'Well, you cannae possibly keep doin' that in the ATS. There's a market not far from here; I could pop out and get you some new clothes – unless you feel you can come with me now the money's no longer a concern?'

Having nailed the floorboard back into place using the heel of her shoe as a hammer, she briefly admired her handiwork before putting the rug back over it. 'You see?' she said, pointing. 'No one'll ever know, and you can come back for it whenever you're ready.'

Gina was swinging her arms into the sleeves of her coat. 'I don't ever want to see that money again!'

'Are you sure? I know it's caused you a lot of worry, but at the end of the day can you really afford to leave it there? Because I cannae see the services payin' much, and that money could be the start of a whole new life. You might even be able to set up your own business.'

'Doin' what?'

'Anythin'! You could start your own bakery, or tea rooms, or whatever takes your fancy with that kind of money.'

'If you put it like that . . .' said Gina slowly.

'How else can you put it?' said Tammy. 'A lot of people would give their right arm to have that sort of cash, and at least you'll only use it for good.'

'If we do come back for it . . .'

'We? It's your money.'

Gina followed Tammy out of the room. 'Strictly speakin' it's neither of ours, but if it weren't for you it would be at the bottom of a river, or even ashes in a grate.' They walked out of the hotel, and she smiled as the spring sunshine touched her face. 'I'd forgotten how good it feels to be outside!'

Tammy tucked her arm through her friend's. 'It's

nice to see you out and about. Carlisle is a lovely city; it's a shame you've not had the opportunity to go explorin' until now.'

'Better late than never, as they say,' said Gina. 'And now that I've got shot of most of that dough there'll be no stoppin' me!'

The two women spent an enjoyable morning buying Gina everything that was necessary before making their way back to the hotel. 'I've really enjoyed our shoppin' trip,' said Tammy, as she opened the door to their room. 'What do you think of Carlisle?'

Gina eyed her thoughtfully. 'I thought Carlisle was great, but I don't know how you can be so relaxed; if I were you I'd be constantly lookin' over my shoulder.'

'I've been keepin' my eye on the papers, and as there's been no mention of my dad I'm guessin' they've still not found him – either that or they think someone else was responsible for his murder and me and Mammy legged it while we had the opportunity.'

'From what you've told me about him, I'd put my money on the latter,' said Gina. 'They've probably got a list of suspects as long as their arm!'

'I just hope they don't wrongfully accuse someone, but as you say, they'll be spoilt for choice when it comes to culprits, so pinnin' somethin' on someone that's innocent isn't very likely.'

'I'm sure your Rory would vouch for your inno-cence,' said Gina. 'He sounds lovely.'

Tammy drew a deep breath. 'He is, which is why I do

my best to keep him out of my thoughts, because I cannae bear the way I treated him, even if I did have no choice.'

Gina took her new clothes out of her bag and put them into the drawer below Tammy's. 'And how do you feel about what happened to your dad? Because I dare say you loved him despite his temper.'

Tammy gazed out of the window to the street below. 'I suppose I must have, deep down, but only because he's my father. It's hard to love someone when they've never shown you any affection. On the one hand, I'm angry that he couldn't find it in his heart to love his own daughter, and that I'm in this predicament because of him. On the other, I'm angry because I wouldn't be alive if it weren't for him, yet I'm responsible for takin' him out of this world.'

Gina shook her head fervently. 'You cannae think like that. If he'd not acted the way he did, none of this would've happened. Had he been a proper father, you'd never have been forced to run away in the first place, so you really mustn't blame yourself for his death, because it's not your fault.'

'If we'd known he was comin' home earlier than planned, we'd have left before he got back.'

'Why did he come back, do you suppose?'

Tammy shrugged. 'I wondered if he'd got wind of our plans somehow, cos he's never home that early normally.'

'I suppose at the end of the day what's done is done, and you can either drive yourself potty dwellin' on the past, or put on a brave face and embrace the future.'

'Brave face it is then,' said Tammy. 'I just hope and pray to God that me mam's doin' the same wherever she may be, because not knowin' how she is – or where, for that matter – is worryin' me sick.'

By bus and then by train Grace had eventually arrived in Liverpool, and even though she'd only been away from Dennis for less than a fortnight she was already enjoying her new-found freedom. With no one to tell her what to do or when to do it she was making all her own decisions, content in the knowledge that there would be no repercussions should she make the wrong choice. For the first time in years, she was able to finally be herself. If it hadn't been for the worry over what might have happened to Tammy since leaving Clyde-bank, Grace would have been truly happy, but that was the cost of love.

Finding work as a seamstress had been a breeze when she didn't have a jealous husband holding her back, and being able to spend her money on whatever she wished without having to explain herself was truly liberating. Thanks to her place of work, finding a home had been just as easy. Suspecting that Grace was running away from a violent husband, one of the women who was present when Grace called in at the tailor's to ask about a job had pulled her to one side so that she might have a quiet word.

'Am I right in thinkin' that you've only just arrived in Liverpool?' Annie had asked.

Grace felt her cheeks begin to bloom. She had a feeling that Annie was about to ask her where she'd come from, and she wasn't keen to start answering questions regarding her recent past.

'I have, aye,' she replied. 'Is that a problem?'

'Not at all. I was just wonderin' whether you've found anywhere to live yet?'

Grace raised a hopeful eyebrow. 'Why, do you know of somewhere?'

'Maybe. You see, I run a women's sanctuary on Scotland Road. There's no need for you to go into detail, but does it sound like summat you'd be interested in?'

Grace breathed an inward sigh of relief. 'Very much.'

Annie nodded knowingly. 'Judgin' by your accent you're a long way from home, but even so should we expect any unwelcome callers?'

Grace shook her head. 'I'd rather not go into the whys and wherefores, but no one's goin' to come lookin' for me.'

'That's all I need to know.' Annie held out her hand. 'Welcome aboard.'

She had taken Grace to her new home after work that same day, and Grace had immediately noticed the array of photographs pinned to a cork board by the front door. She asked Annie who the men were.

'Husbands, boyfriends, fiancés or fathers who aren't welcome at the sanctuary,' said Annie. 'We keep their photographs here so that we can check before we open the door.' By way of demonstration, she walked over to the peep hole and peered through it.

'I understand husbands, boyfriends and fiancés, but fathers?'

'They don't always handle it well when they hear

their little girl's fallen pregnant out of wedlock,' Annie told her plainly.

'Oh,' said Grace, her cheeks colouring slightly. 'I didn't realise.'

'You have to be broad-minded if you live here,' Annie went on, 'because we welcome one and all, no matter their circumstances, and should a pregnant woman decide she wants to keep her babby we do all we can to help her financially as well as emotionally. The same goes if she wants an abortion.'

'Do you get many women in that predicament?' asked Grace, hoping that she was sounding interested rather than judgemental.

Annie pulled a rueful grimace. 'More since the war broke out. People have become impetuous, and it's the girls who are left with the consequences while the boys go back to war with no intention of acceptin' their responsibilities!'

'That's dreadful,' said Grace quietly. 'How can they just turn their backs like that?'

'Lots of different reasons,' said Annie.

'And yet there they are, bravely goin' off to war with people hailin' them as heroes.'

'Because they are! But they're also very young. A lot of them, I'm sure, don't expect to come back, which is why they're keen to become a "real man"' – Annie had placed air quotations around the last two words before continuing – 'even if they're not quite so keen to live up to their responsibilities.'

'The country's goin' to be in a rare old state once this war's over,' said Grace.

'I'm afraid you're right, cos the war is just the beginnin',' agreed Annie. 'The aftermath might be just as bad for those fortunate enough to be left.'

Having handed his notice in down the docks for the second time, Rory had wasted no time in signing up at the recruiting office. 'I don't care where they send me, as long as it's far away from here,' he had told the man who was taking everyone's details. It hadn't taken long for his posting to come through, and soon he was on his way to Padgate after passing his medical and educational tests to qualify as a flight mechanic.

Sitting on the train, he stared dully out of the window as they headed to their destination. Still numb from his loss, he had barely any recollection of the past few weeks. His supervisor down at the docks had tried to persuade him to stay on, but Rory hadn't been interested.

'I see her everywhere I go,' he told the older man. 'I'm a danger to myself as well as others when I'm unable to concentrate on the job in hand.' He had unfortunately proved his case when working his notice. He had been guiding a large cargo onto the dock when he found himself staring at a woman in the distance. He knew it couldn't be Tammy, but even so he found it impossible to tear his gaze away until he heard the cries of the men on the deck above him as the load overshot the mark and slipped from its hook, releasing half the contents into the water below.

Understandably, the men who were responsible for the cargo were not best pleased, and after a frightful row as to who was going to pay for the perished goods Rory was sent home, not that he was terribly bothered.

'I hope you get your act together before you start servicin' planes,' one of the men shouted after him as he left the docks, 'cos you'll have more to worry about than lost cargo otherwise!'

Rory had wondered himself whether he'd be able to concentrate on the job in hand while servicing aircraft, but he hoped that being far away from Clydebank and everything that reminded him of his belle would be enough to allow him to focus properly.

Now, as the train pulled into another station, he glanced at his fellow servicemen. *I wonder how many of them are here because they want to fight for their country, and how many are here because they're lookin' for a better life with more opportunities?* He rolled his eyes. How awful did things have to be for someone to decide that going to war with Hitler was better than their life back home?

He leaned his head against the carriage window. Losing Tammy had changed his whole life and he had no idea whether he'd ever feel whole again, but one thing was certain: he wasn't going to be able to pick up the pieces for a long time yet, because he didn't want to. *I just want to be with Tammy*, thought Rory miserably, *and if hurtin' this way makes me feel closer to her then it's worth the pain!*

Chapter Seven

Tammy and Gina had come to the end of their basic training, and were reminiscing over a plate of sausage and mash in the NAAFI.

'Thank goodness I bought new knickers before leavin' Carlisle,' said Gina as she sliced one of her sausages into pieces. 'I don't think I could stand to wear those awful khaki things they give us without my own on underneath!'

Tammy grinned. 'I thought they called them passion-killers because they look awful, but after wearin' them for a bit I reckon it has more to do with the itching!'

Gina scooped some mashed potato onto her fork. 'I bet the Waafs' knickers don't itch half as much as ours.'

'Their uniforms are certainly much smarter,' conceded Tammy, 'if that's anythin' to go by.'

Gina pointed to the roots of her hair, which were beginning to show their natural colour after being dyed. 'As we'll be gettin' a bit of leave before we're sent to our new postin', would you mind dyein' my hair back to its original colour, please?'

To an outsider this might sound as though Gina was unhappy with her yellow hair, but Tammy knew better. If Gina wanted to go back to her original colour it meant that she was no longer living in fear of pursuit by the Billy Boys; news which was music to Tammy's ears.

'It'll be my pleasure! I far preferred you as a brunette to a blonde anyway; it suits you better.' Her eyes fell to Gina's waist, which was considerably trimmer than when they'd first met. 'You look completely different from when I first saw you.'

Gina beamed as she smoothed her hands over her face. 'All thanks to the early mornin' starts and plenty of exercise – even if I do whinge about it – and a meagre diet! Some of the girls have mentioned my cheekbones, which feels strange because I didn't even realise I had any until recently!'

'Well, there's no way the Billy Boy who saw you would recognise you if he met you now.'

'Not that I'd ever want to go back,' said Gina. 'I've never had so many friends or as much freedom as I have in the ATS. Back in Clydebank I was livin' hand to mouth, so could never afford to go to the cinema, or dancin', but it's easy to do that here, especially if you go to the ones on camp.' She sighed happily. 'No rent or food bills to pay – unless you eat here in the NAAFI, of course.'

'Which we often do because the grub's nicer,' Tammy reminded her.

Gina waved a dismissive hand. 'Even so, I'd have joined ages ago if I'd known it was goin' to be this good!'

'I'm really hopin' my mam joined one of the services,' said Tammy as she mopped up the last of her gravy with a slice of bread. 'Not only would she fit in well, but I'd feel better knowin' that she was bein' taken care of, which is daft because she's a grown woman, but I think she needs a bit of lookin' after with everythin' she's been through.'

'What do you think she'd make of you becomin' a driver?' said Gina.

A slow smile graced Tammy's cheeks. 'She'd be delighted to know that I'd made it into the ATS, never mind the driving school, and she'd be proud of me for makin' the best of my life despite everythin' that's happened.'

'I must say, I think you've done a marvellous job of puttin' the past behind you,' said Gina. 'I dare say a lot of it's a front, but no one here would ever guess the truth behind your joinin' up.'

'I've not really,' Tammy admitted. 'It's all for show, because I daren't let my real emotions rise to the surface. I'm tryin' to block out all the negatives, and focus on Christmas Eve when I really hope to see me mam again. I don't care if I don't have any leave between now and then as long as I get Christmas Eve off.'

'I don't know what I'm goin' to do with my leave,' said Gina. 'It's not as if I've got anywhere to go.'

'You could always come to Liverpool with me,' said Tammy. 'I know my mam would love to meet you.'

Gina's face lit up, albeit hesitantly. 'Really? Only I don't want to intrude when you won't have seen each other for so long.'

'You'd not be intrudin',' Tammy assured her. 'Far from it.'

'Then I'd love to!'

Tammy pushed her tray to one side. 'I just wish you could've met Rory. I know the two of you would have got on like a house on fire.'

'Me too, but Rory's part of your past, and you simply *have* to concentrate on the future if you're ever to move forward from what happened. It's the same with me, and even though I've never had a boyfriend, I'm hoping I will in the fullness of time.'

'You've changed your tune,' Tammy noted. 'I thought you said you weren't interested in men?'

'That's before I joined the ATS, back when I thought I couldn't get one, but I've come on leaps and bounds as far as my confidence goes. When we first arrived I used to get out of puff doin' me laces up, never mind runnin' round the yard, but not any more. I can run rings round my former self nowadays!' Gina said proudly.

'You'd certainly be able to give the Billy Boys what for should you ever see them again.'

'I dunno about that, but I'd certainly be able to outrun them!' chuckled Gina. She took a sip of her tea before adding, 'I'm surprised we never heard anythin' about that feller they killed in the caff. You'd think it would be all over the news.'

Tammy shrugged. 'Maybe they moved the body before it could be found?'

'But why didn't they do that straight away?' mused Gina. 'Surely it would have been better to do it there and then rather than wait a while.'

'Maybe the café owner had upset them somehow, and they wanted to send out a message: mess with the Billy Boys and you wind up dead. The polis wouldn't be able to pin anythin' on them, so they had nothin' to worry about on that score, until they realised they had a witness. Once they saw you, they probably realised you were on your way to the polis station, and got rid of the body. After all, no body, no proof.'

'But surely someone would have noticed that he'd gone missin'?'

'Of course they would, but no one's goin' to mention it for fear the Billy Boys will come after them.'

'So just like that, he disappears with no record of his death?' said Gina in disbelief.

'No one wants to be next in line, so it's either keep your mouth shut or join him at the bottom of the Clyde, or wherever he may be,' said Tammy. 'It's dreadful, of course it is, but don't forget you didn't report it for that very reason.'

Gina's cheeks took on a pink tinge. 'Touché!'

'I'm not sayin' I blame you,' said Tammy hastily, 'cos I'd have done the same – in fact I did worse – but you can see where they're comin' from.'

'When you put it like that, then yes, I suppose I can.'

'I really am surprised about them not findin' my dad, though,' said Tammy thoughtfully, 'cos there's no reason why *he* shouldn't be in the papers.'

Gina took care to lower her voice so she couldn't be overheard. 'You are *sure* about him bein' dead?'

'No one could have survived after bein' hit on the head with an iron the way I hit him.'

A frown creased Gina's brow. 'But you did check to make sure that he wasn't breathin'?'

Tammy thought back to that fateful night. 'Mam asked if he was dead, and he definitely looked as though he was, but to make sure I checked for a pulse and found nothin', so I tried to see if he was breathin', but' – she stopped speaking as she tried to put her experience into words – 'the whole thing was terrifyin'. I didn't really know what I was doin', and the thought that someone could pop round at any second didn't exactly help matters.'

'Why would someone have come round?'

Tammy tried to think why she'd been under the impression that someone might come looking. It was then that she recalled Edie Brodie banging on the floor above their ceiling. She looked up sharply. 'Whenever we started arguin' or shoutin' Edie upstairs used to bang on the floor of her apartment with a broom. It was her way of tellin' us to keep the noise down. I remember her doin' it when Dad first came home, because he shouted at her to shut up. She's reported us in the past for bein' noisy, and I suppose I was worried she might do the same again, because if she did the polis might have called round to have a word, and had they done that they'd have discovered my father's body with us still in the room, and how could we have explained ourselves then?'

131

'But if you're wrong, and he's not dead, then you're runnin' for nothin'.'

Tammy's brow rose towards her hairline. 'On the contrary. Not only did he not want us to go in the first place, I dare say bein' walloped over the head with an iron won't have endeared us to him either. Never mind the fact we left him for dead, not to mention my takin' the housekeepin'.'

'So you're damned if you do and damned if you don't,' said Gina.

'Exactly.'

'Just as well you left when you did. And with us doin' our trainin' in Surrey, we couldn't get further away from Clydebank if we tried!'

'It'll certainly help to take my mind off everythin' that's happened, includin' Rory,' Tammy admitted.

'So, are we agreed?'

'On what?'

'On findin' ourselves a couple of fellers?'

Tammy sighed. 'I know I'll probably want to at some point, but not just yet, or not for me, at any rate.'

'In that case, you can be my wingman. Or should that be wingwoman?' Gina chuckled.

Tammy smiled. 'And do you know the sort of feller you're after?'

'He has to have all his own teeth . . .' began Gina, but before she could go on Tammy gave a shriek of laughter.

'Whose teeth do you expect him to have?' she stuttered.

'You know what I mean!' said Gina, although she too was chuckling as she continued, 'and he has to be clean, and fun-lovin' – I cannae abide men who are serious all the time. I want someone who can laugh at himself; someone who doesn't take himself too seriously, and loves me for me.'

'Sounds like a smashin' chap, but what should he be like looks wise – apart from the teeth, of course?'

'Oh, ha ha! I only mentioned the teeth because it's a sign of good hygiene and I don't want a man who cannae be bothered to look after himself, because if that's too much trouble how can he look after me?'

'Jolly good point!' said Tammy. 'So what about everythin' else? Eye colour? Hair?'

Gina shot her a shrewd glance. 'I'd prefer him to have hair, but as long as he's a nice man who takes care of himself, I'm not really worried what he looks like.' She eyed Tammy curiously. 'I know I said you had to move on from Rory, but out of curiosity, what does he look like?'

Tammy gazed into the distance as she conjured an image of her beau in her mind's eye. 'He has dark curly hair, deep brown eyes that always look happy, and a dimple right in the middle of his chin. And in case you're wonderin', he has all his own teeth, and they're nice and white too.'

'He sounds gorgeous,' said Gina, 'but it's only fair, with a looker like you on his arm.'

'Me?' said Tammy, surprised that anyone should describe her as good-looking.

'Aye, you! What with your beautiful auburn hair, sparkling green eyes and cute little freckles, you're a real catch!'

'You do realise you've just described Little Orphan Annie, don't you?'

'Little Orphan Annie is a child, not a woman,' said Gina reasonably, 'and she doesn't look anythin' like you! Your hair's long and your curls are sleek, and you've got the most beautiful skin.'

Tammy blushed. 'And a face like a traffic light, whenever I get embarrassed,' she said, fanning her cheeks with her hand.

'Well, I think you're lucky,' said Gina, 'and what's more you'll have to fight the fellers off with sticks when they realise you're unattached.'

'I shall bat them in your direction,' said Tammy. Getting to her feet, she pushed her chair back in before heading over to the large tub of water where they washed their cutlery – or irons as she and Gina had discovered they were known in the army.

'I wonder if the people who teach us to drive will be male or female?' said Gina.

'Let me guess, you're hopin' for a male, am I right?'

'It would be nice,' said Gina, 'especially if he's kind and doesn't shout at you when you get it wrong – unlike our drill sergeant who likes nothin' better than to holler my name at the top of his lungs.'

Tammy's face dropped. 'I don't think I'd like to be taught by him in the confinement of a car – I'd be a nervous wreck! Surely they wouldn't allow someone like that to teach us?'

Gina crossed her fingers. 'I sincerely hope not.' They stepped out of the NAAFI, and began making their way to the Nissen hut they shared with twenty other women. 'Someone like that Gregory would be nice,' she added.

Tammy chuckled beneath her breath. 'That explains all those trips to the stores.'

Gina tried to deny her friend's statement, but the blush racing up to her neckline was speaking for her. 'You make it sound as though I'm always buyin' stuff.'

'Put it this way: you'll save yourself a small fortune when we move to Camberley, as will a lot of the women, I should imagine.'

Gina grinned sheepishly. 'Unless they have another one like Gregory in Camberley! Now wouldn't it be grand if we had someone like *that* to teach us how to drive!'

* * *

4TH MAY 1941

The ground shuddered as yet another bomb fell on the city of Liverpool. Cowering in the street shelter along with the rest of the women from the home, Grace turned as one of the younger women, a girl by the name of Millie, pushed her hand into hers.

'It's all right, lass. We're safe in here,' Grace assured her.

'What a world to bring a child up in,' said Millie miserably. 'Why can't they just sod off and leave us alone?'

'Because some men just aren't like that,' said Grace.

'They won't be happy until they've destroyed everythin' and everyone around them.'

'They've already taken my Neil,' said Millie. 'Cos of them my babby will have to grow up without a father.'

'But he or she will grow up feelin' loved,' said Grace, 'you'll make sure of that.'

Another bomb thudded, so close Millie squealed with fear. 'Goodness only knows what this is doin' to my poor babby. The nurse reckons stressful situations are bad for them.'

'Take some nice deep breaths,' Grace advised. 'I'll do some with you.'

Together they breathed in and out slowly, and it wasn't long before Millie was nodding. 'Thank you. I do feel a bit more relaxed.' She smiled. 'I bet you'd have been a great mammy.'

Smiling back, Grace averted her gaze. *If I were a great mammy I'd know where my daughter was and who she was with*, she told herself as the dust sifted down through the planked ceiling of the shelter. *But as it stands I haven't the foggiest.* She felt her tummy jolt as an image of Tammy trying to hide from the Luftwaffe appeared in her mind's eye. *That's even if she's still alive*, Grace thought, *cos bombing's been heavy right across the country.* She found her fingers automatically going to her mouth, but one look at her nails showed there was nothing left to nibble. *If I could just see her, or hear her voice even, that would be enough for now, but there's no way that's goin' to happen because she hasn't a clue where I am.* She sighed ruefully. *I should have arranged to meet up well before Christmas; I don't know what made me think it best to wait nine months when it could easily have been one.* She felt her cheeks warm. *Because you thought it would take longer than that to establish yourself somewhere*, she told herself, *and besides, Tammy's got a sensible head on her shoulders; she won't do anythin' stupid or rash.* She felt Millie's hand tighten in hers and wished it were Tammy's. *Only seven months to go*, thought Grace, *and if she shows up at the Liver Building I'm never goin' to let her out of my sight again!*

* * *

JULY 1941

Having completed his basic training at RAF Padgate, Rory had been sent to the No. 1 School of Technical Training in RAF Halton where he was to be trained in aircraft maintenance.

'Why on earth you chose to work down the docks when your real passion is all things mechanical is beyond me,' said Jimmy, one of his fellow recruits. 'Quite frankly, you're knockin' spots off the rest of us.'

'I didn't exactly choose to work down the docks,' said Rory, 'it was either earn money or become destitute.'

'Just as well for you we went to war then, innit?' said Jimmy. He gave a short, mirthless laugh. 'Funny how things work out, don't you think?'

Rory took a spanner out of his toolbox. 'How do you mean?'

'If we hadn't gone to war, you'd have spent the rest of your life down the docks earnin' peanuts, but now that you're gettin' some qualifications under your belt, who knows? You might even end up runnin' your own garage one day.'

'Every cloud, eh?' said Rory, in a tongue-in-cheek fashion.

'It's the only way to look at it,' said Jimmy. He gave Rory a speculative look. 'So, you didn't join up to get your qualifications? Only I sort of assumed you had, what with you bein' in a reserved occupation an' all.'

Rory rested his arm up against the frame of the aircraft. 'I signed up on the day I lost my belle durin' the March blitz.'

Jimmy lowered his gaze. 'Sorry, mate. I didn't realise . . .'

'Don't worry about it. You weren't to know.'

'Had you been together long?'

'Childhood sweethearts,' said Rory. 'She died on the day that we were meant to run away together.'

'Sounds like true love,' said Jimmy.

'It was.' Rory went on to tell Jimmy how they'd planned to move far away from her father and start life anew. 'We had it all worked out,' he finished, before adding, 'If it hadn't been for the bombing, I wouldn't be here now.'

'You say you joined up because you lost Tammy, but why exactly?'

'I needed to get away from Clydebank because there were too many reminders of what should have been. But not only that – I want to send the Luftwaffe to hell for what they did to my belle. Why should the Nazis get to live on, when they took my Tammy?' He patted the spanner against the palm of his hand. 'I don't care what happens to me as long as we win.'

'It's the same for me,' Jimmy began, then hastily explained himself after seeing Rory's face drop. 'Don't get me wrong, my family are safe and sound – thank God – but I want them to stay that way, which is why I joined.'

'You've children?'

'Two boys, six and eight.' Jimmy glanced around him. 'I hope to God they never have to do owt like this in order to protect their families.'

'It doesn't bear thinkin' about, which is why we've got to make sure we do a proper job this time.'

'We will,' stated Jimmy confidently, 'cos we can't afford not to. And if it's any consolation, I'm sure you'll find love again.'

Rory's features darkened. 'No thanks! I'd rather not fall in love at all than go through that again.'

'Some might say that life without love isn't worth livin',' said Jimmy, resting his chin between his forefinger and thumb while he tried to remember the saying. 'What was it now? Oh, yes. It's better to have loved and lost than never to have loved at all.'

Rory pulled a disbelieving face. 'Take it from one who knows, it's better to never have loved at all than feel the pain of your loss.'

Jimmy raised his brow. 'Are you sayin' you wish you'd never met Tammy?'

Rory thought this through before answering. 'I'm sayin' that given my experience I'd rather not fall in love again, but would I deny my only love? No.'

'You do know that you could feel that again, though?' said Jimmy cautiously.

'They say we all have one true love,' said Rory. 'If that's right, then I can't have another, can I? And if I did, then what's to say that summat wouldn't happen to break my heart again?'

'But that's life,' said Jimmy. 'You have to take a chance because no one knows what's around the corner.' He paused. 'You said that the two of you fell in love when you were children?'

'That's right.'

'Well, who's to say that you won't fall in love with some pretty Waaf whilst on base? From what I remember love sneaks up on you when you're least expectin' it. Or at least it did in my case. I'm guessin' it was the same for you – unless it was love at first sight?'

'Not love at first sight,' admitted Rory. 'We were friends first . . .' He hesitated. They'd met on the playground during their lunch break. She'd been playing hopscotch, and he'd been playing marbles with his pals. *It was the way she cried out with triumph when she won*, he thought now. *Her smile was so totally and utterly beguiling.* He recalled how that smile had deepened as she caught Rory watching her. *She was a little minx and I knew I had to go over and say hello, so I waited until her game was over and asked her if she wanted to play. She said she liked my Kong so I gave it to her, even though it was my prize one.* He paused. Had it been love at first sight? Could you even call it love at the tender age of eleven? *I knew nothin' about her, but from what I saw that day I knew I wanted to get to know her. At first we only saw each*

140

other in class, and at playtime, but when we got to know each other better we started meetin' after school, and that's when I learned the truth about her rotten father and the reason for her bruises. He felt a pang of anger as he recalled how he'd wanted to protect her even then. *She was so small, so fragile, and her skin was like porcelain, meaning the bruises easily caught the eye, yet the school did nothin', despite the fact that it was blatantly obvious she was being beaten. No one likes to get involved,* he reminded himself now, *but they should, because if they had, Tammy wouldn't be dead, and Dennis would be behind bars.*

'Rory?' Jimmy's voice cut through his thoughts.

'Maybe it *was* love at first sight,' concluded Rory, 'but either way, one's thing's for certain: I'll never fall in love like that again.'

Tammy blushed as she and the driving instructor – Mick to his pupils – both reached for the gear stick at the same time.

He flashed her a dazzling smile as his hand rested on top of hers. 'If you're happy that it's in neutral, you can take your foot off the clutch, but do it slowly mind, cos I don't want to end up in the officers' mess.'

Still blushing, she wobbled the gear stick from side to side before carefully pulling her foot off the clutch.

He eyed her approvingly. 'Well done! Always make sure it's in neutral *before* you take your foot off the clutch, cos had there been another vehicle – or a person – in front of the car a few moments ago you'd have careered straight into them.'

She grimaced apologetically. 'There's so much to remember, and all of it matters.'

'All vehicles can be lethal weapons in the wrong hands,' said Mick, 'which is why this course is so important.'

'I thought it would be just a case of learnin' how to start, steer and stop,' admitted Tammy. 'I didn't realise cars had gears and clutches.'

'And as you've already learned, they're the hardest to get to grips with,' said Mick. 'But you're gettin' there, you really are.'

'Does it get any harder than this?' she asked as she selected first gear to practise pulling forward.

'Nah, just bigger,' he said, before signalling for her to move on. 'Once you get the hang of it, you won't give it a moment's thought.'

She laughed. 'I doubt that.' She pulled the Imp forward before slowly applying the brake. 'Don't you get fed up of teachin' people the same thing over and over?'

'Not at all, although I do think your pal's suggestion was a good one.'

'Gina? What did she say?'

'That they should pay us danger money.'

A giggle escaped Tammy's lips. 'Was that before or after she'd run over your pal's foot?'

'After,' said Mick, 'but in her defence, Donny should know better than to daydream where there's people learnin' to drive.'

'Is he all right? Only I haven't seen him in any of the cars lately.'

'His pride took a good bashin', and his foot's still

pretty bruised, but all in all he came out of it quite well. Certainly better than he would have had she been in a wagon.'

'Poor Gina. She felt terrible.'

'She's come on well since,' said Mick, 'or so I'm told.'

'She's probably the most vigilant of all of us,' Tammy agreed.

'How do you find life in the ATS?' he asked conversationally, as Tammy continued to practise engaging first gear and pulling forward.

'I love everythin' about it,' replied Tammy simply, 'from sharin' a hut with all my pals to learnin' new skills.'

'You don't mind havin' someone else rule your life?'

She shot him a sideways glance before quickly returning her attention to the road ahead. 'My father told me what to do and when to do it, or feel the back of his hand. The ATS is positively nurturing compared to him.'

His face dropped. 'Is that why you joined up?'

She tried to banish the guilty blush from her cheeks. 'I'm not sure I'd have done so otherwise, although I suppose I would have eventually, of course.'

'I can't imagine what it must be like to consider the army an easier option than livin' at home.'

Keen to move the discussion away from her father, she deftly changed the subject. 'How about you? What were you doin' before joinin' up?'

'I was trainin' to be an accountant.'

She blew her cheeks out. 'Blimey! I didn't realise you were a clever clogs!'

He smiled appreciatively. 'I dunno if I'd go that far.'

'You are compared to me,' said Tammy firmly. 'I was never any good at maths when I was in school.'

'Not that it's done me much good, thanks to Hitler,' said Mick dolefully.

'This isn't forever, though,' said Tammy brightly. 'You'll be able to go back to bein' an accountant once the war's over.'

He was gazing at her with twinkling eyes. 'I hope I'm not bein' too forward, but do you mind my askin' if you have a boyfriend?'

The vehicle lurched forward as Tammy took both feet off the pedals without thinking. Pulling the handbrake up, Mick was the first to speak. 'Maybe I should've waited until you were in neutral before asking.'

'It was my fault,' said Tammy. 'I should've been concentratin'.'

A faint hue tingeing his cheeks, Mick told her to put the car into neutral and try again. She did so, and as the car crept slowly forward she answered his question as honestly as she knew how.

'I had a boyfriend before I joined up, but we're not together any more.'

'Did he not like the idea of you joinin' the ATS?'

'It's complicated,' she replied truthfully. 'I wish things could've been different, but sometimes even love just isn't enough.'

He raised his brow. 'Sounds like it was a serious relationship.'

'Very much so.'

He eyed her curiously. 'Would I be right in sayin' that you're very much still in love with him?'

'I don't think I'll ever love anyone else,' she said frankly.

'That would be a shame.'

Keen to take the attention away from herself, she turned the tables. 'How about you? Have you got anyone special in your life?'

He cast an eye around the multiple servicewomen in view. 'I'm still lookin' for the arrow to my bow.'

'Very romantic! You must have the girls fallin' at your feet with lines like that.'

'But not you?'

She smiled. 'Been there, done that, no desire to retrace my steps just yet – if ever.'

Mick smiled. 'More's the pity.'

Tammy pulled the handbrake into position. 'How was that?'

He nodded. 'Very good. Carry on like this and you'll have passed your trainin' in no time, unfortunately for me.'

Tammy wagged a chiding finger. 'You're a charmer, that's what you are.'

He looked to his next pupil, who was waiting patiently. 'I say it as I see it.'

Tammy checked in her wing mirror before opening the car door. 'Shall I see you tomorrow?'

He drew the sign of the cross over his breast while jerking his head pointedly in the direction of the woman now walking towards them, an anxious look furrowing her face. 'I certainly hope so.'

145

Laughing softly, Tammy wished him luck before heading off to meet Gina. Nearly every woman on the base had chosen Mick as the man they most wanted to land, but not one of them had got him to bite, until now. Seeing Gina waiting for her outside the door to the cookhouse, she strode towards her.

'How'd it go?' asked Gina, following her pal into the building.

'All right, until Mick asked me if I had a boyfriend.'

Gina emitted a shrill squeal. 'He didn't!'

Tammy wriggled her forefinger into the ear Gina had squealed down. 'Not that it did him any good, mind you.'

'If the others find out, you'll be the most envied woman on the base! Especially Imelda. She's like a bitch on heat when it comes to Mick Turner.'

Tammy snorted with laughter. 'Gina!'

'What? I'm only tellin' the truth! She even told me how many kids she'd like to have with him.'

Tammy continued to chuckle beneath her breath. 'Blimey!'

'Shame you're not interested, cos he's one heck of a catch.'

Tammy stopped laughing. 'Unlike me,' she said quietly.

'What are you talkin' about? Any man would be lucky to have you on his arm!'

They joined the queue, and Tammy lowered her voice so that only Gina could hear. 'Do you really think they'd be interested if they knew what I'd done?'

Gina rolled her eyes. 'Well, obviously, you don't *tell* him any of that.'

'So, you're suggestin' I start the relationship on a lie on top of everythin' else?'

'Not at all. I'm sayin' you don't have to tell him everythin', which I'm pretty sure is different from lyin'.'

They reached the head of the queue and got their food, then found a table on the far side of the hall.

'You make it sound so easy, but he's bound to ask me about my parents at some stage,' Tammy continued. 'And what am I meant to say when he does?'

Gina finished the chip she'd already started before replying. 'You tell him all he needs to know: that you and your mother are estranged from your father.'

'Only it's more than that, isn't it? And while I'm about it, what am I meant to do if I bump into someone I used to know when I lived in Clydebank? It didn't cross my mind at first, but the more women I see, the more I worry that one of them will recognise me.'

Gina lifted the pastry lid off her pie and grimaced at the lack of filling. 'Now there you have a point. I suppose you could always do what I did, cos I bet you'd look loads different with a smidge of mascara and a new do,' she said. 'Why don't you give it a go?'

Tammy wrinkled her nose. 'I've never liked the thought of puttin' stuff on my eyelashes, but I'd happily try a new do. What do you think would suit me best?'

Gina screwed her lips to one side as she gazed thoughtfully at Tammy's hair. 'How about tryin' to straighten it somehow?'

Tammy's eyebrows shot upwards. 'I've more chance of flyin' to the moon than straightenin' my hair.'

'Mascara's quick to apply,' Gina told her. 'I know you say you don't like it, but have you ever tried?'

'No-o,' said Tammy slowly. She picked up her knife and tried to examine her reflection in the blade. 'I cannae see that it would make that much difference, but I suppose anything's got to be worth a shot.'

Gina rubbed her hands together enthusiastically. 'I'll help you put it on ...' but Tammy was shaking her head fervently.

'Sorry, Gina, but I'm not havin' anyone go near my eyes with a mascara wand!'

Clearly disappointed, Gina took a bite of her pie and chewed thoughtfully before swallowing. 'What about pluckin' yer eyebrows? Mavis looked very different when she did hers.'

Tammy envisaged the two faces of Mavis. 'I think you might be on to somethin' there, cos she looked much better after she'd had them done.'

'So new eyebrows; what else?'

'I wonder if partin' my hair on the other side would help?'

'We'll give it a go when we go back to the hut,' said Gina. 'It's a shame you haven't any weight to lose, because that really does change the way you look.'

Tammy gestured towards Gina's ever-shrinking waistline. 'You're certainly half the woman you used to be!'

Gina wrinkled the side of her nose. 'And yet I'm still single!'

'Because you're waitin' for the right man to come along,' Tammy reminded her.

'I suppose that's one way of lookin' at it. Now, let's finish up here so that we can start work on your new look.'

'Don't you think it might seem a bit odd if I suddenly start lookin' different?'

Gina smiled. 'In case you hadn't noticed, we're the only women in our hut who *haven't* started usin' makeup.'

Tammy furrowed her brow; now that she came to think about it, Gina was right. 'I wonder why the others have?'

Gina grinned. 'His name is Mick.'

It was much later that same day and Tammy had her fingers firmly placed over her eyebrows, protecting them from being plucked. 'I've changed my mind,' she told Gina, who was still holding Sophie's borrowed tweezers.

'I barely touched you!' objected Gina. She glanced at the tweezer tips. 'I got a few hairs out at most!'

'You're meant to pluck the hairs, not the skin!' said Tammy, still covering her brows.

Sophie – who had been watching quietly – stood up. 'Would you like me to have a go? I've done some of the other girls' so I've had plenty of practice.'

Tammy eyed the tweezers doubtfully. 'Only if you promise not to nick me.'

Sophie smiled as Gina handed her the tweezers. 'I promise.'

Gina watched as Sophie began to shape Tammy's brows. 'Golly, you're quick,' she said. She glanced at Tammy, who had her eyes closed. 'You'll be done in no time.'

Having tried her hardest not to breathe for fear that the tiniest movement might cause the tweezers to slip, Tammy began to relax as Sophie moved on to the next brow. 'I'm not goin' to say it's not painful, but at least there's no blood,' she said, examining her fingertips.

Gina shot her an accusing look. 'You make it sound as if I cut you to ribbons!'

'That's how it felt,' said Tammy, a faint smile tweaking her lips.

Sophie finished the second brow and stepped back to inspect her work. 'They look pretty even to me.' She fetched the handheld mirror which one of the other girls had brought onto the base and offered it to Tammy. 'Do you want me to take any more off?'

Tammy admired her new look. 'No thank you. I must say, you've done a marvellous job, Sophie.'

Sophie performed a small curtsey. 'My mam taught me to do mine a while ago, so I had plenty of practice before I got here; and as they say, practice makes perfect! If you like, I can do them again for you when they grow back.'

'That would be lovely. Thank you. How long will it take for them to grow back?'

'Around six weeks.'

'Six weeks!' cried Tammy. 'I don't want to go through this every six weeks!'

'Don't worry. You don't have to have them done

again if you don't want to, but most women change their minds once they start growin' back.' She turned to Gina. 'Would you like me to do yours?'

Gina glanced at Tammy, who looked a whole lot better for having her eyebrows plucked, even if her skin did look tender. 'Are you sure you've the time?'

Sophie indicated the chair which Tammy had just vacated. 'Don't worry, it won't take long.'

Feeling that she could hardly refuse after encouraging Tammy to have hers done, Gina sat down and screwed her eyes shut.

'Try to relax,' Sophie advised. 'I can't shape them properly if you don't.'

Gina did as she was told, and Sophie set to work. 'It gets easier the more you do it,' she explained to the girls, while whisking the hairs from Gina's brow, 'because the hair grows back finer each time.'

'So it won't hurt as much?' said Tammy, who was still admiring her reflection.

'Exactly,' said Sophie, adding, 'What made you both decide you wanted to get them done?'

'Everybody does it,' said Gina. 'We thought we might try experimentin' with mascara, too.'

'I just fancied a different look,' said Tammy somewhat truthfully. 'I might try stylin' my hair a different way, too. Have you any suggestions?'

Sophie turned her attention from Gina's eyebrow to Tammy's auburn locks. 'You could try pinnin' it up and back. You'd see more of your face that way.' She jerked her head towards her bed. 'I've got a few hair-clips that you can use to practise.'

Tammy set about clipping her hair into place, while Sophie stood back to admire her work on Gina's eyebrows. 'That wasn't too bad, was it?'

'Not at all, but I doubt I'll ever be as quick as you,' said Gina, picking up the mirror so that she could admire her new look. 'Blimey! I look totally different!'

'We both do,' said Tammy, turning her head from side to side. 'What do you think of my efforts so far?'

Sophie nodded approval. 'You look much better with your hair pulled back.' Taking Tammy's hairbrush, along with a few more clips, she stood, poised in readiness. 'May I?'

Tammy held the mirror up so that she could watch while Sophie styled her hair. 'Be my guest.'

Sophie got to work and within a few minutes she had pinned the rest of Tammy's hair up so that not a wisp hung down. 'You've such a beautiful neckline, it's a shame to hide it away.'

Gina was staring at Tammy open-mouthed. 'You look ever so grown up,' she said. 'Quite sophisticated, in fact.'

'It's amazin' what a few pins and a bit of eyebrow shapin' can do,' agreed Sophie. 'You've a beautiful jawline, too.'

Tammy blushed. 'Thanks, Sophie. You've performed miracles.'

'Just you wait until Mick sees you,' said Gina with a grin.

Sophie raised her brow. 'Got your eye on him, have you?'

'More like the other way round,' Gina told her.

'Lucky girl,' said Sophie. 'Is this the reason for the spruce-up?'

'Nope, I really did just fancy a change,' said Tammy.

'She turned him down,' Gina supplied.

'Crikey, you must be the only woman on camp who'd do that,' said Sophie. 'What gives?'

'Just not ready for another relationship.'

'Nursin' a broken heart, eh? Well, you're not the first, and you won't be the last the way this war's headin'.'

Tammy changed the subject. 'Thanks for doin' this,' she said. 'You should train as a beautician when you leave the services, cos I reckon you're already halfway there.'

'That's not a bad idea,' said Sophie. 'I can use the girls on camp as my guinea pigs.'

'If you can make me look like Tammy, I'm more than happy for you to practise on me,' said Gina.

The door to their hut opened and a woman by the name of Doreen leaned through. 'Are you ready, Sophie?'

Sophie picked up her jacket. 'Coming.' Tammy looked to Gina as the door swung shut behind her.

'Do you think people will recognise me?'

'I doubt it. You don't look like someone who grew up in a tenement; you look far too classy for that.'

'That's good to hear,' said Tammy. There was a pause before she added, 'I wonder what Rory would think if he could see me now?'

'He'd think that you were the belle of the ball, and he'd be right.'

'I wish I could see him again,' said Tammy softly. 'Just so I'd know that he was all right.'

Gina took her by the hand and gave it a small squeeze. 'He'll be fine.'

'I hope so, cos I really want him to be happy.'

'Just knowin' that you got away from your dad will be enough to make him happy, and even though he'll find it tough he'll move on with his life, just as you have with yours.' She lowered her lashes. 'I don't wish to sound mean, but you did say that you were goin' to try and forget about Rory so that you could move on with your life.'

Tammy sighed. 'I know, but I cannae help but wonder sometimes, especially when I do things like this.'

'I just don't like to see you dwellin' on the past, when you've such a bright future ahead of you.'

'I know.' But even though Tammy knew that Gina was right, it didn't stop her from wishing things had been different.

Chapter Eight

Grace walked slowly through the crisp autumn leaves which carpeted the pavements as she made her way home from work. Spending the last six months not knowing where her daughter was, or how she was getting on, had taken its toll. Add to that the various sightings of her ex-husband – every one of which had proved to be a case of mistaken identity – and it was hardly surprising that her work colleagues and house-mates, one of whom was currently trying to catch up with her, had become aware that things weren't quite right.

'Grace! Hold up!'

Turning, Grace smiled at Annie, who was holding her hat on her head as she raced along the pavement behind her. 'Sorry, were you callin' me?'

Annie fell into step beside her. 'Not to worry. You've obviously had a lot on your mind of late.'

Surprised that anybody had noticed her preoccupation, Grace shot her friend a sidelong glance. 'What makes you say that?'

Annie arched her brow. 'You live in a house full of women who've been through the mill in one way or another, which makes them good at spottin' when summat's wrong, and we've all noticed that you seem to be worried for some reason.' She hesitated. 'Has someone said or done summat to upset you?'

Grace shook her head fervently. 'Not at all. They've all been wonderful.'

'Is it the number of young girls lookin' for somewhere to hide until they can deal with their unwanted pregnancies? I know that weighed heavily on your mind at first.'

'I suppose it does upset me a little.' Without thinking, she went on, 'I would hate to imagine my own daughter was goin' through summat like that.'

Annie shot her a sidelong glance. 'You've a daughter?'

Paling, Grace cursed herself inwardly for slipping up, but it was too late now. She'd just have to go with the flow and see where it took her.

'Aye, but I've not seen her since March.'

'Could you not go and visit her?' said Annie. 'If money's an issue, we'll happily club together to cover your rail fare.'

'That's really kind of you, but I'll be seein' her on Christmas Eve,' said Grace, adding, 'or at least I hope I will.'

Annie walked on in silence for a few minutes, before asking the question uppermost in her thoughts. 'And if you don't?'

Grace felt a lump form in her throat. 'Then I shall go

there every Christmas Eve for the rest of my life in the hope that she'll show up one day.'

'Go where?' said Annie softly.

Grace drew a deep breath – if she couldn't trust Annie, she couldn't trust anybody. 'The Liver Building. That's where we arranged to meet after we ran away from her father.'

'Why on earth didn't she come to Liverpool with you?'

'Because I thought I was doin' the right thing at the time, but the way I feel now she should've come with me and to hell with the consequences.'

Taking her in a one-armed hug, Annie looked around for somewhere suitable for them to have a quiet chat, and spied a tea shop across the way. She led Grace over the road and through the door, just as the heavens opened, and chose a table in the corner of the café. Sitting in the chair opposite Grace so that her friend was obscured from the other diners, she ordered a pot of tea along with two teacakes, and waited for the waitress to go before handing Grace a spare handkerchief. 'Let it all out, love. We all need a good cry from time to time, and I'd wager this one's long overdue.'

Grace dabbed her eyes as she thanked Annie for the handkerchief. 'I've been tellin' myself that she's OK and can look after herself, but she's never been through anythin' like this before.'

'And you have?'

'No, but I'm a lot older than her.'

Annie rubbed the nape of her neck. 'You don't have to tell me if you don't want to, but it's hard for me to

157

help when I haven't the foggiest what happened to separate you in the first place.'

They stopped talking as the waitress placed their order on the table, before going off to serve the next customer, and then Grace stared at Annie as though she very much wanted to tell all, but was too scared of the consequences. 'I wish I could, but I can't.'

Annie held her hand across the table. Grace had made it clear from the start that she wasn't in any danger of being followed, but how could she be so sure when they'd obviously run away from her daughter's father in the first place? And what would make the two of them split up if they knew they had nothing to fear? *Because they were afraid of someone other than the father*, thought Annie, *but that hardly makes sense when Grace has already said it was the father they were runnin' away from*. Totally flummoxed, Annie put herself in Grace's shoes. *I ran away with my daughter, and we got split up, but I'm not scared of my husband pursuin' either of us, because he can't for some reason or other. But what would stop him?* The answer hit her so hard it nearly knocked her off her feet. She stared at Grace, stony-faced. 'So, it's not your daughter's father you're afraid of comin' after you, because you know he can't,' she said slowly, while keeping a careful eye on Grace's reaction. 'It's the scuffers what you're scared of. Am I right?'

Grace felt an icy chill enter her stomach as she stared back at Annie, who was looking at her with certainty. Annie had heard too many stories for Grace to try to pull the wool over her eyes when she already knew the truth. She nodded meekly.

'So, am I also right in sayin' that you split up cos you thought you'd draw less attention that way?'

'Aye, and even though I know it was the right thing to do at the time, it doesn't stop me from worryin' as to the consequences.'

'So, what happened exactly? Was it some sort of horrible accident, or . . . ?' She left the question hanging.

'Tammy was stoppin' him from stranglin' me,' Grace said, so softly that Annie had to strain to hear her correctly.

'And now the two of you are payin' the price for his violence,' she sighed sadly. 'You aren't the first and you certainly won't be the last – unfortunately.'

'I just wish I knew where she was so that I could check if she's all right,' sniffed Grace. 'It's the not knowin' that's the hardest.'

'I take it you lied about your name when you came here?'

Grace grimaced. 'We'd been plannin' to leave for a long time; we even had fake papers made. Had we left the house just five minutes earlier Dennis would still be alive and we'd still be together.'

'Sod's law,' said Annie. 'But at least with new identities, you should remain below the radar.'

Grace eyed Annie with shocked admiration. 'How can you take all this in your stride? I've just dropped the biggest bombshell and you've not batted an eye!'

'I'm sorry to say that your story's not unique. In fact, it's been experienced by many, many women before you. Wife-beaters always follow the same path, normally with one of two endings: either the wife dies after one beatin' too many, or she manages to escape only to find herself on the end of a noose for murder.' She gave Grace an approving glance. 'You're one of the lucky ones, and you're right: your daughter's better off without you for the time bein'.'

'What if she's been caught by the polis?' Grace said woefully.

'Then she'd be all over the news,' replied Annie, 'and as they say, no news is good news!'

'Do you really think she's all right?'

'With you for a mother, I don't see how she could go wrong.'

Grace gave her a wobbly smile. 'Thanks, Annie.'

'What are you thankin' me for?' cried Annie. 'I've not done owt.'

'For not judgin' me, and for puttin' my mind at rest,' said Grace, 'and that means a lot, believe you me!'

'Don't mention it; it's what I'm here for. I should imagine you've been tyin' yourself in knots keepin' this to yourself.'

'I was too scared to tell anyone for fear of what they might say.'

'All that aside, how do you really feel about seein' your daughter?'

'On the one hand I cannae wait to see her again, but on the other, I'm terrified she might not turn up.'

'You know, if I were in her position, I think I'd have applied for the services. Would she do summat like that, do you think?'

'Very much so. Why d'you ask?'

'It's the only thing I could think of that would keep her away – the services are renowned for bein' a bit stingy when it comes to givin' people leave around Christmas time.'

'Oh, heck. I hadn't thought of that.'

'I'm sure she'd get a message to you somehow,' Annie assured her. 'But it's summat to bear in mind.'

'A message to say she's safe and well would mean a lot, but seein' her in the flesh would make my Christmas!'

Annie patted Grace's hand in a reassuring manner. 'We'll help you all we can, and in the meantime we'll keep everythin' crossed for Christmas Eve.'

Archie blinked after getting Edie to repeat herself.

'Considerin' it was pitch black and all hell was breakin' loose, I wouldn't take the word of *anyone*, let alone Stella Warbeck!' he said incredulously.

'She told me straight,' said Edie, 'and what's more I believed her. What possible reason could she have to lie?'

'I'm not sayin' she was lyin',' said Archie hastily, 'I'm sayin' she was mistaken.'

'So that's it, is it? Murder's been committed and you're goin' to stand there and do naff all about it!' She tutted beneath her breath. 'You're as bad as the polis.'

Offended by this accusation, Archie puffed out his chest. 'If you think I'm about to start accusin' folk of murder when there's no proof . . .'

She pointed to the collapsed building behind her.

'You want proof? Then start searchin' through that lot. I know what I heard that night, and they was shoutin' blue murder – until they went quiet, that is.'

He rolled his eyes. 'I'm always tellin' the kids that I'll kill them if they don't stop playin' on the bomb sites, but I don't actually mean it! It's a turn of phrase – an empty threat, if you will. Christ, the courts would be packed to the rafters if they took idle death threats like that seriously.'

'Only it's not idle, is it?' said Edie. 'Not when it comes to folks like the Blackwells. We all know what that family's like, especially *him*.'

'Exactly! There isn't a man, woman or child this side of Clydebank that hasn't heard them screamin' blue murder at some time or other. It's the way they are; it don't mean to say they've turned into murderers overnight.'

'People snap, we've all seen it, and there's not a doubt in my mind that Stella saw what she saw,' said Edie defensively.

'Before you go wastin' everyone's time, why don't you go down the docks and ask if anyone's seen him there?'

She folded her arms in a defensive manner. 'Why should I?'

He rolled his eyes in disbelief. When it came to gossiping fishwives, Edie and Stella – as well as a few others who lived in the tenement blocks – were up there with the best of them. 'Because you're the one that's insistin' he's still alive when he evidently isn't!'

'Not me; Stella's the one who said she saw him!'

'Then let Stella search for him,' snapped the warden. 'In case you hadn't noticed, there's a war on, and I've only got so much time on my hands!'

'I thought better of you, Archie Simmons.'

He stared at her in disbelief. 'What more do you want? They've been through the rubble, and while they found several victims it was impossible to tell who was who. Please don't go stirrin' the pot unless you've actual proof. Now if you don't mind, I've a job to get on with, which doesn't involve goin' off on a wild goose chase.'

'On your head be it,' said Edie through thin lips. 'Don't say I didn't warn you!'

She walked stiffly away, leaving Archie to continue grumbling about matters that were out of his control. *Stupid bloomin' woman*, he thought as he turned the corner, *what does she expect me to do? Insist we have a nationwide search for someone who's dead?* His mind turned to Rory, and how the younger man had insisted that Dennis would sooner see his wife and daughter dead than watch them walk away, but even if he was right, and Dennis had done the unthinkable, what proof did they have? He shook his head. Edie was making him doubt himself. Dennis had died in the bombing and that was an end to it. He sighed. But what if Stella *had* seen Dennis? Edie was bound to tell others what Stella had said and if Stella was right, and Dennis really had killed his family before running off, what then? Edie was bound to tell someone that she'd told him about it, so if he failed to act on her words he could be held culpable for not doing something sooner in

163

order to catch the murderer. He reached a conclusion. He would go down the police station and tell them what he'd heard. It would be up to them if they wanted to do anything about it, and Edie and Stella wouldn't be able to accuse him of not doing his bit.

* * *

OCTOBER 1941

Tammy rubbed her hands together as she sat in the cold staff car waiting for her passenger, an officer by the name of Carter whom she was going to drive all of three miles up the road.

So much for drivin' bein' a glamorous occupation, she thought bitterly as she huffed on her hands. *Sittin' in freezin' cold cars for hours on end isn't just mind-numbingly borin', it's lonely to boot!* Her thoughts turned to Gina, who to Tammy's relief had also been posted to Camp Woodbury but was driving the larger vehicles, which meant she was never short of people of her own rank for company.

I'd rather be on the fire engine, Tammy thought now. *It might be a darned sight more dangerous than drivin' stuffy officers from A to B, but at least I'd be with my pals.* She was so engrossed in her thoughts she never saw the approaching officer until he'd already opened the back door.

Plonking himself down on the back seat, he leaned forward with a broad grin. 'Sorry. I didn't mean to wake you!'

Believing that he really thought she'd been asleep

at the wheel, Tammy was quick to put him straight, finishing with an apology for not having seen him coming.

His eyes twinkled mischievously as they connected with hers in the rear-view mirror. 'Relax! I was pulling your leg, although I wouldn't blame you if you had snatched forty winks, considering you've been waiting for me the past four hours. Sorry about that, by the way; these meetings don't half drag on.'

Tammy glanced in her rear-view mirror for a second time as she pulled the car up in front of the guard, who waved them through. *Handsome for an officer*, she thought. *Young, too.* She quickly looked away as his eyes met hers again.

'It's all part of the job,' she replied with a smile.

'That's very good of you to say . . .' He hesitated. 'Sorry, what was your name again?'

'Corporal Lloyd,' said Tammy automatically.

He grimaced. 'Can we drop the formalities? I'm Cecil, and you are?'

Tammy felt her cheeks warm; no officer had ever asked for her Christian name before. 'Tammy.'

'Pleased to meet you, Tammy. So tell me: how's the ATS treating you?'

If any of her peers had asked her that question Tammy would have had no problem in answering, but hearing an officer take an interest in her life was so unusual that she found herself almost at a loss for words.

'It takes a bit of gettin' used to,' she said eventually, 'but I rather enjoy havin' a regular routine, and I love

165

drivin' cos it gets me out and about in the beautiful Devonshire countryside.'

She saw the moonlight glance off his teeth as he shot her a dazzling smile. 'You forgot to mention meeting all the handsome and fascinating officers, such as myself!'

Realising that he was having fun with her, Tammy smiled back. 'So I did!'

His grin broadened. 'I dare say you need a good sense of humour given the stuffy old walruses you're forced to drive around.'

Much to his delight, Tammy stifled a giggle as an image of one particular officer entered her mind. What with his large stomach and bushy moustache he had very much resembled a walrus. 'I wouldn't let them hear you say that!' she replied, trying not to laugh.

Cecil winked at her. 'If the cap fits!'

Tammy felt her cheeks grow ever warmer as she gazed at the road ahead, occasionally flicking her eyes to the rear-view mirror. 'You're very different from the other officers I've met.'

Cecil sounded relieved. 'Thank goodness for that. All this "knowing your position" nonsense really gets my goat.'

'I bet you don't say that to the men under your command.'

'That's different, but it doesn't mean I talk down to them, because I never have and never would. Those fellers are laying their lives on the line to protect our country, and for that they deserve the utmost respect, no matter who's giving the orders.'

She cast him an approving glance. 'I think a lot more officers could do with takin' a leaf out of your book.' Having travelled the short distance, she drew up to the gate and waited for the guard to examine their passes before allowing them through. 'Are you new to Woodbury? Only I cannae say as I remember seein' you round and about the camp.'

He shifted in his seat, causing the scent of his aftershave to waft towards her – it was Old Spice, one of her favourites. 'Nigh on eighteen months, but I'm rarely here. I think the other officers find ways to get rid of me, because they're not keen on my views.'

Tammy pulled the car up in front of the office. 'Talkin' of views, are you goin' to allow me to open the door for you, as is expected of me?'

'No I am not,' said Cecil with verve. 'It should be me that opens the door for you, not vice versa!'

Tammy wagged a reproving finger. 'You'll get me into trouble!'

Cecil grinned playfully. 'I'd never get a lady like yourself into trouble. Not that I wouldn't be tempted, mind you!' He winked as Tammy's eyes rounded. 'Thanks for the ride, Tammy. I'll see you tomorrow.'

'Tomorrow?'

Closing the car door behind him, he called out over his shoulder as he headed towards the office. 'Tomorrow!'

Tammy stared after him. Was it her imagination, or was he flirting with her? *Of course he was flirtin' with you*, she told herself. *Why else would he have made that comment about gettin' you into trouble?* The sound of a car horn brought her attention back to the present, and she waved a hand of acknowledgement to the driver who wanted to get past. Hastily putting the car into gear, she drove over to where the rest of the staff cars were parked and found a space.

I cannae wait to tell Gina about Cecil, she thought, *but I've simply got to get summat to eat first cos I've not had a bite since brekker this mornin'*. Her thoughts turned back to the handsome officer as she headed for the NAAFI. *I wonder what he meant when he said he'd see me tomorrow? If it was anyone else I'd take it as a throwaway comment, but there was summat about the way he said it that makes me think . . .* She paused to thank the soldier who'd held the door open for her, and then, joining the queue, she heard Gina hail her from across the way.

Waving back, Tammy bought herself a cup of tea and a corned beef and tomato sandwich before joining Gina at her table, where her friend eyed her with fervent curiosity as she took the opposite chair. 'Oh aye?' Gina remarked. 'And just what's happened to make you look like the cat that got the cream?'

'I didn't know I did,' said Tammy, surprised.

'Well you do, so somebody's obviously put a smile on your cheeks,' said Gina. 'Question is, who?'

Tammy wagged a warning finger at her friend before taking a sip of her tea. 'Promise me you won't go readin' things into summat that aren't there?'

Gina grinned. 'What's his name?'

'Cecil, but it's not what you think.'

'Who's Cecil when he's at home?'

'He's the officer I picked up this evenin'.'

Gina's eyes were out on stalks. 'You cannae fancy an

officer! Not only is it not allowed; how *old* is he?' She paused briefly before continuing, 'And you certainly shouldn't be callin' him by his first name!'

'He's not old, and I don't fancy him.' Her cheeks ruddied as the last words left her lips, forcing her to be truthful. 'All right, so I do fancy him; not that I intend to do anythin' about it, because he's an officer and I'm not. Not that I think it would bother him, mind you.'

Gina chuckled incredulously. 'What on earth did he say or do to make you so giddy?'

'I am *not* giddy,' objected Tammy, 'but if you must know . . .' and she went on to tell Gina of their conversation.

'I hope he was jokin' when he said the bit about gettin' you into trouble given half the chance!' said Gina stoutly. 'You don't want to get involved with a womaniser.'

Tammy looked at her in surprise. 'Is that what you think he is?'

Gina raised her brow. 'Don't you? Bein' all nice and friendly; askin' you to call him by his first name? Officers just aren't like that, unless they want to get into your bloomers.'

Tammy snorted on a chuckle. 'I don't wear bloomers!'

Gina rolled her eyes. 'You know what I mean!'

The smile disappeared from Tammy's lips as Gina's words sank in. 'Do you really think he was sayin' all that stuff just to get me to drop my drawers?'

'Maybe.' Gina arched an inquisitive eyebrow. 'But you know him better than me; what do you think?'

'I didn't think so at the time, but there again, maybe I was bein' naïve.' As she finished speaking, Tammy envisaged the handsome officer standing in front of her, his eyes gazing into hers as he leaned in for a kiss . . . and his face morphed into Rory's.

Seeing her friend physically recoil, Gina eyed her sharply. 'What?'

Tammy relayed the scene, adding, 'I should be ashamed of myself.'

Gina stared at her uncomprehendingly. 'Why?'

'Because I shouldn't even be thinkin' of another man, yet here I am daydreamin' about a feller I've only just met.'

'Why shouldn't you be thinkin' of another feller? Good God, Tammy, it's been seven months since you and Rory split. You cannae stay single for ever!'

'I know, but despite my determination to keep him from my thoughts, I never truly believed that I'd find myself thinkin' of anyone other than him!'

Gina cast her a sympathetic glance. 'I dare say you never imagined yourself in a lot of the predicaments you've been in of late, but that's life for you. You need to go easy on yourself, Tammy. None of this was your fault, and it's unhealthy to dwell on the past.'

'I just wish things were different.' She looked up at Gina from underneath her lashes. 'Do you suppose Rory's talkin' to other women?'

Gina tried to speak as kindly as she could. 'I really couldn't say, but I'm sure he will in time. Does that bother you?'

'A little bit,' said Tammy, 'but it would be wrong for

me to expect him to stay single because of what should have been.'

'And the same applies to you,' said Gina softly.

'But the thought of movin' on breaks my heart, because it will mean that me and Rory are really over.'

'I hate to break it to you, but you already are.' Gina hesitated before continuing in more sympathetic tones. 'Let me put that another way. Do you genuinely believe there's any chance of you and Rory gettin' back together?'

Tammy heaved a resigned sigh. 'I'd like to think so, but how on earth can we if we can't even communicate?'

Gina wrinkled her forehead. 'I know you say you cannae write to him, but it's been a long time since you saw him last and I'm sure they won't be botherin' to watch his mail any more – that's if they were in the first place, of course. Why not send him a short note lettin' him know how sorry you are and that you wish things could've been different? If you sign it with a false name, say O'Mara, he'll still know full well who it's from but no one else will, not after all this time.'

'Do you really think I should?'

'I don't see why not. And if Cecil asks you out in the meantime, I suggest you say yes.'

'But shouldn't I wait for Rory to reply first?'

'You need to get out,' said Gina bluntly, 'and with someone other than me.'

Tammy didn't feel so sure. 'But wouldn't that be leadin' Cecil up the garden path?'

'Good God, Tammy, it's not like you'd be acceptin' a proposal of marriage!'

Tammy laughed softly. 'I s'pose not.'

Gina smiled kindly at her. 'Havin' a meal out with a member of the opposite sex isn't a crime, Tammy. It's just a nice thing to do, or at least I expect it would be if I ever got the chance!'

'Of course you will!'

Gina eyed her quizzically. 'You said summat earlier that's rather intrigued me.'

'Oh?'

'About your bein' naïve when it came to the opposite sex.'

'So I did. Why?'

'I thought you were quite experienced when it came to men.'

Tammy choked on her mouthful of tea. Coughing frantically, she regained her composure before staring at Gina wide-eyed. 'What on earth made you think that?'

'Rory,' said Gina simply. 'Unlike yours truly, you've had a boyfriend, which means you know a lot more than I do when it comes to datin'.'

Tammy looked perplexed. 'I don't know about that; Rory and I were friends for a long time before we became boyfriend and girlfriend.' She smiled. 'I don't think many fellers would wait as long as he did before havin' a smooch.'

'Why did it take so long? Were you shy?'

Tammy laughed. 'We were kids! He taught me how to play conkers for goodness' sake! From what I remember we went from conkers to marbles to holdin' hands, and on from there. I'm not sure when the turnin' point came exactly; it just sort of happened.'

'So, did Rory never officially ask you out?'

'No. I think we both assumed we were boyfriend and girlfriend after our first kiss.'

'Oh,' said Gina, clearly disappointed that her friend wasn't quite the authority she had believed her to be. 'How did that come about – the kiss, I mean?'

'It was Christmas Day and we'd gone ice-skating on Dalmuir lake. Rory was actin' the goat, tryin' to pirouette, and he was actually doin' quite well until he went down.' She giggled at the memory. 'He looked so funny with his arms and legs spinnin' like windmills; it was a miracle he didn't break anythin'.'

'He was lucky,' agreed Gina, who had experience of falling over on ice herself.

Tammy smiled wistfully. 'He certainly was, because that's when we had our first kiss. I'd been helpin' him get to his feet when we both went over. We started to laugh, and I remember Rory was gazin' at me like I was the only girl in the world.' She sighed wistfully. 'And that's when it happened.'

'It sounds romantic.'

'I suppose it was, but I was only fifteen.'

'Fifteen!' Gina almost choked. 'I'm nigh on twenty and I've never so much as held a feller's hand.'

'Age doesn't come into it. I think it's far more important to wait for the right one to come along, which is what happened to me and Rory.'

'Just suppose that for whatever reason things don't work out with you and Rory, do you think you'd be nervous to start courtin' again?'

'I think even more so; it'd take a long time for me to

be open with anyone else, because of the skeletons in my closet, and I cannae see any man bein' prepared to hang on for that long.'

'He will if he thinks you're worth the wait,' said Gina reasonably.

Tammy yawned behind her hand. 'Even when he must have goodness knows how many other women who'd give their right arm to be with him?'

'I take it you're referrin' to Cecil?'

Tammy nodded.

'Is he really that handsome?'

'Very much so.' Tammy stood up from the table. 'I dunno about you, but I'm ready to hit the hay.'

Gina joined her as they made their way out of the building. 'I'll have to keep my eye out for him, because right now he sounds too good to be true.'

'Too good to be true?' said a voice from behind them. 'Should my ears be burning?'

Tammy shot round to find herself looking into the twinkling eyes of Cecil.

Blushing to the roots of her hair, she fought desperately for something to say, and was glad when Gina chipped in. 'Not unless your name's Frank Sinatra.'

'Old blue eyes himself, eh?'

'The one and only,' said Gina, who was trying to buy Tammy time to think of something to say.

'He'd certainly give me a run for my money on the dance floor.' He turned his attention to Tammy. 'I must admit I was a tad hasty earlier when I said that I'd see you tomorrow. I take it you'll be on duty?'

Tammy glanced briefly at Gina before replying. 'Aye, but . . .'

He clapped his hands together. 'Splendid! Then I shall definitely see you tomorrow.'

'It's not up to me.'

Cecil waved a nonchalant hand. 'Don't worry, I'll sort it out.' He smiled, causing two deep dimples to puncture his cheeks. 'Good night, ladies.' Touching the peak of his cap, he walked away.

'Oh, my good God,' said Gina, her jaw practically hitting the floor. 'I can see why he's got you all of a doo-dah.'

'So it's not just me, then?'

'I should cocoa, the man's drop-dead gorgeous!' said Gina, fanning her face with her hand.

'So, what do you think, is he a dreadful flirt or genuine?' Tammy asked, as they watched the officer walk away.

'I'm not sure,' Gina said as she turned to Tammy. 'But you're right about women givin' their right arm to be with him, cos I reckon he could woo practically every one of us off our feet, including me!'

'Exactly! So why ask *me*?'

'You must've said or done summat to impress him – either that or he's fallen for them beautiful green eyes of yours via the rear-view mirror!'

'Unless I'm just another woman to cross off his list.'

Gina raised an eyebrow. 'You'll find out soon enough when you see him tomorrow.'

'Well, if he thinks he can get into my drawers with a

flash smile then he's another think comin',' said Tammy resolutely.

'Maybe it's not just your eyes that he finds so attractive,' Gina mused, 'maybe it's your feisty nature. Some men like a challenge.'

'How could he possibly know what I'm like after one short car ride?'

'A lot of women would clam up if an officer spoke to them the way he did to you, but you didn't.'

'Only because he put me at my ease. I wouldn't be like that with any other officer,' Tammy pointed out.

'And he might not speak like that to any other driver,' retorted Gina.

Tammy held the door of the hut open for her friend to pass through, and they gathered their wash kits before heading for the ablutions. Popping her toothbrush back into her bag, Tammy examined her freshly brushed teeth in the mirror while she waited for Gina to finish.

'For all I know I might not be the one who gets to drive him tomorrow.'

Gina gave her a very knowing look as she put her things away. 'Oh, you'll be drivin' him all right, he'll make sure of that.'

Tammy said nothing as they walked back to their hut. Wishing Gina a good night, she pulled the sheets back and climbed into bed. *He paid you attention, which made you feel special,* she told herself as she snuggled down to sleep. *Had any other man done the same . . .* she paused. There had been plenty of others who'd shown an interest, but she'd made it plain that she didn't want to know, which reminded her of a conversation she'd had with Gina.

'You may as well have "back off" tattooed across your forehead,' Gina had quipped one evening as she and Tammy took a turn on the dance floor of the NAAFI. 'It took that poor feller ages to pluck up the courage to ask you to dance but he soon changed his mind after you gave him "the look".'

'What look?' asked Tammy, who hadn't the foggiest idea what Gina was referring to.

'You narrow your eyes like this,' said Gina, demonstrating.

Tammy was shocked. 'I don't . . . do I?'

'Why else do you think they always change their mind at the last second?'

Now, as she lay in her bed, it occurred to Tammy that the men she'd scared off might have seen her as too much of a challenge. She turned her thoughts to Rory, who hadn't changed his mind even when her father had thrown everything in their path to try to break the relationship up. *Rory must have seen me as a challenge because of my dad, but instead of running away he rose to it.* She thought back to the times she had crept out of the house to meet him, knowing full well that her father would be furious if he found out. It had been nerve-racking as well as terrifying, but above all it had been thrilling, and she knew from Rory's response that he had felt the same. Defying her father had become her main goal in life and she very much enjoyed getting one over on him, as did Rory. Doing what she wasn't meant to gave her a real sense of freedom, and she knew that organising the fake documents had been rewarding not just for her, but for Rory too. Unsettled, she fell into deep thought. Would Rory have been as interested in her had her father not put so many obstacles in their path? Was he with her purely for the thrill of the chase? The answer to that lay with Rory.

And with that thought uppermost in her mind, Tammy drifted to sleep.

After several changes of heart, Archie finally made his way to the police station a good few days after Edie had told him of Stella's claims. The constable behind the desk instantly brightened as he walked through the door. 'Hello, Archie. What brings you to this neck of the woods?'

Having removed his ARP helmet, Archie ran the brim through his fingers. He hated the thought of wasting police time, but if the rumours were true . . . He gave the constable an apologetic grimace. 'You know that I'm not one for gossip, Calan – I like to leave that to the ladies – but summat's come to my attention and I thought I'd best tell you about it; cover my back type of thing.'

Calan nodded his understanding. 'Fire away.'

Archie went on to tell the constable of the supposed sighting of Dennis Blackwell, along with the comments of young Rory regarding the possible murder of Dennis's wife and daughter. 'I'd never normally listen to anythin' Edie and her cronies have to say, because I know better than to take heed of idle gossip, but on the other hand . . .'

'What if she's tellin' the truth?' agreed Calan. 'We'll certainly keep an eye out for him, but I very much doubt there's anythin' in it, because we haven't had Dennis Blackwell in here since the March blitz, so it very much looks as though he perished along with the rest of them what stayed in Jellicoe House – God rest their souls.'

Relieved that Calan had laid his worries to rest, Archie placed his helmet back on his head. 'Thanks, Calan. I knew it was a pile of tosh.'

As he spoke, another constable appeared from one of the rooms at the back of the building. 'What's this about a pile of tosh?'

Archie waved a nonchalant hand. 'Nothin', Reg, just Edie and Stella blowin' off again.'

'They reckon Dennis Blackwell's alive and kickin',' Calan explained.

'He certainly was the last time I seen him,' said Reg.

Archie crossed his fingers. He felt guilty enough over his actions – or rather the lack of them – since talking to Edie Brodie as it was, without the rumours proving to be true. 'When was this?'

'After the all-clear had sounded on the first night of the March blitz,' replied Reg promptly. 'He come in here, reekin' of booze; claimin' that he'd been the victim of an attempted murder. Someone had obviously given him a damned good hidin', cos his head was all bandaged up, but attempted murder?' He gave a disbelieving snort. 'Ten to one he'd come off worse in an argument he'd started—'

Calan broke in. 'Sounds like Dennis.'

'Exactly! Which is why I told him to go home and come back later when he'd sobered up.'

Archie paled. 'Are you positive this was *after* the all-clear sounded?'

'No doubt about it. He wanted me to take his statement, but I couldn't on account of havin' to man the desk while everyone else was off fightin' fires. He threatened to report me to my superiors before stormin' off in a huff – not that he ever did, of course, more than likely because he'd sobered up.'

'Have you seen him since?'

'Not personally, but I've heard a few people sayin' he's been seen round and abouts the area.' Seeing the warden's face cloud over, he continued hesitantly, 'Is there somethin' we should know?'

Archie pulled a rueful face. 'I hope not, but . . .' He went on to tell them everything he'd learned since that fateful night.

Reg and Calan were both looking doubtful. 'Surely he wouldn't want to report it, should that have been the case?' Reg queried.

'Unless he wanted to cover his back so that people believed him to be the innocent party,' said Calan, who was the more experienced officer of the two.

'My thoughts exactly,' agreed Archie. 'If he comes in here sayin' he wants them to get done for attempted murder, he can feign surprise when he hears they died in the bombing.'

'But he couldn't have known that the Luftwaffe were goin' to hit his place,' said Reg reasonably. 'Nobody could.'

'Very true, but seein' as Dennis came by *after* the raid had finished, he knew he had nothin' to fear,' said Archie.

The constable sighed heavily. 'I think we'd best keep an eye out for him, so we can have a word in his shell-like.'

'What about his wife and daughter?'

'I'll put a missing persons' report out on them, see if we come up with anythin', but I cannae do more than that. They've already taken the bodies out, and by all accounts you couldn't tell one from another, but we'll just have to try, because the courts will want proof. No bodies, no proof.'

Archie sighed. 'That's what I figured. Let me know if you find anythin' out, won't you?'

Calan nodded. 'Will do.'

Having received her instructions earlier that morning, Tammy checked her appearance before heading out to the car with Gina, who was eager to catch a glimpse of the handsome officer during the hours of daylight.

'Blimey, he's already there,' she said. 'You're not late, are you?'

Tammy shot her a sidelong glance. 'I'm never late! He's early,' she added with reproval.

'Eager,' noted Gina, before adding, 'He's even more handsome than I thought.' She winked at Tammy – 'Don't do anythin' I wouldn't' – before peeling off and leaving her friend to greet Cecil while she went about her business.

Cecil smiled at Tammy as she approached the car.

'For a minute there I thought we were going to be chaperoned.'

She returned a fleeting smile as he swung his kitbag down from his shoulder. 'I see you've got everythin'.'

He opened the back door and placed his pack on the seat, then joined Tammy in the front of the car. 'I thought I'd best take everything seeing as I'm not coming back, or at least not for the foreseeable.'

Despite her conversation with Gina the previous evening, Tammy was disappointed to learn that he would no longer be on the same camp as herself. 'I didn't realise you were bein' posted to Faringdon,' she said as the guard waved them through.

He raised his eyebrows. 'Does that mean you'll miss me?'

She shook her head, smiling. 'I hope they realise what they're lettin' themselves in for.'

'That I'm an utter delight, you mean?' He chuckled softly. 'Why else would they have demanded my presence?'

She shot him a sidelong glance. 'If it were any other officer sayin' that to me, I'd think he was bein' serious.'

'And you'd probably be right,' said Cecil. 'In my experience, the more pips they have, the bigger the God complex.'

Tammy gasped out loud, then broke into laughter. 'Yesterday you described them as stuffy old walruses; today they're gods. Talk about movin' up in the world!'

Cecil roared with laughter. 'I was right about that sense of humour of yours, too!' His blue eyes twinkled as he gazed at her. 'It's a shame I'm being posted to Faringdon, but that doesn't mean we can't see each other again.'

The traffic lights ahead of them turned red, and Tammy pulled the car to a halt before turning to face him. 'Of course not! Our paths are bound to cross every now and then.'

He furrowed his brow. 'I think we've got our wires crossed.'

Unsure as to what he was getting at, but not wanting to hazard a guess in case she was wrong, Tammy said: 'Oh?'

'I'm talking about me taking you out on a date. If that's all right with you, of course?'

Tammy's cheeks bloomed as the driver behind her sounded their horn to make her aware that the lights had changed to green. Hastily putting the car into gear, she pulled forward. 'And what would your superiors think if they knew you'd asked me out on a date?'

'Because I'm an officer and you're not?'

She nodded. 'I'm sure they'd prefer you to date someone of equal rank.'

'I couldn't give a monkey's what they'd prefer. It's up to me who I date, not them.' He paused momentarily before continuing, 'When I marry it'll be for love, not the number of pips she has on her epaulettes.'

Tammy felt herself melting under his words. He certainly knew the right things to say to win a woman's heart, not that she was about to tell him that. 'I'm sure you'll have no difficulty in findin' the right woman,' she said.

He winked at her. 'You think I'm a bit of a catch, then?'

'I think you've a silver tongue that will have the women fallin' at your feet.'

'But not you?'

She furrowed a single eyebrow. 'Are you this persistent with every woman you meet, or just the ones out of your reach?'

His brow lifted towards his cap as a half-smile creased one side of his face. Tammy was a tough nut to crack, which made her interesting. 'I'm curious to know what it is you do think of me.'

'It's hard to say, because I don't really know you.'

But he wasn't going to let her off that easily. 'From what you've seen of me, then?'

'As I can only go off my own experience, I have to wonder if you're like this with all the women.'

He clapped his hands together. 'I knew it! You think I'm a womaniser!'

Even though he'd hit the nail on the head, it didn't stop the blush from forming on her cheeks. 'Only because I don't know what you're like with other women,' she said defensively.

'I guess you can only judge a book by its cover until you've delved between the pages, so maybe I cannae blame you for that when I've been so forward, but I can assure you I'm not like this with every woman I meet.'

She glanced at him from under her lashes. 'You're not?'

'Look, I don't want to come across as big-headed,

because you know what I think of people who believe in their own hype, but officers don't generally have to chase women. If anything, it's the other way round.'

'So why me?'

'Because you're not impressed by my pips, and I want someone who wants to date me for who I am, and not my rank.'

Tammy stared at him. He'd more or less voiced what she'd said the previous evening, except she'd used the word 'challenge' instead of pips. She voiced her thoughts.

'Do you see me as some sort of challenge?'

He looked genuinely shocked. 'Just because you don't fall at my feet? God, no! I see you as a woman who knows her own mind and doesn't want a man just for his money.' He turned to face her. 'There's only one way I can prove myself to you, and that's for you to let me take you out for dinner.' Seeing the dubious look on her face, he held his hands up in mock surrender. 'No strings attached, and I promise to have you back before lights out.'

'And if I say yes?'

'Then we shall have a delightful evening getting to know one another.'

Tammy cursed herself inwardly. She'd told Gina she had no intention of dating for a long time yet, but here she was considering that very idea. The trouble was, she really liked him. He was nothing like any man she'd met before – including Rory – and she found herself being helplessly drawn to him. She wondered what Gina would say if she told her of their proposed date.

A smile twitched her lips. Gina would be delighted to hear that Tammy hadn't stuck to her guns, and was making an effort to move on with her life.

'Just a meal?'

He gave her a lopsided grin. 'I don't mind pitchin' in for a couple of drinks.'

She giggled with good humour. 'Where?'

The lopsided grin split the other cheek. 'Where do you fancy?'

'The Maltsters Arms is popular with the girls on camp.'

'Good choice. When are you free?'

'I'm off on Wednesday . . .'

'Then Wednesday it is. Shall we say eighteen hundred hours?'

She felt her heart quicken in her chest. If she answered yes, there'd be no going back. She pulled up outside the gate to the Faringdon base. If she didn't jump in with both feet, she knew she'd end up backing out. 'I'll see you there.'

He wound his window down and showed his pass; Tammy did the same and the guard waved them through.

Pulling up outside the office, she eyed him seriously. 'I hope I'm doin' the right thing.'

He grinned. 'What harm can come from a meal out?'

'That's what worries me,' she said as he collected his kitbag from the back seat of the car.

'Don't you trust yourself around me?' said Cecil with a wink.

Tammy scoffed at the very idea, but deep down she

knew that he was right. She'd fallen for him hook, line and sinker, and she was worried about going out with him no matter how innocent his intentions. *I'm not ready to start courtin', but I don't know whether I'll be able to help myself around him,* she thought now, *because there's summat about him that makes me go weak at the knees. Not that I'll be tellin' him that!*

'Tammy?'

She snapped out of her trance. 'Sorry?'

'I was only joking.'

She smiled. 'I'll see you on Wednesday.' Turning the car round, she gave him a brief salute as she drove back towards the gate, which the guard had already opened.

When she arrived back at Woodbury she wasn't surprised to see that Gina was awaiting her arrival, but there was something wrong with the way she was looking at her. Far from the eager expression Tammy had expected to see, Gina was looking decidedly worried. She wound down the car window. 'What's wrong?'

Wordlessly, Gina handed her an envelope which had been resealed with Sellotape. Tammy turned the envelope over in her hands, and saw the three simple letters which had been written across the back. *R.T.S.*

She looked up at Gina, tears brimming in her eyes. 'Does this mean what I think it means?'

Gina grimaced. 'I don't know, but . . .'

'Well, he's obviously read it because it's been opened,' said Tammy, 'so as far as I can see it can only mean one thing. Rory doesn't want to know and what's more I don't blame him.'

'I'm so sorry,' said Gina. 'I should never have encouraged you to write.'

'It's all right,' said Tammy. 'It's better that I should know.'

Gina pulled an awkward-looking smile. 'At least you can move on now.'

'I suppose some might say the timin' couldn't be better, what with me just agreein' to go out for dinner with Cecil.'

Gina smiled more happily. 'Fate?'

'Maybe,' Tammy said, tapping the envelope against the palm of her hand. 'But regardless of this letter nothing's changed between me and Cecil: no strings attached.' She went on to describe their conversation in its entirety.

Gina nodded thoughtfully. 'I reckon he must be the real deal, because he'd have to be pretty horrid to lie to that extent.'

'I tend to agree with you, but who's to say he'll still like me once he gets to know me better?'

'Me!' cried Gina. 'He'd be mad not to.'

'We'll see,' said Tammy calmly. 'When it comes to the future, I've learned not to count my chickens before they've hatched.'

They were just about to walk into the administration block, when a woman came out of the door. Her arms heavily laden with books, she was attempting to balance a pile of paperwork on top.

'Looks like someone's got their work cut out for them,' said Gina, as they stepped to one side to allow the woman to pass.

'Do you need a hand?' Tammy asked.

The woman stopped abruptly, and lowered the pile of books in her arms. Staring wide-eyed at Tammy, she grinned. 'Well, if it isn't Tamara Blackwell. I knew I recognised that voice!'

Chapter Nine

Tammy was stunned into silence as she came face to face with her old school pal Bonnie McCleod. Terrified that Bonnie might say something even more incriminating, she hastily pulled her to one side, a finger to her lips.

'I can explain . . .' she began, but Bonnie interrupted.

'I should jolly well hope so! You do realise that everyone back home believes you to be dead?'

Tammy blinked. 'Why on earth would they think that?'

Bonnie adjusted the burden in her arms. 'Because of what Edie Brodie and her mate Stella Warbeck have been tellin' everyone.'

Still flummoxed, Tammy raised her arms in a helpless manner. 'Which is?'

'Edie reckons your dad did you and your mammy in, and your bodies are underneath the rubble of Jellicoe House.'

'Rubble?'

Bonnie rolled her eyes. 'After it got bombed, of course!'

Tammy stared at her. 'When was this?'

'First night of the March blitz.'

Also feeling somewhat confused, Gina broke into the conversation. 'If Edie believes Tammy and her mam to be under the rubble of Jellicoe House, why does she think her father's not with them?'

'Because he's been seen round and abouts by a few people,' said Bonnie, as if this was obvious.

Stunned, Tammy began to feel faint. Swaying on her feet, she looked as though she were about to fall until Gina rushed forward and caught her by the arm. 'Steady on there!'

Still feeling light-headed, Tammy turned her attention back to Bonnie. 'Are you positive it's my dad they've seen, and not just someone who looks like him?'

'There's no doubt about it. From what I hear, Stella was the first person to spot him, and she told the polis, but a few have seen him since.'

'And there's no doubt that it was my dad they saw?' reiterated Tammy, who couldn't believe what she was hearing.

'Yes!' said Bonnie. 'I don't see why you're surprised—' She stopped suddenly as something she had overheard came to the forefront of her mind. 'Although there was that rumour . . .'

'What rumour was this?'

'I don't believe it, of course, in fact nobody does, but they're saying your dad told the polis that someone had tried to do him in before leavin' him to die . . .' She left the sentence hanging in the hope that Tammy would finish it for her.

Tammy felt a chill run through her body. She had no

idea how her father had managed to survive such a blow to the head, and at the time she would have sworn on her own life that he was dead, but with several witnesses to testify otherwise it seemed that not only was he alive, but he'd also been spreading rumours that she was the one responsible for his attempted murder. Bonnie might not have said so, but it was obvious that she thought Tammy could have had something to do with it. Tammy knew that the longer she stayed silent the guiltier she looked, and took a moment to compose herself. Telling a part-truth was better than trying to deny everything, and if her father really was still alive, then it would be his word against hers.

'I swear to God I was only tryin' to stop him from killin' Mammy,' she began, and went on to tell Bonnie what had happened on that fateful night. She did not say they had left him for dead, but instead ended with: 'So we legged it before he came to, because we knew that he'd kill her for sure when he did.'

Bonnie tutted in disgust as she placed her load down on the wall. 'I know I shouldn't speak ill of my elders, but your old man takes the biscuit, he really does! Fancy him tryin' to play the part of victim when he was the aggressor all along! Mind you, maybe that's why he never said it was you or your mammy, because he knew no one would believe him. He probably only went down the polis station in the first place in case you'd reported *him* for attempted murder!'

'That sounds exactly like the sort of thing my dad would do,' agreed Tammy.

'My mammy said she'd have left him years ago had she been daft enough to marry him in the first place – no offence to your mammy,' Bonnie added hastily.

'None taken,' said Tammy, 'but it's easier said than done when he was threatenin' to kill her if she even *thought* of leavin' him.'

Not altogether shocked to hear that Dennis would've made such threats, Bonnie spoke in curious tones. 'So, what happened to change her mind?'

Gina nudged Tammy as a couple of women from their hut began to walk in their direction. Following her line of sight, Tammy continued in hushed tones. 'We managed to get hold of a couple of fake IDs so that we could start afresh.'

Bonnie's eyes grew wide. 'Are you sayin' you entered the services under—'

'Yes,' hissed Tammy in a voice that told Bonnie to go no further. The girl tapped the side of her nose in a conspiratorial fashion.

'Sorry. Message received and understood!' She hesitated briefly before whispering, 'So, what do I call you now?'

'I'm Tamsin Lloyd now, so you can still call me Tammy, just not Tamara Blackwell,' said Tammy, who was thoroughly relieved to see that Bonnie understood the need to talk in lowered tones.

'Very clever!' said Bonnie approvingly. 'They always say that you should never judge a book by its cover, and that's certainly the case as far as you and your mammy are concerned. There was me thinkin' the two of you wouldn't say boo to a goose, yet there you both are actin' like a couple of spies! Quite frankly, you're wasted in the ATS; they should have you workin' undercover!'

'No thank you,' said Tammy with verve. 'I nearly passed out when I bumped into you, so imagine what I'd be like under interrogation!'

Bonnie chuckled. 'Perhaps not, then.'

Feeling slightly better, Tammy smiled. 'I hope I don't need to stress how important it is that you don't tell another livin' soul that you've seen or spoken to me – not because of Dad and his stupid rumours, but if he got wind of the IDs, God only knows what he'd tell the ATS, and where would we be then?'

Thrilled that she was being included in the conspiracy, Bonnie said 'Mum's the word' before pretending to zip her mouth closed.

'Thanks, Bonnie. I'm sorry that you've been dragged into this.'

She waved a nonchalant hand. 'Don't worry about it; I think it's rather exciting! Not that you see it that way, I suppose.'

'Not with *him* after us,' said Tammy firmly.

Bonnie looked around her as though searching for someone. 'Talkin' of "us", where is your mammy?'

With Bonnie believing that Tammy and her mother had run off before her father could chase after them, Tammy answered without thinking. 'I don't know.' It was only after the words had left her lips that she realised how suspicious it must sound. After all, if the pair of them had planned to run away all along, why did she now not know the whereabouts of her mother? She hoped that Bonnie hadn't picked up on her faux pas, but it seemed that very little got past her former school pal, who looked at her in surprise.

'How can you not know?'

Tammy thought on her feet. 'Mam thought it would be best if we split up, because it would be harder for Dad to find us that way. We've arranged to meet in a few months' time.' Much to her relief, the smile returned to Bonnie's lips.

'Golly, you really thought this through, didn't you?'

'We'd been plannin' it for months,' admitted Tammy.

'Given the way he is, why do you suppose he's not come after you?'

'I reckon Tammy wallopin' him one made him think twice,' said Gina, who swiftly introduced herself to Bonnie and then continued, 'Bullies only bully those who are weaker than themselves. Tammy has proved she's anythin' but weak, so he's decided to get even in the only other way he can think of: by accusing them of attempted murder.'

Bonnie's face clouded over. 'Rotten pig! I'll never forget the day he tried to pick a fight with our Gavin!'

Tammy rolled her eyes. She had thought her days of having to apologise for her father's behaviour were long gone. 'I'm so sorry, Bonnie.'

'There's no need for you to apologise. It was your father that was bullyin' school kids when he was three sheets to the wind, not you!'

'Typical of Dad to pick on someone half his size. Was Gavin all right?'

195

'He was a bit shaken up, but nothin' major. Turns out your dad was too drunk to take a proper swing, so Gavin ran off while he had the chance.'

'I don't know what's wrong with him, I really don't,' Tammy began before being interrupted by Gina, who didn't like to see her friend so down.

'That's enough talk about your dad. You don't have to worry about any of that, not any more. As long as Bonnie here stays true to her word, there's no reason why you should ever see or hear from him again.'

Bonnie held a hand to her heart. 'I promise I won't say a word,' she said solemnly.

Tammy smiled gratefully. 'Thanks, Bonnie. It means a lot, it really does, but who's to say I won't bump into someone else from Clydebank? I had thought that changin' the way I did my hair would make me less recognisable, but you knew it was me straight off the bat!'

Bonnie grimaced. 'I recognised your voice before I clocked it was you.'

'Oh, great! My voice is summat I cannae change!'

'Everyone knows what your dad's like,' said Bonnie. 'If you do meet anyone, and explain it to them like you did to me, I cannae honestly see them tellin' him. Let's face it, he was hardly what you'd call popular.'

Tammy glanced anxiously around her. 'It's not so much my father that I'm worried about. I'll lose everything if the ATS find out that I joined up under a false identity.'

Bonnie's cheeks coloured, as she thought about the moment she could have triggered just that. 'Well, at least you'll not have to worry about me for much longer, because I shall be leavin' for Norwich in a couple of hours, along with this little lot and one of your officers.' As she spoke she picked the books and paperwork back up.

Tammy brightened. She very much liked Bonnie, but she was also extremely worried that the other girl might accidentally refer to her as Tamara in front of one of her colleagues. 'Perhaps it's just as well, given the circumstances,' she said in an apologetic manner.

'I wouldn't say anythin' intentionally, but accident or not, once the cat's out of the bag there'll be no puttin' it back.'

'And that's what worries me,' said Tammy. 'If I've bumped into you, I could just as easily run into someone else from school and they might shout my name for all to hear!' She put a hand on her tummy, which was fluttering anxiously. 'I don't suppose you know how many of the girls joined up?'

'Quite a few, but nearly all of them are working in ROF Dalmuir, making anti-aircraft guns. Last I heard, Kitty Williams was in London workin' as a secretary for the War Office.'

'So, mine and Kitty's paths should never cross, at least,' said Tammy, crossing her fingers.

'I wouldn't have thought so, but she isn't the problem.'

Tammy's heart sank. 'What is?'

'Not what, but who.'

Fearing the worst, Tammy lowered her gaze. 'Please don't tell me . . . Ella?'

'I wish I could, but I can't.'

197

Tammy's shoulders sank. 'If she sees me, I'm screwed!'

'The most you can hope is that she tries to avoid you,' said Bonnie frankly, 'cos the last thing you need is her pokin' her nose into your business.'

Gina was looking from Bonnie to Tammy. 'I take it there's no love lost between you and this Ella?'

'She hates me,' Tammy said.

'Why?'

'Rory,' said Tammy simply. 'Ella reckoned he should be with her and she didn't care who knew it.'

Gina winced. 'Oh dear. That doesn't bode well.'

'Exactly! She'd crow it from the rooftops if she ever found out the truth behind my leavin' Clydebank. She'd say it was proof that she'd been right all along, and she'd want everyone to know it.'

'Right about what?'

'That I wasn't good enough for Rory,' said Tammy simply.

Gina snorted her contempt. 'Don't be ridiculous! You've done your best by Rory; I know it, as do you, and I don't give two figs what the likes of this Ella have to say on the matter, because they don't know the facts if they think otherwise!'

'I second that,' said Bonnie loyally. 'You've not a bad bone in your body. Never have had, never will have.'

Tammy smiled. 'Thanks, Bonnie. You've been a tonic, you really have. It's been lovely to see you again after all this time. I just wish it was under less stressful circumstances.'

'Hardly your fault,' said Bonnie reasonably. 'But let's

not rake over old ground. How have you found your time in the ATS?'

'Top notch, compared to life with Dad. Apart from the food, of course.'

'I think that probably goes without sayin',' agreed Bonnie. She hesitated. 'While I think about it, whatever happened to Rory? I seem to remember that the two of you were as thick as thieves at one point.'

Rather than tell Bonnie that Rory had returned her letter to him, Tammy shrugged. 'We grew apart.'

'That's a shame. He was a lovely lad.'

'Tammy has herself a date with an officer,' said Gina, who was keen to move the subject away from Tammy's past.

Bonnie's jaw practically hit the floor. 'You haven't!'

Tammy rolled her eyes. 'I don't know that I'd call it a date as such, more of a friendly meal out.'

'You lucky duck,' said Bonnie. 'Is he here?' She was craning her neck in the hopes of spying said officer.

'He was, but he moved to a new base this mornin',' said Tammy, adding, 'Have you a boyfriend?' in a bid to steer the conversation away from herself.

Bonnie shook her head. 'I'm on the road most of the time, so I never really get to meet people. In fact, this is the longest conversation I've had since qualifying as a driver.'

'Oh, Bonnie, that's awful! Do you ever get lonely?'

'Not really. I get to visit lots of different places.' She glanced around her. 'This place is like a palace compared to some. I bet you hardly get any rats.'

Tammy's brow shot towards her hairline. 'Surely you're joking? The army wouldn't allow rats on camp!'

'I wish! I've seen some as big as cats,' said Bonnie.

Gina looked nervously around her. 'I don't like mice, never mind rats!'

'They tend to keep out of the way of humans,' said Bonnie. 'I've only come face to face with them on a couple of occasions, usually on camps that've been deserted for a long time.'

Gina gripped hold of Tammy. 'I'd die if I came face to face with one! What did you do?'

'Got out of its way,' chuckled Bonnie. 'Believe me, it was as eager to get out of there as I was to have it gone!'

'Didn't it come back?'

'Not after we blocked the holes up,' said Bonnie matter-of-factly. 'But believe it or not, they're as afraid of you as you are of them.'

'I hope I never get posted anywhere else,' said Gina. 'I don't think I could cope with rats even if they were *more* scared of me than I am of them.'

Bonnie looked towards the NAAFI. 'I don't suppose you've had your lunch yet?'

Tammy followed her gaze. 'No, but we'd better get our stories straight first, in case anyone asks how we know each other, because it's pretty obvious that we do.'

Gina had a brainwave. 'How about we say that you and Bonnie met each other down one of the shelters durin' the March blitz! That way you wouldn't have to go any further into your relationship.'

'Perfect!' said Bonnie.

The girls headed to the NAAFI where they each bought a sandwich. Sitting at a table at the far side of the big room, they listened to the tales of Bonnie's various outings while discussing the war in general.

'We cannae lose,' said Gina. 'We just cannae.' She looked at Bonnie. 'You must have a better understanding than us as to what's goin' on, what with you travellin' the length and breadth of the country.'

'Nobody tells me anythin',' Bonnie assured them. 'They sit in silence for the entire journey.'

'They usually do that to me too,' said Tammy, 'which is what makes Cecil so different.'

'Unique!' agreed Bonnie. She glanced at the watch on her wrist. 'I'd best get this lot to the car.'

'We'll give you a hand,' said Gina, gathering some of Bonnie's paperwork while Tammy picked up a pile of books. Thanking them for the help, Bonnie led them over to her car.

'And thanks again for keepin' everythin' under your hat,' said Tammy, as she placed the books she'd carried in the boot of the car. 'I should imagine it will be difficult for you not to tell people back home that you've seen me, but . . .'

Bonnie smiled. 'Some things are worth keepin' shtum over, and this is one of them.' She took Tammy in a brief embrace. 'Look after yourself.'

'Same goes for you, and if you hear anything about my dad . . . ?'

Bonnie pulled off a mock salute. 'You shall be the first to know, and that's a promise.'

'I'd like to keep in touch, but I'm guessin' it's not so easy for you to receive letters when you're always on the move?'

Bonnie shrugged. 'I'm based at Clifton. Not that I ever go there much, but when I do there's always a pile of mail waitin' for me.'

'Well, I'll write to let you know how we're gettin' along,' said Tammy. 'It'll be fun to have a pen pal.'

Bonnie's attention was drawn to a very strait-laced-looking officer who was walking towards them. 'Looks like this one's mine.'

'Safe journey,' said Tammy as she and Gina stepped back from the car.

'I look forward to reading my first letter,' Bonnie called over her shoulder as she hurried to open the door for the approaching officer.

'Me too!'

'And Tammy?'

'Yes?'

'I'm pleased the rumours weren't true.'

* * *

NOVEMBER 1941

Rory pulled up the collar of his greatcoat as he jogged across the base to the NAAFI. He'd come up with every excuse under the sun to avoid the dances and parties held at the base, but Jimmy's persistent nagging had taken its toll and finally Rory had given in, saying that he'd give it a go.

'You can't say you don't like them when you've

never even been,' Jimmy had said reasonably. 'If you feel the same way after tonight, then I promise to never mention it again.'

The conversation had taken place while they were discussing their plans for Christmas, and Rory had revealed he had no intention of asking for any leave.

'Wallowin' in self-pity won't do you or those that have to live with you any good,' Jimmy had pointed out.

'I don't see how it affects anyone else,' Rory had said, only to have Jimmy put him straight.

'You spend most of your workin' day walkin' around with a face that'd turn fresh milk sour, and it brings down the morale of everyone around you,' he'd said, glancing round at the empty beds in their hut. 'Some of these lads might not make it to the end, and I'm pretty sure they'd rather get there with a smile on their face than spend their last few months feelin' miserable.'

Rory grimaced. 'Sorry. I didn't realise my mood was dampenin' the spirits of others.'

After glaring at him, Jimmy had looked at one of the beds in particular. 'If you spent less time dwellin' on the past, you'd realise that there's folks here with problems as big as yours, if not bigger.'

Rory had followed his gaze. 'You mean Ernest? I heard him havin' a bit of a cry the other night, but I assumed he was feelin' homesick. There's a lot of that in the services.'

'He lost his entire family durin' the May blitz,' said Jimmy in leaden tones. 'Everythin' and everyone he loved; gone in the bat of an eye, and he's not even eighteen.'

Rory looked at Jimmy, astounded. 'How old is he?'

'Sixteen. He lied to get in even though his mam objected. The last time they spoke he told her that he was old enough to do as he pleased, and that he'd never speak to her again if she continued to try to get him discharged.'

Rory rubbed his hands over his face. 'Bloody hell!'

'Exactly! She wasn't goin' to give up on her son just like that, so *she* continued to try and *he* stayed true to his word. On the one hand, his stubbornness saved his life, but I don't think that really matters when he has to live with the fact that he never spoke a kind word to his mother from the day he signed on.'

'Why didn't the RAF discharge him, if they knew he was too young to be here?'

'They turn a blind eye because they need the man-power. I dread to think how many men we'd be down if they sent everyone who's under age back to their families.'

'Men?' said Rory. 'They're still boys!'

'Exactly! So, now that you know what's what, how about you try and crack a smile once in a while?'

Now, as Rory entered the NAAFI – which was packed to the rafters – his eye was drawn to Jimmy, who was waving to gain his attention and jerking his thumb towards the bar. 'Will Bartons do you, or would you prefer summat else?'

'I'll have whatever you're havin'.'

Having ordered two pints of Bartons, Jimmy continued to talk to Rory as the barmaid poured their drinks. 'So, what do you reckon, then?'

Rory followed his gaze to the dance floor where the revellers were packed in like sardines. 'It's certainly popular.'

'You should take a turn on the floor; you never know, you might actually enjoy yourself.' Jimmy stopped speaking as the barmaid placed their drinks on the counter, and raising his own glass he said 'Cheers' before taking a large swig.

Rory followed suit, only unlike Jimmy he drained his glass of the first alcohol to have passed his lips in one go.

It was the following morning and Jimmy was leaning over Rory's bed, a huge grin on his face. 'Why, if it isn't RAF Halton's answer to Fred Astaire!'

Rory groaned, then winced. He had a pounding headache; his mouth was as dry as the Sahara, and his eyes were refusing to open. 'What happened to me?' he mumbled, much to the mirth of those around him.

Jimmy pretended to be deep in thought. 'Do you mean before or after you started the conga?'

Rory's brow furrowed as he tried to recall the events of the previous evening. He remembered getting to the NAAFI and tasting alcohol for the first time, but for the moment that was where it ended. His frown deepened as he wondered why Jimmy had made the comment about his starting a conga, and suddenly an image of himself placing a woman's hands on his hips as he set off around the dance floor flooded his mind. 'Oh, God!'

Jimmy's grin broadened. 'I don't think he'll be able to help you, not after the way you behaved last night!'

Ernest came up beside Jimmy, a broad smile on his face. 'You should be pleased with yourself; you were the life and soul of the party!'

Rory opened his eyes just enough to peer at the youngster. 'I didn't realise it was a party?'

'It wasn't, until you showed up,' chuckled Jimmy. 'I don't think I've ever seen the NAAFI that lively, not even on New Year's Eve!'

Rory sat up slowly, a hand to his head. 'What else did I do?'

Jimmy sank down on the bed opposite Rory's. 'You introduced the RAF to Pennying, although I rather think some of the toffs had played it before.'

Rory looked momentarily confused before realisation dawned. 'Oh . . . my . . . God.'

Jimmy gave a sigh of satisfaction. 'I'd never heard of it until last night. Funny thing; you may have been the one to introduce it, but you had more pennies dropped into your drink than anybody else!'

Ernest leaned forward. 'What's Pennying when it's at home?'

Rory groaned. 'You drop a penny into someone's drink, and if they don't notice they have to down it in one.'

'To save the King from drowning!' laughed Jimmy.

Rory held a hand to his forehead. 'No wonder I feel ill. I've only ever seen the lads down the docks play that. Was that it?' Seeing the look of delight on Jimmy's face, he groaned. 'Please don't tell me there's more to come.'

'I'm afraid so. You then decided it would be great

fun to have a game of blind man's buff, and you were right cos everyone joined in.'

'Blind man's buff doesn't sound too bad,' ventured Rory hesitantly.

'Depends on who you grab and where you grab them,' grinned Jimmy, much to Rory's angst. He tried to lick his lips, but his mouth was too dry.

'I need a drink.'

'You also need to shake a leg, if you're not to be late for your date with the lovely Helena.'

Rory whipped his head up, causing a sharp stabbing pain to rip through his skull. 'Please tell me you're pullin' my leg?' he begged, holding his head between his hands.

Jimmy raised his eyebrows but said nothing.

Rory racked his brains as he tried to think who this Helena was, and exactly what he'd said to her. He conjured an image of a blonde woman with sparkling blue eyes and a smile which lit up the room. He looked at Jimmy. 'She wasn't a blonde by any chance?'

Jimmy roared with laughter. 'Just how many girls did you invite to the flicks?'

Rory's heart sank. 'I didn't know I'd invited anyone!'

'Helena's a brunette, although I did see you talkin' to a stunnin' blonde at one point, so I suppose you might well have asked her out too.' He glanced at the clock above the door. 'You really should get a move on if you're to make it to the ten o'clock showin'.'

Rory groaned inwardly. He really didn't want to go and meet this woman, but he could hardly stand her up. Swinging his legs out of bed, he grabbed his wash-bag. 'Shan't be a mo.'

A slow smile formed on Jimmy's cheeks. 'Of course, it's up to you, but personally speakin' I like to put clothes on before I venture outside.'

Hoping that Jimmy was joking, Rory glanced down, only to see that his mate was telling the truth. Holding his washbag to hide his modesty, Rory walked back to his bed in a crab-like fashion. 'I never sleep in the buff normally!' he said as he swapped the bag for underpants.

'You obviously had a change of heart last night,' chuckled Jimmy, before adding, 'So, you're goin' to go ahead with the date then?'

'No,' said Rory as he headed for the ablutions, 'I'm only goin' so that I can explain myself and hope she understands.'

'Maybe see how you feel when you get there. You never know, it might do you some good to have some female company – it certainly did last night!'

Aware that he had little time in which to get ready, Rory hastily brushed his teeth before having a shave in cold water. Cursing as the razor nicked his skin, he stared at the blood which began to trickle down his cheek. If this was how you felt after having a night on the tiles, he couldn't understand why some of the dockers made it a weekly, if not nightly, event. With small pieces of toilet paper peppering his face, he headed back to the hut.

'Blimey! You look like someone's been usin' your face as a dartboard!' chuckled Jimmy.

'I feel like it too,' said Rory, dragging his trousers on.

'Are you really not going to the film? It seems a shame to let Helena down at the last minute, especially when you've nowt better to do.'

'You know why,' said Rory dully.

'If you knew the Rory I met last night, you'd know that it would be a crime to keep someone like him locked away,' said Jimmy. 'He brought a smile to everyone's lips and he even managed to make them forget their woes, which is a priceless quality to possess!'

'He obviously showed no respect for his loved ones who are unable to party with him,' said Rory stiffly. 'Not such a nice guy in my book.'

'And how do you think those loved ones would feel if they could see him wastin' his life on what should have been?' said Jimmy softly. 'Do you *really* think they'd approve?'

Rory knew that Jimmy was right, but he wasn't going to admit it. 'Why are you so bothered?' he asked, his jaw flinching.

'Because life's too short, mate,' said Jimmy kindly. 'You of all people should know that.'

'But you're askin' me to act like nothin's happened!' Rory protested.

'No, I'm not. I'm askin' you to live your life while you can. I know you feel as though you're disrespectin' your Tammy's memory if you so much as smile, but you're really not, you know.'

Ernest broke an awkward silence. 'I've been feelin' the same way – like I shouldn't laugh or smile because my folks are no longer here – but last night helped me to realise that bein' miserable doesn't mean I'm mournin' their loss. It means I'm not livin' my life to the full, which in itself is disrespectful, because I'm not valuin' life itself. You helped me see that when I saw how happy you could be, and how much you lifted the spirits of others – includin' me. All I could do was think of what my mam and dad would have said if they'd seen everyone havin' fun last night, and I knew they'd be laughin' and jokin' alongside us. And it's thoughts like that which keep their memory alive.'

'The lad's right. Not makin' the most of your life is a crime,' said Jimmy. 'I've seen people waste years mournin' for those who'd do anythin' to have their own lives back.'

Rory glanced at the clock; it read five minutes to ten. 'I'll see you later,' he said, and dashed out of the hut.

'Do you think any of that sunk in?' Jimmy asked Ernest.

'I hope so, cos I could do with another night like that,' said Ernest. 'Quite frankly, I think we all could!'

As Rory hastened towards the camp cinema, he hoped there would only be one woman waiting outside, and that he would recognise her. *I'll tell her I'm sorry for asking her out while drunk*, he told himself, *but what then? Do I go ahead with the date so as not to let her down, or do I tell her that I'm still gettin' over the loss of my belle? I don't wish to do her a disservice by lettin' her think this could be the start of summat special, but on the other hand* . . . He saw a petite brunette waving to gain his attention.

'Helena?'

She grinned. 'I didn't know whether you'd remember!'

He smiled sheepishly. 'My friends reminded me this morning. I'm sorry if I did or said anythin' out of order last night.'

She waved a nonchalant hand. 'Nonsense! You were the perfect gentleman, and a real hoot to boot! My sides are still achin' from havin' laughed so much.'

'What on earth did I do to make you laugh?'

'You didn't specifically do anythin' per se, but you chortled a lot yourself, and you have a pretty infectious laugh. I guess you're just one of those people who are fun to be around.'

Given the past few months, Rory highly doubted he could be described as fun to be around, but he wasn't about to tell Helena that after everything Jimmy had said about bringing people's mood down. 'As long as I didn't do anythin' to embarrass myself,' he said instead, hoping very much that she wouldn't say anything to the contrary.

'Not at all! You're jolly good at gettin' folk to join in, and last night proved it really is a case of the more the merrier!'

He glanced towards the camp cinema. 'I've no idea what they're showin' for the ten o'clock viewin' . . .'

'*21 Days*,' said Helena promptly. 'Have you seen it?'

He shook his head. 'You?'

'Yes, but I don't mind seein' it again.'

Having fully intended to let his date down gently, now that he stood in front of her Rory found he hadn't the heart to cancel on someone as lovely as she. 'Are you sure? We could do summat else if you'd rather?'

'Such as?'

'We could grab a bite to eat in town.' He smiled apologetically. 'I could do with eatin' summat stodgy, to soak up some of last night's beer.'

She chuckled softly. 'I'm not much of a drinker myself.'

'Me neither!' said Rory. 'Last night was the first time I ever drank alcohol – I think I might have got carried away.'

'So how would you rate your first glass of alcohol, out of ten?'

'Eight for the taste, but nil for the after-effects, so I won't be in a rush to repeat the experience.'

Helena jerked her head in the direction of the main gate. 'If we leave now we can catch the bus into town.'

'And you're sure you don't mind?'

Thinking that Rory might be trying politely to wriggle out of their date, she smiled kindly. 'Unless you'd rather call it off altogether? I'd understand if so, given that you can't remember much about our previous meeting.'

Rory felt his cheeks warm. 'From what I've been told, the Rory you met last night was the life and soul of the party, but that's not me at all. I'm not sayin' I don't like to have fun, cos I do, but I'm not normally the instigator.'

'Everyone's different when they've had a drink,' said

Helena, 'but if you're happy to continue with the date, then I am too.'

Rory drew a deep breath. 'I think it's only fair to let you know that I'm still gettin' over the loss of my long-time girlfriend.'

She nodded wisely. 'That makes sense. I wondered why a handsome, charmin' feller such as yourself was still footloose and fancy free!'

'Last night was the boys' way of bringin' me out of my shell – lettin' me hair down so to speak.'

'Well, it certainly worked!'

He eyed her levelly. 'Look, I'd really like to take you out to lunch, by way of sayin' thank you for bein' so understandin', but I wouldn't want to give you the wrong impression, because I honestly don't think I'm ready to start courtin' again quite yet.'

Helena shrugged his comment off. 'Don't worry about the date thing. I'm happy to go out as friends.' She hesitated before continuing. 'It sounds as though you really loved your last girlfriend?'

'We were childhood sweethearts,' said Rory, 'and we'd still be together if it weren't for the Luftwaffe.'

She stopped walking abruptly. 'Oh, Rory, I am sorry. I thought by "loss" you meant you'd split up, not . . .' she made a forward motion with her hand, 'you know.'

'I think that's why I drank so much last night. I hate to say it, but it felt good to forget, even if just for a little while.'

'Do you regret your decision to go to the dance?'

Rory flagged down the approaching bus. 'I did when I woke up, but not so much after talkin' to you.'

She brightened. 'Really? How come?'

'I thought I'd made a fool of myself, but that's not the impression I'm gettin' from talkin' to you – unless you're just bein' kind, of course.'

'You were a complete gentleman,' said Helena. 'You should stop bein' so hard on yourself.'

A faint smile twitched his lips. 'So I've been hearin'.'

'But are you goin' to take any notice?'

Rory strode towards the first available double seat and stood back so that Helena could sit by the window. 'I'll certainly try, because I don't want to sully her memory by bein' miserable all the time, cos that's not the feller she fell in love with, and I know that she'd be disappointed to see me not livin' my life to the full.'

'Sounds as though you've had an epiphany.'

'Believe it or not, it was a lad six years my junior who made me see the light of day.'

'Good for him!' said Helena. 'You said that you and your belle were childhood sweethearts. Did you meet while you were both in school?'

'I was eleven.'

'Just like me and my old flame, although we were just in our teens when we met,' said Helena. 'I thought it was true love until he left me for my best friend.'

Rory's eyes widened. 'He did what?'

'As it turned out, Adam was only with me cos he fancied her, but she wasn't interested – or not until we left school and he got a job workin' at a solicitor's. It seems he was a much more attractive package with a wad of money in his back pocket.'

214

'Didn't he care that she only wanted him for his money?'

'Not really. After all, he only wanted her because she was a busty blonde – even if it did come out of a bottle.'

'Oh.'

'Exactly. When I think about it, they're far better suited than Adam and I were, because they're both materialistic, and I'm not at all like that. I want to fall in love with someone for who they are, not the things they have, and I want him to fall in love with me for the same reason.'

He seemed surprised. 'I thought that's what everyone wanted.'

'With hindsight, I always knew she was after a rich hubby,' she mused, 'so it shouldn't have come as such a surprise when they got together.'

'Did they start a relationship behind your back?'

'They say not, but I think they did. After all, you notice these things, don't you? The furtive glances when they think no one else is looking . . . and they were always unavailable on the same days, which I think was the biggest clue.'

'Sounds like you're better off without them both! Have you been on any dates since you and Adam broke up?'

Helena laughed. 'This is the first one – or it was!'

'I'm so sorry. If I'd known . . .'

'No apology necessary. I'd rather you were honest than string me along.'

The bus trundled to a halt, and Rory stood up so Helena could get off before him. He might not have had any intention of going on a date, but meeting her had done him the world of good. *I couldn't think of a better person to go on a non-date with,* he thought as they descended on to the pavement, *and even though we're startin' out as friends, who knows where our friendship might take us given the fullness of time?*

Chapter Ten

It was an hour before her dinner date with Cecil and Tammy was eyeing her reflection in the mirror in a critical manner.

'You look perfect!' Gina assured her. 'I really don't see why you're so worried.'

'Because I've never been on a formal date before,' said Tammy, removing a hair clip, only to put it back in virtually the same spot. 'I've got no idea what's expected of me, or whether I've put too much makeup on . . . first impressions are everythin'.'

'True, but it's a bit late for first impressions when you've met each other three times already,' Gina pointed out. 'Besides, accordin' to you this isn't a date, but a meal for two people who are gettin' to know each other better.'

Tammy shrugged. 'So call it a pre-date date, but I'm still clueless as to what's expected of me.'

'Nothing's expected of you,' Gina told her. 'Just be yourself and have a good time.'

'That's all very well for you to say, but we both know I cannae possibly expect him to take me out without expectin' at least a kiss goodbye at some stage or other.'

'Ah, but by then you'll know whether you like him as a friend or whether it's summat more than that,' said Gina. She looked at the clock on the wall of the hut. 'It's time you were off.'

Tammy followed her gaze. 'For all I know he might not even turn up.'

Gina gave a short, sarcastic laugh. 'Oh, he'll turn up all right, you needn't worry about that.'

Tammy gave an inward groan. 'Do you ever feel as though you've bitten off more than you can chew?'

'Look at it this way. Worst case scenario: you have a nice dinner with a handsome officer, only to find that he's not the one for you, and you go your separate ways.'

Tammy opened the hut door and she and Gina stepped out into the cold autumn evening. 'I suppose when you put it like that, I really don't have anythin' to lose!'

'Meeting an officer for dinner.' Gina smiled as she walked Tammy to the bus stop just outside the camp gate. 'That's the sort of thing us mere mortals can only dream of!'

Tammy took no notice. 'How old do you think Cecil is? I don't think he can be more than what, twenty-five?'

'I'd say that's near the mark,' said Gina, 'which, as we've already pointed out, is awfully young for an officer – unless you're born with a silver spoon, of course.' She hesitated, her eyes rounding like saucers. 'Do you think he's rich, on top of everythin' else?'

'I doubt it, cos he certainly doesn't act that way, and he's very much against all of that stuffy "I'm above you because I'm an officer" nonsense, which in my opinion is typical behaviour of those born into wealth.'

Gina smiled wistfully. 'He really is dreamy, isn't he?'

'Let's just hope there isn't a hidden side to him,' said Tammy. She waited for the approaching bus to come to a complete halt before turning to Gina. 'Wish me luck!'

'Good luck!' said Gina, adding as Tammy boarded the bus, 'Not that I think you'll need it, mind you!'

Tammy sat down in the first vacant seat and scooted across to the window to wave to Gina, who was mouthing the words 'Have fun' as the bus pulled away.

Until Bonnie's appearance the previous day, Tammy had worried she would never be able to court again, what with the weight of her father's murder hanging over her head, but hearing that Dennis was very much alive had changed her perspective entirely. She and Gina had touched on the subject the previous evening when they'd gone for a stroll around the perimeter fence.

'I might be off the hook as far as murder goes, but it's obvious that Rory still thinks I'm a real heel!'

'So what do you intend to do? Cos the way I see it, you're stuck between a rock and a hard place. If you were to go back to Clydebank to put Rory straight, Dennis would have you arrested for attempted murder, and even if they didn't believe him, they'd have to ask a few questions to check out your story, and once they do a background check and find you joined the ATS under a fake ID . . .' She pulled a grim smile. 'They'll believe your plans to have been premeditated, which could make it look as though you intended to do him in all along.'

Tammy buried her face in her hands before slowly drawing them down to her chin. 'You're right,' she said miserably. 'No matter what happens, I cannae escape the past; in fact it just keeps gettin' worse, and I didn't think that was possible!'

'Least said, soonest mended,' said Gina. 'You cannae undo the past, so you're better off leavin' sleepin' dogs lie.'

'Somethin' you've been tellin' me since the beginnin',' said Tammy. 'When did you get so wise?'

'When I made the biggest mistake of my life,' said Gina with a mirthless chuckle. 'I'm just lucky that I didn't have the same baggage as you, else I'd also have a lot more to worry about.'

Now, as the bus pulled up at the station, Tammy waited for it to come to a halt before disembarking and making her way in to the Maltsters, where Cecil stood up to greet her. 'I did wonder whether you'd change your mind,' he said, pulling out a chair for her.

'I won't say that it didn't cross my mind,' she admitted, 'but I'm glad I didn't.'

'That makes two of us.' He handed her a menu. 'I'll get us a couple of drinks while you take a look at this.'

'That would be lovely. I'll have a lemonade, please.'

He pulled off a mock salute. 'Right you are. Shan't be a mo.'

Tammy glanced around the pub interior before turning her attention to the menu. She'd never been taken out for a meal before, and with Cecil pulling her chair out as well as fetching the drinks she was feeling rather special.

'Here's your lemonade.' Cecil placed the drink down in front of her. 'The barmaid said she'll come and take our orders when we're ready.'

Tammy smiled. 'The fish and chips looks nice, but then again so does the sausage and mash.'

'I've had both in the past,' said Cecil, 'but I'm a sucker for fish and chips.'

'Me too,' admitted Tammy, 'but as you've had both, which would you recommend?'

'The fish and chips, and if you're up for a pudding you can't go wrong with their rhubarb crumble and custard.'

Tammy stared at him. 'That is my favourite pudding of all time!'

He indicated to the barmaid that they were ready to order, then gazed at Tammy with twinkling blue eyes. 'Seems like we've got a lot in common so far.'

'Garden peas or mushy?' the barmaid asked as she took their order.

'Mushy,' they both replied, much to their amusement. Making a note of their choice, the barmaid left them to it.

Tammy eyed Cecil thoughtfully across the table. 'Favourite film?'

'*The Maltese Falcon*. I love a good mystery. You?'

'*Gone with the Wind*.'

He pulled a reproving face. 'I'm all for romance, but I'm not keen on romantic films.'

She pulled a downward smile while making a note to herself that he was telling the truth despite knowing her preference, which could only be a good thing.

Cecil took a sip of his beer, then wiped the froth from his top lip. 'What was your life like before you joined the ATS?'

She stared at the bubbles rising up the side of her glass of lemonade. 'What would you like to know?'

'You obviously hail from Scotland, and judging by your accent I'd say you were Glaswegian. Is that right?'

'Clydebank,' said Tammy, in the hope that this would satisfy his curiosity.

'Close enough. Have you any siblings?'

'No. You?'

'Alas! I've two brothers – both older than me – and a younger sister.'

She smiled. 'I've often wondered what it would be like to have siblings.'

'Take it from me, you're better off on your tod!' he said with a wink.

'So, you've not got three best friends all livin' under the same roof as yourself?' Tammy asked, in disappointment.

He coughed on a chuckle. 'Only an only child would think that way. Having older brothers means your parents are always drawing comparisons.' He wagged a reproving finger while doing what she took to be an impersonation of his father. '"Clive was always top of the class. You should take a leaf out of his book." Or

"James had won the tennis championship twice when he was your age." Then there's always the games that your darling sibs like to play, such as the classic Stop Hitting Yourself.'

She laughed. 'I don't think I've ever heard of that one.'

'That's because you don't have siblings – but trust me, it's only fun for older brothers!'

'Where are they now?' She barely paused before guessing the answer. 'Are they officers too?'

'Yes but in different services. Clive's in the Navy and James the RAF.'

'That's a pretty talented family you've got there. Are your brothers like you, or do they think themselves a cut above the rest?'

'Same as me. Our parents would have our guts for garters if we ever got above our station. The ones that believe they're superior tend to think that anyone under the age of fifty is still wet behind the ears.' He paused to thank the barmaid, who had put their plates in front of them. 'You should have heard the response when a few I knew learned about the thousands of women joining up.'

She sliced her knife into the crispy batter. 'I should imagine they thought the war was as good as lost already.'

'That's exactly what they thought.' He shook his head in disbelief. 'I couldn't believe what I was hearing, so I gave them a piece of my mind, not that they appreciated it.'

She looked up from her meal. 'What did you say?'

'That theirs was a typical response from those at the

top who hadn't had to work their way up the ranks first. I also told them that we'd be up a certain creek without a paddle if it weren't for the WAAF, the Wrens and the ATS – not to mention the auxiliary nurses!'

'What was their response?'

'That women were only good for two things and one of them was cooking.'

Annoyed, Tammy stabbed her fork into a chip. 'I wish I could say I'm surprised, but I'm not. You only have to see the look on some of their faces when they realise it's a woman driving them to their destination to know what they're thinkin'. I had one of them head back to his office after proclaiming that he wasn't ready to leave, despite the fact he'd turned up to the car with his briefcase in hand. He returned a good half an hour later with the same briefcase, but instead of gettin' into my car, he got into the car behind me. Needless to say, it was being driven by a man.'

'Absolutely ludicrous. And what's worse, they're in charge!'

She sprinkled salt over her chips, gazing at him across the table. 'Do you think that's why you're drawn to a woman of lower rank than your own – so that you can put two fingers up to those who would disapprove?'

'No, although it's a definite plus,' he said with a wink.

She laughed out loud. 'It's good to know I have my uses!'

He grinned mischievously. 'Fishing for compliments, eh? All right then, I asked you out because you're a fascinatin' woman, who utterly beguiles me.'

Her cheeks colouring hotly, Tammy tried to smile. 'I'm glad to hear I pass muster.'

He raised his eyebrows. 'You passed muster from the moment I saw those beautiful emerald-green eyes of yours in the rear-view mirror.'

She felt her cheeks grow even warmer, but rather than let her embarrassment get the better of her she tried to make light of his answer. 'And is that all it takes?'

He eyed her levelly. 'No. There's more to you than the depth of your gaze.'

The depth of your gaze, thought Tammy. *Wait until Gina hears that one!* 'You cannae possibly know what I'm like just from seein' my reflection in the rear-view mirror.'

He leaned forward ever so slightly as he continued to gaze at her. 'They say that the eyes are the windows to the soul. Maybe I can see straight into yours.'

Tammy felt as though her heart was singing, but one thing was niggling her. *He says all the right things, but how can someone so wonderful – not to mention handsome – still be single?*

He wiped the corners of his mouth with his napkin. 'Why do I get the feeling that I'm being interrogated without you having to say a word?'

She lifted her gaze from her half-empty plate to look up at him shyly. 'I suppose I'm just wary because I've never done anythin' like this before. Certainly not with someone like you.'

He eyed her incredulously. 'Are you telling me that you've never been on a date before?'

'Not really. I've only ever had one boyfriend, and we were just kids when we met, so stuff like this was way beyond our purse-strings, even after we'd left school.'

He rubbed his chin thoughtfully. 'There's no way he'd have been the one to break things off, which means that you did. Yes?'

She grimaced guiltily. 'Yes. But I'd rather not go into the whys and wherefores, if it's all the same to you.'

He leaned back in his seat. 'Is there no going back?'

She locked eyes with him. 'Never.'

'Then that's all I need to know.' He scooped the last of his mushy peas onto his fork. 'So, tell me about your life in Clydebank. I know you don't have siblings, but I'm guessing you had parents?'

'There's not much to tell,' said Tammy, hoping to be able to keep as close to the truth as possible without going into too much detail. 'I'll be seein' my mammy at Christmas, but I don't care if I never see my father again – in fact I'd prefer it that way.'

He pulled a rueful smile. 'Sounds like he won't be getting any prizes for best father in the world any time soon?'

'Definitely not! My mother, on the other hand, deserves every prize that's goin', cos I don't know where I'd be without her.'

'Is she still with him? I only ask because you said you'd be seeing your mother at Christmas, but . . .' He left the sentence unfinished.

'No. She left Clydebank the same day as me.'

'Where are you meeting?'

'Liverpool.'

He paused, a forkful of fish poised before his lips.

'What made her choose Liverpool? Not that there's anything wrong with it; I'm just curious.'

Aware that she'd accidentally given him the impression that her mother had moved to Liverpool, Tammy decided to go with the flow. 'It's where her grandparents hailed from, plus it's full of opportunities.'

'Wise choice.'

'That's enough about me. Let's talk about you.'

'What do you want to know?'

'How come you're still single?'

He gave her a cheesy grin. 'I know what you mean! It's unbelievable that a man with my good looks and charismatic nature is still on the shelf, yet here I am!'

'If any other officer had said that to me I'd have thought he really felt that way. How come you seem comfortable at poking fun at yourself?'

'I suppose having two elder brothers constantly referring to me as an annoying little twerp helped to keep me grounded.'

Tammy giggled. 'What a pair of meanies. I'm sure you were nothin' of the sort!'

'Twerp's a form of endearment coming from them,' said Cecil with a chuckle. 'You have to be able to take a good ribbing in our family.'

'You still haven't answered my first question.'

'I've never really thought about it, but I suppose the odd dates I've been on have never amounted to anything, and since I started my career in the army I've tended to distance myself from the fairer sex.'

She used her last chip to pick up the remaining juice

from the mushy peas before posing her next question. 'Why?'

'First off I never met the right woman, and secondly the women I did meet scared the heck out of me.'

Tammy finished her last chip before saying, with an air of surprise, 'You? Scared of women? Why do I doubt that?'

He placed a hand across his chest as though she'd wounded him. 'I might look big and tough across a table, but face me with a bunch of marriage-hungry females and just watch me run!'

Tammy gasped before collapsing into yet more laughter. Holding her napkin up to her lips, she looked at him affectionately. She might not know him very well, but she couldn't help but find the handsome officer endearing.

He gave her an accusing stare through eyes that laughed. 'You know exactly what I'm talking about. Tell me I'm wrong!'

Still chuckling, she tried to straighten her face. 'I do know the sort of women you mean, but you make them sound like a pack of hungry wolves!'

He pointed at his lapel. 'You wear a uniform like this, and you'll know what I'm talking about. I swear by all that's holy they couldn't tell you what colour my eyes are – all they see is an officer's uniform, and the money that goes with it!'

Tammy tried to dismiss from her mind the countless overheard conversations when women in her hut had fantasised about what their life would be like if they landed an officer. The fancy jewellery and the swanky occasions they would attend; to the huge house they believed went with the rank. 'I'm sure they see you as more than some kind of trophy.'

'I think they can smell my fear,' he said, sending Tammy off into fits of renewed giggles. 'They can! Either that or they can see the sweat pricking my forehead from ten feet away.'

Holding on to her side, which was beginning to ache with laughter, Tammy waved a hand for him to stop. 'Now I know you're exaggerating, because the man that got into the back of my car the other night was not scared of talkin' to me, far from it. You had a great deal to say for yourself.'

'Ah, but that's because you're different!' he said, tapping the side of his nose in a gesture of wisdom. 'When I looked into your eyes I didn't see a fox after its prey, I saw a woman who hadn't the slightest interest in me.' He clicked his fingers. 'If that isn't attractive, I don't know what is!'

'So, you *do* see me as a challenge, then?' said Tammy, as she placed her napkin down.

'No. I see you as a woman who knows her own mind and is confident that she doesn't need a man on her arm in order to make it in life, and that's the sort of woman I'm after. Not someone who only cares about what I can provide.'

Tammy mulled his words over. She'd never really thought about it before, but now that he'd brought it up she realised that he was quite correct. 'My father was a violent bully who liked to keep women in their place. If living with him taught me one thing, it was that if I want to make it in life, then I need to be able to stand on my own two feet.'

'And that's the difference between you and the other women I've come across,' said Cecil approvingly. 'Most of them are after a man to provide for them, but not you.'

She gave him a wry smile. 'They say that most men are after a woman to replace their mother. Is that true of you?'

He feigned shock. 'No woman could replace my mother!' Seeing Tammy laugh, he chuckled himself before continuing. 'All joking aside, my mother is a wonderful, loving, caring woman who can't cook for toffee. So I'm not after a replacement mother, if only because I don't fancy having indigestion for the rest of my life.' He twinkled at her. 'I bet you're a good cook.'

She rolled her eyes. 'Not accordin' to my dad I'm not, but then again, he doesn't think much of anythin' anyone does unless he's the one who's done it. And I don't believe your mother cannae cook for one minute.'

He pointed to his stomach. 'Everyone moans about military grub bar me and my brothers; there's a reason for that!'

'She cannae do worse than the army's version of corned-beef hash!'

He kissed the tips of his fingers as though having savoured a particularly delightful morsel of food. 'It's one of our favourites.'

Shaking her head, she looked at him steadily. 'I don't know whether you're pullin' my leg or bein' serious.'

He placed his hand over his heart in a solemn manner. 'I swear to almighty God that my mother can't cook anything that's still edible once she's had her wicked way with it!'

Tammy giggled as the barmaid removed their empty plates. 'Don't you take anythin' seriously?'

'I try not to!' He glanced at the barmaid before looking back to Tammy. 'Pudding?'

'I hope that's not a term of endearment,' said Tammy, much to his delight. A smile crossed his face.

'I wouldn't dare!'

Tammy smiled at the barmaid. 'I'll have the rhubarb crumble and custard, please.'

'Make that two, please.' He waited for the barmaid to go before asking, 'So how do you think our first getting to know you dinner has gone?'

'You tell me. So far I've learned that you have a great sense of humour, and you don't like to take life too seriously, am I right?'

He gave her a quiet round of applause. 'Ten out of ten.'

'But you cannae possibly be like that all the time, because nobody is. I want to meet the annoyin' little twerp before makin' a decision.'

'He's in here somewhere,' said Cecil softly. 'He might come out to play if you're good.'

She shook her head again, smiling. 'At this rate, I'd expect you to propose with a bunch of trick flowers and a ring that squirts ink!'

He grinned. 'It would certainly be cheaper!' Seeing that she was still smiling, he straightened his face. 'I can be serious, I just don't want to be, not with everything that's going on in the world right now.'

The scent of rhubarb and custard filled their nostrils as the barmaid placed their puddings on the table. 'I do love a good crumble,' said Tammy, 'especially when it's drowning in thick custard.'

'Me too. You can't beat a bit of comfort food.'

They ate their puddings in relative silence; only when Tammy had finished did she ask, 'So where do we go from here?'

'Well, I don't fancy dancin' on a full stomach, so how about a walk around the park?'

'And what if somebody sees us?'

'What if they do?'

'They might tell your fellow officers.'

Cecil grimaced. 'I don't care if they do. I doubt if they need another excuse to look down their noses at me.'

'Only because you're younger and smarter.' She smiled. 'And, dare I say it, better lookin'?'

He laughed softly. 'I knew I'd get you to admit it sooner or later!'

'They see you as a threat – the young blood that's snappin' at their heels ready to take over.'

'I don't think they see me that way at all; they're too arrogant for that.' He signalled to the barmaid that he'd like to pay the bill before pressing on. 'I'll tell you something for nothing: it'll be a cold day in hell before I behave in that manner.'

'That's because you know what it's like to be on the receivin' end,' said Tammy. Getting to her feet, she dug her purse out of her handbag ready to pay her half of the bill, but before she could say so Cecil had already paid.

'This is my treat, because I was the one who asked you out for dinner. Besides, I'd never let a lady pay for her own meal,' he said as he held out her coat for her to put on.

Tammy pushed her arms into the sleeves. 'Thanks, Cecil, but I don't want you to feel that you always have to be the one who pays.' Realising that she'd implied they might go out more than once, she felt the blush race up her neckline. 'That's if we did go out again, of course,' she added hastily.

'I rather hope we will,' he said, taking his umbrella from the stand and holding the door open for her. 'Unless you still think of me as a womaniser who's out to see how many women he can bed before the war's won?'

'Perhaps not *all* of them,' she joked as she stepped out onto the pavement, taking care to avoid the puddles.

Cecil pushed open his umbrella and held it over the two of them. 'Rain, rain, go away . . .'

She smiled. 'If only that worked.'

He looked to the overcast sky. 'It doesn't look as though it's going to let up any time soon, certainly. Would you rather call it a day?'

'A little rain never hurt anyone,' said Tammy. She made to unfurl her own umbrella, but putting his hand over hers, Cecil encouraged her to take his arm instead.

'No point in us both having wet brollies.' He winked

at her before continuing, 'I hope you don't think I organised the bad weather just to get closer to you.'

Tammy laughed. 'What was that you were sayin' the other day about a God complex?'

Cecil roared with laughter. 'I really need to learn to think before opening my mouth at times. No wonder you thought I had a high opinion of myself!'

'And what a good job it was that you invited me out to dinner, so that you could prove me wrong!'

A half-smile tweaked his lips. 'So, you don't think too badly of me then?'

'Let's just say that you're beginning to change my thinkin'.'

'It's a start.' He looked down at her. 'Have you thought about what you'll do after the war's over?'

'Aye. I'd like to start a business with my mammy.'

'Ambitious,' he said with approval. 'What sort of business?'

'Tailors,' said Tammy promptly. 'Makin' new and mendin' old clothes, that sort of thing. You?'

'I'll stay in the army – assuming I make it out the other end, of course.'

Tammy's heart plummeted into her shoes as the words left his mouth. How could he talk about his own possible death in such a matter-of-fact way? Keen to change the subject, she asked him whether he thought he'd like a family.

'Very much so,' said Cecil, who was watching the raindrops fall from the brim of the umbrella. 'Definitely a boy and a girl, or two of each. You?'

'One of each would be nice.' Thunder rumbled in the

distance. 'Sounds like it's gettin' closer. Do you think we should call it a day? Only I don't much fancy bein' caught out in a thunderstorm.'

'Rain might be romantic, but not thunder,' Cecil agreed.

She looked up at him curiously as they headed for the bus stop. 'You think rain's romantic?'

'Of course! With rain comes new life. What can be more romantic than that?'

The smile returned to her face. She wanted to ask him whether he used these lines on all the girls, but decided to keep quiet and give him a chance. *No matter what situation you put him in, he always says the right things*, she thought now. *Is that because he's speakin' from the heart, or because he's learned the right things to say?* She looked up at the underside of his clean-shaven chin. The only way to know the answer to that question was to give him a chance and go on from there, and she could only do that by agreeing to meet him again should he ask. She tutted to herself. If there was one thing she could be sure of, it was that Cecil would ask to see her again. The question was, when would they stop going out as friends and start doing so as something more?

They reached the bus stop and he hailed the approaching bus. 'So, when shall we two meet again?'

'Shakespeare,' said Tammy, 'or near as damn it. I'd have to check my diary, but off the top of my head I know I'm free on Saturday, if that suits you?'

'I'll be busy most of the day, but I could take you for dinner and dancing come the evening.'

'Shall we say eighteen hundred hours outside the Maltsters?'

He glanced up as a sheet of lightning illumined the sky. 'Perfect!'

Tammy bade him goodbye as she boarded the bus. Waving to him from the warmth of her seat, she wondered how Gina would react to the news that they would be seeing each other again in just a few days' time. *She'll be cock-a-hoop, but not surprised*, thought Tammy as another sheet of lightning lit the night sky, *because even though she had her reservations to begin with, she too was beginning to think the same way as I do now. After meeting him tonight there's not a doubt in my mind that he's true blue. If anythin' I'm the one who's holding back, because I'm not Tamsin Lloyd, but Tamara Blackwell, and even though I didn't kill Dad I left him for dead and that in itself is just as bad. If Cecil were to learn the truth he might feel very differently about me. Which leaves me with a dilemma: do I sit tight and hope he never discovers the truth, or do I hope he sees things from my point of view? The longer I leave it the harder it will be, so I'd better make my mind up soon.* She paused. *On the other hand, how can he make an informed decision until he gets to know me better?* She heaved a sigh. There was only one person with whom she could talk this through, and that was Gina!

Archie was on his way back from the market when he decided to pop into the police station to see if there was any news of Dennis Blackwell.

'It seems our friend Dennis has disappeared into thin air,' Reg informed him. 'He's not been seen by anyone, anywhere, for a long time now. It could be that he's found somewhere new to live, or he might have had an argument with the wrong person and found himself at the bottom of the cut. Personally, I'd be more inclined to go with the latter because I know what an argumentative bugger he can be.'

'But what about his wife and daughter?'

Reg grimaced. 'I had a word with the firefighters, and none of them are prepared to say whether the bodies they found were male or female, never mind who they might have been.'

Archie leaned against the counter. 'Which is much as I thought, but regardless of any of that we cannae just let him get away with murder, because I'm positive that's what he's done.'

'And well you might be, but neither can we accuse someone of murder when we can't produce a body,' said Reg. 'Or not one that's recognisable, at any rate.'

Desperate to see Dennis held to account, Archie racked his brains for a solution. With the police unwilling to take the matter further he would have to hope that putting the man under a bit of pressure might cause him to slip up, but in order for that to happen Archie would have to find him first. 'Just a thought, but has anyone gone to look for him down the docks? If he's got a new place to live, he might well be back in work.'

Reg raised an eyebrow. 'Nobody's stoppin' you from lookin', but we haven't the resources to send anyone off on a wild goose chase, and like it or not that's exactly what this is.'

Archie pushed himself away from the counter. 'Fair enough. I'll take a wander; see if anyone's heard anythin'.'

Reg eyed him sternly; Dennis had no respect for the police, never mind a warden. 'Just you be careful. Dennis wasn't a placid soul before he lost everythin' and I cannae see that his current situation would've improved him much, so mind what you say. He won't take kindly to accusations.'

'I won't be confrontin' him,' said Archie, crossing his fingers at the fib, 'I just want to see what's what.'

Reg wished him luck, and Archie headed for the docks. Surveying the melee, he caught the attention of one of the dockers who was having a quiet smoke. 'I'm lookin' for Dennis Blackwell. Do you know him?'

The man's face dropped instantly. 'Unfortunately, yes; I'm down two bob because of that rotten git. What do you want with him?'

'Just interested to see if anyone knows where I can find him.'

The man stubbed his cigarette butt out with the toe of his boot. 'If you don't mind my askin', why the interest? I cannae imagine you'd have much to do with the likes of him.'

Archie waved a dismissive hand. 'I like to keep tabs on who's livin' where in case of an air raid.'

The man gave him a disbelieving stare. 'Look, you don't have to tell me if you don't want to; I was just bein' curious. Loads of people have beef with Dennis – I just wondered what yours was.'

Archie wasn't prepared to set forth his suspicions for

fear that word might reach Dennis, and with fore-warned being forearmed he had no intention of giving the other man the heads-up. 'Will you let me know if you see him?'

The docker shrugged. 'I will, but I doubt we'll be seein' him round these parts again.'

'Oh?'

'Rumour has it he was last seen boardin' a train – well, I say boardin', but it looked more like stowin' away, apparently.'

'Any idea where he was going?'

'Somebody said summat about Llangollen. But who really cares, as long as he doesn't come back. Good riddance to bad rubbish, that's what I say. He's somebody else's problem now.'

'But what about your money?'

'He cannae give me what he's not got, and it's a small price to pay if it means I never have to see his ugly mug again.'

Archie thanked the man for his help before heading away from the docks. *Why the hell would Dennis be goin' to Llangollen, of all places? It's not as if he has family there, or not that I know of.* He hesitated as another thought sprang to mind. Wasn't Grace from somewhere in Wales? Feeling a sense of unease, Archie found his feet automatically walking in the direction of the train station. If he could confirm that Dennis had indeed gone to Llangollen it would mean that, far from murdering them, he believed that Grace and Tammy were still alive, in which case Archie would have to find a way to warn them he was on their trail, if it wasn't already too late for that. He would ask the guards if any of them remembered seeing a man fitting Dennis's description boarding one of their trains. As he neared the station he came across a familiar face.

'Hello, Henry. How's tricks?'

The tramp known as How d'you do Henry gave Archie a gappy smile. 'How d'you do, Archie? What brings you to the station? You off anywhere nice?' He noticed the warden's distinct lack of luggage and amended his question. 'Or are you here to meet someone off a train?'

Archie shrugged. 'Neither. I guess I'm here out of desperation.'

'Oh?'

Archie rubbed a hand across the back of his neck. 'I'm lookin' for a feller by the name of Dennis Blackwell. I don't suppose you've seen him?'

Henry pulled a disgruntled face. 'No, and what's more I'd rather keep it that way.'

Archie was intrigued. He'd half expected the tramp to say he didn't know Dennis, but this was clearly not the case. 'What's he done to you?'

'Apart from the odd kick as he passes me by?' said Henry sarcastically. 'Nothin'.'

Archie shook his head angrily. Henry wouldn't harm a soul, so why would Dennis kick him when the man was clearly down on his luck? He said as much to Henry, who simply shrugged.

'It's the way some folk are. They think we're beneath them and they can treat us how they like because we haven't got a home to sleep in.'

240

'Believe you me, you're a long way above Dennis, and I reckon he knows it, too. That's probably why he strikes out.'

'He doesn't need an excuse,' said Henry. He paused, a frown wrinkling his forehead. 'Sorry, but why are you lookin' for Dennis here?'

'Because he was seen boardin' a train not long after the blitz.'

Henry appeared doubtful. 'Are you *sure*?'

Something about the way in which Henry had asked the question made Archie hesitate. 'Positive. Someone seems to think he was bound for Llangollen, which is where Grace came from, and if that's true . . .' He shook his head without finishing the sentence.

'And you don't know who saw him?' asked Henry slowly.

'Not a clue.'

'And you are positive it was Dennis they saw?'

'I must admit I was dubious when I first heard he was still alive, but it was someone in the polis who told me, and if you cannae believe the polis who can you believe?'

Henry scratched the top of his head, chuckling softly to himself. 'So they didn't murder him, then.'

Archie tutted angrily. 'No, if by "they" you mean his wife and daughter, despite the fact he's tellin' everyone they tried to. It was a pack of lies.'

Henry looked around before eyeing Archie acutely. The warden had always been kind to him; never one to turn his back, or pass by without handing him a few coins. Henry regarded Archie as a prince amongst men, someone to be trusted. 'Maybe not quite the pack of lies you think.'

Archie stared at him open-mouthed. 'Go on.'

Henry told him how on the night of the blitz he'd been asleep not far from the train station when he was woken by two women talking in hushed tones.

Archie listened in incredulous silence while Henry spoke his piece. 'So they legged it thinkin' they'd done him in by accident!' Archie breathed at last.

'It would appear so.'

'But they'd no need to run, because not only is Dennis not dead, he's not in Clydebank any more.'

'Shame they don't know, really,' mused Henry.

'Isn't it just!' said Archie. 'Thanks, Henry.' He paused. 'Have you told anyone else what you heard that night?'

'Nah. People don't tend to make small talk with tramps.' He smiled, then exclaimed as Archie pushed a crisp ten bob note into his palm. 'What's that for?'

'For bein' you, Henry.' Archie paused. 'Is there any-thin' else I should know?'

Henry thanked him before pocketing the money. 'They did say summat about meetin' up at the Liver Building on Christmas Eve, wherever that is. I think they said midday?'

'Brilliant! You won't tell this to anyone else, will you?'

'My lips are sealed,' said Henry loyally.

Archie smiled, but he was worried that Henry, after one too many drinks, might still tell people of their conversation. *So I must set the record straight before he has a chance,* thought Archie, bidding Henry goodbye and heading back to the police station.

Gina was eagerly awaiting Tammy's arrival, and she wasn't disappointed when Tammy entered the hut, a grin splitting her cheeks.

'Well, I can see from the look on your face that every-thin' went tickety-boo,' she said, patting the empty space beside her. 'So tell me, what did you do?'

Tammy unbuttoned her coat and hung it up. 'We had a lovely meal, and talked a lot.' She smiled wistfully. 'And I mean a lot!'

'That's good! Certainly better than sittin' opposite someone who's got nothin' to say for themselves.'

'There was no fear of that – not only did he have a lot to say, he always said the right thing,' and Tammy went on to tell her friend some of the things he'd said which had made her heart sing.

When she had finished, Gina pretended to swoon. 'Goodness me, he certainly knows how to woo a girl! But is he a genuine guy who speaks from the heart, or . . . ?' She left the question hanging.

Tammy didn't hesitate. 'I truly believe he's a nice guy, who wears his heart on his sleeve; the only thing I'm unsure of is the way he tends to make light of every situation.' She remembered how straight-faced he'd become when talking of those above him. 'Or nearly every situation.'

'And is that such a bad thing?'

Tammy sat down next to her friend. 'Not per se, but you cannae go through life as if it's one long joke, and that's rather the impression he gave me.'

'But you did say you'd caught a glimpse of a serious side?'

'Aye, when he was talkin' about the other officers and their view of him. He got quite serious then.' Tammy began to unlace her shoes. 'But that was the only time.'

'That's how some folk deal with the war,' supposed Gina, who was failing to see the problem. 'Better to laugh than cry type of thing.'

'He did say summat along those lines, which is all well and good,' conceded Tammy, 'but I need to know that if somethin' does go wrong for me he won't try to make light of it, or brush it under the carpet, but do everythin' he can to help.'

'And do you not think he would?' asked Gina dubiously. 'Because I cannae see how he'd reach the rank of officer if he were the type to let people down.'

Tammy mulled Gina's words over. Considering that Cecil had worked his way up the ranks and not just gone in as an officer, her friend had a point, and a valid one at that. She nodded. 'When you put it that way, I suppose you must be right.'

Gina furrowed her brow. 'You almost sound disappointed. Are you sure you're not tryin' to put a spanner in the works so that you can wriggle out of seein' him again? You were full of the joys of spring when you walked through the door just now, but that changed when you started to talk about how wonderful he is and I cannae see why.'

Tammy pulled her shoes off and stared at them as though deep in thought. 'When I started to tell you how wonderful he was, I think it made me face up to reality.'

'Which is?'

Tammy absentmindedly picked an errant piece of fluff from her skirt. 'Cecil isn't the problem; I am.'

'What? Why?'

Tammy lowered her voice so that only Gina could hear what she was about to say. 'Because sooner or later I'm goin' to have to tell him who I really am, and what then?'

'If he loves you he'll understand,' said Gina in an equally quiet voice. 'Besides, you don't have to tell him that you left your dad for—'

Tammy cut her off before she could finish the sentence. 'If I'm goin' to be honest then I have to tell him *everythin'*, warts an' all.'

Gina raised a speculative eyebrow. 'And do you think I'm ever goin' to tell anybody about my encounter with the Billy Boys?' She shook her head vehemently. 'Not on your bleedin' nellie!'

'So you're never goin' to go back for the money, even though it could change your life?'

'It's not my money,' said Gina, before immediately spoiling the effect by adding, 'I don't know.'

'Because if you do, you'll have to explain to whoever it is you're with where it came from,' said Tammy resolutely.

Gina's brow creased. It was something she'd not given any real thought to, until now. In her head, she quickly ran through several different scenarios as to how she could have come into such a large sum, but all of them sounded too far-fetched for words. 'All right, so maybe it's not as easy as all that,' she conceded.

245

'Not if you love and care for someone,' said Tammy. Holdin' on to secrets can be the death of a relationship; you only have to look at me and Rory to know that. If I'd been able to tell him the truth from the word go we'd still be together now. One mistake,' she said ruefully. 'That's all it took.'

'A mistake that was out of your control,' Gina pointed out, before adding, 'None of us are in charge of our own lives now we're at war. There's not a woman in this hut who hasn't either lost someone they love or met someone who has, and although that might unite us in one respect we all deal with grief differently, and while some of us will come out the other side stronger, many of us won't. But one thing's for certain: we'll all be different from how we were before war broke out.'

'The world will never be the same again,' said Tammy, 'and all because of one man!'

'The power to inflict misery on billions, including your own countrymen,' agreed Gina. 'Kind of puts your own problems in perspective, doesn't it?'

'It does,' said Tammy, 'and I'm goin' to have to do a lot of soul-searchin' before I make a decision about any man, because I don't intend to go through life leavin' a trail of broken hearts in my wake.'

Gina responded quizzically. 'Does that mean you think Cecil's fallen for you? I'd tend to agree, cos I reckon it was love at first sight – on his side, at any rate.'

Tammy drew a deep breath and let it out slowly. 'I don't know about love at first sight, but he's certainly very keen, so if that's anythin' to go by I'd say yes. But only time will tell.'

'Did you find out much about his family?' Gina enquired in a casual manner, although deep down she was keen to know more about Cecil's parents and whether they were rich or not.

'He has two older brothers – both officers – and a younger sister.'

'So he *did* enter the army with a silver spoon—' Gina began, only to be cut short by Tammy, who told her Cecil's opinion of officers who came into the army that way.

'So he's not rich, then?' Gina sounded disappointed. 'Never mind.'

'I'm rather hopin' he's not,' said Tammy, chuckling. 'We're already poles apart regardin' rank, and if he's well-to-do on top of everythin' else I don't see how we could possibly work out.'

'Just because he's rich and you're not?'

'Exactly. I know they say that opposites attract, but sometimes people can be too different.'

'And sometimes they can be a perfect match no matter their differences,' said Gina. 'So please don't write your relationship off before it's properly begun.'

'I won't,' Tammy assured her. 'I'm goin' to stick to the original plan of takin' things slowly and seein' where we end up.'

'Good! Because believe it or not, Tammy, you deserve to be happy!'

Chapter Eleven

Having been on her feet for most of the day, Grace removed her shoes and rubbed her aching arches before heading to the sink to fill the kettle. Hearing the door open behind her, she turned to see Annie walking into the kitchen.

'Are you makin' a cuppa, or is that for your feet?' asked Annie as she joined her by the sink. 'Only I'm gaggin' for a cuppa, so I'd be grateful if you'd put a bit extra in if you were only thinking of a footbath.'

'Both,' replied Grace, adding, 'It doesn't sound as though you've had a good day.'

Annie rubbed her hands over her face before resting her chin on the tips of her fingers in a prayer-like fashion. 'How right you are! In short, my day's been ruddy awful! Little Millie Hepworth's father turned up, threatenin' to drag Millie out by her hair and take her for a back-street abortion.'

Grace tutted. 'Poor kid. She must've been scared out of her wits!'

'Quite frankly, I'm surprised she didn't go into labour there and then,' admitted Annie.

Grace's eyes rounded. 'He didn't actually get in, did he?'

Annie looked horrified. 'No, he did not! I told him to do one as soon as I saw him through the spyhole, but that didn't stop him gobbin' off at the top of his lungs.' She continued in a rueful manner. 'Millie was in tears listenin' to the vile accusations that come out of his mouth, poor mare.'

Grace shook her head. 'I dread to think.'

Annie spoke through thin lips. 'Accordin' to him she's a whore, a liar and everythin' in between.'

Grace put the kettle on to boil. 'How can anyone say that about their own daughter?'

'It's cos he thinks her actions have brought shame on the family,' said Annie bluntly, 'but the only person who's done that is him!'

Grace put her hands on her hips. 'Millie's only ever had one partner and that's the father of her child, God rest his soul.' She quickly drew the sign of the cross over her breast.

'And you'd think her dad'd show some compassion considerin' the father of his forthcomin' grandchild died while servin' his country!' snapped Annie. 'Which just goes to show that he's more bothered about himself than anyone else.'

'Neil's parents are thrilled that Millie's carryin' his child,' agreed Grace. 'Why can't he be the same?'

'Because he reckons no one will want her now that she's goin' to be a single mother.'

'The sooner she gives birth the better,' said Grace vehemently. 'At least then she'll be able to take the babby to live in Portsmouth with Neil's parents.'

'Just a shame she couldn't have gone there before the birth,' agreed Annie.

Grace lifted a bowl from under the sink. 'That's a thought. Why isn't she there already?'

'She wants to see if her father will change his mind once he's seen his grandchild,' said Annie, 'but I think there's more chance of him flyin' to the moon than that happenin'.'

Grace heaved a sigh. 'He's a fool to himself; the same as my husband.'

'Doesn't appreciate what he's got,' conceded Annie, before going off on a slight tangent. 'I bet you're countin' down the weeks till you see your daughter again.'

'Not long now,' said Grace. 'I've a mixture of emotions, cos whilst I cannae wait to hug her and hear what she's been up to, I don't know for certain that she'll even turn up. Quite frankly, I go from excited one minute to feelin' sick with dread the next.'

'Well, all I can say is that if she's anythin' like her mam, she'll have done you proud,' said Annie loyally.

'As she always does,' said Grace. 'I just hope she's had as much luck as me when it came to startin' her new life.'

Annie took the steaming kettle off the stove and poured some of the water into the bowl before placing the rest back on to boil. 'Have you any idea what your plans are after meeting up?'

'If she's able, I'm hopin' she can come back here and join me in the laundry.'

Annie scooped tea leaves into the pot and poured on the boiling water. 'Do you not think she'll have a job to get back to? I mean, she can't have survived this long without money, and I'm assumin' she'll have found a place to live as well, which makes the services the most likely option.'

'As long as she's happy that's all that matters, although I'd really love her to come and live with us if at all possible,' said Grace, pouring a little cold water into the footbath she had put on the floor beside one of the kitchen chairs.

'I'm really lookin' forward to meetin' her.' Annie poured the tea into two cups and handed one to Grace.

'She's a good kid,' said Grace as the warm water began to soothe her aching feet. 'I just wish I'd left Dennis years ago. Things would've been very different if I had.'

Annie cooled her tea down by gently blowing on the surface. 'For a start you can't possibly know how things would've been, and had you been able to, leaving him is exactly what you'd have done. But you couldn't, and you know that.'

'I do, but she's my daughter, and it should've been me protectin' her, not the other way round.'

'And had he had her by the throat instead of you it would've been,' insisted Annie. 'You need to stop bein' so hard on yourself!'

Grace smiled. 'Isn't that what bein' a mother is all about? Worryin' yourself sick that somethin'll happen to your child, and beatin' yourself up when it does.'

Annie thought about this for a while before eventually

nodding. 'Sounds like it to me, but perhaps we'd best not tell Millie that!'

Grace chuckled softly. 'They're worth it, though. Every grey hair, every wrinkle, every sleepless night.'

Rory jerked his head in acknowledgement to Jimmy, who had just entered the Nissen hut, then turned his attention back to the mirror and continued to straighten his tie.

'Off out again?' remarked Jimmy, shrugging his jacket off.

'I've nowt else to do,' said Rory. 'Besides, I wouldn't want to disappoint the ladies.'

Jimmy chuckled softly as he hung his jacket onto a wooden hanger. 'I've never seen anyone do a one-eighty like you. You've gone from a moanin' Minnie to the biggest tomcat in town!'

Rory caught Jimmy's gaze in the mirror. 'As long as I'm not hurtin' anyone.'

Jimmy held his hands up in a placating fashion. 'I'm not judgin'; just an observation, that's all.'

Rory held his gaze. 'I'm not in the market for a girlfriend, and I make sure they know that before I take them out. That way we all know where we stand.'

Jimmy removed his shoes before lying down on his bed. Picking up his copy of *And Then There Were None*, he began to leaf through it until he reached the place where he'd left off the previous evening. 'If I were in your position I'd have stuck with that Helena.'

'But you're not,' said Rory, somewhat stiffly.

Jimmy stuck his finger in the book to mark the page.

'I thought you made the perfect couple, and she was ever so keen on you.'

'Which is why I ended things – not that there was anythin' to end, mind you.' Rory gave up adjusting his tie and turned to face Jimmy. 'And as I've already told you, I'm still not ready for a relationship.'

'The way you're goin' you'll run out of women before the war's over, and what will you do then?'

Rory shrugged his indifference. 'Does it really matter, if they're not right for me?'

Jimmy stared at him in disbelief. 'How can you possibly know whether they're right for you or not when you don't give them a chance?'

'I knew Tammy was the one for me straight off the bat.'

'You'd known each other since you were kids, and by all accounts you were friends for a long time before you got together,' Jimmy pointed out.

'What's that got to do with the price of fish?'

'It means you're not givin' any other women a chance, and I reckon it's because you're frightened of what might happen if you do.'

Rory screwed his cap on his head. 'You're right, Jimmy, I am. I've already nursed one broken heart, thank you very much, and the way the war's goin' it could easily happen again, should I be fool enough to start another relationship.'

Jimmy put his book down and swung his legs over the side of his bed so that he could address Rory properly. 'You're lookin' at this the wrong way round.'

'I am?'

'Yes. You're seein' things from a negative point of view when you should be makin' hay while the sun shines!'

'I am!' Rory protested. 'I love goin' out and havin' fun with no expectations on either side at the end of the evenin'.'

'But you can't do that for ever!'

Rory eyed Jimmy thoughtfully. As far as he could see his actions had nothing to do with his friends, so why was Jimmy getting so hot under the collar? He decided to say so. 'Why are you so bothered, anyway? I cannae see as it makes any odds to you.'

Many different retorts went through Jimmy's mind, none of them pleasant. He was taking his own emotions out on Rory, and being churlish, which wasn't fair. 'Because I'm jealous,' he said truthfully.

Rory blinked; of all the things he'd expected Jimmy to say, being jealous wasn't one of them. 'But I thought you loved your Beryl?' he said.

'I do! And I'd love to be able to take her out the way you take them girls, but that's impossible with us bein' hundreds of miles apart.'

'Then you must see why I don't want to settle down!'

'Of course, and please ignore me. I'm just findin' it hard because I can't forget about my wife and dance with another woman the way some of the fellers do. I suppose seein' you havin' fun every night is a painful reminder of how far I am away from the woman I love. So anyway,' he went on in upbeat tones, 'who are you takin' out tonight, and where are you takin' her?'

'Carmel, and we're goin' for a bite to eat at the Boot and Shoe in Flintham.'

Jimmy smiled wistfully. 'Proper grub!'

Rory gave his reflection one last glance in the mirror before heading towards the door. 'Don't wait up!'

He heard Jimmy bid him goodbye as the door swung closed behind him. He didn't like to see his friend down in the dumps, especially after Jimmy had been the one to coax him out of his shell in the first place. He turned his thoughts back to Helena and their brief relationship. He had told Jimmy that he had ended things because Helena was too keen on him, but in truth he had also found himself falling for her, so had decided to cut the relationship dead in the water before things went any further.

'Oh,' had been her dispirited response. 'I thought we were gettin' along quite well.'

'We were, but I guess I'm not ready for another relationship just yet,' Rory had said, albeit regretfully.

'Well, I appreciate you tellin' me sooner rather than later,' Helena had conceded, 'but I can't pretend I'm not disappointed. It would be different if we had nothin' in common.'

Rory had wanted to protest against his own words, to say that she was right and they did have a lot in common, but that would only have confused her even further and he cared for her too much to do that.

He turned his thoughts to Carmel. *She's definitely not lookin' for anythin' permanent*, Rory reminded himself, *so there's no chance of either of us gettin' hurt*.

'Just a bit of dinner and a film, or dancin', whichever you'd prefer, and it'll be my treat,' he'd told Carmel as she counted out his change. 'No strings attached, no expectations, just two people havin' a bit of fun. What do you say?'

Carmel's answer had been 'yes', as had many others from women he'd asked out in a similar manner. There was no kiss at the end of the evening, no promise to meet up again, just a casual goodbye and thanks for a lovely time. Some of them had watched him walk away as though they hoped he would turn back and say something else, but he was careful to make sure he kept on walking because he didn't want to give anyone false expectations.

Carmel will be no different from the others, Rory told himself now, *and I shall make sure it stays that way, because they're a crackin' bunch of girls who deserve a lot better than me.*

Tammy was on her way to meet Cecil for a bite to eat in the Copper Kettle café. They'd met twice since their first dinner together, and even though he hadn't yet asked her out on an official date she knew it was only a matter of time before he did. She glanced out of the window as the bus approached the stop before hers while she pondered the question uppermost in her thoughts: what would she say if he asked her for a date outright? If she turned him down there would be no reason for them to continue meeting, and she would miss his company dreadfully, but was that enough of a reason for her to agree to go on a serious date? *I'm goin' to have to cross that bridge when I come to it, because I cannae see myself reachin' a decision before it happens. He's a lovely chap, with a good heart, and as for bein' handsome . . .* she broke off mid-thought as she remembered Cecil smiling at a coat clerk who had stared back at him entranced . . . *I don't think there's a woman on the planet who wouldn't think that.* So what was the reason for her indecision? It couldn't be Rory, because that was well and truly over. So what was it, then? Guilt? Or the worry that Cecil might expect more from her than she was ready to give?

She lowered her gaze to her lap. She already knew the answer, but didn't like to admit it. No matter what he might say, he came from a family of high achievers who would undoubtedly despair if they knew their son had begun courting a woman who'd not risen past the rank of corporal. She envisaged the officers whom Cecil so despised. He might call them a bunch of stuffed shirts, but if they ever found out about his relationship with her she hadn't a doubt in her mind that they'd not mince their words when it came to voicing their displeasure, and what then? Would he dump her for someone else? Or would he ignore them and live with the consequences? And if so, could they force the two of them apart?

She rolled her eyes. Of course they could. All they had to do was send him to the opposite side of the world and that would be the end of that, but was it something that Cecil had thought of, and should she mention it to him, just in case he hadn't? Or should she just go on as before and see how things panned out? There was only one answer: she should tell him what

257

she thought and advise him to have a really hard think about what it would mean for his future if he was seen dating someone of her rank.

Seeing her stop draw near she got out of her seat and pressed the bell, her tummy giving a nervous flutter as she spotted Cecil waving to gain her attention as he crossed the road to greet her.

Observing the serious look on her face as she stepped down from the platform, he eyed her studiously. 'You look as if you've lost a pound and found a penny. Has something happened?'

'I've been givin' our friendship some thought,' she began, and saw Cecil's face fall like a stone.

'Oh dear. Why do I not like the sound of this?'

She gave him a grim smile. 'Haven't you stopped to think about what people would say if we started seein' each other in a romantic sense?'

'Not this old chestnut again!'

She curved her hand through his outstretched arm. 'I know you say that it doesn't bother you what other people think, but what about the ramifications?'

A smile twitched his lips. 'Do you think they'll send me to my room without any supper?' He had expected her to laugh, and was surprised to see her features cloud over.

'No, I'd expect them to send you to the other side of the country, if not the world,' she replied gravely, and felt him falter mid-pace. 'Has it not even crossed your mind?'

He pulled a downward grimace. 'It hasn't. I mean, I know they wouldn't approve, because they don't seem to approve of anything, but it didn't occur to me they'd take things that far.'

'And what about now?'

He fell into silent contemplation before reaching a conclusion. 'I'd like to think they wouldn't be so petty, not with the way the war's going, but in reality?' He shook his head sadly. 'They're so bothered about appearances that nothing they do would surprise me.'

'And not just the army either,' said Tammy meekly. 'There're your parents to consider too.' He started to interrupt, but Tammy pressed on. 'I'm sure they're wonderful, loving, kind-hearted people, but we're polar opposites when it comes to our backgrounds. My father's a docker, but I'm guessin' yours is . . . what? An officer?'

Cecil laughed. 'You couldn't be further from the truth, although I can see why you'd think that. But it's my mother who comes from a well-to-do background. My father's a builder, and has been all his working life.'

Tammy looked at him in surprise. 'Your mother's the posh one?'

'Does that surprise you?'

'Normally, if you hear of someone marryin' money, it tends to be the other way round.'

'Like who?'

She tried to swallow her smile. 'Cinderella.'

Cecil roared with laughter. 'Have you any examples that aren't fictional?'

She released his arm as they entered the café. 'Actually, no. But as far as society's concerned it's always the women who need rescuin'. Why is that, do you suppose?'

Cecil gave her a very knowing look while removing his coat. 'Cinderella and Snow White were written by men. So was Tarzan.'

'No wonder women have such a hard time provin' themselves when men are writin' nonsense like that, and women are readin' it,' said Tammy huffily.

'The trouble is that most women do want a man to rescue them.' He held his hands up in self-defence. 'Just so you know, I would never describe you as most women.'

Tammy wanted to object, to say the women in her hut were fiercely independent, but she could hardly do that after hearing the way they talked about marrying men of means. She handed her coat to Cecil to be hung up along with his own, and said reluctantly, 'It pains me to admit it, but I think the majority of women want it both ways.'

'How do you mean?'

'They want to be independent and paid the same as men while still havin' a man sweep them off their feet. Does that make sense?'

'Ah! The good old knight in shining armour,' said Cecil, pulling out a chair for her at their table.

'Exactly! And the services don't exactly help matters,' Tammy continued. 'I've spoken to some of the girls who work on the ack-acks; did you know they don't train them to fire the guns because they're *women*?' She blew her cheeks out in disbelief. 'Where's the sense in that?'

Feeling that he had to apologise on behalf of men, Cecil opened his mouth to speak, but Tammy pressed on before he had the chance.

'The women line the whole thing up, work out the trajectory, the aim, the whole nine yards, and the only thing the men have to do is point and shoot!'

Cecil was desperately trying to swallow his smile for fear that Tammy would think he was laughing at her. 'You're quite right, and I swear I'm not laughing at you, I'm smiling because in just one sentence you've shown how bigoted and senseless their opinions are.'

'And why are we only allowed to fly planes from base to base?' Tammy went on. 'What's wrong with goin' overseas like the men?'

His face straightened in an instant. 'There are some things you really shouldn't wish for.'

Seeing the shadow that had darkened his features, she continued slowly, 'Maybe you're right, and perhaps I should be grateful, but what would be the difference between a male and female bomber pilot? Nobody wants to see the sights they see, or do the things they do, but they do it because they don't want to be under Nazi rule, and sex shouldn't come into it. Because in some ways that makes us as bad as them.' She shook her head ruefully. 'Segregation is a terrible thing.'

Cecil agreed wholeheartedly. 'It starts wars.'

A slight frown creased her brow while she tried to remember what had got them onto the subject in the first place. 'I seem to have gone off at a tangent.'

He smiled. 'You've passion – which is one of your many qualities that I find attractive.'

Blushing, she glanced across to the waitress who was hovering in the background. 'We haven't even looked at the menu. Do you know what you want?'

He cast a quick eye over the chalk menu board which hung behind the counter. 'Faggots and chips. You?'

'I'll have the same, please.'

He beckoned the waitress over and gave their order before turning back to Tammy. 'Do you miss your traditional Scottish dishes, being down in this neck of the woods?'

'I have porridge every mornin'.'

'I was referrin' to that delicacy known as haggis.'

The colour faded from her cheeks. 'There aren't many things I won't eat, but haggis is one of them. In fact the very thought . . .' She tried to banish the image from her mind.

He grinned. 'Why ever not?'

'Why'd you think?' She paused before adding, 'You do know what haggis is, don't you?'

He began to reel the ingredients off on his fingers, beginning with sheep's lungs, but Tammy was holding up a hand for him to go no further.

'You'll stop right there if you want me to eat my dinner!'

He chuckled softly. 'I've never had it myself, but I believe my parents tried it while in Edinburgh on their honeymoon.'

'And?'

'Mum thought much the same as yourself, but Dad thought it was great.'

She smiled. 'It seems your mother and I have at least one thing in common.'

An impish grin creased his cheeks. 'Well, that and the fact that you both find me adorable, of course!'

She rolled her eyes in a good-natured fashion. 'I can see why you made the rank of officer.'

He held a hand to his heart as though he'd been wounded by her words. 'Low blow!'

She eyed him curiously. 'How did your mother and father meet?'

'He was doing some work for her father.'

Tammy seemed somewhat surprised. 'What did he make of their relationship?'

He grinned. 'Pops was pleased because Dad gave him a discount.'

Tammy burst out laughing. 'Typical!'

He leaned back in his seat so that the waitress could lay their plates on the table, along with the cutlery and condiments. Biting into a chip, Cecil chewed it thoughtfully before continuing. 'Pops was what you'd call a hands-on type of man. Whether it was tinkering with engines or laying slabs, he'd have a go at pretty much anything, so when Dad began his work Pops was right beside him asking all sorts of questions, and even giving it a go himself – not that he could lay bricks to save his life, mind you, or not in a straight row at any rate.'

'He sounds like a really nice, down-to-earth kind of feller,' observed Tammy as she sliced her faggots into quarters.

'He is. He believes a spade's a spade and it's what's

on the inside that counts, which is why he never held Dad's profession against him.'

'A rare breed indeed,' noted Tammy, adding, 'What a pity it is that there aren't more like him in the world. You should hear some of the officers I drive about. I dread to think what they'd say if they knew we were doing this.'

He gazed at her, a forkful of chips poised before his lips. 'Will they ever have to know?'

She very much wanted to throw caution to the wind, but that would be a silly thing to do. She gave him a fleeting smile. 'It only takes one person to tattle-tale.'

'Our word against theirs?'

'You mean lie?'

He shrugged. 'They don't show us any respect, so why should we show them any?'

'Because they might end up movin' you, just to be on the safe side.'

'They don't need an excuse to do that,' said Cecil. 'Sometimes I think they move us around just because they get bored with seeing the same old faces.'

'So damned if we do, and damned if we don't.'

'Exactly. So why not stop worrying about what may or may not happen, and just get on with enjoying our lives?'

Because I'm lyin' to you, said Tammy's wretched inner voice. *So even if they wouldn't object, we cannae possibly form a decent relationship when I'm only tellin' you half-truths.* Aware that he was waiting for her to respond, she desperately tried to think of a plausible reason for turning him down, but the truth was she didn't want to.

'I suppose if you put it that way . . .'

He wiped his lips with his napkin as his eyes glittered with expectation. 'Are you saying what I think you're saying?'

Tammy felt her tummy flutter. 'That depends on what you think I'm saying.'

'That we can stop meeting as friends and actually give it a go?' Realising that this was not an appropriate way of asking a woman to be your girlfriend, he slapped his forehead with the palm of his hand. 'No wonder they think that romance is dead!' He cleared his throat. 'Tammy Lloyd, will you go on a date with me?'

Tammy's head was screaming at her to turn him down, but her heart said: 'I'd love to!'

Tammy was expertly darning the toe of her stocking when Gina entered the hut.

'Spill the beans!' said Gina as she sat down on the bed next to her.

Tammy did as she was instructed and Gina squealed with delight. 'That's the best thing I've heard in donkey's years! I don't know what made you change your mind, but I'm glad you did!'

'I didn't change my mind exactly,' Tammy admitted, 'it was more of a spur of the moment type of thing. I had a multitude of reasons to turn him down, but I couldn't bring myself to voice any of them!'

'Are you happy you did it, though?'

'Very,' said Tammy, continuing in quieter tones, 'If it weren't for my conscience I'd be ecstatic!'

'Not that again,' said Gina with a heavy sigh. 'You cannae keep punishin' yourself for summat that wasn't your fault!'

'I don't like lyin',' said Tammy flatly, 'especially when it's to people I really like.'

Gina wrinkled her nose. 'You told a white lie, which is very different.'

Tammy eyed her appreciatively. 'That's ever so kind of you to say, but I'm not sure it works that way.'

'If the Nazis came lookin' for me and they asked you if you knew where I was, would you tell them the truth or would you lie?'

'Lie, of course!' cried Tammy, looking shocked that Gina would even ask such a question.

'Glad to hear it!' said Gina. 'So if it's all right for you to lie under those circumstances why isn't it all right for you to lie about the night you were runnin' for your life? What's the difference?'

'I suppose there isn't any,' said Tammy. 'But I'll have to tell him the truth one day, especially if he asks me to marry him.'

'You can cross that bridge when you come to it,' said Gina, continuing with a grin, 'You're courtin' an officer!'

Tammy's smile matched Gina's. 'I know!'

Archie slowed as he neared the police station. His gut reaction had been to tell the police everything he knew so that the women would be free to come back to Clydebank, but then he realised that in order to do that he would have to admit that Dennis hadn't been lying, and that would put a very different spin on things. *The polis would have to hunt Grace and Tammy down for attempted murder*, he thought now, *but I cannae see why two women who wouldn't normally say boo to a goose would suddenly turn into cold-blooded killers. If I were to lay money on it I'd say that they were defendin' themselves. But it'll be his word against theirs, and with bloomin' How d'you do Henry givin' his version of what he overheard, they might have to come down on the side of Dennis, because innocent people don't run!* He sighed heavily. There wasn't a doubt in his mind that the women were innocent, but what if the judge didn't see it that way? He cast his mind back to the conversation he'd had with Reg about Dennis bursting into the police station to report his attempted murder. That was ludicrous in Archie's eyes, because anyone who knew Dennis would know that the police were the last people he'd turn to for help.

He had a sudden thought. With that being the case, why on earth *had* Dennis gone to the police? *Because Grace and Tammy had managed to get away and he was most likely worried that when they felt safe they'd go straight to the polis to tell their side of the story*, thought Archie now, *and Dennis knew if he didn't get in first the polis would take their word over his, leavin' him to look like the guilty party he was.*

Archie drew his cigarette pouch out of his pocket and began rolling a cigarette with absent-minded precision. The right thing to do would be to walk into the police station and tell them everything Henry had told him, but Henry's love affair with alcohol might mean that the polis wouldn't take him at his word. On the other hand, if he didn't go in, Grace and Tammy would be living in fear for the rest of their lives when there was no need. He licked the cigarette paper and smoothed it down as he continued to think things through, then took a box of matches from the same pocket and struck one. Holding the flame to the tip of his cigarette, he heard a familiar voice hail him from the steps of the station.

'Archie! What brings you here?'

Archie exhaled a plume of smoke as he placed the matches back in his pocket. 'Just passin'.'

'Did you ever find out what happened to Dennis?'

Archie had made up his mind. He gently blew on the end of his cigarette, causing it to flare. 'Left town, by all accounts.'

'Probably for the best. You know we'd never have been able to prove anythin'.'

'I know,' agreed Archie. 'I just hate to see an injustice, that's all.'

Reg clapped a hand onto Archie's shoulder. 'Me and you both, but what can you do?'

Archie smiled grimly as he walked away. *Keep my mouth shut, until I've spoken to them myself, that's what I can do!*

* * *

DECEMBER 1941

Grace lifted the collar of her thick woollen coat against the sharp, cold rain, which was coming down like stair rods.

'Did we really have to buy a tree today of all days?' she asked Annie, who was huddled beneath their shared umbrella.

'Too right we do! Look about you.'

Grace lifted her head above her coat collar just enough to take a quick look round at the market, which was empty of customers. 'What at?'

'Exactly! No customers means no sales, no sales means low prices!'

'I just hope it's still got some needles left on it by the time we get it back,' said Grace, as she and Annie began to hunt for the smallest tree on offer.

'What about that one?' said Annie, pointing to one which was drooping under the weight of the rain.

Grace looked for the stallholder who was huddled in the doorway of one of the buildings. She waved to gain his attention, then quickly pushed her hand back into the warmth of her jacket.

The man threw his cigarette stub into a puddle as he jogged over. 'Ladies!'

'How much for that one?' asked Grace, pointing to the tree, which had just given up the struggle and fallen over.

He screwed his lips to one side. 'Four bob?'

Annie gaped at him. 'Four bob? For that?'

He shrugged. 'Three bob then?'

Grace shook her head. 'We won't give you a penny over a bob and you're lucky to get that.'

'No chance!' he began, until he saw Grace start to walk Annie away. Heaving a sigh, he relented. 'All right. A bob it is!'

'And you can throw in one of them wreaths for half price whilst you're about it,' said Grace, fishing her kiss-clasp purse out of her handbag.

'And why would I do that?'

Grace looked around her. 'Because unless the weather changes, these might be the only sales you make today.'

Grumbling that they were taking advantage of an honest feller trying to keep a roof over his family's head, he held his hand out for the money before handing Grace one of the wreaths.

'How're we goin' to get it home?' said Annie as she eyed the tree, which was as broad as it was tall.

'You take one end and I'll take the other,' said Grace as she hooked the wreath over her arm. 'I have to say I think it's wonderful that you all chip in for Christmas the way you do.'

'Some of the girls have never had a proper Christmas,' said Annie as they lifted the tree – which couldn't have been more than three foot high – off the ground.

'I used to do my best to make it as Christmassy as possible when we were livin' with Dennis,' said Grace, 'but I had to mind what I bought cos he'd only accuse me of robbin' from the housekeepin'.'

Annie gave a small exclamation as her end of the tree slipped out of her grasp. Picking it back up, she apologised to Grace and plodded on, doing her best to avoid the large puddles which had accumulated on the pavement. 'Why have kids if you don't want them?' she said.

'Lookin' back, I think he wanted a wife, a child, and

a home, because to him that would mean he'd made it in life,' said Grace. 'But when push came to shove he didn't actually want any of that except the home.'

'I think that goes for a lot of men,' said Annie, 'or at least it does for the ones I encounter, but that probably comes from livin' in a women's shelter.'

'I've said it once and I'll say it again: I think it's marvellous what you do for the girls,' said Grace. 'I dread to think where they'd be without you.'

Annie smiled. 'I get pleasure out of knowin' they're safe and happy. Maybe it's because I never had any kids of me own.'

'Or maybe this was your callin',' mused Grace. 'If you believe in that type of thing.'

'Maybe.' Annie stepped off the pavement in order to cross the road. 'When you say you tried to make it as Christmassy as possible, what did you do exactly?'

'Not much,' admitted Grace. 'Certainly no tree, because he'd never have allowed that, but he was all right with paper chains provided they were cut out of old newspapers, although he made it plain he couldn't see the point.'

'What about dinner, though?' ventured Annie. 'Surely he let you do summat special for that cos he'd benefit from it too?'

'Dennis isn't interested in food; alcohol's his love,' said Grace. 'If I could afford meat with what was left of the housekeepin', then it'd be offal or sausages at best, and he'd even begrudge us that.'

'You must really be lookin' forward to givin' your Tammy a proper Christmas,' said Annie.

'Very much so! And I'll chip in extra to cover the food—'

Annie was shaking her head. 'Don't be daft. We have it quite good with so many of us livin' under the same roof, and some of the women are amazingly inventive when it comes to makin' the food stretch. There's not a year gone by when we haven't had a feast what was fit for a king.'

Grace was intrigued. 'It sounds wonderful!'

Annie smiled. 'It is. For Christmas dinner we have veggies, bread sauce and stuffin' with the murkey—'

'Don't you mean turkey?' Grace interrupted.

Annie laughed. 'I wish! Murkey is stuffed mutton, which may not sound much but once Maisie and Cammie have had their way with it it's really quite delicious. On Boxing Day we do sausage rolls, bubble and squeak, sarnies, and any leftovers from the day before.' She hesitated before adding, 'Maisie does a lovely Christmas pud.'

'Christmas pudding?' cried Grace. 'What with?'

'Dried fruit, amongst other things; Cammie's a real whizz when it comes to bulkin' things out usin' root veggies.'

Grace shook her head sadly. 'It comes to somethin' when I eat better in a shelter than I did in my own home.'

'Alcohol's pricey,' said Annie, 'but not enough to stop some of them drinkin' it. If you ask me they should make it even more expensive, cos that way men like Dennis couldn't afford to get drunk, and without drink there wouldn't be half the domestic violence there is at present.'

Grace laughed sarcastically. 'A world without alcohol? He'd have taken his own life a long time ago!'

'Do you ever think back to the day you left?' Annie asked, adjusting her grip on the tree.

'All the time, because I wish we'd done things differently,' admitted Grace. 'And I'm still waitin' for the long arm of the law to come down on my shoulder.'

'I don't understand why there's been nowt about the murder in the news,' said Annie. 'I know there's a war on, but you'd think it worthy of a headline.'

'It does seem odd, but I suppose I should be grateful for small mercies. Maybe I've got someone up there lookin' after me,' said Grace.

They had reached the steps of the shelter, and stood the tree down while Annie opened the door. 'It's been ages since the blitz,' she said. 'I doubt they could prove anythin' now even if they caught up with you.'

'That's the only explanation I can think of,' Grace agreed. 'Dennis was always rubbin' people up the wrong way; pinnin' his murder on just one person would prove nigh on impossible with so many suspects to choose from.'

'Only wouldn't it be kind of obvious, what with you and Tammy bein' missin'?'

'I thought that, but even if someone else had done him in, the polis would believe we'd legged it in case we got the blame.'

'Sounds plausible.' Grace froze as she spied a man watching them from across the street. 'Annie . . .'

Annie looked at Grace over her shoulder. 'What?'

'That man . . .'

'What man?' said Annie, whipping round and looking to Grace, who had gone white.

'I thought it was *him*,' said Grace. 'I'd swear he looked just like Dennis until he turned away.'

Annie's brow furrowed. 'He looked different from the back?'

'Dennis has black hair, not ginger. I couldn't see the man's hair under his cap until he turned.'

'You're lettin' your paranoia get the better of you again,' said Annie.

'I know. I seem to see him everywhere I go these days.'

'He's gone,' Annie assured her. 'But if you'd rather I met Tammy on your behalf . . .'

'It's fine,' said Grace. 'I just need to get a hold of myself. Let's forget about him and get inside.'

Annie gave the little tree a shake to rid it of the rainwater before they took it in. Propping it up in the corner of the hallway, they stood back to cast a critical eye over their purchase, which was leaning to one side.

'Perhaps it's just as well we've not got a lot of baubles,' mused Annie. 'It doesn't look as though it could take a lot of weight.'

'If we place more of them on one side than the other, it might stand up straight,' said Grace, shrugging her coat off her shoulders and hanging it on the coat rack.

'Good idea. They do say that less is more,' agreed Annie. 'Which is why I don't think we should attempt to put any candles on it.' They shared a mental image of the small tree speckled with candles, which would almost certainly set light to the branches above, once dry.

'Definitely no candles,' said Grace.

'We've probably still got some of last year's paper chains in the attic,' said Annie. 'But we can always make more.'

Grace looked at the picture rail which ran the length of the hall. 'We can put the things the kids make at school along the picture rail, and criss-cross the paper chains from one side of the ceiling to the other.'

'And we can go to Princes Park and take some cuttings from the holly trees,' said Annie, hanging her coat next to Grace's.

'I cannae wait to see the look on Tammy's face when she sees how festive everythin' looks. I just know she's goin' to be here; I can feel it in my bones.'

'It certainly is goin' to be a Christmas to remember,' concurred Annie, 'and for once it's goin' to be for all the right reasons!'

Chapter Twelve

Rory had just finished his shift and was heading for the NAAFI when a familiar face caught his eye. Normally he wouldn't have dreamt of gaining her attention, but it had been so long since he'd seen anyone from home that he couldn't help but jog over.

Turning to see who'd put their hand on her shoulder, the woman hesitated before smiling. 'Rory! What on earth are you doin' here?'

Rory pushed his hands into his pockets. 'I joined up straight after the first day of the blitz – you?'

'I joined up a couple of months later,' said his former classmate, eyeing him thoughtfully. 'I must say I'd have thought you'd have stayed down the docks, what with dockers being exempt from joinin' up.'

He lowered his gaze. 'I couldn't stay in Clydebank after what had happened.' Unsure whether she knew to what he was referring, he looked up. 'With the Black-wells, I mean.'

Her brow rose slowly. 'I don't see why. It's not as if you have anythin' to be ashamed of.'

Rory blinked. 'Why should I be ashamed? And more to the point, what of?'

Ella stared at him. 'Don't you know?' Without waiting for him to reply, she continued, 'Of course you don't. You'd have been well gone before the rumours started circulatin'.'

'What rumours?'

'About Tammy and her mammy tryin' to murder Dennis!'

Rory stared at her in annoyed disbelief. Trust Ella to make up a load of nonsense. 'What on earth are you goin' on about? You know damned well Grace and Tammy wouldn't do anythin' like that.'

'Wouldn't they now? Shows what you know! I have it on good authority that they bashed Dennis over the head before leavin' him for dead,' said Ella smugly.

Rory's cheeks paled. Had they really done Dennis in before making good their escape? And if so, why on earth hadn't they come straight to him? He scolded himself inwardly. This was another of Ella's stupid theories that she liked to make up when she didn't have all the facts. She and Tammy had never got on at school, and this was certainly not the first time she had invented nonsensical stories about people she didn't like.

Not appearing to notice Rory's reaction to her news, Ella pressed on. 'I must say, I wasn't entirely surprised. I've always thought that Tammy to be tuppence short of a shilling.'

Rory fixed her with a steely look. 'You really shouldn't spread rumours when you haven't a clue what you're talkin' about.'

'I'm only repeatin' what I heard,' said Ella defensively.

'Makes a change,' said Rory stiffly, before adding, 'Let me guess. Stella and Edie have been busy on the tom-toms again?'

She shot him a scathing glance. 'I don't listen to the likes of them, and I resent the accusation of spreadin' unfounded rumours when I heard it straight from the horse's mouth.' She paused. 'Well, maybe I didn't hear it from Dennis himself, but I cannae believe the polis would lie about a thing like that.'

He eyed her in disbelief. 'Are you seriously tryin' to tell me that the polis have been spreadin' gossip about Dennis?'

She sighed irritably. 'It's not gossip. Dennis was the one who told them!'

Rory gaped at her. 'You must be *sixpence* short of a shillin' if you believe Dennis made it out of Jellicoe House alive!'

'I don't care what you think,' said Ella haughtily, 'the facts speak for themselves, and if the polis say that Dennis turned up at the station claimin' to be the victim of an attempted murder, then who am I to question them?'

Rory stared at her blankly. 'Who on earth told you this pile of codswallop?'

Ella bristled. 'It is *not* codswallop. If you must know, it was my aunt who told me; she cleans down the polis station.'

Rory's jaw clenched; he could hardly believe what he was hearing. If Dennis really had survived, then he wasn't the one who'd been the victim of attempted murder. He cast her a sceptical glance. 'And you're tellin' me that the polis believed him?'

She shrugged her indifference. 'I've no idea, but I say where there's smoke, there's fire, and with Tammy and her mammy no longer in Clydebank there can only be one conclusion!'

'Being?' said Rory stiffly.

'That there's some truth in what they're sayin',' said Ella.

'So it hasn't occurred to anyone that Dennis is the one who's done the murderin'?' said Rory, who couldn't understand why any locals would listen to Dennis.

'Of course it did, but they didn't find their bodies, so . . .'

He stared at her incredulously. 'Did you not see the ferocity of them incendiary bombs? You'd not . . .' He'd been about to say that you wouldn't possibly have been able to identify anyone's body after the fires, but he couldn't bring himself to say the words once the mental image had appeared in his mind's eye.

Ella guessed why Rory had gone quiet, but that didn't stop her from pressing on with her own thoughts. 'But why accuse them of murder if he was the one who'd done the murderin'? Surely it would've been wiser to keep shtum and blame their deaths on the Luftwaffe?'

Rory held a hand to his forehead, which was

beginning to ache. 'How on earth should I know? Dennis isn't exactly the sharpest tool in the box; who knows what goes on in that empty skull of his?'

'Unless the rumours are true,' said Ella, somewhat cautiously. She liked Rory, always had done, and she didn't wish to incur his wrath, especially as he was no longer involved with the awful Tammy.

Rory blew his cheeks out. 'So, you're sayin' they all made it out in one piece and that's why he went to the polis, but if that's the case, why didn't Grace and Tammy also go to the polis?'

'Would you do that if you were guilty of attempted murder?'

His question had been simple enough, but Ella's reply rocked Rory to the core of his very being, mainly because she was right. *But where does that leave me?* he thought. *They knew I was waitin' for them, so why run off leavin' me not knowin' what was goin' on? More to the point, what would have happened had Archie not stopped me going into the house when the sirens went off? And what would I have discovered if I had?* He imagined himself entering the house and finding Dennis spark out on the floor. *How could they have run off, leavin' me to pick up the pieces?* Another more rational voice had the answer though. *They'd have been scared out of their wits, which means they wouldn't have been thinkin' straight.*

Ella had taken Rory's silence as an admission of agreement. 'You think I'm right, don't you?'

He shook his head, but couldn't look her in the eye. 'I think that people do all kinds of strange things when they're frightened. I also believe neither Tammy nor

Grace would attack Dennis unless provoked to do so. If anything has happened – and I'm not sayin' it has, mind you, but *if* it has – then there will be a perfectly reasonable explanation for it.'

She glanced away. 'I seem to remember that you and Tammy had quite a thing for each other at one point. Am I to take it that's no longer the case?'

He stared at her levelly. 'How can it be when I believe her to be dead?'

'Which is a bit odd in itself,' continued Ella. 'I'd have thought she'd have come straight to you, given the closeness of your relationship. I must say, I'm surprised she didn't.'

Not as surprised as me, thought Rory to himself, but out loud he said: 'This is a complete waste of time. As far as I'm concerned Tammy and Grace are still at Jellicoe House, and that's where they'll stay until I see evidence to prove otherwise.'

'So you're not with anybody?'

He stared at her incredulously. After everything that had been said, all Ella wanted to know was whether he was available or not. 'You can't just forget about someone when you love them as much as I loved Tammy.' He hoped that would draw a line under the conversation.

She nodded. 'They do say that time's a great healer. I just hope you don't waste too much of yours hangin' on to the hope that you might see her again. Not after the way she treated you.'

'And what has she done to me?'

'Left you high and dry without a clue as to what's

become of her. I'd never do that to somebody, not if I loved them I wouldn't. If you ask me, that precious pair wanted rid of Dennis, and as soon as they got what they wanted they ran off into the night and to hell with everyone else.'

Rory wanted to say that Tammy would never treat him in such a manner, but how could he when the evidence was indicating otherwise? He rubbed the back of his neck. 'As I've already said, people act out of character when they're scared. I don't think Grace or Tammy would've hung around to chat if they thought Dennis was after them, do you? What's more, if either of them did do somethin' to hurt Dennis it wouldn't have been on purpose, but in self-defence.'

She shrugged. 'Life's too short to worry about those who don't care about you, that's all I'm sayin'.'

'Well don't, because you don't know what you're talkin' about,' Rory snapped.

'You always were blinded by that one,' said Ella. 'I see nothing's changed, even when you're faced with the truth.'

Rory made as if to turn on his heel. 'You wouldn't know the truth if it smacked you in the face! And I know for a fact that you hated Tammy with a passion, which is why you're spieling your spiteful nonsense when she's not here to defend herself.'

Ella clenched her fists as she watched his retreating back, her eyes narrowing. 'You know I'm right. That's why you're runnin' away – because you cannae bear to hear the truth!'

Rory continued to walk until he passed the NAAFI.

All thoughts of food out of his mind, he continued on to the exercise yard where he began to jog slowly round the perimeter. If he didn't get some of the pent-up anger out, he feared he might swing for someone.

I've never hit a woman in my life, and I never will, he told himself as he began the second lap of the yard, *but that bloomin' Ella pushes people to breakin' point, she really does.* He speeded up, determined to outrun his treacherous thoughts. *She genuinely thought she was speakin' the truth, and you know it.* A bead of sweat ran down his temple. *No matter how worried or scared Tammy was, she could've written to let me know she was all right, because even if the polis had taken Dennis at his word they'd have known I had nothin' to do with it because I was convinced that Dennis had killed* them! No matter which way he looked at it, he couldn't help but wonder if there really was some truth behind Ella's words. He'd never have thought it before today, but had Tammy only used him to get the fake papers? Had she and Grace planned to do a runner all along? He shook his head. He was letting his imagination get the better of him. *You know for a fact that they didn't leave Jellicoe House until after Dennis got there, and that was hours after you gave them the papers. Had their intention been to jump ship as soon as they got their hands on the IDs, they'd not have been at home when Dennis left work. Listening to idle gossips such as Ella, Edie or Stella is a stupid thing to do – when you know how much they like to elaborate on the truth.* For all he knew, Dennis had never set foot in a polis station; in fact the more Rory thought about it now, the more ludicrous it seemed. *It's nought but Chinese whispers gone wild*, he thought as he slowed back down to a brisk jog. *And I should've known better than to talk to Ella in the first place, when she's never been anythin' other than horrible to Tammy. Well, I shan't give her the pleasure again, that's for sure!*

Tammy was reapplying her lipstick, while taking great care to use it sparingly.

'There was nothin' wrong with it the first time round,' said Gina pointedly.

Tammy flicked her eyes to Gina's mirrored reflection as she paused in her application. 'I looked too wanton.'

Gina rolled her eyes. 'You most certainly did not. You looked lovely!'

'Well, I thought I did, and I have to be careful that I don't give Cecil the wrong impression,' Tammy continued, blotting the barely visible lipstick with a piece of tissue paper.

'Cecil's lovely,' said Gina. 'He'd never consider you wanton; and he wouldn't be takin' you on a date if he did.'

Tammy mulled this over while she continued to do her makeup. 'I suppose you've a fair point, but even so I don't want to appear too eager.'

'That's a different matter, but I don't think there's anythin' wrong with makin' an effort. It just shows you care.'

Tammy heaved a sigh. 'I know; so why am I gettin' my knickers in a twist?'

'You're nervous, which is natural. I expect I'll be the exact same way – if I ever get to go on a date, that is.'

'Of course you will. I'm sure Harry will pluck up the courage sooner or later.'

Gina wrinkled her nose. 'I'm still not convinced our meetings are anythin' other than coincidental.'

Tammy eyed her dubiously. 'Put it this way: do you bump into any other fellers as often as you do Harry?'

'No, but if he really does like me, then why doesn't he just ask me out instead of followin' me from place to place? Quite frankly, I find it a bit creepy!'

Tammy tutted, wagging a reproving finger. 'He's not creepy. He's just shy, much the same as yourself.'

'Only I don't follow him round,' said Gina levelly.

'I should hope not! It's the men that are meant to do the chasin', not the women, and don't forget, he doesn't know that you'll agree to go on a date with him. For all he knows you might turn him down point-blank.'

'Who says I'll agree to go on a date with him?'

Tammy raised her brow. 'Are you sayin' you'd turn him down?'

'Well, no, but . . .' An annoyed frown appeared on her face. 'We weren't talkin' about me. We were talkin' about you and why you feel so nervous when you've been out with Cecil a few times already.'

Tammy heaved a sigh; she had rather hoped that their previous conversation had been put to bed. 'I haven't any idea, but I do know one thing: I'm beginnin' to wish I hadn't agreed to go on this date.'

'But you get on so well together,' Gina had begun when the owner of the lipstick Tammy was using cut her off without warning.

'What are you doin'?' she cried, seeing Tammy wipe

the lipstick from her lips. 'That stuff's not cheap, you know – or easy to come by, for that matter!'

Tammy twisted the lipstick back down at once. 'Phyllis, I'm sorry, but I guess I'm not a makeup kind of gal. I've tried wearin' it on a few occasions but it just doesn't feel right, almost like tryin' to fit a square peg into a round hole, if that makes sense?' She barely gave Phyllis time to respond before pressing on. 'And I never wore lipstick when Cecil took me out to dinner, so why am I thinkin' about it now?'

'You don't need makeup,' conceded Gina. 'I, on the other hand, need all the help I can get, so if you've finished with that lippy?'

'You don't need it either,' Tammy pointed out. 'Harry certainly doesn't think so, cos he'd not be chasin' you otherwise.'

Gina turned to Phyllis. 'You've been on a few dates – have you any advice for Tammy?'

'Just be yourself,' said Phyllis. 'That's what I do.'

'Only you never seem to see them more than a few times before movin' on to the next. Do you not like any of the fellers that take you out?'

'Oh yes, very much, but I'm not lookin' for a long-term relationship.'

Gina put the lid back on the lipstick and handed it back. 'How come?'

'I don't want to have my heart broken,' said Phyllis simply. 'You never know what's goin' to happen from one day to the next with the war an' all, and I've seen plenty of girls wavin' their beaus goodbye with a tear in their eye, only to never see them again, either because the feller's met someone else, or . . .' She didn't need to finish the sentence; they all knew what she meant.

'That's a very sensible outlook to have, but what happens if you fall in love with one of them?' Gina wanted to know.

'That's why I keep it to a three-day maximum,' said Phyllis. 'I can't bear the thought of gettin' close to someone only to have them taken away from me.'

Tammy gazed at her reflection in the mirror. What Phyllis said made sense, and it was part of the reason why she hadn't wanted to date Cecil in the first place; not after losing Rory. But surely it wasn't healthy to deny yourself the chance of falling in love on account of what ifs? She said as much to Phyllis.

'I'm not sayin' I want to be on my own for ever,' was the reply, 'only while the war's on.'

Gina looked to Tammy, who was continuing to stare at her reflection. 'What about you, or is it too late?'

Tammy heaved a sigh. 'I don't know about love, but . . .' She turned her gaze to the clock above the door of their hut. 'Oh heck! I didn't realise that was the time! I'll miss the bus if I don't get a move on.'

Gina got to her feet. 'C'mon, I'll walk you to the stop.'

Tammy bade Phyllis goodbye as she and Gina hurried off.

'What do you think about what Phyllis was sayin'?' Gina asked as they hurried towards the gate.

'She's certainly got her head screwed on, but I don't think it's good to live your life based on what ifs.' Catching the unbelieving look on her friend's face, Tammy continued, 'And while I know I'm hardly one

287

to talk, Cecil is proof that *not* fallin' for someone is easier said than done. Not that I'm sayin' I have, mind you, but you know what I mean.' She gave Gina a sidelong glance. 'I hope her words haven't put you off sayin' yes to Harry when he asks you out?'

Gina rolled her eyes. 'If he ever does!'

'He will. And does it really matter if it takes him a little longer to pluck up the courage if he proves to be the right one for you?'

'I s'pose not. I just don't want to be the last one on camp to not have been kissed,' said Gina. 'Like I'm some sort of child!'

'Kissin' a feller doesn't make you a grown-up,' said Tammy, 'so you can put that thought out of your head for a start.'

'But it sort of does, though,' said Gina, 'because it's all part of growin' up, isn't it? First you get a boyfriend, then you get married, then you have kids.'

Tammy turned to face her. 'And is that what you want from life, or just what you think you should aspire to?'

Gina shrugged. 'Isn't that the same thing? I thought most women want to get married and settle down.'

'Not all of them,' said Tammy thoughtfully. 'Take Amelia Earhart, for example.'

'Wasn't she married?'

'Aye, but she was so much more than a married woman!' enthused Tammy. 'Her accomplishments paved the way for the female pilots of today!'

'Is that who you want to be like? Amelia Earhart?'

'I certainly want more from life than just to be someone's wife,' said Tammy. 'Before everythin' went belly-up I had my sights on me and Mammy openin' our own tailor's, and I'd still like to do somethin' along those lines. If my mother had had money of her own she'd have found it a lot easier to leave Dad, which is precisely why he made sure she didn't have any.' She held out a hand to catch the bus driver's attention. 'Whatever I end up doing with my future, I know one thing: the decision will be independent of any man!'

Gina smiled. 'And you wondered what it was that attracted Cecil to you!'

Tammy smiled back. 'Good job he appreciates a woman who can stand on her own two feet!'

Gina stood back to allow Tammy to jump on board. 'Say hello from me.'

'I will! T.T.F.N!'

Tammy took a seat near the window and waved to Gina as the driver pulled away from the kerb. Taking the fare from her purse, she handed it to the clippie before settling down to enjoy the ride. Gina's ideal of getting married and having children had made her think of the women in their hut whose sole purpose in life was to find a man to take care of them, and while it was none of Tammy's business what Gina did with her future she rather hoped she'd managed to make her friend see that there was more to life than being a typical housewife. *I couldn't think of anythin' worse*, Tammy thought now as the bus gathered speed. *Mammy was convinced she needed a man if she were to get anywhere in life, which is why she agreed to marry my father. I know she says she'd hoped there would be more opportunities for her in a big city like Glasgow, but why did she feel that she needed a man in order to get there?* After a moment's thought, she told herself cynically, *Because that's what men want us to think. You've only got to look at the way officers look down on the servicewomen to know they don't have any respect for them.* A vision of Cecil formed in her mind's eye. He certainly seemed to think differently from his peers, but how would he feel if she were to tell him that she wanted to be independent once the war was over? Would he encourage her, or would he expect her to toe the line and fall into the role of the good housewife? *These are the things that should be talked over before puttin' a ring on your finger,* Tammy told herself. *If Mammy'd had this conversation with Dad, she'd have run a mile in the other direction, because someone as opinionated and bigoted as him wouldn't have been able to lie convincingly. He'd have laughed in her face, and told her to stop havin' such fanciful notions.* She could feel her blood beginning to boil. There was no way on earth she was going to end up like her mother, and even though she didn't think Cecil would dream of treating her in such a fashion, she knew her father would never have told her mother that he planned on controlling every part of her life, because she'd not have agreed to marry him otherwise. *Most men would think it too soon to be talkin' of the future,* she thought, *but surely it's best to find out whether you're singin' from the same hymn sheet from the get-go rather than face heartbreak further down the line?*

She found her thoughts automatically turning to Rory and whether his new belle – if he had one – was as independent as herself. She tutted beneath her breath. How many times had she said she was going to forget about Rory and leave the past behind? *Actions speak louder than words*, Tammy thought now, *and you've already got the ball rollin' by agreein' to go out on a date with Cecil*. She gazed blindly out of the window. It was all very well for her to think that, but banishing Rory from her thoughts might prove impossible.

Seeing her stop loom into view, she waited for the driver to pull up before leaving her seat. Wrapping her belt tightly around her waist, she stepped out onto the snowy pavement, noting as she did so that the snow came over the tops of her shoes. *Wellies would've been a better option, but not so practical for dancin'*, thought Tammy. She smiled as an image formed in her mind of Cecil whisking her around the dance floor in her wellies, while the other officers looked on in disgust.

Cecil was already waiting for her when she reached the café, and she waved a greeting as she stepped through the door. 'Have you been waitin' long?' she asked, unbuttoning her coat.

He stood up to pull her chair out for her. 'Only around five minutes. How's tricks with you?'

'Same old same old, although I did have a thought-provokin' chat with Gina before gettin' on the bus.'

'Oh?'

Tammy told him of their conversation regarding Gina's life expectations, finishing with: 'I'm hopin' I made her see that there's more to life than that, but I suppose it's each to their own. Some women are happy to fit the norm.'

'To be the perfect wife and mother,' concurred Cecil. 'If that's what Gina wants, there's nothing wrong with that, but it's not enough for women like the aforementioned Amelia Earhart.'

'Which brings me to my next question.'

She paused while the waitress came over to take their order, and after a quick scan of the menu they chose their meals along with a pot of tea for two.

'You said something about another question?' said Cecil as soon as the waitress had left their table.

'The war makes life move so much faster than it used to and while I'd never have asked a question like this before, I think it only wise to ask it now.' She paused, gathering her thoughts. 'What do you want from a wife, Cecil? Do you want someone whose sole ambition is to cook, bake and clean, while you go off to defend your country? Because if so, that's not me. I want – or rather, I *need* – my independence.'

'You want your own job and your own money?'

'My own *money*,' said Tammy. 'I don't want to rely on my husband for anythin'.'

'I've never really thought about it,' said Cecil slowly, 'but I suppose I don't have a strong opinion either way. It's your life and you should live it as you see fit.'

'So you'd not object to me wantin' to stand on my own two feet, then?'

'Not in the slightest. In fact, I think it should be encouraged.'

'Me too! I cannae think of anythin' worse than bein' chained to the kitchen sink while poppin' out babbies like peas.'

Cecil winced. 'Sounds painful!'

She chuckled softly. 'It would be for me, and not just in the physical sense either.'

He reached across the table to hold her hand. 'I'm not going to sit here and say that I don't want to get married and have kids one of these days, because that would be a lie, but neither would I expect my wife to stay at home if she had something else in mind.'

Tammy couldn't help but notice how smooth his hands were. 'So you'd support a wife who wanted to work?'

'I would indeed, but there would have to be a happy medium, because I certainly wouldn't want a wife who was never home.'

'Quite right too. Marriage should be about give and take,' applauded Tammy. She eyed him fondly. 'I think most men would've run a mile if I started talkin' about marriage this early in the relationship.'

He grinned. 'I'm not most men.'

'I'm beginnin' to realise that.'

'Besides, we've already discussed how many children we want.'

'Ah, but that was different: we were just two friends talkin',' Tammy reminded him. 'Any topic of conversation is fair game between friends.'

'Good point.'

He sat back as the waitress put their plates of food on the table, along with the pot of tea. Tammy continued to talk as she sprinkled salt over her chips. 'Have you any plans for Christmas?'

'I wish! But I'm afraid I have to work.'

Tammy passed him the salt before picking up the

vinegar. 'That's a shame. I know my mam would've loved to have met you.'

He waved a dismissive hand. 'Not to worry. There's plenty of time for me to meet your mum, and for you to meet mine too, come to that.'

Tammy pulled a doubtful face. 'I think you have less to fear from meetin' my mammy than I have from meetin' yours!'

He cut his knife through the thick pastry of his chosen pie. 'I thought we'd already been through this?'

'We have, but you've never seen me out of my uni-form, and—' She stopped short as Cecil attempted to quell his laughter.

'And there I was thinking that you were a good girl!'

Her cheeks flushing as she realised what she'd said, she made an attempt to redeem herself. 'You know full well I was referrin' to my civilian clothes!'

Apologising for his mirth, he twinkled at her from across the table. 'You're worried your clothes won't be good enough for her?'

Tammy nodded shyly.

'What do you think my father wore when he first met her? A pinstriped suit and oxford shoes?'

She shot him a cynical glance. 'Of course not, your dad was in his work clothes when he met your mother. The circumstances are very different.'

'Ah! So you think he kept his pinstripes and brogues for evening attire? My dad wore the clothes of a work-ing man, which weren't in the least bit posh.'

'I've only got one dress,' said Tammy. 'Dad didn't think I needed any more than that.'

'And I'm sure you look lovely in it,' said Cecil, 'but please don't think you have to dress to impress my parents, because you really don't.'

'I just worry that your mother's expectin' someone more worthy of you than me.'

He rested his knife and fork on his plate. 'My mother will love you, because you don't believe in convention but think out of the box – just like her. Not only that, but you know your own mind – another of my mother's qualities. And to top it off she'll love you because I . . .' His voice trailed off, before coming back quietly. 'You mean a lot to me.'

Realising that she was staring at him, Tammy quickly averted her gaze. Had he been about to say that he loved her? Every nerve in her body scoffed that it was far too early for him to profess his love, but maybe that was why he'd stopped himself.

'My mother will think the world of you too,' said Tammy, adding, 'although she'll probably need to see you with her own eyes before she believes that you're an officer.'

He grinned. 'I'd like to be a fly on the wall when you break the news. She'll probably be horrified, thinking that you're dating some old walrus with an ego the size of his waist!'

Tammy laughed. 'That's what Gina thought when I first told her about you.'

Cecil roared with laughter. 'I hope you put her right.'

'Of course I did! And I shall do the same with Mammy if she should get hold of the wrong end of the stick.'

'And do you think that an officer will be good enough for her little girl?'

Tammy pretended to mull this over. 'Obviously she'd want someone of higher rankin', but beggars cannae be choosers.' She broke into laughter as he pretended to look downhearted. 'Of course she'll think you're good enough for me.'

'That'll teach me to fish for compliments! I think I'd better quit while I'm ahead,' chuckled Cecil. 'Are you still up for a dance after this, or would you prefer the cinema?'

Remembering the wellies, she put it to him to see what he'd say.

'As long as you don't stand on my toes, I don't care what you wear on your feet!'

Her smile broadened. 'You can rest assured I wouldn't turn up to a date in wellies. I'd rather have toes like ice cubes than do that.'

'Spoken like a true woman!' said Cecil. 'Always putting appearance over comfort! You ask any feller that question and you'll get the same answer: they'd rather wear wellies and have dry feet, and to hell with what anyone else thinks!'

She glanced under the table before looking back up with a wry smile. 'So what stopped you?'

He pulled an impish grin. 'I don't own a pair of wellies.'

Tammy laughed at this obvious fib. 'See? You men are just as vain as us women!'

He held up his hands. 'Guilty as charged!'

The bell above the door rang, signalling another

customer, and Tammy turned to see a young woman shaking the snow from her umbrella as she entered the café. Looking out of the window, she spoke to Cecil over her shoulder. 'Just look at the snow! Isn't it beautiful?' She turned back to see him staring at her with affectionate eyes.

'I've never seen anything more beautiful in my entire life,' he said, without breaking his gaze.

She waved him away. 'Sweet talker!'

'Truth teller,' he rallied.

'I'm not goin' to win this one, am I?' said Tammy.

'Not a chance!' He glanced at her empty plate. 'Room for a pudding?'

'I dare say you have, so it would be rude of me not to keep you company,' said Tammy, a smile twisting her lips.

'Bread and butter pudding do you?'

'Yes, please.'

Cecil beckoned the waitress over and gave their order. Clearing the table of the used plates, the woman left them to talk.

'I hope I can still cut a rug after I've finished eating my pudding,' said Cecil. 'What is it about rationing that makes you feel as though you can't say no to food?'

'Not knowing when you'll be offered it again,' said Tammy simply. 'I know I've got a lot less picky since the war started – although as you already know, I draw the line at haggis.'

'What about good old-fashioned tripe?'

She shot him a scathing glance. 'When I say a lot less

picky I'm referrin' to normal food, not an animal's innards.'

'Fair enough!' He looked at the snow, which was falling thick and fast. 'It's really coming down now.'

'The base will send people out to clear the roads,' said Tammy, adding, 'I'm glad I'm not on duty tonight.'

'Have Woodbury put their decorations up yet?'

Tammy thought about the Christmas tree in the NAAFI and the fun they'd had decorating it. 'They certainly have.'

'I hope your tree is better than the one we've got,' said Cecil. 'Ours looks like it fell off the back of the lorry and got dragged the whole way back.'

Tammy laughed gently. 'I'm sure it cannae be as bad as all that, and it definitely cannae be any worse than the decorations – or rather lack of them – we used to have when I lived at home.'

'What, nothing?'

'Only newspaper paper chains,' said Tammy. 'There was one time when I got a sprig of holly from the tree in our school yard, but Dad went and sold it down the pub.'

Cecil looked horrified. 'Surely you can't have been that hard up for money?'

'When someone's drinkin' every penny they earn you can,' replied Tammy simply.

He shook his head angrily. 'How could he do that to his own child?'

'Because he didn't believe in Christmas. He said it was an excuse to spend money on stuff that didn't matter. Not that it stopped him from spendin' the day down the pub, mind you.'

Their puddings arrived and Cecil scooped the custard back to allow it to cool down while he continued to talk. 'Men like that don't deserve a family.'

'I couldn't agree more.'

'Do you ever wonder what he's doin' now that you and your mammy are no longer on the scene?'

Tammy quickly banished the vision of her father lying on the kitchen floor, blood oozing from his head. If Bonnie was to be believed, and Tammy rather thought she was, then Dennis would be drinking himself into an early grave just as he always had. She said as much to Cecil.

'He sounds like an alcoholic.'

'If he wasn't workin' he was drinkin'. If that makes him an alcoholic, then yes, that's exactly what he is. I don't think there was a day went by when he didn't have a drink.'

'Thank God you got away from him when you did.'

'He probably feels the same way, cos with me and Mammy both gone his money's all his own, and even though he'll have to cook and clean for himself, I think he'd prefer that to havin' us around. The only thing he'll miss is bein' able to say he's got a wife and child.'

'They say there's nowt so queer as folk, and that certainly seems to be the case with your father,' conceded Cecil. 'Quite frankly, I'm amazed you've turned out as well as you have, all things considered.'

'If I have then it's down to Mammy; she's the one who taught me right from wrong.' Tammy gave a mirthless chuckle. 'She had a brilliant example in Dad when it came to wrongdoing. All she had to do was point at him and say don't do that.'

Cecil smiled. 'And yet you can still joke about it, which says a lot about your spirit.'

'It's either laugh or cry; I choose to laugh.' She indicated his clean bowl. 'Would you like the rest of mine, only I think my eyes are bigger than my stomach.'

He reached across the table and scooped up her bowl. 'You'll never see me turn down seconds!'

'I think that applies for most men,' said Tammy as she watched him enjoy the rest of her pudding. 'Apart from Dad, that is, unless it's a round of drinks.'

'I prefer good food to ale, and my dad's the same,' said Cecil.

'I wish my dad had been more like yours,' said Tammy, 'but then again, I wouldn't be here with you if he was, so I suppose you could say every cloud . . .'

'Good or bad, he's made you the woman you are today,' Cecil agreed. 'I think we're all shaped by our parents' beliefs and morals.'

Tammy blew her cheeks out. 'I hate to think what beliefs Hitler's parents must have had; I know they couldn't have had any morals.'

'How different would all our lives be if he'd never been born?' supposed Cecil.

'If only!' She smiled at the waitress who'd come to collect the empty dishes and present them with the bill.

As before, Tammy made to get her purse out of her bag, only to have Cecil motion for her to stop. 'I know what you said, but I'm afraid when it comes to paying for meals and the like I'm still pretty old-fashioned.'

'Are you sure?'

He handed the waitress the money, along with a generous tip. 'Positive. Besides, I could hardly ask you to pay for half when I ate most of your pudding!'

'Fair point,' said Tammy, sliding her arms into the sleeves of the coat he was holding for her. Buttoning herself up, she turned to thank him as he passed her umbrella over. 'I'm glad I brought this,' she said, indicating the snow which was still falling thickly.

'There's something romantic about a walk in the snow, don't you think?'

'I seem to remember you sayin' the same about rain,' Tammy reminded him, 'and look how that turned out.'

He pulled a rueful face. 'Walking in the rain is lovely; thunderstorms not so much,' he said, 'but it's different with snow. Snow is always beautiful.'

They stepped outside and Cecil unfurled his umbrella over the two of them. Holding his arm, Tammy looked at the people hurrying about their business around them. 'If you were to ask these people how the war has affected their Christmas, I'd wager a lot of them would say it's made things worse because they cannae afford the things they'd normally buy. And even if they can buy them, they're rationed, so Christmas is far more meagre than before. But I could tell them that when you've never had a proper Christmas in your life, even the small things seem enchanting.'

'I think a lot of people could do with taking a leaf out of your book,' said Cecil as they walked towards the

301

dance hall. 'The upper classes never have to worry about not having enough because most of them can afford to buy off the black market. It's wrong that the rich get richer and the poor get poorer, yet that always seems to be the way.'

'I suppose it depends on how you define bein' rich,' said Tammy. 'I think if your family and friends are safe and well, that makes you a rich person. Material things are all well and good, but they don't dry your eyes, or help you get through the bad times, or give you a cuddle when you're feelin' down.'

'If you were to say that to some of the fat cats in business suits they'd think you insane, because they believe that money can buy everything from lunch to love, and anything in between,' said Cecil. He hesitated. 'I know my family have money, but Mum and Dad always taught us that your health and happiness are more important than your bank balance.'

'Having money does make a difference, though,' said Tammy, 'because if you have money you can afford to pay a doctor, or a dentist, and put coal on the fire to keep you toasty durin' the winter months, and so on and so forth.'

'So what are you saying exactly?'

'I guess it depends on what you spend your money on. After all, those that can afford good health care live longer than those who can't.'

Stepping slightly ahead of Tammy while still keeping the umbrella over her, Cecil opened the door to the dance hall for her to pass through before shaking the snow from his umbrella and stepping inside to join her.

'You're right, but it's a shame it has to be that way. Everyone should have access to doctors and dentists no matter their financial circumstances.'

Tammy handed her jacket to the clerk and waited for Cecil to do the same. Taking the ticket which married up to their belongings, he tucked it safely into his pocket as they strolled over to the bar.

'Lemonade for me, please,' said Tammy when the barmaid came over to greet them. Knowing how Tammy felt about alcohol, Cecil ordered the same.

'Why aren't you havin' a beer? I thought that was your tipple of choice?' Tammy smiled as they took their drinks over to a table.

'I prefer soft drinks when I'm with you,' said Cecil. Sitting down on the chair next to hers, he turned to face her.

'Why?'

'I suppose I don't want you to worry that I might be like your father after a drink or two, so I'd rather go without.'

'Your puttin' my feelin's first shows that you're nothin' like my father,' said Tammy. 'And while we're about it, Dad never stops at one or two, he only stops when he runs out of money, so please don't deny yourself a beer on my account.'

He rested his hand over the top of hers. 'Alcohol has played a big part in your life, and not a good one, so I'll stick to lemonade if it's all the same to you. Besides, I'm really not that fussed about alcohol. All it does is give you a headache and the excuse to make a fool of yourself.'

'I've never touched a drop – for obvious reasons – although I'm surprised to hear you say that it gives you a headache, because I thought it must make you feel great for Dad to love it as much as he does.'

'Drink the right amount and it can make you forget your worries, or so I'm told, but what's the point in that when your worries will still be there when you wake up the next morning?'

'Dad didn't have any worries, or none that I knew of,' said Tammy, 'so goin' on that basis me and Mammy should've been the ones drinkin', because we had a lot more to worry about than him.'

Cecil was staring at Tammy as though he'd just had an epiphany. 'You said before that you didn't think your father really wanted a family?'

'I did. Why?'

'Having a family is a huge responsibility; your father might've turned to drink as a way of coping.'

Tammy paused. What Cecil said actually made sense. 'So you think he was runnin' away from his responsibilities by gettin' drunk every night?'

'Exactly! I'm not saying that you or your mother are to blame, because it wouldn't matter who he'd married; it was marriage and fatherhood itself he couldn't cope with. Not that that's any excuse, mind you.'

'Too right it's not! He should've remained a bachelor, not ruined the lives of innocents.'

'I've not a doubt in my mind that I want to be a dad,' said Cecil warmly. 'But I'd not go ahead and marry someone just because I thought that's what was expected of me.'

'Society has a lot to answer for,' said Tammy. She smiled as the band struck up one of her favourite tunes. 'I love this one!'

He held his hand out to her, and together they walked to the dance floor. 'I've only ever danced with the girls, and I've always been the one who led, so I don't know how good I'll be at followin' your lead,' said Tammy as he took her onto the floor.

He grinned. 'Try not to fight me, and I'll do my best to guide you rather than steer.'

Chuckling softly, she nevertheless felt herself stiffen under his touch as she tried to follow his lead, so rather than struggle his way around the floor he suggested, 'Tell you what, how about you close your eyes? That way you'll *have* to rely on me.'

Thinking this a good idea, she did as he asked and found that it instantly changed everything. Not only was he now guiding her around the floor, but she became more aware of his body next to hers, the strength in his arms, the warmth of his hands, and the smell of his cologne.

'That better?' said Cecil, completely unaware of the effect he was having on her.

'Lots,' murmured Tammy, who was very much enjoying this new experience.

From that moment they hardly left the dance floor, and by the end of the evening Tammy was no longer having to close her eyes.

The band struck up the last tune of the evening, which happened to be a waltz.

'The old *one*, two three,' said Tammy as Cecil slid his

arm around her waist. Having started the evening worried that he might try to kiss her, now she placed her cheek against his chest without hesitation. *If Gina could see me now, she'd be crowin' with delight,* she thought. *I hope that bloomin' Harry asks her out soon, cos I'd love to go on double dates with them.*

'Penny for them?'

She smiled. 'I wish this wasn't the last dance of the evenin'.'

'Me too. But there's always next time.'

She glanced up at the underside of his chin. 'I'd like that.'

'Does that mean you think our first date's gone well?'

'Very well, wouldn't you say?'

Cecil leaned back so that he could look into her eyes. 'Extremely.'

She watched his eyes travel to her lips. Was he going to kiss her? Did she mind? Tammy knew she would be disappointed if he didn't, and as his lips met hers she felt her body melt under his touch. With his hand caressing the nape of her neck, Tammy wished the moment would never end, but when the band fell silent and the house lights went up, Cecil broke away as if on cue.

'Well, that was a nice way to end the evening.'

She smiled shyly at him as his fingers entwined with hers. 'I wish we could spend our first Christmas together.'

'Me too, but I think hell would have to freeze over before they gave me leave over the Christmas period.'

'What about New Year?' said Tammy. 'I'll be back for that.'

'I don't see why not. Have you anything in mind?'

She glanced down at their hands before looking back up with a smile. 'I'd quite like to go dancin'.'

He brought her hands to his lips and kissed the backs of her knuckles. 'I was just thinking the exact same thing.'

'So that's settled then. And I've got one evenin' off before I leave for Liverpool – this Wednesday comin'. Do you think you'd be free to meet up somewhere?'

He slid his arm around her shoulders and began to walk her towards the cloakroom. 'I think I can manage that. What would you like to do?'

'How about we watch a movie? Summat light-hearted for preference.'

'Only if you allow me to take you out for dinner first.'

'I knew there'd be food involved somewhere along the line, but yes, that would be lovely. Same place as today?'

He handed the coat clerk his ticket. 'As it's a special occasion, I say we go to the Maltsters Arms because that was the first place we went to together.'

Tammy looked puzzled as Cecil held her coat up for her to put on. 'What special occasion is this?'

'It's our second date, and the last one until New Year,' said Cecil. 'If that isn't a special occasion I don't know what is.'

Tammy waited for him to don his own coat before

sliding her arm through his elbow. 'I still think you could do a lot better.'

He clicked his tongue. 'You need to stop putting yourself down.'

She shrugged. 'Force of habit.'

'But why? You're beautiful, kind and honest. Heck, you've got to be the most genuine person I've ever met!'

Tammy felt her cheeks flush hotly, and was glad to get outside where it was too dark for him to see her properly. Wishing for the ground to swallow her whole, so that she wouldn't have to react to his comment, she was grateful when he spoke again.

'If this is anything to do with you and your ex, you should put it out of your mind. We've all got a past, and I dare say mine's nothing to be proud of, but that's all part of growing up, isn't it? You make your mistakes when you're younger, and learn from them.'

'Things didn't end as well as they could have,' said Tammy truthfully. 'If I could turn back the hands of time I'd do things differently.' *Although how, I don't know*, she thought in the privacy of her own mind.

'There you are! You've learned from your mistakes; no one can ask more of you than that, so stop being so hard on yourself.'

She glanced up at him. She knew she had no right to question him about his life prior to meeting her, but curiosity was getting the better of her. 'You said something about not being proud of your own past?'

'I've no skeletons in the closet regarding girlfriends,

but I could've tried harder than I did in school. Got better grades, and played truant far less than I did.'

Tammy stared at him disbelievingly. 'Truant? You? I don't believe it!'

He cocked an eyebrow. 'Do you really not? Think about it.'

Tammy did just that. As far as she was concerned Cecil was a hard-working, dedicated officer who ... she hesitated, then said slowly, 'Given the way you feel about your fellow officers, and your descriptions of the fat cats of society, I'd say you didn't deal with authority well, is that right?'

'Bingo! I rebelled against anyone who thought they could tell me what to say or do, which included teachers and even the police.'

Tammy gazed at him open-mouthed. 'What did your parents think?'

He gave her a shrewd smile. 'Dad applauded me, but not Mum. In fact, it was only because of her that I started to toe the line.'

'What did she do?'

'She told me that we have rules and regulations for a reason, and that without them the world would fall into chaos.'

'Wise words indeed,' said Tammy, 'because that's exactly what's happened.'

'I always thought that rules were there to be broken, and I still feel that way to a certain extent.' He paused before correcting himself. 'Although maybe not so much about the rules, but more about bigoted opinions. The world is a very different place from what it was when

309

Queen Victoria was on the throne, yet some of these old fellers are still living life as if we were under Victorian rule, and I hate that, because as a race we should be progressing, not sitting stagnant. I hope this war will teach people that things have to change and biased opinions can't be tolerated any more, because this is what happens when someone decides they're better than everyone else.'

'You should run for Prime Minister,' said Tammy, only half joking.

Cecil laughed. 'No thanks. I'm no good at lying and you've got to be top notch at that to be in government.'

She sighed quietly as they reached her bus stop. 'I wish I hadn't dallied so much about us gettin' together,' she said as she held out a hand to the approaching bus.

'Better late than never!' said Cecil. 'I'll see you at the Maltsters on Wednesday. Nineteen hundred hours all right for you?' Giving her the briefest of kisses, he stepped back as the bus drew to a halt.

'Thanks for dinner – and the dance,' said Tammy.

He bowed slightly. 'My pleasure!'

Taking her seat on the bus, she waved to him as it pulled away.

Cecil is dreamy, handsome, and grounded, she thought to herself as the bus crept along the snow-covered roads. *Rory will always be my first love, but with life takin' me in a different direction from our original plan I'm glad I met Cecil when I did. As for his believing me to be the most genuine person he's ever met, I shall have to do as Gina suggested. Never tell him the whole truth about my new identity, but leave Tamara Blackwell where she belongs, because I'm really not that girl any more. He's right: I should stop punishin' myself for the past and look to the future. And the way to do that is by embracing the present!*

Chapter Thirteen

The thought of Tammy's still being alive had weighed heavily on Rory's mind. If Ella was right and she really had survived the blitz, then he could only assume that the rumours which Dennis was putting about were also true. After all, if Tammy really thought she'd killed him, running away before the authorities could catch up with her was the only sensible thing she could've done. True, she could've met up with him as planned, but she'd have been taking one hell of a risk in doing so, given that the argument and potential murder had taken place only hours before they were due to meet up. If that were the case, he wished she'd at least written to him explaining things, but was that asking too much? After all, the postmark on any letter would have betrayed her whereabouts, and what was she even meant to say? All she could tell him without implicating herself in her father's murder was that she was alive and well, and that was about it. She certainly couldn't give him an address to respond to; nor could she arrange to meet him. Was he being selfish by wishing she'd at least done that? Given that she'd honestly believed her father to be dead, and couldn't possibly have known about the bombing, then he had to concede that she had done the only thing she could do under the circumstances. And in any case, why should she bother to let him know that she and her mother were alive and well when she didn't know about Jellicoe House? She wasn't to know that he thought her to be buried beneath the rubble because she didn't know there *was* any rubble. He drew a deep breath. There was no point in dwelling on the past, because there was nothing to be gained by it. By one twist of fate, he and Tammy were over, and even if he were to bump into her tomorrow there'd be no going back, not now, because no matter her reasons he doubted he could ever get past the hurt of being abandoned by the woman he loved most in the world.

So why was he still keeping the new women he dated – if he could call it that – at arm's length? Was he still pining after Tammy? Hoping she'd turn up and they could continue where they left off? Whether she was right for leaving him in the dark or not, it didn't really matter. Tammy had once said that they were like Bonnie and Clyde, together for ever come what may. But when push came to shove that hadn't been the case. Tammy had left him high and dry while she swanned off into the sunset with her mother. Rory scolded himself inwardly for having such a thought. *Tammy did say that the two of us were like Bonnie and Clyde, but at the end of the day nobody knows what they'd really do if they were faced with such a dire situation, and you've already conceded that she had no choice other than to leave you behind. The Tammy I knew would never have run out on me, but the Tammy I knew wasn't involved in a murder, and anyone who's involved in summat like that is bound to change.*

He glanced at his reflection in the mirror. Tammy had done what she did for a reason, and he must accept her decision and move on with his life whether he liked it or not. But how could he do that when her ghost was always haunting him?

Jimmy entered the hut and gave a groan. 'Blimey, who stole your smile?'

Rory caught Jimmy's gaze in the reflection of the mirror. 'What makes you say that?'

'Your face!' said Jimmy. 'You look as if you've got the weight of the world on your shoulders, but it can't be woman trouble, because you don't have one!'

'I wish I did, because I've really got to start movin' on with my life,' mumbled Rory.

'And so say all of us!' cried Jimmy. 'So, what's stoppin' you? It's not as if you're short on offers.'

'I don't know how to let go,' said Rory truthfully.

'It's easy. You forget about the past, and start a whole new life,' said Jimmy. 'For goodness' sake, lad, look around you. Given the circumstances, people are havin' to do that all the time.'

'Whenever I speak to a woman, I find myself instantly comparin' her to Tammy. I've tried not to, but I just cannae help myself.'

'You can't live your life like that. You need to put Tammy far from your thoughts.'

'Easier said than done,' said Rory. 'I feel as though

I'm on a roundabout; I know I need to get off, but I'm hesitant to jump because it won't stop turnin'. Does that make sense?'

'Perfect,' said Jimmy. 'But there's always the chance that should you time it just right, not only will you escape unscathed, you'll be a whole lot happier for doin' so.'

'It's just knowin' when to jump,' Rory supposed.

'You don't jump until you're sure you've picked the right moment. Or in this case, woman.'

'But how will I know who the right woman is? I thought I'd already found the one, in fact I'd have laid my life on it, and look where that got me!'

Jimmy frowned. 'But you said you thought she died in the blitz?'

Rory sank onto his bed. 'I did, until I met someone who thought otherwise, and if they're right, it would seem my belle left Scotland without sayin' goodbye.'

Jimmy pulled a face. 'Tough call! I'm assumin' she had her reasons?'

'Very much so. Not that it helps me any.'

'Look, son, none of us can predict what the future holds, but the less baggage you have, the better chance you've got of makin' it in the long run. And I think I'm right in sayin' your Tammy came with a fair amount of baggage.'

'She had a complicated life, that's for certain.'

'So, you find a woman who's uncomplicated,' said Jimmy, before chuckling softly to himself. 'What am I sayin'? *All* women are complicated, just some more so than others.'

'So how do I tell them apart?'

'You want someone regular, with no prior boyfriend or family issues.'

One of the men who was standing close by gave a disbelieving snort. 'An uncomplicated woman with no family issues? Jeez, Jimmy, where's he goin' to find someone like that? You're not part of a proper family unless you have issues!'

Jimmy mulled this over. 'Orphans!' he said after a moment's silence. 'They don't have family issues!'

Rory furrowed his brow. 'I'm an orphan, so take it from one who knows: you don't have to be livin' with your family to have issues with them. I don't know who my parents were, but I do know they dumped me at the orphanage because they didn't want me.'

Jimmy grimaced. 'You don't actually know that for a fact, though, do you? I dare say most parents who take their kiddies to an orphanage only do so because they don't have a choice. Just like your Tammy, everyone who's made a tough decision in life also has a backstory.'

'That may be so, but it's left me feeling I don't belong anywhere,' said Rory. 'It's horrible not knowin' who you really are, or where you came from. I thought those days were over when I met Tammy, but to learn that she might have gone off without so much as a goodbye makes me feel like I've been orphaned all over again!' He blew his cheeks out. 'That's why I'm findin' it so hard to move on, and that's why it hurts to know she did what she did, even if she didn't have a choice at the time.'

'Do you think she knows how you feel? If she's still alive, of course?' said Jimmy quietly.

'Without doubt, if she's the woman I thought her to be, and I'm sure she is,' said Rory, 'which makes it all the more painful, because even though I know she must have thought she didn't have a choice, I cannae help but think she could've done summat if she really wanted to.'

Jimmy sank down onto his own bed. 'I can only judge your Tammy by what you've told me, but from what I can gather you'd be hard pushed to find someone as beset by complications as she is, because whatever they are they must be really serious for her to behave in such a manner. Do you agree?'

'You couldn't have hit the nail on the head with any more precision if you'd tried,' said Rory.

'I can see why you haven't wanted to put all your eggs in one basket again as far as courtin's concerned, but you're goin' to have to take a chance sooner or later – either that or die a bachelor.'

'I doubt any of the women on base will want me now,' said Rory. 'Not with my reputation.'

Jimmy rolled his eyes. 'If you think that, then you don't know women! They'll all be eager to be the one who "reformed" you. Don't ask me why, but women love to think they can change a man from a Lothario to a loyal husband who wouldn't even *think* of lookin' at another woman.'

'You'd think they'd run a mile rather than hook themselves to a womaniser like that,' said Rory.

'It's why men who like to play the field can continue

to do so,' said Jimmy. 'Each new woman that comes along is hopin' to be the one that tames him.'

'Cos if they do, it shows how special they must be,' said the other man.

Rory appeared thoughtful. 'So they've not got much in the way of confidence, then?'

'Exactly! A woman who knows her own worth wouldn't step foot near a man like that. Mind you, you're not a Lothario, not really.'

'So what I really want is a woman who spurns my attention,' said Rory reflectively. 'Not one that's not interested in courtin' a Lothario.'

'Spot on!' cried Jimmy. 'You'll have to work hard to persuade her to accept your advances, but that's part of the fun.'

The other man nodded. 'There's no sport in landin' a fish straight off the hook. You need to play the reel; bring them in slow.'

Rory brightened. With the advice of his friends, the future wasn't looking so bleak after all.

With only a few days left before she was due to see her daughter again, Grace was down the market trying to find something suitable to give Tammy as a Christmas present.

It cannae be too flash, because I've not got the money for anythin' fancy, and if she really has joined the services I don't think they will allow her much in the way of necklaces an' that, Grace thought as she moved past a stall displaying costume jewellery to another which sold a variety of sensible clothing. She picked up a thick pair of woollen socks, and some sheepskin mittens which she tried on for size. It might not be the dolls' playhouse which Tammy had always wanted, but it was more than Grace had ever been able to give her in the past. *Tammy's a practical girl, and she'll appreciate warm clothin'*, Grace told herself, *and when all's said and done you can never have too many socks!*

She motioned to gain the stallholder's attention. 'I'd like these, please,' she said, holding up the chosen items.

'Right you are, queen, I'll bag them for you now – unless you've one of your own, of course?' said the woman hopefully.

Grace handed over the money, then opened her net bag so the stallholder could place the socks and mittens inside. Thanking her briefly, Grace moved on to the next stall, where she could hear what sounded like an ongoing argument between the seller and a customer.

Tutting beneath her breath, she crossed over to the opposite stalls to give them a wide berth. She knew times were hard, and indeed she pitied those without a roof over their heads, but she found it impossible to condone stealing, especially when the person being stolen from was living hand to mouth as it was.

Keeping her back to the argument, she asked the man on the vegetable stall if he had any carrots that were past their best. She watched as he rooted round for the worst ones, while listening with half an ear to what was going on behind her.

'I never touched your bleedin' tools!' roared the man

who was being accused of theft. 'What would I want with a knife like that?'

Just hearing the accent, which sounded so very much like her husband's, caused an icy chill to run down her spine. Chiding herself for letting her imagination run away with her, she paid and thanked the man for the carrots before swiftly moving on to a stall which she knew sold vanity items. Picking up a beautiful mother-of-pearl handheld mirror, she positioned it so that it showed the arguing men behind her. *It's been a long time since you've heard a Scottish accent*, Grace told herself, *and with Dennis always shoutin' it's only natural that you should hear his voice in the first you've heard in months.* But she felt her blood run cold when the man gripped the stall with both hands and attempted to turn it over. She'd seen Dennis behave in such a manner on more occasions that she'd care to count, and the very memory now flooded her with fear. Frozen with shock, she let the mirror slip through her fingers, to be caught by the stallholder, who cried out in protest.

'Mind out! The last thing we need is seven years' bad luck!'

Grace fumbled a hasty apology. 'I'm sorry, I didn't mean to, but it's not broken, see?'

The woman tutted angrily as Grace hurried away, not stopping until she reached the safety of the shelter. Closing the door behind her, she made sure to slide the bolts across before calling out for Annie, who came at a brisk trot.

'What is it?' Annie's eyes were wide with worry.

'I thought I saw Dennis down the market!' said Grace, tears trickling down her cheeks. She wrung her hands. 'Not that I saw his face, but his voice, his behaviour' – she waved her hands in a theatrical manner – 'everythin' about him reminded me of Dennis.'

Annie tried not to sigh. Grace's supposed sightings of Dennis were now happening on a daily basis, and Annie was certain it was due to her impending meeting with Tammy. 'When you say you *thought* you saw him, is it the same as every other time you've "seen" him recently?'

Grace gave a watery sigh. 'I don't know. I suppose it could be, but I legged it before I had a chance to see him properly.'

Annie placed an arm around her shoulders. 'It's only your mind playin' tricks on you, just like it has been every other time. You know as well as I do that Dennis is dead.' Still seeing the doubt in Grace's face, she added, 'Tell you what, how about we get you a nice cup of tea, and you can tell me all about it. Maybe a chat will help put your mind at ease.' She called out to one of the girls to fetch Grace's bags as she walked her through to the kitchen.

'I feel so stupid, because I didn't actually *see* anythin'; I just heard a Glaswegian arguin' with one of the stallholders,' Grace explained as Annie sat her down by the table. 'I recognised the accent from the very off, but I couldn't believe it was him, so I picked up a vanity mirror to take a look and saw him tryin' to flip the stall of the man he was arguin' with, which is just the sort of thing Dennis would do.'

'So you didn't see his face?' asked Annie, worried that her friend's paranoia was sinking to new depths.

'No. I was that scared I dropped the mirror and legged it.'

'I know you turned me down the other day when I offered to go and meet Tammy in your stead, but are you sure you don't want me to? I really don't mind, and I'm worried you're goin' to give yourself a heart attack before you've been reunited.'

Grace began to shake her head before changing her mind. 'I know you think I'm paranoid, but I've got a really bad feelin' about all this. I know I didn't see his face, but there was somethin' about the way he held himself, and his temper, and the way he talked which made me think it was him, and what if I'm right? I'd be forever kickin' myself for not trustin' my gut. I don't know how he could have found out where I am, and it may well be coincidence that he's here – assumin' it even is him, of course – but no matter whether I'm bein' silly or not, I don't believe in temptin' fate and that's exactly what I'd be doin' if I went to meet her. So if you don't mind?'

'Don't worry. I'm more than happy to do that for you,' said Annie. 'What does she look like?'

'A younger version of me,' said Grace, 'but there's goin' to be hundreds of people out and about on Christmas Eve. Are you sure you'll be able to spot her?'

'There'll only be one person lookin' for their mam,' said Annie. 'And as this won't be the first time I've done this sort of thing, I've every confidence I'll have her back here in no time.'

Grace eyed her curiously. 'You've done this before?'

Annie smiled. 'There've been a few occasions when one of the girls has made contact with a trusted member of the family. I always go to meet them just to be on the safe side.' She shrugged. 'They're easy enough to spot once you've done it a few times.'

'How?'

'The look of bein' lost while searchin' for a familiar face,' said Annie. 'They stand out like a sore thumb, because everyone else knows where they're goin'.'

'In that case, I'd be ever so grateful if you'd do it. I'm pretty confident the polis know nothin' of what happened to my husband, but I really don't want to draw attention to myself. Not when I'm so close to seein' Tammy again.' *Cos I just know summat's goin' to go wrong*, thought Grace now. *Either I'm goin' to give myself a heart attack, or I'll get myself arrested, or Tammy's not goin' to be there.* She closed her eyes as she tried to banish the last thought from her mind. *She'll be there*, Grace told herself. *Cos I don't know if I can carry on if she's not.*

Tammy nudged Gina as Harry scanned the long queue of people outside the stores, as if searching for someone. 'Don't look now, but your stalker's just arrived,' she quipped.

A blush sweeping her face, Gina chided Tammy for making fun. 'I swear I'm goin' to scream if he doesn't ask me out soon, cos this is gettin' ridiculous, and your teasin' doesn't help.'

'Hello, Harry!' called Tammy, much to Gina's dismay. 'What brings you here?'

Swallowing, Harry waved back. Tammy could see visible beads of sweat pricking his forehead as he walked towards them. 'I, er, I needed some boot polish,' he said, smiling nervously at Gina.

'You should get to the back of the queue, then,' teased the man standing behind Tammy.

Harry, who was staring at Gina as though caught in a trance, said, 'Not for me thanks,' much to the mirth of everyone in earshot.

'Take no notice of them, Harry,' said Gina, shooting a chiding glance to those around her. Harry's throat bobbed as he smiled shyly back at her.

'I've been meanin' to ask you . . . well, that is to say . . . I've been wonderin' . . . although of course you don't have to if you don't want to . . .'

Gina stared blankly at him. 'Sorry?'

He ran a nervous tongue over his bottom lip before trying again. 'Do you come here often?'

Tammy pinched her nose to quell the laughter that threatened to spill out as Gina looked towards the stores room. 'Quite often, yes.'

Seeing the queue ahead of them move forward, the man behind Tammy spoke up again. 'For cryin' out loud, lad, will you just ask the lass out? Either that or step out of the queue so the rest of us can get on with our day?'

Tammy smiled sympathetically as Harry's cheeks burned ever brighter. 'Leave the lad alone, Derek,' she scolded as she and Gina closed the gap in front of them. 'It's hard enough without you addin' your tuppence-worth.'

His ears matching the colour of his face, Harry took

a deep breath before closing his eyes. 'Can I take you out for dinner some time?' The words finally out, he opened his eyes and stared anxiously at Gina.

'As in a date?' Gina asked cautiously.

'Yes – unless you'd rather not . . .' Harry began, but Gina, who was beaming from ear to ear, cried 'Yes' before he could talk himself out of it.

Harry stared at her, a slow smile spreading across his cheeks as they made arrangements to go out the following evening, and Derek winked at Tammy. 'Thank Gawd for that!'

Still beaming, Harry gave Gina a small wave good-bye before he tripped over his own feet as he headed back down the queue.

Waiting until he was out of earshot, Tammy turned to Gina with an air of excitement. 'Well?'

'Well what?'

'Where are you meetin' him and when?'

'We're meeting the same time and place as you and Cecil, because he has a few errands to run first. You don't mind, do you? Only I don't want to wait for him on my own.'

Tammy rubbed Gina's shoulder in a reassuring manner. 'Of course I don't. If it wasn't your first date, I'd suggest you join us.'

'Maybe after a few dates we will? I honestly never thought he'd actually ask me.'

'That makes two of us,' said Derek as they slowly moved up the queue. 'I think havin' a lass on his arm will do him some good, cos he's not what I'd describe as "one of the lads".'

That's one of the things I like about him, thought Gina. *After all, who wants a Lothario for a husband?*

Cecil picked up the purse and clicked the kiss-clasp open and closed several times before placing it in his pocket. He knew that the clasp on Tammy's purse was unreliable, after she told him how she'd recently scattered loose change on the floor of the bus when she'd gone to pay the clippie.

Having no idea what sort of purse Tammy would like, he'd gone for one that was both simple and functional; hoping that she would approve of his choice, he had been pleased when the sales assistant affirmed his taste.

'I'd be thrilled if my boyfriend bought it for me,' the woman had said. 'Whoever she is, she's a very lucky girl.'

Now he watched one of the corporals driving towards the main gate; it would be far quicker for him to cadge a ride to Woodbury rather than catch the approaching bus, but Tammy's recent words had given him food for thought.

It shouldn't matter that she's a corporal and I'm an officer, he thought now as he stuck his hand out to flag down the bus, *but I know the top brass won't see it that way.* The bus came to a halt and he jumped aboard, paying his fare before taking a seat. *Although what difference it makes to them I don't know.* He pictured himself introducing Tammy to his fellow officers, and the look of disdain on their faces as they realised who she was. *They think others will judge them by the company I choose,* thought Cecil, *but I'd rather be with Tammy than them any day of the week! All they do is sneer at those below them, which is rich considering the lower ranks are the ones taking all the risks. And they're the same when it comes to the women; far from appreciating the amazing work they do, they see them as an embarrassment – something to be ashamed of.* He pictured the officers he knew and the women they'd chosen to marry. *Not one of them has married a working woman; they're too conceited for that. Instead they go for the women that come from money – preferably with a title – because that's what matters to them!* A frown creased his brow. Such men were no better husbands than Tammy's father. *They'd be far happier if they married women such as Tammy; what a pity it is they're too arrogant to either know or care.* He paused as this thought caught up with him. *I couldn't think of a woman I'd rather marry,* he told himself. *She's perfect in every way. Witty, intelligent and beautiful to boot, what more could a man ask for?*

It was the evening of Gina's first date with Harry, and she was sitting on the bus with Tammy as it headed into town.

'Are you nervous about meetin' him?' Tammy asked as she watched Gina twist the strap of her handbag around her fingers.

'A little bit, but I'm mainly excited,' Gina confessed. 'I never thought this day would come, and now it's here I don't know what to do with myself.'

'Have fun and enjoy yourself!' said Tammy. 'I know it's early days, but I already think that you and Harry make a lovely couple.'

Gina smiled. 'We do, don't we? I know he's a bit shy, but I find it quite endearing. Certainly better than those that consider themselves to be cock-of-the-walk.'

'He's far from that.' A look of nostalgia took over Tammy's features. 'We've come a long way since leavin' Clydebank. I for one certainly didn't think we'd be goin' into town to meet our beaus nine months after joinin' the services!'

'Nor me!' said Gina. 'But aren't I just glad everythin' worked out the way it did. Our lives could have been very different had we chosen different routes!'

'I couldn't agree more,' said Tammy. 'And with the past behind us, there's nothin' to stand in our way. I see bright futures ahead for both of us, although yours will undoubtedly be brighter than mine should you go back for the . . .' she mouthed the word *money*.

Gina's face grew dark. 'I've been thinkin' about that a lot lately, and I wish to goodness I had burned it or chucked it in the river rather than hide it where it could be traced back to us,' she said. 'That' – here she also mouthed the word before continuing aloud – 'will only bring misery. You've only got to look at how it was obtained in the first place to know that.'

'I've been thinkin' the same thing,' admitted Tammy, 'but I imagine we're safe enough, because there must've been a whole host of people staying in that room since we were there, so even if it's been found I don't think they could trace it back to us.'

'Unless the receptionist remembers us,' said Gina. 'It was written all over her face that she didn't think us capable of payin' to stay somewhere as swanky as that.'

Tammy's eyes widened as she remembered the snooty receptionist who'd questioned Gina's heritage. 'I hadn't thought of that. What do you suppose we should do?'

'There's not a lot we can do at the moment bar keep our fingers crossed,' said Gina. 'But if I can think of a way to get rid of it without gettin' caught I'll be sure to let you know.'

'We've got away with it up to now,' said Tammy. 'We'll just have to hope our luck continues to hold.'

The bus came to a stop and the girls thanked the driver as they stepped onto the pavement. 'Just think: if tonight goes well, you and Harry will get to spend your first Christmas together.'

'I was thinkin' about that while I was lyin' in bed this mornin',' said Gina. 'I can't not give him a pressie, but what do you buy for someone you don't know very well?'

'How about sweets?' suggested Tammy. 'Everyone likes sweets.'

'Thanks, Tammy, that's a great idea! If I could knit and sew like you I'd have knitted a scarf like the one you've made for Cecil.'

'I just hope he likes it.'

'I think he'd like anythin' you made for him because it came from you,' said Gina. She felt her stomach lurch as she saw Harry waving from outside the pub. 'Wish me luck!'

'Good luck – not that you'll need it,' Tammy assured her. 'And remember: have fun!'

'Ditto!'

Tammy pulled off her scarf as she stepped into the warmth of the pub. Seeing Cecil already nursing a drink at the bar, she went over to join him. 'Have you been here long?'

'Around five minutes.' He gestured to where they could see the snow falling outside the window. 'Was that Gina I saw you with just now?'

Tammy beamed. 'It certainly was! She's just gone off on her first ever date, with a lovely chap by the name of Harry.'

'Ah! The shy chap, am I right?'

'That's the one! Fancy you rememberin' that!'

He took her coat from around her shoulders and hung it up on the clothes horse which stood beside the bar. 'I like Gina, and I get the impression she's been a good friend to you.'

'She has that.' Tammy looked to the barmaid, who was waiting patiently to take her order. 'I'd like a lemonade, please.'

'And I'll pay,' said Cecil, withdrawing his wallet from his pocket.

'You spoil me,' said Tammy, as he counted out the correct change.

'You deserve to be spoilt,' he said, taking her drink from the barmaid. Glancing round, he indicated a table close to the fire. 'Shall we?' He waited for her to take the lead before following behind with their drinks.

'I always feel like such a lady when I'm with you,' said Tammy as he set down their glasses and pulled her chair out for her.

'Good. Because that means I'm behaving like a

330

gentleman, which would please my mother greatly. And talking of mothers, you must be awfully excited about seeing yours on Christmas Eve.'

'Unbelievably so!' said Tammy, who after a quick glance at the menu had already made up her mind to try their pie and mash for a change. 'I cannae wait to give her a big hug!' *Providin' nothin's happened to prevent her from comin'*, she added, in the privacy of her own mind.

'Have you arranged anywhere to stay?'

'Not yet. I thought I'd see whether she's got room to put me up for a night or two. With precious little time together, I'd rather stay with her, even if it means I have to kip on the floor.'

'You have to make the most of every second,' concurred Cecil, who was still perusing the menu.

'Which is why I'm determined to see more of her come the new year.' Tammy hesitated. Should she give him his gift now, or would it embarrass him if he hadn't got her anything in return? As she was wondering what to do the barmaid came over to see if they were ready to order.

'I'll have the pie and mash, please.'

Cecil smiled up at the barmaid. 'And I'll have the faggots, please.'

Tammy waited until the woman had left before turning her attention back to Cecil. 'You know how we won't be seein' each other again before Christmas?'

'I do, which is why I got you a little something.' As he spoke he pulled out the purse, which was wrapped in coloured tissue paper, and handed it over. 'Merry Christmas, Tammy.'

It was plain to see by the pleased look on Tammy's face that she was delighted with his choice. 'It's lovely, Cecil! What made you think of a purse?'

'I knew yours was a bit iffy,' said Cecil, 'and I didn't want you travellin' to Liverpool with no money because you'd lost yours on the floor somewhere.'

Placing her handbag on the table, she took out the brown paper bag which contained the scarf she had knitted and handed it to him. 'Merry Christmas to you too, Cecil. I hope you like it.'

Cecil gave an approving smile as he wrapped the scarf round his neck. 'It's perfect, but I wouldn't expect anything less coming from you! You truly are gifted, you know.'

Pleased that he was happy with her present, Tammy smiled. 'It's very kind of you to say that, because I really wanted to get you somethin' you liked.'

He grinned. 'And I really wanted to give you that purse before I had an accident and someone found it on me!'

Tammy laughed out loud. 'I hadn't thought of that!' She eyed him fondly. 'I'm so glad that you turned out to be everything I thought you were. If it wasn't for your peers everythin' would be just perfect.'

'And while I'd love to be able to shout about you from the rooftops, I don't trust them not to try and put a spanner in the works, so I think you were right in suggesting we keep our relationship quiet, just for the time being.'

Tammy pulled a guilty grimace. 'I'm afraid it's nigh on impossible to live with a bunch of women without them knowin' the ins and outs of your personal life, but the ones that know about us have all promised faithfully that they'll not breathe a word, and I believe them.'

'They're a good bunch at Woodbury, and if any of them do slip up, then who knows? It could be for the best.' He nodded with approval as the barmaid placed their food down on the table. 'A meal fit for a king,' he said, as the woman headed back behind the bar.

'You can keep your caviar,' said Tammy, before adding, 'Not that I've ever tasted it, but who wants to eat fish eggs?'

'I tried it once, at one of the officers' dos,' said Cecil, who was mixing the gravy into his mash. 'I didn't think much of it at all.'

'That's because you're a meat and two veg man,' said Tammy. 'Do you think you get that from your father?'

'Possibly. He certainly doesn't like fancy food.'

They ate the meal in relative silence, only commenting on the fullness of the pie, or the smooth mashed potato. Once they'd finished, Cecil raised his brow. 'Pudding?'

She laughed. 'Order me whatever you'd like and you can have the other half.'

Grinning, he called the barmaid over and ordered two portions of spotted dick, and asked her to bring the bill at the same time. 'They say the way to a man's heart is through his stomach,' said Tammy, 'I think that's certainly true in your case.'

'Not in my dad's, though,' said Cecil. 'Not with Mum's cooking.'

'If that was the case, what do you think did attract him to your mother?'

'Her heart,' said Cecil at once. 'Dad said she spoke from the heart, and that her voice was that of an angel.'

Tammy gazed at him. 'Well, the apple certainly didn't fall far from the tree. You've definitely got your father's way with words.'

'Does that matter if the meaning behind them is genuine?'

'Not at all! I just cannae believe my luck at times.' Her inner voice was quick to remind her that she had had bad luck as well as good, causing her to add, 'Although there are times when I don't want to believe it.'

'You mean when you have bad luck?'

'I do indeed. Except for meeting you, I always seem to have bad luck.'

The waitress returned and placed the puddings down on the table, leaving the bill beside Cecil's plate. 'I think most people feel that way,' he said, as he fished out the correct money. 'Except for the bit about meeting me, of course.'

'You eager for the off?' said Tammy.

'We've not got long before the next showing starts at the cinema,' said Cecil. 'You know what it's like: if I waited until the end of the meal before paying we'd end up missing the beginning of the film.'

They both fell silent as they tucked into the delicious pudding, and when Tammy had eaten her fill she handed the rest of hers over to Cecil, who quickly polished it off. Standing up, he held Tammy's coat for her to put on before donning his own.

'Why does the time always fly when I'm with you?' she asked as he held the door open for her.

'Because you're enjoying yourself,' said Cecil. 'I know that because it's the same for me.'

'I hope it doesn't go that fast when I'm with Mammy,' confessed Tammy as they walked arm in arm to the cinema.

'It'll pass in the bat of an eye,' said Cecil. 'Everything that's long awaited always does.'

'I wonder how Gina's date with Harry's goin'?'

'Are you worried for her?'

'Only in the sense that I feel like a mother whose daughter's gone on a first date,' said Tammy. 'Which is silly, I know, because she's perfectly capable of lookin' after herself. It's just that she's such a lovely girl, and I want everything to be perfect for her.'

He laughed. 'You sound just like a mother. Which is no bad thing.'

'Why d'you say that?'

'Because you've obviously got a natural maternal instinct,' said Cecil, 'which means you'll make a brilliant mother.'

'I'd be pleased if I was half as good as my own mammy.'

They entered the cinema, and Cecil bought the tickets.

'I wish you'd let me pay once in a while,' said Tammy as the usherette showed them to their seats. 'I can hardly fight my corner for equality when you pay for everythin'.'

'And spend the next ten minutes picking coins up off the floor?' chuckled Cecil.

'Ah, but I have a nice new purse now, thanks to you,' Tammy reminded him.

'And that's where your money shall stay as long as I'm around,' said Cecil. 'And as I'm on considerably better pay than you, you can think of it as equalling us out.'

They took their seats and Tammy smiled as he slid his arm around her shoulders pulling her close. *He's too much of a gentleman to try and kiss me when we're sitting cheek by jowl with so many people,* she thought as the cinema lights dulled. *More's the pity!*

She was glad they'd chosen a comedy, but sad at the same time because once again the time went by in a trice. With the credits rolling, she turned to Cecil. 'I'm goin' to have to hurry if I'm to catch my bus.'

He smoothed his hand over the back of her head. 'I wish we had longer.'

'Me too. And even though I'm lookin' forward to seein' Mammy, I wish she was comin' here so that I could get to spend Christmas with you both.'

'Maybe next year?'

Tammy swallowed. Everyone in the services thought it bad luck to talk about the future when the present was so uncertain.

Hearing the silence that followed his suggestion, he guessed her thoughts as he got up from his seat and held his hand out to her. 'I don't believe in tempting fate either,' he said, as he walked her along the row of seats. 'If your time's up, it's up. It makes no odds what you say or do.'

'That may be so, but I'm willing to try anythin' and everythin' to help keep us safe,' said Tammy. 'And if that's followin' a bunch of superstitious nonsense, then so be it.'

'So, you do believe in tempting fate?'

'Kind of. I guess it's a bit like the bad luck thing.'

He stepped out onto the pavement and turned his collar up against the cold wind that was blowing icy air down the nape of his neck. 'Now that I think about it, maybe you're right. My believing that I had to pay the waitress sooner rather than later, for fear she'd be too busy and we'd miss the start of the film, was a bit like tempting fate, I suppose.'

She smiled primly. 'See? Not just a pretty face, am I?'

His eyes twinkled in the moonlight as they met hers. 'Indeed not.'

It didn't take them more than a few moments to reach the bus stop, and as she looked down the road for the bus she saw Gina and Harry approaching. 'They're holdin' hands!' she hissed. 'It must've gone well!'

Cecil placed his arms around her waist, pulling her close. 'In that case I'd best kiss you goodbye before they get too close.'

Tammy felt her heartbeat quicken in her chest as the warmth of his lips sent her tummy into a wave of somersaults. She wished they could have longer together, but she would make sure they spent every spare minute in each other's company after Christmas. At the sound of approaching bus wheels driving through the wet slush, Cecil broke away.

'Always on time when you don't want them to be,' he said despondently.

Tammy jutted her bottom lip out in a regretful manner. 'Isn't it always the way?'

He looped an arm over her shoulders as Gina and Harry neared. 'You must be Harry?' he said, using his free hand to shake Harry's.

Turning puce at being addressed in such an informal manner by an officer, Harry's Adam's apple bobbed nervously in his throat. 'Yes, sir,' was all he could manage. Gina bade Cecil a quick hello and goodbye before following Harry onto the bus, and Cecil turned his attention back to Tammy.

'Merry Christmas, Tammy. Say hello to your mother for me, won't you?' He kissed her briefly on the lips before stepping back as she boarded the bus and took a window seat so that she could wave to him until he disappeared from view.

'I've never had an officer call me by my first name before,' said Harry, whose cheeks were returning to a more natural colour.

'Cecil's different from the others,' said Tammy. 'Did you have a nice evening?'

'Lovely,' said Gina, who was trying to swallow her smile.

'Grand,' agreed Harry, his cheeks beginning to ruddy once more.

Seeing the sloppy smiles that adorned their faces,

Tammy knew she'd be better off waiting until they got back to the relative privacy of their hut if she wanted to get anything other than small talk from Gina. Turning so that she faced the front of the bus, she daydreamed about Cecil and the dates they would have when she returned. *We shall spend every spare moment of our time together*, she thought; *maybe even go on double dates with Harry and Gina.* Wondering how Harry would cope if he were to spend an evening of dinner and dancing in the company of an officer, Tammy decided that Cecil would soon put him at his ease. *Once he gets to know Cecil he won't feel nearly so uptight around him.* She then envisaged the many other officers she'd come across and how different Cecil was compared to them. *You've struck gold, Tammy Lloyd; Cecil Carter is one in a million!*

Back at the camp, the girls bade Harry goodbye, and Tammy waited until he was out of earshot before demanding the nitty-gritty.

'I thought I'd have the devil's own job gettin' a word out of him,' said Gina, 'but he's very different when he's on his own.'

'Oh?'

'Aye. He talked about his parents, and his time at university.'

Tammy was impressed. 'University? Is he a bit of a boffin, then?'

Gina nodded. 'Very much so. He's hopin' to become a lecturer when the war's over.'

'Gosh! He must be a brainbox!'

'His family sound wonderful, and he wasn't at all fazed by my bein' an orphan.'

Tammy furrowed her brow. 'Why would he be?'

Gina gave a half-shoulder shrug. 'Nobody wants someone else's cast-offs.'

Tammy's face grew stern. 'Don't ever describe yourself that way, because it's just not true. My Rory was an orphan, and you couldn't hope to find a lovelier man than he.'

'Goodness. I don't know why, but I assumed he was from a proper family.'

Tammy wrinkled her nose. 'A lot of people might describe my family as proper, with two parents and a child, but it just goes to show how deceptive appearances can be.'

'Like Cecil and Harry,' supposed Gina, 'because they don't look how they actually are.'

But Rory did, thought Tammy now; *what you saw was what you got.*

'You're thinkin' about him again, aren't you?'

Tammy blushed. 'When you say him . . .'

'Rory,' said Gina.

Tammy grimaced meekly. 'I do try not to, honestly I do, but I just cannae help myself.'

Gina smiled kindly. 'What will be will be. It's only natural for you to think of him, I realise that now, because I cannae stop thinkin' of Harry when we've only been on one date!'

Tammy smiled back. 'When you watch these romantic films it all looks so easy, but it's far from that. Love can be complicated.'

'All you can do is be yourself and see what happens. It might prove to be a tough ride, but it'll all work out in the end,' said Gina, 'cos true love always shines through!'

Eager to make sure that he was there in plenty of time, Archie had arrived in Liverpool the day before Christmas Eve. As soon as he stepped off the train he'd asked one of the railway guards for directions to the Liver Building and was pleased to learn that it wasn't far away. However, he was disappointed to discover that the impressive building had more than one entrance. Pacing the outer perimeter, he came to the conclusion that if he were going to meet someone he'd choose the grandest entrance: the one closest to the canal. With that settled he went off to find somewhere to lay his head for the night, as well as buy himself some supper.

Having found a boarding house nearby, he bought himself a round of sandwiches and took a stroll into the city, where he followed a crowd of people to St George's Hall and through the gates of the public grounds. Liverpool was proving to be far more impressive than Clydebank; so much so that it led him to wonder whether Tammy and Grace would want to return to the city they once called home. *Not that it matters if they don't,* Archie reflected, *cos even with Dennis gone I suppose the place holds bad memories for them, but at least I can tell them they don't have to spend the rest of their lives lookin' over their shoulders, which I should imagine is an awful way to live.*

***

CHRISTMAS EVE 1941

Tammy felt the excitement rise as the train pulled into Lime Street Station. The train ride hadn't been as long or indeed as arduous as the previous journeys she'd undertaken by rail, but it seemed to her as though it had taken forever to reach Liverpool. Eager for the off, she had collected her small suitcase from the rack above her head and was making her way to the carriage door before the train had come to a complete halt. Jiggling anxiously, she craned her neck to see where the guard was, and was relieved to see that he wasn't far away.

Clutching the suitcase in her hand, she took a few deep breaths as she tried to steady her nerves. *Everythin's goin' to be just fine, she* told herself as the guard opened the carriage door; *you're worryin' over nothin'.*

Descending onto the platform, she caught the attention of a rail worker and asked for directions to the Liver Building, repeated them back to him a couple of times, and thanked him before setting off at a brisk trot. So keen was she to get to the point of rendezvous, it seemed no time at all before she saw the grand building loom into view. *With a bit of luck Mammy will be there already;* she thought as she hurried on. *What a surprise she'll get when she learns that I'm a driver in the ATS who's bagged herself an officer! I just hope she's had half the luck I have, and it would be wonderful if she too has joined the ATS, because then if we're lucky we might even end up on the same camp.* Her face dropped as another, more urgent thought announced itself. If her mother had joined the services she might not have been as fortunate as Tammy when it came to having Christmas off.

Unless she's done the same as me, Tammy thought, *and given up the rest of her leave in exchange for these two days.* She nodded to herself. When it came to decisions Tammy and Grace were like peas in a pod, and she had no doubt in her mind that her mother would have done exactly that.

Grace paced the hall as Annie got ready to meet Tammy.

'Are you sure you'll be able to recognise her?'

'Positive. Now stop your worryin', I'll have your Tammy back before you can say knife.'

Grace sighed heavily. She knew she was being cowardly by not going to greet Tammy herself, but the thought of going outside on such a momentous day was giving her the heebie-jeebies, because she'd convinced herself that Tammy was not going to show up. Not that she'd admit that to Annie, of course. *I couldn't bear it if I were the only one who turned up, because I would know for certain then that my darling daughter might not have made it, and I could never forgive myself for that.*

Keen to ensure that he was outside the entrance to the Liver Building in plenty of time, Archie had arrived an hour before many people were about, and was now standing at the top of the steps to the main entrance, a position which he considered afforded the best vantage point possible. His arms folded, he went through the plan one more time. As soon as he saw Grace or Tammy he would make himself known and tell them the good news. What he'd do after that he wasn't quite sure, because it depended on how long it took them to turn up. If they were late, he'd have to dash so that he didn't miss the train back to Scotland, but if they were early . . . maybe tea and a bun somewhere?

The poor things are in for the shock of a lifetime, thought Archie as he kept a keen lookout, *but at least they won't have to live in fear of the polis any more* . . . Suddenly, he spied a woman who he thought could be Tammy. Keen to ensure that he didn't approach the wrong person, he subjected her to a long hard look until, convinced he'd identified her correctly, he hurried down the steps to greet her.

Unsurprisingly, Tammy was alarmed to see a man waving to gain her attention as he hastened towards her. Hoping it was something to do with her mother, she responded cautiously, only recognising him when he drew near.

'Good God!' she exclaimed. 'What are you doin' here?'

Archie quickly explained the conversation he'd had with How d'you do Henry. 'So you see, you're not wanted for attempted murder or anything of the sort, and if rumours are to be believed your father's no longer in Clydebank, so it would be safe for you to return should you wish to do so, especially after the polis have heard your version of events!'

The colour flushed Tammy's face. 'I'd heard rumours that he was alive, but I wasn't sure whether to believe them until now.' She held a hand to her stomach while fixing Archie with a look of grave concern. 'I swear I was just tryin' to stop him from stranglin' me mammy. I had no intention—'

Archie cut her off short. 'I know you wouldn't have done anythin' to him on purpose. It was obvious to everyone that he must have been the aggressor, cos he always was. I'm only here to let you both know that you can stop runnin'.'

She eyed him incredulously. 'You came all this way just to tell us that?'

He nodded. 'It seemed wrong that you and your mammy were on the run when you'd done nothin' wrong while he was walkin' round scot free tryin' to make out that you were the ones to blame.' As he spoke he led the way back up the steps, explaining as he went that the top was the best spot to see people from. 'I'll watch the west side; you watch the east,' he said. 'That way we should spot her quite quickly.'

Hurrying up the steps of the Liver Building, Annie began to scour the area for a young woman matching the description Grace had given.

'She's like me: auburn hair, green eyes and pale skin,' Grace had reiterated, 'only her hair's curlier than mine.'

Now, as Annie scanned the melee below, she realised that spotting Tammy might be difficult if she was wearing a hat or a scarf like so many of the women in the throng of people hurrying back and forth. With only a few minutes to go before the clock struck noon, she began pacing the top step like a cat on a hot tin roof. Grace had told her to go to the main entrance, but had she told her daughter that nine months ago? Even if she had, they'd both been under a huge amount of stress when making their plans, so either one of them

345

could've got the meeting time or the destination confused. Hearing the clock strike twelve, she nigh on
jumped out of her skin.

Stop panickin', she told herself. *The trains haven't run
on time since the war began, and what with it bein' Christmas Eve the situation will only have worsened. It could be
another hour before she arrives, so for goodness' sake get a
grip and stop expectin' the worst!*

As she turned to pace the steps again, she collided
with a man who was looking as anxious as she felt.
Apologising briefly, she sidestepped him, and that's
when she saw the young woman in ATS uniform looking out uneasily over the crowded street. Annie stared
hard at the auburn hair beneath the woman's cap.
Keeping her fingers crossed, her heart was in her
mouth as she approached the red-head. 'Excuse me?'

The woman turned to face her, and Annie saw the
same smiling green eyes she saw whenever she looked
at Grace. 'Tammy?'

Fearing that something awful must've happened to
her mother, Tammy stared at the stranger ashen-faced.
'Where's my mammy?'

Annie held up a reassuring hand. 'Don't worry, she's
safe and well. She sent me here to meet you because
she had quite a scare yesterday – I'm Annie, by the
way, a friend of your mam's.'

Archie had hurried across to join them, and Tammy
quickly introduced him to Annie. 'Archie was our ARP
warden when we were livin' in Clydebank; and Archie,
this is Annie. She's a friend of Mammy's.'

Archie furrowed his brow. 'Sorry to ask, but did I hear you say that you're here instead of Grace?'

Annie smiled. 'I was just explainin' to Tammy that Grace had a bit of a fright yesterday. It was somethin' and nothin', but we thought it best if I came to greet Tammy cos she's a bag of nerves at the moment.'

Tammy eyed her anxiously. 'What kind of a scare?'

'She thought she saw your father, and even though she knows it couldn't possibly have been him, it's put her on edge.'

Tammy looked at Archie, then turned back to Annie. 'I'm not sayin' she did see him, but it might not be as impossible as she thinks.'

Annie stared at her, somewhat confused. 'Sorry, but what did you just say?'

'It turns out he wasn't dead after all,' said Tammy. She looked to Archie with a questioning expression, and after a brief pause the warden told them everything he knew.

Annie's eyes rounded. 'Flippin' 'eck, talk about a turn-up for the books! Maybe your mammy was right not to leave the shelter.'

'She needn't worry about Dennis,' said Archie. 'Apparently he was last seen boardin' a train to Llangollen and nobody's seen or heard from him since.'

Tammy was looking skyward as though expecting to see the Luftwaffe. 'Annie, when you say shelter . . . ?'

'Oh, not an air raid shelter,' Annie said quickly. 'This is a home for women who've landed on hard times for one reason or another, but mainly because of men. I met your mammy when she was looking for a job and invited her to join us.'

Tammy was relieved to hear that Grace was safe and well, but hearing that her mother thought she'd seen Dennis the previous day was enough to give her kittens even though she felt it couldn't possibly be true. 'Can we talk while we walk? Only I'm that excited to see her!'

'Of course!' Annie smiled at Archie as they descended the steps. 'I must say, I think it's awfully good of you to have come here like this. There's not many men who would go to the lengths you have.'

'Just tryin' to right a wrong,' said Archie gallantly.

'Living in the shelter means I can be a bit quick to tar all men with the same brush, and that's wrong of me, because I know there are some good ones out there, like you.'

'And my Cecil,' said Tammy.

Archie shook his head. 'I could've sworn he said his name was Rory . . .'

The comment was so out of the blue it brought Tammy to a halt.

'You saw Rory?'

The warden shrugged. 'Yes. It was Rory what told me how he was helpin' you and your mammy run away from your dad. Poor beggar, he was breakin' his heart outside Jellicoe House.'

Tammy felt her cheeks bloom with guilty shame. 'Poor Rory. I would've done anythin' to have him come with us, but not under the circumstances in which we had to leave.'

'You did what you had to do,' said Archie. 'I under-stand that now more than ever, and I'm sure he will too, if you ever see him again.'

Rather than tell him about the returned letter, she said: 'He's better off without me. Too much water has passed under the bridge since I left Clydebank.'

'For which I feel partly responsible,' murmured Archie as they continued on their way.

'You?' cried Tammy in surprise. 'How on earth did you come to that conclusion?'

'I knew what Dennis was like. If I'd stepped in sooner none of this would've happened and you'd still be in Clydebank with Rory.'

Tammy was quick to put him straight. 'And just suppose you had? My dad would have accused you of havin' feelin's for my mammy and clocked you one; her too, come to that. I appreciate you wantin' to help, but in truth you'd have only made matters worse, which is why most people chose to not get involved.'

'That may be so,' said Archie grimly, 'but I'm not proud of myself, especially given that Rory wanted us to check that you and your mammy were out of the house when the sirens were goin' off, and I refused to even look.'

'And a good job you didn't, cos me and Mammy were long gone by that time, and probably Dad too, so you and Rory might both have died for no reason.'

'I know you're only tryin' to make me feel better, and perhaps you're right, but I'm still not proud of myself for turnin' a blind eye for all them years.'

'You've a conscience,' said Annie, 'which puts you

349

above people like Dennis, and Tammy's right when she says he might have turned on you, because we've had women in the shelter whose saviours have been murdered for tryin' to do the right thing.' She gestured to a large house ahead of them. 'This is us.'

Archie stopped. 'Then this is where I say my good-byes. If I hurry I should be able to catch the next train back to Scotland.'

Tammy stared at him open-mouthed. 'You're not stoppin'?'

'I've done what I came to do,' said Archie. 'Besides, I really don't want to miss my train.'

'But surely a cup of tea?' Annie insisted.

'Sorry, but I daren't. Knowin' my luck, it'll be early for once!'

'Can you not even say hello?' said Tammy. 'I know my mammy would want to thank you for lookin' out for us.'

Archie had already half-turned. 'There's really no need. Tell her I'm sorry for not doin' summat sooner.' And with that he left.

'It's a shame he didn't stop to say hello,' said Annie as she placed her key in the lock. 'I know he feels guilty, but your mam never blamed anyone for not steppin' up.' As she spoke she opened the door, only to stare in horror at the sight which met them.

'A little late to the party,' growled Dennis, as light glinted off the knife which he was holding to Grace's throat, 'but like they say, better late than never, hey?'

Chapter Fourteen

Tammy moved to rush forward but stopped quickly as her father lifted the knife higher up Grace's neck.

'I don't understand,' she cried. 'We thought you were in Llangollen!'

Looking somewhat surprised to learn that his daughter seemed to know what he'd been up to, Dennis merely shrugged. 'I was, but as you two obviously weren't I went back to Clydebank.'

'So how the hell did you know where to find us?'

He grinned evilly. 'You've How d'you do Henry and a skinful of alcohol to thank for that. He never could keep his mouth shut after a few drinks.'

But Tammy was still confused. 'But Henry couldn't possibly have known where Mam was livin'.'

Keeping her eyes locked on Grace, who was looking as guilty as sin, Annie spoke in hollow tones. 'Grace?'

A tear trickled down Grace's cheek. 'I'm so sorry. I know I shouldn't have, but I was so worried you wouldn't recognise her.'

Annie lowered her gaze. 'You came to the Liver Buildin'.'

Dennis grinned wickedly. 'Like a lamb to the slaughter, luckily for me, cos had she stayed put I might never have got me money back.'

'So you saw us with Archie,' said Annie softly.

Dennis's grin broadened. 'I know when I'm outnumbered.'

Looking somewhat confused, Tammy cut in. 'What money?'

'The housekeepin' money you nicked when you left me for dead,' thundered Dennis. 'And don't even think of lyin' because I found the jar empty just before the bombs began to fall.'

Tammy stared at him incredulously. 'You came all this way for two bob?'

'It was the only money I had,' snarled Dennis. 'Two bob might not be much to you, but it was the difference between startin' again or endin' up on the streets for me.' He dug the flat of the blade into Grace's throat. 'And with no money I was left destitute.'

Annie held up a hand. 'I'll get you your two bob . . .' but Dennis was shaking his head.

'They owe me at least ten quid given everythin' I've lost.'

'Ten quid!' cried Tammy. 'Where the hell are we meant to get that kind of money?'

He shrugged. 'Not my problem.'

Tammy stared at her father. Getting bombed out of his home would've taken its toll, but it wouldn't have stopped him from going back to work and renting somewhere new, and she said as much, finishing with: 'I don't get it. Why spend so much time and effort chasin' two bob which you could easily earn down the docks?' She paused before adding, 'Not to mention the stuff you pinched as a sideline.' Suddenly, realisation dawned. 'So that's why you come home early that day! You were given the sack for pilferin' stock!'

'That's where you're wrong!' snarled Dennis. 'I never took nothin' what wasn't mine!'

Realising that he hadn't denied the dismissal, Tammy rallied. 'Well, they didn't sack you for no reason!'

'They accused me of stealin' a wallet when I found it,' said Dennis. 'And everyone knows the rule of finders keepers.'

'Does any of this really matter?' interjected Annie, who was eager for Dennis not to become more agitated than he already was. 'When all's said and done, Tammy and Grace haven't got that kind of money!'

A bead of blood bloomed on Grace's neck as Dennis pierced her skin with the tip of the blade. 'Then get it!'

Wondering where they could lay their hands on such an amount, a vision of the hotel room in Carlisle entered Tammy's mind. Gina had said she'd do anything to get rid of the money without getting caught, and if Dennis took it they would be killing two birds with one stone. She fixed her father with a wooden stare. She hated the thought of giving him something he didn't deserve, but she'd do anything to get him away from her mother, and this could mean they'd see the back of him for good. 'You can have the money, but you'll have to go to Carlisle in order to get it.'

Dennis laughed in her face. 'You must think I was born yesterday!'

'Not at all,' said Tammy, 'I know where there's a stash of cash hidden in a hotel in Carlisle.'

Dennis eyed her with disgust. 'And you expect me to let your mammy go and trot off to Carlisle on your say-so, do you?'

Tammy shook her head. 'I expect you to let my mammy go and take me to Carlisle, because I know where the money's hidden.'

'And jump the train at the first opportunity, no doubt,' said Dennis, continuing in damning tones, 'I think not.'

'I'll go with him,' said Grace, who was eager to protect her daughter while doing her best not to swallow.

'But you don't know where it is,' said Tammy, aghast at the thought of her mother going anywhere with Dennis alone.

He narrowed his eyes. 'I knew it! You're lyin'!'

Tammy shot him a look of pure hatred. 'No, I'm not! Because unlike you, I don't lie! We hid the money under one of the floorboards in room twenty-three.'

Dennis paused as he stared back. He knew his daughter of old, and he could see by the look in her eyes that she was telling the truth, but why hide the money instead of taking it to a bank? He asked Tammy as much.

'Because I haven't got a bank account!' snapped Tammy. 'And before you ask, I'm not cartin' the best part of a hundred quid round Britain with me either!'

Dennis lifted the knife away from his wife's neck.

'How the hell did you get your hands on that sort of money?'

'That's of no concern to you,' said Tammy. 'You either want it or you don't. Which is it to be?'

'I want it all right,' said Dennis greedily, 'but your mammy's coming with me, so if you're sendin' me on some wild goose chase it'll be her that pays the consequences. Same goes if you call the polis.'

Tammy held her hands up. 'No tricks, I swear.'

Dennis lowered the knife so that it was just below Grace's ribs. 'C'mon then, tell us where it is.'

'Room twenty-three, the Crown and Mitre Hotel, Carlisle. There's a loose floorboard under the bed nearest the window. You'll find the money hidden in a satchel between the joists.'

'What happens if someone's stayin' in the room?' said Annie, who would rather iron out any issues before Dennis left the house with Grace.

Dennis looked to Tammy for the answer.

Tammy turned to Annie. 'Have you a telephone?' Annie nodded, and Tammy turned her attention back to her father. 'Then the answer's simple. Phone the hotel and book room number twenty-three. Should they ask why you want that room in particular, make up a lie. You're good at them,' she finished sarcastically.

Hooking his arm around his wife's waist so that the knife was still below her ribcage, he followed Annie through to the telephone and made the call.

'Please don't tell me you're playin' for time,' Annie hissed to Tammy, 'cos I dread to think what he'll do should he turn up to the room to find there's no money.'

'Oh, it's there all right,' said Tammy, adding quickly, 'I'll tell you where it came from when he's not around.'

Dennis reappeared. 'If I find out you're playin' silly beggars . . .'

Tammy shot him a withering look. 'Why the hell would I do that? It may not have grabbed your attention, but my mammy means everythin' to me and I wouldn't do anythin' to risk her life.'

Grumbling incoherently, Dennis jerked his head at his daughter. 'I've got no money for the train, or for the hotel.'

Tammy immediately opened the purse which Cecil had bought her and fished out enough for those expenses. She was about to hand it over when she had another thought. 'How do I know you're not goin' to harm Mammy once you've got the money?'

He grinned nastily. 'You don't, but then again, what choice do you have?'

'I'll come with you . . .' Tammy began, but he was shaking his head.

'No you won't. I know first-hand what the two of you together are capable of. It'll just be me and your mammy.'

Realising that she was about to lose control of the situation, tears pricked Tammy's eyes. 'Please don't hurt her. I've done everythin' you've asked, and more.'

Grace smiled bravely. 'If he killed me, there'd be nowt stoppin' you from goin' to the polis. He'll not risk the noose if he has the money.'

A tear trickled down Tammy's cheek as she watched

her mother leave the house, with Dennis's knife still wedged below her ribs.

Archie paced the platform as he waited for the train to arrive. He had wanted very much to see Grace to say that he was sorry for not having intervened when he'd had the chance, but somehow he didn't feel his apologies would be enough. *I was all too willing to turn the other cheek because I didn't think it right to get involved in someone else's marriage,* he thought bitterly, *but now it seems Grace could have died as a result.* He thought of his reaction to Edie and Stella's accusations down the air raid shelter, when in fact Grace had been fighting for her life just a few hours before. *I accused them of bein' gossips, even encouragin' that poor lad to not listen to a word they had to say, and why did I do that when I knew they could well be tellin' the truth?* The answer hit him like a brick. *Because you couldn't bear to think of Grace in that situation, and by acknowledgin' their words you'd be acknowledgin' the fact that you should've done somethin' sooner.* He heaved a sigh. Grace was safe, though no thanks to him, and that's all that mattered. The train pulled into the station, and he waited for the passengers to descend, which they did in dribs and drabs. Heading over to one of the empty carriages, he noticed a man and a woman who appeared to be having difficulty boarding. *What are they doin'?* he thought as he watched them try to board the train without breaking contact with each other. Assuming that the woman must have mobility problems, he headed over to lend a hand, and that's when he realised that the woman was in fact Grace, and the man Dennis. Determined never to stand idly by again, he was on the brink of intervening when he saw the glint of the knife blade.

His heart pounding in his chest, he looked around to see if he could catch sight of Tammy or Annie, but they were nowhere to be seen. His mind raced as he tried to work out what could have happened for Grace to be in such a position, but there was no time to waste. If he wanted to help her, he would have to try to get a seat in the same carriage. Lifting his collar to hide his face, he pulled down the tip of his hat and boarded the train. He saw where Grace and Dennis were sitting, hurried to the seat which was back to back with Grace's and sat down as causally as he could so as not to gain their attention, wishing fervently that he knew what was going on. The only answer he could come up with was that Dennis must've found out where Grace was living and intercepted her before Tammy and Annie got back. *Poor Tammy won't have a clue that her mother's with her father,* thought Archie now, *but what a good job I didn't go in for that cup of tea, else I might have missed the train and none of us would know where Grace was, or who she was with!*

Tammy had given her parents a five-minute head start before hurrying to the station with Annie, who was eager to be sure that Tammy boarded the train without her father's knowledge. 'There's no tellin' what he'll do if he sees you,' she told Tammy as she jogged alongside her.

'Which is why I fully intend to stay out of sight,' said Tammy. 'I know where the hotel is, which is more than he does, so I should be able to get there before them and make sure he doesn't hurt her. I know better than to take him at his word.'

When they reached the station, Annie and Tammy made sure they kept out of sight whilst they scoured the crowded platform. First spotting Archie, and then Grace and Dennis, Annie gasped, 'Oh, no!'

Tammy, who was still looking for her parents, turned to face her. 'What?'

Annie indicated Archie. 'I'd forgotten about him. What if he says or does summat to panic your dad?'

Tammy groaned inwardly. 'We're just goin' to have to hope he doesn't do anythin' rash. I'm sure he knows Mam would never willingly go with Dad.' They watched Archie stride towards her parents before suddenly hanging back, and she breathed a sigh of relief. 'Thank goodness for that. I thought he was goin' to wade in feet first for a minute there!'

'Look at the way he's lifting his collar and pulling the peak of his hat down,' said Annie. 'He definitely knows summat's up.'

Tammy felt relief sweep over her. 'He's sittin' in the seat that's back to back with Mam's! There's no doubt about it: he's stayin' close by to see if he can do somethin' to help. What do you reckon? Should I take the seat next to him?'

Annie looked at Tammy, who had borrowed one of Annie's headscarves to hide her flaming red hair and an overlarge mackintosh to cover her uniform, before shaking her head. 'Still too risky. Dennis won't be expectin' a man, but he'll definitely be keepin' an eye out for you, because he knows you won't be happy to leave him alone with your mam.'

'I wish I could speak to him – Archie, that is – because that way the two of us could put our heads together and come up with a plan to save her.'

Annie took a pencil and paper from her handbag and began to write hastily. She handed the note to Tammy. 'Make your way down the carriage in the direction where your mam and dad won't see your face, and hand the note to Archie as you go past.'

Tammy read the note, which simply said, *I'm in the next carriage behind you. Tammy*. She pushed the note into her pocket before hugging Annie goodbye. 'Thanks for everythin', Annie. I'll be sure to let you know what happens.' Turning on her heel, she hurried towards the carriage, making sure to keep her head lowered.

Boarding just before the guard closed the doors, she made her way between the rows of seats and dropped the note onto Archie's lap without breaking stride. She entered the next carriage and chose a window seat which faced the same way as her mother's.

Waiting for the train to get underway she resisted the temptation to look over her shoulder, but when Archie failed to show up after a good ten minutes had passed an awful thought occurred to her. What if the note had dropped off Archie's lap and fallen beneath the seat? Worse still, what if her father found it?

Beads of sweat pricking her brow, she was relieved

when Archie sank into the seat next to hers. 'What's goin' on?' he hissed.

Keeping her voice barely above a whisper, Tammy quickly explained the situation, finishing with '. . . we need to stop him before he takes her to the hotel.'

'So there's no money?'

Tammy sighed wretchedly. 'The money's there all right, but what's to stop Dad killin' me mam before leggin' it? That kind of money could get him a long way from Blighty, cos he knows the sort of people whose silence can be bought.'

Archie lifted an eyebrow. 'Is there any point in my askin' where you got the money from in the first place?'

She flashed him a fleeting smile. 'Take my word for it, you're better off not knowin', but safe to say I had nowt to do with it, and the girl who did come across it has paid a heavy price for pickin' up the wrong satchel!'

'That will do for me.'

'Trust me, no one innocent is missin' that money. What worries me is how we're goin' to get me mammy away from me dad with no one innocent gettin' hurt.'

'It needs to be done as publicly as possible,' said Archie, 'and without givin' Dennis a clue as to what's takin' place until it's too late.'

'Hit him from behind type of thing,' said Tammy.

He turned to face her slowly, as though he'd had a revelation. 'Now that might not be such a bad idea!'

Having spent the entire train journey wishing he'd gone to the toilet before encountering Grace, Dennis was relieved when the train pulled into Clydebank station. If they hurried he would be able to use the hotel's facilities as soon as he'd confirmed the money was in the room.

Prodding her with the tip of the knife, he growled at her to get up. 'Just remember, I know where to find Tammy, so don't even think about tryin' to run off.'

Grace got to her feet, and with the knife still close to her ribs she walked in front of Dennis to join the queue of people waiting to disembark. As soon as the guard opened the door the people ahead of them quickly filtered onto the platform, and with Grace having to descend before Dennis he had no choice but to temporarily remove the blade from her ribs. With one foot in the air as he prepared to step down, Dennis was alarmed to find himself sprawling face down on the platform as someone – far heavier than Grace – barrelled into the back of him. Cursing as the knife flew from his grasp, he was about to get to his feet when he saw Tammy and Archie standing over him.

'What the—' Dennis was beginning, when Archie bellowed, 'Somebody stop him! He's got a knife!'

Furious beyond words, Dennis grabbed his knife, only to see a policeman making his way through the gaping passengers. Scurrying to his feet, he spat in Tammy's face. 'Go to hell!'

Tammy turned to her mother, who was white with shock as she watched Dennis push his way through the crowded platform. 'Are you OK, Mam?'

In reply, Grace took her daughter in a tight embrace. 'I'm so sorry, luv.'

Wiping her mother's tears, Tammy smiled through

her own. 'Don't be daft. What've you got to be sorry about?'

Archie gave her a knowing look. 'Aren't you forgettin' summat?'

'Of course!' Tammy turned back to her mother. 'I won't be a minute; I've got to make a quick phone call.' She hurried away, and Archie turned to the policeman, who was approaching with caution.

'Is everythin' all right?'

Archie gave him an apologetic smile. 'Not to worry. I thought I seen some feller with a knife, but I guess I was mistaken.'

Grace appeared confused as the policeman walked away. 'Why didn't you tell him the truth?'

Archie tapped the side of his nose. 'Because I believe in karma!'

Cursing his treacherous daughter for foiling his plan, Dennis was determined to get to the money before Tammy. *She's done all this just so that she could get to the money before me,* he told himself as he stopped a stranger to ask for directions. He grimaced as the smell of urine reached his nostrils. When he'd fallen from the train he'd lost control of not just the knife, but his bladder along with it. Slowing down as he approached the hotel, he did his best to smooth his hair down and make himself look more presentable.

Walking to the desk, he told the woman – who was regarding him with distaste – of his reservation and waited for her to fetch the key. Throwing the money onto the desk he snatched the key from her hand, muttering 'Snotty cow!' beneath his breath. The woman watched him climb the stairs and enter the door to the room, before heading through to the back of reception.

Desperate to see whether his daughter had been telling the truth, Dennis wasted no time in moving the bed and pulling the rug back before using the knife to prise the floorboard up. To his surprise the satchel was there, and the briefest of glances was all it took for him to see that she had not been lying to him. Scarcely able to believe his luck, he toyed again with the notion of using the hotel's facilities, but quickly dismissed the idea. Tammy's attitude at the shelter, along with the way she'd attacked him coming off the train – he had no doubt it was she who had barrelled into him – was enough to persuade Dennis that she was also the one who'd struck him over the head before leaving him for dead back in Jellicoe House.

Clutching the satchel, he trotted back down the stairs and threw the key on the counter as he passed reception, mildly puzzled as to why the receptionist was not questioning his decision to leave so early. All became clear when two police officers emerged from the office behind her.

'It's mine!' yelled Dennis as they cuffed him. 'I don't know what that bitch told you but the satchel and everythin' in it's mine.

Opening the bag, one of the officers raised his brow. 'Are you sure about that?'

Dennis nodded fervently. 'I won it playin' the pools in Liverpool.'

The other officer looked inside the satchel and tentatively removed the knife with his gloved hand. 'I'll wager you didn't win this on the pools.'

Dennis stared in horror at the knife, which still bore the dried blood from its last victim. 'That ain't mine!' he protested.

The officer appeared confused. 'Then why did you say it was?'

'Because I didn't know it was ruddy well in there, did I?' Dennis roared. 'It's obvious I've been set up.'

'What makes you say that?'

Dennis shot him a scathing glance. 'Don't give me that. I know you were tipped off.'

The policeman pulled a face. 'We had a phone call from the hotel months ago to say that one of their maids had discovered the money, but I'd hardly call that a tip-off.'

Dennis stared at him in utter disbelief. 'If you knew about the money, why is it still there?'

The officer smiled. 'I know you probably believe the police are stupid, but we're really not, you know. It's obvious someone was going to come back for that money; all we had to do was wait.'

Dennis could hardly believe what he was hearing. People booked rooms all the time; he said as much to the constable.

'Aye, they do that,' said the constable, 'but they don't normally ask to book a room by its number. Not unless there's a reason for it, of course.'

Dennis's face fell. When he had booked, the woman on the other end of the phone had asked if any room would do and he'd said it had to be room twenty-three. When she asked why, he'd told her to mind her own business.

'I can tell you whose money it really is,' Dennis began, but the policeman was laughing softly.

'And why would we believe you, when you swore blind it was yours in the first place?'

'Because this time I'm tellin' the truth,' pleaded Dennis. 'You've got to believe me! I know what this must look like, but that's down to them what tried to set me up.'

'Ah, the anonymous tip-off, who never tipped us off?' said the policeman as he led Dennis out of the hotel to the waiting paddy wagon.

'I ain't gettin' done for murder,' said Dennis as he was guided into the back of the van. 'You ain't goin' to hang me for somebody else's crime! I may be a lot of things, but I'm not the sort to go round stabbin' people!' The policeman pushed him down onto the bench and he let out a yelp as he sat on something sharp. Leaping up, he watched the blood ooze from his trouser leg.

His brow rising, the policeman gingerly slid his hand into Dennis's pocket and pulled out the knife Dennis had used to threaten his wife. 'God forbid we should think you the sort of feller to go round carryin' knives,' said the policeman sarcastically.

It was well into Christmas Day before Tammy, Grace and Archie walked back into the shelter.

'I'm glad you phoned from the train station,' said Annie as she poured the tea into four cups, 'but that

366

hasn't stopped me from worryin' he might head back to Liverpool now he knows where you live.'

'I dare say he won't give us a second thought now he's got the money,' said Tammy. 'Good riddance to bad rubbish.'

Annie looked to Archie. 'I'm glad you came back with them, but what made you change your mind?'

Archie glanced fleetingly at Grace before turning his attention back to Annie. 'I wanted to make sure that Dennis didn't hop back on the same train as them,' he confessed, 'but mainly because I don't really fancy goin' back to Clydebank yet where I could face some uncomfortable questions.'

Annie looked at him quizzically. 'Such as?'

'Why I went harin' off to Liverpool in the first place,' said Archie. 'If the polis talk to How d'you do Henry, they'll know that he told me about Tammy and Grace still bein' alive, and that in itself will raise all kinds of other questions, none of which I have an answer for. Or not one that I'd want to give, at any rate.'

Annie gave him a knowing smile. 'And is that the only reason why you don't want to go back?'

Blushing slightly, he glanced briefly at Grace, who was smiling at him. 'I also thought it might be nice to accept Grace's kind offer of spendin' Christmas with you all; save me bein' on me tod.'

'You may find that you prefer Liverpool over Clyde-bank,' said Annie, who hadn't missed the furtive glances he kept flashing in Grace's direction. 'I'm sure you'd get a job here easily enough should you wish to do so.'

Archie gave her an embarrassed smile. 'I suppose it

wouldn't harm to ask; it certainly beats goin' back to Clydebank.'

'But what about your work; your home?' said Tammy. 'Surely you cannae just up sticks like that?'

He shrugged. 'When I'm not workin' as a warden, I work for the railway, and I can do that here just as easily as I did in Clydebank. And I cannae see a problem with my stayin' on at the b&b until I find a room to rent.'

Grace smiled. 'You'd do well in Liverpool.'

He smiled back. 'I think so too.'

Barely able to contain the grin that was threatening to split her cheeks, Annie got to her feet. 'Now that we've sorted that, who's up for a bit of Christmas dinner?'

Tammy, who couldn't wait to see the feast which awaited them, stood up from her chair. 'Yes please! I've been lookin' forward to this all mornin'!'

They followed Annie through to the kitchen, where a whole host of women, young and old, were putting the last touches to the meal. Archie's eyes lit up as he scanned the fare on offer. 'Is that bread sauce?'

'It certainly is,' said Annie, and she pointed to each of the other dishes in turn. 'Leeks in white sauce, stuffin', various veggies, Yorkshire puds, fried cabbage with black pepper, roast potatoes, and murkey.'

He gazed at the food in admiration. 'How on earth did you manage to get all this?'

Grace beamed proudly. 'It's the beauty of so many women livin' under the same roof. We've all been savin' our coupons, and puttin' our rations together in readiness for today.' She glanced at Tammy, who was looking equally happy. 'Maisie's even done a real Christmas pud, includin' the brandy sauce, believe it or not.'

The expression on Archie's face caused everyone to laugh. 'No wonder none of you need a man to get by. You're doin' a much better job on your own!'

The comment got him a round of 'Hear, hear's!

'I wish I could've brought Cecil to meet you, Mam,' said Tammy as they watched the women laying the table.

'From what you told me about him on the train he sounds wonderful,' said Grace, before adding, 'Does that mean you're completely over Rory?'

'I put Rory out of my mind a long time ago,' confessed Tammy, before a guilty bloom called her out as a liar. 'Or rather I tried to, once I realised he'd returned my letter without comment, but he keeps comin' to the forefront of my thoughts no matter how hard I try to forget him.'

'Poor Rory. He must've felt terribly hurt and betrayed to have turned his back on you like that.'

'And I don't blame him, which is why I shall respect his decision,' said Tammy. 'But that doesn't mean to say that I can just move on as though I haven't a care in the world, not when I'm not bein' entirely truthful.'

'Truthful about what?'

'My new identity, amongst other things,' said Tammy. 'For a start, I cannae tell Cecil that I entered the services under fake ID because it would put him in an

369

awkward position, what with him bein' an officer an' all. I cannae even be honest with him about my time here with you, because he'd want to know where the money came from and that would mean implicatin' Gina.' She sighed. 'Our relationship is built on numerous lies, only he doesn't know it.'

'Why do you have to tell him the truth about changin' your name?' said Grace. 'It's not as if it's made any difference to who you are.'

'Because I don't like lyin' to him,' said Tammy miserably, 'and it *has* made a difference to who I am, because I *never* used to lie!'

'And just suppose you end things with Cecil, what then? Are you never goin' to date again? Or are you goin' to go back to bein' Tamara Blackwell, in order to feel at peace with yourself?'

Tammy flinched at hearing her old name. 'I *never* want to go back to bein' a Blackwell.'

'So why not embrace Tammy Lloyd? Because that's who you are, and once you're married your name will change again anyway, but that won't mean that you do.'

'But what do I tell him about this Christmas? I really don't want to add another lie on top of the rest.'

'Tell him the truth: that your father kidnapped me, and you and Archie came to my rescue.'

'Even though it's not the whole truth?'

Grace folded her arms across her chest. 'Did you see your father collect that money from the hotel?'

Tammy looked perplexed. 'You know I didn't.'

'Then how can you be sure he did?'

'And if he didn't how can I be sure he won't come lookin' for his pound of flesh further down the line?' said Tammy glumly. 'Because if he does, Cecil will learn the truth, and what then?'

'You cannae live life like that,' said Grace. 'Besides, you've beaten your father on two separate occasions and I don't think even he would be stupid enough to go for third time lucky. If he's not retrieved the money then that's his lookout, but we both know what he's like, and there's not a doubt in my mind that he'll have gone for it.'

Tammy imagined her father taking the bag from under the floorboards and opening it. She gasped, causing her mother to look at her in alarm.

'What?'

'There was a knife covered in someone's blood in that satchel!'

Grace laughed. 'If your father's seen it, all sorts of scenarios will be goin' through his head, the biggest of which bein' that you killed someone in order to obtain the money.'

'It's not funny, Mammy!'

'Oh yes it is! Don't you see? Not only did you wallop him when he attacked me, but then you go and kill someone for a stash of money. Once your father sees that knife he'll not come within a hundred miles of you.'

'But I'm not a murderer . . .' Tammy began, before Grace interrupted.

'*He* doesn't know that, does he? And why are you so bothered about what people think of you? I can kind of understand your concern as far as Cecil goes, but your dad? Surely you don't care what he thinks?'

'I don't want him to think I'm anythin' like him, because I'm not.'

'Your father wouldn't come to anyone's rescue the way you have,' said Grace, 'and he'd certainly never put his family before his own safety as you did. The two of you couldn't be less alike, and he knows that.'

'I hope so.'

Grace changed the subject. She had noticed Archie merrily chatting to some of the younger women, and she indicated this to Tammy. 'What do you make of him wantin' to stay in Liverpool?'

'I think his excuse for not goin' back is just that, an excuse,' said Tammy. 'If you ask me there's only one reason for him wantin' to stay in Liverpool and I'm standing next to her.'

Grace felt her cheeks grow warm. 'That's what I thought.'

Tammy arched an eyebrow. 'And?'

A slow smile formed on Grace's cheeks. 'Did you hear me say anythin' to discourage him?'

Tammy's eyes widened. 'But you hardly know him!'

'I know that he could've let sleepin' dogs lie when he was in Scotland, but when he realised what was what he was determined to put things right and he needn't have done that. Also, he could've told the polis about his conversation with How d'you do Henry, but he didn't do that either, because he wanted to tell us first. A lot of people might've thought we deserved every-thin' we got, but he didn't. All in all, he's a good man, with a kind heart, and I don't have to explain my past to him because he already knows and he *still* likes me, warts and all. In short, I know enough about Archie to know I could do a lot worse.'

'And that's my trouble with Cecil,' said Tammy. 'He doesn't know everythin' about me.'

'No one knows everythin' about anyone,' said Grace. She gazed at Tammy thoughtfully. 'Are you *sure* this has nothin' to do with your feelin's for Rory?'

Tammy sighed. 'I tell myself that I'm over him, but I don't know if I truly am. I often wonder what would happen if I were ever to run into him again. A lot of water has passed under the bridge since I wrote to him; he might feel differently now.'

'It sounds to me as though you're livin' your life on "what if"s, and you cannae live like that. Nobody knows what's round the corner; you should know that better than most. You might never find out what happened to Rory, so you must live your life for today, cos as the sayin' goes, none of us are guaranteed a tomorrow.'

'I'll never forget him,' said Tammy quietly.

'And no one's suggestin' you should,' said Grace. 'I know you're uncertain of where your true feelin's lie, but it'll all come out in the wash sooner or later. These things always do.'

'How do you mean?'

'You might find that you don't love Cecil as much as you did Rory, and if that's the case your relationship will come to a natural end.'

'And what then?'

Grace held up a hand to calm her daughter. 'You might find someone you love more than Rory *or* Cecil.'

'Do you think it possible to be in love with two men at the same time?'

'I do indeed, but I also think you'll find you love one just a wee bit more than the other. But either way . . .'

Tammy finished the sentence for her. 'It'll all come out in the wash!'

'Precisely! And you know that business about you not wantin' to tell Cecil about you changin' your name?' Tammy nodded. 'If he truly loves you he'll not bat an eye, especially when he hears your reasonin' behind it.'

'But what if I tell him and he reports me?' said Tammy. 'I could be court-martialled.'

'Ah, but you'll only tell him when you know the time is right,' said Grace wisely.

'I suppose I hadn't known Gina long when I told her about my fake identity,' mused Tammy.

'True, but you knew she had a satchel full of money and a bloodied knife in her possession,' said Grace, 'so she had as much to lose as you, should either of you decide to tell tales on the other. Not only that, but the discovery made you kindred spirits, because you'd both been forced into a dreadful situation through no fault of your own.'

'I just hope I'm not stringin' Cecil along, because he's too nice for that.'

Grace motioned for Tammy to join her at the table as everyone started to take their places. 'Just suppose you hadn't done any of the things you have but gone about everythin' the right way, yet six months from now you discovered that you and Cecil weren't as perfect a match as you'd first believed. Would you think of yourself as havin' strung him along for all that time?'

'No. Because no one knows whether they're right for each other at the beginnin' of a relationship.'

'Bingo! So, what's the difference between that situation and this?'

Tammy sighed. 'Because things didn't end naturally between me and Rory, and I don't think they would have, had Dad not come home when he did.'

'So you are still in love with him, then?'

Tammy blew her cheeks out. 'I think I must be, because I wouldn't feel so awful about my behaviour otherwise.'

'That's called havin' a conscience, but either way, only time will tell whether you and Cecil have a chance of makin' it,' said Grace as she spooned some sprouts onto her plate before passing the bowl on to Tammy. 'And I think Cecil would rather take the risk than have you end things on the basis of "what if".'

Tammy passed her mother the bowl of bread sauce after taking a scoop for herself. 'He's been ever so patient with me. He even took me out on a just friends basis so that we could get to know each other better before gettin' into a relationship.'

Grace arched an eyebrow. 'He sounds very considerate.'

'He's put me first all the time we've known each other,' said Tammy. 'He even respects my wish not to go into the ins and outs of mine and Rory's break-up.'

'Picture yourself standing with Rory and Cecil in front of you.' Grace licked an errant bit of bread sauce off her thumb. 'You have to choose one; the other will be heartbroken. Who do you choose? And don't go off sympathy, or loyalty – go off what your heart tells you.'

With Annie saying grace, Tammy tried to do as her mother advised, but it was no use. Saying a brief 'Amen', she turned to her mother. 'No matter how hard I try, I cannae separate my heart from my head.'

'And that means you're not ready to make a decision yet,' said Grace calmly. 'You'll know when you are.'

'How?'

'Your heart will let you know!'

After the best Christmas of her life, Tammy was on her way to Lime Street station with an entourage of women from the shelter.

'You've been a real inspiration to some of these girls,' Annie told her as they avoided the puddles on the rain-wet pavements.

'I have?'

'Don't sound so surprised! You've proved that a woman can make it on her own no matter the odds stacked against her.' said Annie. 'You've seen your dad off twice, and you're forgin' a promisin' career in the services. I've heard a few of them discussin' the idea of joinin' up, and that's down to you.'

Tammy blushed. 'Even after everythin' I did in order to get there?'

'*Especially* after everythin' you did! A lot of these

women aren't here just because they're escapin' a violent relationship – they could go anywhere to do that – but because they believed they couldn't make it on their own. You're livin' proof that's not the case! You've shown them that life can still go on, but it's up to them to make that happen.'

'I think a lot of it might be more by chance than anythin' else in my case,' said Tammy. 'I don't know where I'd have ended up if it hadn't been for Gina.'

'I expect she feels the same way,' said Annie. 'And, whether by fluke or by fate, it doesn't really matter. You both made a future for yourselves without the aid of a man, and the girls find that inspiring when they've had men tellin' them the exact opposite all their lives.'

Tammy glanced to her mother, who was walking side by side with Archie. 'I never thought I'd see Mam with another man, but I'm glad she found Archie.'

'He's a rare find indeed,' Annie agreed.

Tammy eyed her curiously. 'Have you never been tempted?'

Annie shook her head fervently. 'Not because I don't believe in love or owt like that, but . . .' She shrugged. 'Your mother once said that the shelter is a vocation for me and I rather think she's right, because if I wasn't here I don't know what would happen to a lot of these girls. You could say the shelter is my love, and I can't bring a man into the mix because it wouldn't be fair to him *or* to the girls.'

'I suppose the important question is are you happy?'

'Very much so!'

Grace turned to wait for them. 'I wish you didn't

have to leave so soon. Is there any chance the ATS might post you closer to Liverpool?'

'There's always a chance, unless I ask them, of course,' said Tammy. 'They don't like to do things unless it's their idea.'

'Well, I could always come and visit you in Woodbury,' said Grace. 'I'd get to meet Gina and Cecil that way.'

Tammy beamed. 'They'd love to meet you, and it would be nice for you to see where I live – not that I could take you around the camp or anythin' like that, but I could take you into the town; show you where Cecil takes me dancin' and our favourite pubs and cafés.'

Grace linked her arm through Tammy's. 'I thought you were grown up when we parted, but you've matured a lot more since then.'

'It's bein' free of Dad,' said Tammy. 'When I was with Rory we daren't breathe for fear that he would find out, but it's not like that with Cecil. I feel as free as a bird when I'm with him.'

'And as an officer, he can show you the kind of life you'd never have had with Rory.'

Tammy gave her mother a sidelong glance. 'I know, and I cannae help but feel guilty about that, even though Rory's status in life had nowt to do with my feelin's for him.'

'But as you've already said, Rory's made his own feelin's clear. It doesn't matter how much you love someone if they don't feel the same way, and it sounds as though you've found someone very special in Cecil.'

'He's not the same as the other officers,' said Tammy. 'Cecil thinks the war will bring about a lot of changes, or rather he hopes it will, because he says he's sick and tired of seein' women bein' treated as second-class citizens when they pull their weight as much as the men.'

'An officer *and* a gentleman,' said Grace. 'You really have found a diamond in the rough!'

Dennis sat with his head in his hands as he explained the situation to the police officer yet again.

'It was my daughter that set me up. Her name's Tamara Blackwell. She was the one what told me where the money was. Why won't you believe me?'

'Because we only have your word for it,' said the constable.

Another officer chimed in. 'And when we phoned your local constabulary they confirmed your daughter and your wife had died in the March blitz.'

'How can they be dead when I've just sat on the same train as them?' snapped Dennis. A sudden thought occurred to him. 'Can't you ask the other passengers? They'd vouch for me! And while you're about it, check that knife for my fingerprints, cos you won't find a single one.'

'Firstly, I'm not goin' to waste my time goin' off on some wild goose chase, and secondly I'd be surprised if we found any prints on that knife, because no one would be stupid enough to leave any behind!'

Dennis shot them both an acute glare. 'If you cannae find any prints on the knife, and you cannae find a murder to link it to, then what the hell am I doin' in here?'

'You were in possession of a hell of a lot of money which doesn't belong to you,' said the first officer.

'Finders keepers,' said Dennis with lightning speed.

'A bit more than that when you knew exactly which room to find it in,' said the second officer, adding, 'not to mention the pools you supposedly won it on!'

Dennis deftly ignored the last comment. 'And just how the hell did a maid find money underneath a floorboard? If that isn't iffy, I don't know what is! If you ask me she's in on it with my wife and daughter!'

The officer viewed him through narrowing eyes. 'When you hammered the floorboard back into place, one of the nails nicked a waterpipe. It took a while for the water to seep through, but when it did they traced the leak back to the pipe.'

'I never nailed the flamin' board back in place,' thundered Dennis. 'It was Tammy what did that.'

The constable looked at his partner. 'I've heard of poltergeists movin' things, but hammerin' a floorboard back into place?'

'You're goin' to have to let me go sooner or later,' glowered Dennis, 'cos you ain't got anythin' on me.' *And when you do*, he thought, *I know exactly where I'm headed!*

Chapter Fifteen

It was New Year's Eve and Tammy and Gina were getting ready for their double date with Cecil and Harry.

'How does Harry feel about spendin' the evenin' with Cecil? He looked like a deer in the headlights when they first met.'

'Poor Harry, he does tend to wear his heart on his sleeve,' said Gina as she ran a comb through her hair. 'I've told him to treat Cecil like one of the boys, but whether he'll be able to or not only time will tell.'

'I must say, I'm really lookin' forward to seein' Cecil. It feels as though I've not seen him for ages!'

'Not surprisin', considerin' all that you've been through since you saw him last.' Gina hesitated. 'Have you decided whether you're goin' to tell him any of it?'

Even though the hut was empty Tammy still glanced around to check they couldn't be overheard. 'I want to, because I cannae keep lyin' to him, but at the same time I don't want to drop you in the mire.'

Gina waved a dismissive hand. 'Don't you worry

about me; I've had a good think and I reckon you should tell him.'

Tammy was looking dubious. 'How come?'

'Because when all's said and done, I didn't do anythin' wrong, and I don't see why either of us should be forced to lie about somethin' that wasn't our fault.' She pushed her foot into the toe of her stocking as she spoke. 'I don't know of a single person who would've handed that money over to the polis knowing what the repercussions would be, and let's face it, no matter how good my intentions, I would've paid a hefty price for tellin' the truth.'

'Exactly! So why do it now?'

'Because back then I was more frightened of the Billy Boys comin' after me than I was of the polis, particularly with them havin' my address, but not any more, especially now the money's gone. I feel bad about not comin' forward as a witness to a murder, but had I done so I'd have had the life expectancy of a lemming runnin' towards a very steep cliff!'

'Are you sure you don't mind me tellin' Cecil? Only once the cat's out of the bag there'll be no puttin' it back.'

'If it means you don't have to tell him any more porkies, that's fine with me, because I know how much you hate concealin' the truth from him. Besides, the money is a pivotal part of your story, because what would've happened to you and your mam without it?'

'I honestly don't know, but things would've turned out very differently, and probably not for the better,' supposed Tammy. 'And had Mam not got on that train,

Archie couldn't have come to her rescue, and they'd not have got together as a result.'

'So, all's well that ends well.'

'For once! But if you don't mind me tellin' Cecil, does that mean that you're goin' to tell Harry?'

'Already have,' said Gina primly.

Tammy stared at her, full of open-mouthed admiration. 'What made you decide to do that?'

'Watchin' you wrestle with your conscience! I couldn't bear to go through that on a daily basis, so I figured honesty to be the best policy.'

'And what did he say?'

'That he didn't blame me for makin' the choices I did, and that he was glad the money was gone.'

'That's it?'

'Yup! I'm so glad I told him, because it was handy to get someone else's point of view, and it was Harry who made me see that most people would do the same in my circumstances, and those that didn't would spend the rest of their lives lookin' over their shoulders, if they weren't dead already.'

Checking her stockings for ladders, Tammy took great care not to create any nicks or snags when putting them on. 'I must admit it's goin' to be a huge relief to be open with Cecil for a change.'

'Have you thought about tellin' him the *whole* truth?'

'Not yet,' said Tammy slowly. 'I've spoken to Mam about it, and we think it best to keep quiet until I know where our relationship's goin'. As Mam quite rightly pointed out, if he loves me it won't make any odds, because it doesn't affect the Tammy he knows, and it will just show him how dire our situation truly was.'

'The way your father hounded you to Liverpool was proof of that,' said Gina. 'There's no doubt about it, had you not changed your names he'd have found you a lot sooner than he did. Someone with that amount of determination won't stop for anythin' or anyone.'

'We definitely made the right decision,' agreed Tammy. She checked her appearance in the mirror before wiping a few pieces of fluff from her leather jerkin. 'Are you ready?'

'As I'll ever be!' Gina donned her cap. 'I said we'd meet Harry by the gate.'

Swinging her handbag over her shoulder, Tammy was the first to leave the hut. 'I'm so glad things are workin' out between the two of you.'

'You were right when you said the right man would come along at the right time,' said Gina as she closed the door behind them. 'Did being away from Cecil make it any clearer as to whether he's the one for you?'

'Still as clear as mud,' Tammy sighed. 'I don't think I'll know for sure until I can be totally honest with him.'

'I dare say Archie didn't make it any easier when he told you about Rory bein' so upset.'

'Aye, but deep down I already knew he was heart-broken; he wouldn't have returned my letter otherwise.'

Gina nodded a greeting to the guard as they passed through the open gate. 'Your father has a lot to answer for, he really does. I hope he gets his comeuppance one of these days.' She smiled at Harry, who was holding his hand out to hail the bus.

'You're in the nick of time!' he said.

Tammy pulled an apologetic face. 'My fault! I should know better than to natter while we're gettin' ready.'

He gestured for the women to board the bus ahead of him. 'A woman's prerogative, surely?'

'Prerogative maybe, necessity definitely,' said Gina as she took a seat near the front.

'Gina told me all about your Christmas shenanigans. You don't half lead an excitin' life!' he said, with the air of someone who was grateful they had no such excitement in their own life.

'Led,' corrected Tammy. 'I'm rather hopin' next year's Christmas will be dull in comparison!'

'I wonder where you'll be this time next year,' mused Gina, adding, 'Where we'll all be, come to that.'

'Mam wants me to go to Liverpool.'

'I wouldn't half miss you if you did,' said Gina, 'and I bet I wouldn't be the only one.'

'I'd miss you too,' said Tammy fondly. 'We started this journey together, and I don't know how I'd feel about life in the ATS without you to keep me out of trouble!'

'And what about Cecil? Surely you'd miss him?'

'Very much, although maybe it would give me time to think about what I really want.'

'Absence makes the heart grow fonder,' said Harry idly, 'or so they say.'

Gina locked eyes with Tammy. 'That's an interestin' point Harry's just made. Is it true, do you think? And I'm not referrin' to Cecil, just so we're clear.'

Tammy lowered her gaze. She knew that Gina was

thinking of Rory, and she had a point. In Liverpool, she'd often found herself thinking that she'd have to tell Cecil this or that when she got back to Woodbury, but she never found herself thinking that way about Rory. Was it because she never expected to see him again, or was her love for him slowly petering out? She eyed Gina levelly. 'I really don't know, although I did miss Cecil terribly when I was in Liverpool, and I cannae wait to see him tonight.'

'Carpe diem,' said Harry.

'Seize the day,' supplied Tammy, for a confused-looking Gina. 'That's what everyone says, and they're right.'

The bus pulled to a halt, and to her delight Tammy saw a fresh-faced Cecil beaming up at her from the pavement below. Hurrying to be the first off the bus, she fell into his arms as he lifted her down from the platform.

'God, how I've missed you!'

'And I you!' said Tammy. 'I've heaps to tell you, though.' She glanced at Gina, who gave her an encouraging smile.

Tammy went on to tell Cecil everything that had transpired in Liverpool, but she allowed Gina to tell him the part about taking the wrong satchel.

Watching his reaction with anxious eyes, she was comforted when Cecil shot Gina a look of sympathetic admiration. 'I think you made a very wise choice, Gina, and thank goodness you did, cos Tammy wouldn't have had bait to lure her father away otherwise.' He clasped Tammy's hand in both of his. 'I know you said he was a bad egg, but to go to all that bother over a measly couple of shillings!' He shook his head in disbelief. 'Although I suppose it was more a question of control than the actual money itself. He wanted to show you that you couldn't get away with taking what he believed to be rightfully his. If he does find the Billy Boys' money, I hope he comes a cropper.'

'I doubt it. He's the luck of the devil, that one,' said Tammy. After a moment's pause, she added, 'Unless he uses it to drink himself to death, of course, which he could quite easily do with that kind of wonga.'

Cecil held the door to the venue open, and they all trooped through. 'Some might say he'd be getting his just deserts after what he put you and your mother through,' he said, taking Tammy's coat along with his own and checking them in with the coat clerk.

'You reap what you sow,' agreed Gina as Harry checked their coats in. 'Fingers crossed he'll leave sleepin' dogs lie.'

'He can't seriously think there's any more to be had,' said Cecil as they approached the bar. 'Even Gina's not that unlucky!'

Gina's eyes grew wide. 'Once was bad enough!'

He caught the attention of the barmaid and they each told her what they wanted before continuing with the conversation.

'That Archie sounds like a decent chap,' said Cecil. 'I'm glad he decided to stay in Liverpool. I expect you are too, Tammy.'

'I sleep a lot better at night knowin' he's not far away from Mammy should she need him,' Tammy admitted, 'and I'm sure he'll be an excellent deterrent should Dad decide to go back.'

Cecil paid for the drinks, with Harry insisting that he'd get the next round.

'I wish I'd been there,' Cecil told Tammy as they wandered over to a nearby table. 'I'd have sent him off with more than a flea in his ear!'

'Then thank goodness you weren't. The last thing I want is for you to get into trouble on my account.'

'Blow that! Wild horses wouldn't stop me from defending you, never mind a bunch of stuffed walruses.' He jerked his head in the direction of the dance floor. 'Fancy a tango?'

Tammy took his hand. 'Do I ever!'

Rory lay on his bunk, reading through his instructions.

'You'll like it in Liverpool,' said Jimmy. 'I haven't been since the May blitz so I should imagine it looks very different now, but even so, it's still a marvellous city, with plenty to see and do.'

Rory sat up on one elbow. 'I'm lookin' forward to it, truth be known. It'll get me away from that Ella if nowt else.'

Jimmy tutted beneath his breath. 'She's a proper little stirrer is that one. Comin' here spreadin' lies, and for what?'

'She always was jealous of my Tammy, but I never thought she'd stoop to those levels!'

'You definitely think she was lyin', then?'

'I questioned it at first, because she seemed so sure of what she was sayin' – so much so she even had me questioning what I know to be true. Cos if Tammy and her mammy had got out of that buildin' alive they'd have come straight to me.'

'People who like to gossip tend to believe their own lies,' said Jimmy, 'but to make you think that Tammy had run out on you when she had no proof whatsoever was a terrible thing to do.'

'She just wanted to paint Tammy in the worst possible light; why else would she believe the likes of Dennis?'

'You've hit the nail on the head,' said Jimmy simply. 'Ella's hate for Tammy was stronger than her care for the truth.'

'Exactly!'

'So, when are you off?'

'Thursday.'

Jimmy shrugged off his jacket and hung it up. 'I hope you come to terms with all that's happened, son. It was lookin' quite promisin' until that Ella threw a spanner in the works.'

'I keep thinkin' how angry Tammy would be if she knew what Ella has been sayin', but then I think about how disappointed she'd be in me for believin' her in the first place!'

'Do you really think she would? Wouldn't most people want to believe that the love of their life wasn't dead after all but was out there somewhere waitin' to be found?'

'I s'pose.' He hesitated. Why hadn't Ella thought of that? Or was she so mired in her own petty prejudice she couldn't see the wood for the trees? He said as much to Jimmy.

'I reckon it's the latter. No one wants to come second place to someone, especially if that someone's dead. If she could make you hate Tammy, she'd not feel as insecure about herself.'

'Stupid thing is, I'd never look twice at Ella,' said Rory. 'First of all, she's not my type, and secondly, I don't like women who gossip.'

Jimmy burst out laughing. 'You've just dismissed ninety-nine point nine per cent of the female population.'

A half-smile creased Rory's face. 'Then it's the point one per cent I'm after.'

'Someone special,' said Jimmy. 'A woman who knows her own mind and isn't swayed by others.' He nodded approvingly. 'Sounds to me as though you're lookin' for a strong, independent type of gal.'

'I like a woman who's not afraid to speak up for herself.'

'My Beryl's like that,' Jimmy grinned. 'She often tells me what I'm thinkin'.'

Rory laughed. 'You've got a good 'un there, Jimmy, I hope you realise that.'

Jimmy undid the laces on his shoes. 'I do indeed, and you'll have a woman like my Beryl one of these days!'

'Tammy will always be my first love, but she won't be my last,' said Rory with a confidence that Jimmy had never seen in him before. 'I'm done lickin' my wounds; it's time I embraced my future.'

'Amen to that!'

Tammy felt as though she were dancing on air as Cecil whisked her around the dance floor.

'My mammy cannae wait to meet you,' she said, resting her cheek against his chest.

'I hope I pass muster, cos I dare say my rank won't cut the mustard if she doesn't like what she sees.'

'No need to worry on that score. She's already decided that you're the bee's knees.'

He twinkled down at her. 'Really? And what made her decide that, do you suppose?'

She slapped him on the arm in a playful manner. 'You know full well who gave her that impression.'

'So, you've been singing my praises then?'

'You could say that.'

'Then I shall have to make sure I live up to her expectations, cos I wouldn't like her to think that I'm anything other than worthy of her daughter's attention.'

'You've taken me on despite my family history, and in Mam's eyes that means a lot. Most men would want to run a mile.'

'Then they must need their heads testing,' he said firmly.

'You still say all the right things,' said Tammy, continuing to gaze into his eyes, which sparkled delightedly.

'I speak my mind, good or bad.' He kissed her softly. As their lips parted, he said, 'Anyone who'd walk away from you because you had a rotten father wouldn't have been worthy of your attention in the first place. You're one of a kind, Tammy Lloyd; I hope you realise that?'

'Much like yourself then,' said Tammy as his arms slid even further around her waist.

'Two of a kind,' agreed Cecil. His lips meeting hers, he gently caressed the nape of her neck.

Wishing that the embrace would never end, Tammy felt a silvery tingle run through her body. It was something she had never experienced before, but it made her feel very much alive.

Leaning back from their embrace, Cecil ran a finger around the inside of his shirt collar. 'Is it me, or is it getting hot in here?'

Tammy smiled shyly. Her lips still tingling from their kiss, she used her hand to fan her face. 'It is awfully crowded,' she said, although she was fairly sure the other people had nothing to do with the heat radiating throughout her body.

He smiled slowly. 'There're other people in here?'

She felt her cheeks grow warmer. 'I don't know whether I'll ever get used to your charm.'

'What can I say? It comes naturally!'

She lowered her gaze before looking back up. 'Mam's asked me to see if I could get a posting to Liverpool.'

He faltered mid-step. 'Oh! And have you?'

'I don't see the point. The services aren't exactly amenable when it comes to such requests.'

'True.' He hesitated. 'I know you don't like the idea of accepting help from an officer, but I don't mind seeing if I can pull a few strings if you'd like me to?'

She looked into his eyes, which drew her in like warm pools of delight. 'You'd really do that, for me?'

He replied without hesitation. 'If you really wanted to go, then yes, I would. I'd miss you like crazy, but I'd rather you were happy there than miserable here.'

Holding his gaze, Tammy shook her head. 'I love my mam, of course I do, but whilst I miss her terribly I'd rather be here with you.'

Secretly surprised, yet thrilled to hear she'd rather be with him, Cecil pulled her in so close there wasn't a sliver of light between their bodies. 'You've just made me a very happy man!'

His words warmed her heart, but they also made her feel a real heel, and she'd had enough of feeling that way. Gina had bitten the bullet by telling Harry everything, and if Tammy didn't do the same with Cecil she would continue to live in limbo. 'Don't go celebratin' just yet. There's somethin' that I've got to tell you first.'

His face instantly fell. 'Uh-oh. Why do I get the feelin' I'm not going to like the sound of this?'

Tammy ran a nervous tongue over her lips. 'Remember when you called me Tammy Lloyd a moment ago?'

He nodded. 'What of it?'

'I'm not,' she said simply.

Cecil furrowed his brow. 'Sorry?'

Taking him by the hand, Tammy led him over to a darkened part of the dance floor where they couldn't be overheard.

'My real name's Tamara Blackwell. My mother and I changed our names when we ran away from Dad because we knew he'd come after us.'

Getting hold of the wrong end of the stick entirely, Cecil raised his brow. 'You say it as though it's a terrible thing, but lots of people change their names by deed poll.'

She felt her heart sink further. Trust Cecil to think that she and her mother would've done everything legally instead of using a backstreet forger. Taking a deep breath, she went on to tell him everything, not excluding Rory's part in the scheme. Waiting with bated breath for his response, Tammy could only hope that she'd made the right decision.

Cecil gave a low whistle. 'You don't do things by halves, do you?'

'It sometimes feels as though I make a complete pig's ear out of everythin' I touch,' said Tammy. 'Hopefully I'm not includin' you in that statement; although I wouldn't blame you if you never wanted to see me again.'

He wrinkled his brow. 'Because you acted in haste? Blimey, if you could get hung for making hasty decisions, we'd all be lined up beside the gallows.'

She felt her heart rise. 'So you don't think badly of me?'

He wrapped his arms around her. 'How could I think badly of you? You didn't mean any of this to happen, and if your father hadn't been a vicious thug you wouldn't have been forced into an impossible situation. It's just rotten luck that he came home when he did.'

A tear trickled down her cheek. 'I cannae believe how well you're takin' all this. I was worried it might be one step too far, especially after my runnin' out on Rory the way I did.'

Cecil pulled an awkward grimace. 'Is that why you said there was no chance of the two of you getting back together?'

Her cheeks bloomed with guilty embarrassment. 'Yes.'

He kissed the top of her head as he continued to hold her. 'I've never known anyone pay such a high price for savin' someone's life.'

With everything out in the open, Tammy couldn't stop the tears from flowing. Taking a handkerchief from his trouser pocket Cecil pressed it into her hand, whispering, 'You've had a rotten time of it, but that's all in the past.'

To his surprise she began to giggle as her tears turned from relief to happiness. 'Mam said that if you were the right man for me you'd understand when I told you the truth, and you didn't bat an eye.'

He cupped her cheeks in the palms of his hands. 'Because I knew *you* from the moment we first met. I only had to look into your eyes to know that you were a decent, honest woman who always stayed on the right side of justice.'

'But I lied . . .' Tammy interrupted.

'To protect those you love,' said Cecil. 'Your father came haring halfway across the country for a couple of shillings! You *knew* you had to do the things you did, because you knew what he was capable of. I'm so glad you trusted me enough to tell me, and I want you to know that no matter what happens between us, I will *never* breathe a word of this to anyone. As far as I'm concerned you're Tammy Lloyd, and you always have been.'

She smiled. 'I don't know what I did to deserve you, Cecil Carter, but boy am I glad I did it!'

He took her in his arms and kissed her, softly at first,

but increasing in intensity as the kiss deepened. So lost were they in the moment, they didn't notice the lights go up.

Hearing someone cough to announce their presence, Tammy turned to see Gina looking awkward. 'Sorry to interrupt, but it's time we were off.'

'Right you are, I'll just fetch our coats,' said Cecil, and went to do precisely that. As soon as he was out of earshot, Tammy filled Gina in on the last ten minutes of their conversation, while her friend listened open-mouthed.

'I thought you weren't ready to tell him yet. What made you decide that tonight was the night?'

'It was hearin' what you said about tellin' Harry about the Billy Boys and how you couldn't bear to live a lie the way I was doing. As soon as Cecil said I'd made him a happy man, I knew I had to tell him the truth because I was never goin' to be able to move on until I did, so I told him everything, including the bit about Rory.'

'And how do you feel now that everything's out in the open?'

'Like I'm walkin' on air!'

'Which explains the long smooch,' Gina chuckled.

'Ever since we bumped into Bonnie I've been terrified that someone would blurt out the truth before I had a chance, but I don't have to worry about that any more now that Cecil knows everythin'.'

Gina couldn't help thinking that Tammy had more than Cecil to worry about should someone else from her past see and recognise her, but she hadn't the heart to burst Tammy's bubble, so she changed the subject.

'Has it helped you to make your mind up on what you'd say to Rory if you were to bump into him?'

Tammy nodded. 'I'd tell him how sorry I was and that I didn't blame him for returning my letter before wishing him luck in the future.'

'So, no lingerin' feelings?'

An image of Rory appeared in Tammy's mind's eye, and she instantly felt her heart begin to ache. She and her mother had talked about being in love with two men at the same time, but even if she did still have feelings for Rory she was with Cecil now. 'Rory will always be my first love, but that's where it ends,' Tammy told Gina. 'I'm done with treadin' the same path; it's time for me to start a new journey!'

* * *

1ST JANUARY 1942

Scarcely able to believe how much her life had changed in the past twenty-four hours, Tammy was waiting for Cecil by the gate to her base. Seeing him pull up in a taxi, she hurried towards him, brandishing the note she'd been handed by her sergeant earlier that morning.

Taking the missive and scanning it quickly, Cecil gave it back to her with a grim smile. 'You've obviously impressed someone with your driving skills.'

Tammy folded the note and put it back into her pocket. 'But I want to stay here, with you!'

He brushed his fingers along her neckline. 'How long have we got?'

She looked up at him, her eyes glistening with tears. 'I leave tonight.'

He pulled her close. 'They don't do things in half measures, do they!'

An even more terrifying thought occurred to her. 'You don't suppose someone's found out about us, do you?'

He shook his head. 'I'd have got it in the neck if they had; this is down to pure bad luck.'

Tammy buried her face against his chest. 'How on earth will we get to see each other now?'

'I'll see if I can get posted close by, but failing that it'll have to be long weekends as and when we can.'

'I suppose that's better than nothin',' murmured Tammy.

'We'll work something out, don't you worry.' He hesitated. 'How did Gina take the news?'

'She's still raging about it now; I think she's going to see someone this afternoon to see if she can come with me.'

'I'm sorry to say that I don't fancy her chances much.'

'And there I was thinkin' I'd had my run of bad luck, but at least this has to be the last of it.'

'How d'you mean?'

'If it's true that bad luck comes in threes, then I've had my quota,' said Tammy. 'First Dad comin' home early, then me wallopin' him with the first thing that came to hand, and now my repostin'.'

'I see!'

'So no more nasty surprises for me!' said Tammy, although she absent-mindedly crossed her fingers as the words left her lips.

'I hope I don't start having bad luck, because I've not had any as of yet.'

'Apart from me gettin' reposted, of course,' Tammy reminded him.

'So that's my first. I just need two more.'

Tammy laughed. 'Bad luck isn't the same as collectin' badges!'

'Let's hope not!'

She looked up at him as he leaned in for a kiss. 'What if someone sees?'

'Let them see. It's not as if they can do anything about it now that you're off to pastures new.'

Falling into the kiss, Tammy wished the moment would never end. As their lips parted, she held his hands in hers. 'I've got to go; I've still got work to do.'

He sighed heavily. 'I ain't half going to miss you.'

'And I you,' she replied, her voice hoarse with emotion.

Pulling her in for one last kiss, he whispered, 'You're very special to me, Tammy Lloyd.'

Her stomach performing somersaults, Tammy beamed back at him, though her eyes were filling with tears.

'As you are to me, and I cannae wait until we see each other again.'

He kissed the back of her knuckles. 'Good luck. Please call me as soon as you arrive so that I know you got there safely.'

'Will do.'

'And try to look on the bright side,' said Cecil sympathetically. 'It's not as if anything else can go wrong now you've had your quota of bad luck!'

'I'm sure everythin' will be just fine,' said Tammy, though it was with a sigh that she added, 'Look out Liverpool, here I come!'

Dear Readers,

I do hope you had a wonderful summer; I know I did! A keen swimmer, I took my first dip in the sea in the first week of May and, although cold, it was wonderful to be back swimming.

Something we've not done in a while is travel in our motorhome. So, this summer, we took a trip down south to visit friends and family. Needless to say, a wonderful time was had by all, proving the theory that it really does do you good to get away every now and then.

But that's enough about me and my shenanigans! Time to talk about the new novel *The Winter Runaway*. I've been holding on to this story for such a long time, and I am so happy I've finally been able to share it with you. I do love a dramatic start to a book that leaves you wondering what on earth has transpired to get the characters to this point in their lives, and *The Winter Runaway* is the perfect example of that. I think we've all been at a moment where things have taken a totally unexpected turn for the worse, through no intentions of our own, and it's always interesting to see how people cope when thrown in at the deep end. And boy oh boy, are Tammy and her mother up to their necks in hot water!

The Winter Runaway kept me hooked the whole time as I was writing it, and I hope you felt the same whilst reading it.

Wishing you all wonderful festive seasons to come and I look forward to catching up next year!

Warmest wishes,

Holly Flynn xx

DISCOVER THE LATEST NOVEL IN THE RUNAWAY SERIES

COMING FEBRUARY 2025

DISCOVER THE WHITE CHRISTMAS SERIES

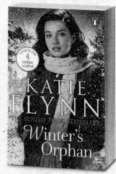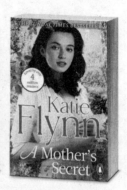

FROM THE UK'S NO. 1 BESTSELLING WWII SAGA AUTHOR

Katie Flynn

DISCOVER THE LIVERPOOL SISTERS SERIES

FROM THE UK'S NO. 1 BESTSELLING WWII SAGA AUTHOR

Katie Flynn

DISCOVER THE ROSE QUEEN SERIES

FROM THE UK'S NO. 1 BESTSELLING WWII SAGA AUTHOR

Katie Flynn

LOVED BY
4 MILLION
READERS

Katie Flynn

If you want to continue to hear from the
Flynn family, and to receive the latest news about
new Katie Flynn books and competitions,
sign up to the Katie Flynn newsletter.

Join today by visiting
www.penguin.co.uk/katieflynnnewsletter

Find Katie Flynn on Facebook
www.facebook.com/katieflynn458

SIGN UP TO OUR SAGA NEWSLETTER

Penny Street

The home of heart-warming reads

Welcome to **Penny Street**, your number **one stop for emotional and heartfelt historical reads**. Meet casts of characters you'll never forget, memories you'll treasure as your own, and places that will forever stay with you long after the last page.

Join our online **community** bringing you the latest book deals, competitions and new saga series releases.

You can also find extra content, talk to your favourite authors and share your discoveries with other saga fans on Facebook.

Join today by visiting
www.penguin.co.uk/pennystreet

Follow us on Facebook
www.facebook.com/welcometopennystreet/